Killing The Royals

A Pickleball Murder Mystery

Congratulations!

Remember to keep dinking.

Gary

2024

By Gary Resnikoff - 2023

Acknowledgments

First to my wife and partner for over 40 years, thank you for always supporting me and tolerating my obsessions; pickleball being just the most recent. I am extremely grateful to Emily Resnikoff and Lori Resnikoff for the awesome editing and story improvements that they provided. Any mistakes are mine for not listening to them. And lastly, thank you Sarah Resnikoff for all the marketing advice. Hopefully you have not found me to be too stubborn.

Disclaimers

This is entirely a book of fiction. Any resemblance to real people or real occurrences is completely coincidental. Rio Viejo does not exist except in the mind of the author. There are, however, a number of towns near the border with Mexico that may sound and feel like Rio Viejo. That being said, pickleball is real and the people who play are real, as is the drama surrounding any activities that involve people. Anyone that has played pickleball for any length of time can relate to the term "The Royals" and who that represents. Some people may have other not-so-endearing terms for these people. It is for that reason that the reader may think they know someone who fits the descriptions of these characters. You may indeed. In fact, if you are honest, you might even admit that you have exhibited the traits attributed to "The Royals" from time to time. It seems no matter where you play or who you play with, there is a group of people who regularly manifest these rude and crude behaviors. It may even come off as entitlement. Sadly, I admit I've been guilty on occasion of such behavior.

Intolerable as these individuals may be, I don't condone murdering them. Please refrain from doing so.

Regarding the tips. The tips were written by me, but know this: I am not a pro, and I don't play one on TV, but I have played and studied the game and watched dozens, if not hundreds, of videos and training tips by real pros. The tips I have chosen seem fairly consistent and universal among most of the teaching pros, so hopefully there won't be any disagreement about them. It is for this reason that you may have already heard many of these tips in one fashion or another. If it appears like one of your tips has appeared here, it is because they are in fact widely accepted and not proprietary to any particular pro. I have found that writing and thinking about these tips has improved my game. So, even if you are an advanced player, hopefully being reminded of these tips will improve your game as well.

One last note. Odd as this may sound, a reader of my previous book, *All in a Day's Work*, asked if I had ever killed anyone. She appeared to be quite serious and when I said no, she looked at me and said, "I don't think I believe you." Let me assure you, I have not murdered anyone and I have no intention of doing so in the near future.

Chapter 1

Like most people, I hadn't been out much the past year. Between my wife battling and finally losing to cancer and COVID scaring the crap out of just about everyone, I really didn't have any desire to interact with other humans. I had Butch, my 80-pound bundle of fur and muscle to walk and talk to, and I had Netflix, Hulu, YouTube, Peacock, and Prime to entertain me. But I missed pickleball. This was going to be the first time in a year that I even walked by the courts.

A block before I arrived at the Gates Tennis Center in Cherry Creek, Colorado, I could hear it, the popping sound of balls against paddles and the raucous laughter from the players. Even though I wasn't planning on playing today, I could feel and taste the adrenaline. When I rounded the corner and saw all twelve courts full, and a crowd milling about waiting to play, I was both excited and dismayed. The last time I played here there couldn't have been more than five courts full at a time. I approached the waiting area filled with benches and tables, flabbergasted by what I was seeing.

"Al," I heard my name called, "Over here."

I turned around to see a man I vaguely knew from playing here in the past running over to me.

"It's me, Robert. Don't you remember me?"

"Of course I do," I said, although I hadn't remembered his name, "How are you?"

"I'm good, buddy. Haven't seen you here in ages. Have you been playing somewhere else?"

"No, I took some time off."

"Oh. Yeah. I remember hearing you lost your wife. Sorry."

"Thanks." Maybe he didn't remember, but my last encounter with Robert wasn't all that pleasant. Robert had a reputation for arguing line calls that didn't go his way, and I had been distraught dealing with Stephanie's cancer and was in no mood for Robert's antics. When he called me out on a call, I lost my composure, and we almost came to blows. Probably would have if not for our playing partners pulling us apart. I left that day and hadn't been back until now.

"Have you been playing?"

"Nope. I just haven't been very interested in playing since Stephanie died."

He nodded, "Understandable." We were quiet for a few minutes, watching the games all around us.

"Sure are a lot more people since the last time I was here. I don't even recognize most of the faces."

"Yeah, man. It's crazy. New people keep coming out every day. The old gang you used to play with now come real early and are out of here before the crowd arrives. It's like this every day. You play a game and then have to sit out fifteen minutes before you can get back on a court. It sucks."

"I've been reading it's the fastest growing sport in the country. Looks like they weren't wrong."

"Well, someone needs to tell them to quit promoting it," Robert lamented, "We don't have enough courts as it is, and we don't need all these newbies coming in here and spoiling it for us."

"Court 6 open. Next group is up," said some guy I had never seen before.

"That's me," said Robert, jumping up off the bench, "Hang around and let's catch up after my game."

I didn't have time to respond as he ran toward his court, along with a group of people I didn't know. At one time I knew just about everyone who played here, but as Robert said, new people were discovering the game every day. Just in the past year, new courts had sprung up all over Denver and it still wasn't sufficient.

I sat on a bench to watch the players and to see where my previous skill level would put me today. Before I took my hiatus, I was considered a 4.0 – 4.5, which put me in the advanced skill level, but not good enough to play with the pros. Now, after a year off, I figured I would be rusty, but was anxious to get on a court and find out where I would fit in.

A pretty, blond woman dressed in a bright floral tennis outfit, probably in her 40's, set her paddle in the rack and approached me.

"Hi there, I'm Joanne," she said, as she held out her hand.

"Al," I replied and shook her hand.

"May I sit down?"

"Of course," I said, and scooted over to make room for her.

"You look new. Have you played here before?"

I had read in one of the hundreds of recent articles about pickleball that it was becoming the new pick-up place for middle-aged people. Was Joanne just being friendly or was this a pickup line?

"I used to play here a year ago but stopped. It sure has grown since I was here last."

"I just started to play a few months ago. I love the game," she said enthusiastically, "I can't get enough of it. Why did you stop coming here?"

I contemplated making up something but decided not to bother. "I took time to take care of my wife when she got ill." I paused and collected myself for the next part. "After she passed away, I guess I just didn't feel ready to come back." I wiped away a tear.

"I'm so sorry to hear that," she said in a very comforting tone, while lightly touching my arm, "Are you OK?"

No one had asked me that since Stephanie died. I immediately liked this person and something about her made me want to open up. "It was cancer. We thought she beat it, but it came back and there was nothing the doctors could do to save her. She and I used to play here before she became ill. She was an excellent player."

"That had to be tough. I had breast cancer myself. Fortunately, they found it early and I'm cancer free now."

I smiled. "That's great. Cancer sucks and I'm glad to hear from someone who beat it."

"Are you here to play?"

"No. I just came by to take a look around. Maybe see some of the people I used to play with. Like Robert," I pointed him out on the court.

"Oh."

The way she said it, I knew something was wrong. "You know Robert?"

"Oh yeah. Everyone here does. He has a bit of a reputation."

I laughed. "He had one when I was playing too. So, I take it he's still a hot head?"

"You might say that. He's always arguing with someone about rules or line calls. I saw him get in a fight just last week. Some people had to break it up. They tried to get him banned from playing here, but so far, no such luck. I don't play with him anymore because he hits too hard and, I hate to say it, he targets women. I got hit in the chest by him. But he isn't the only one like that. There are a few guys that like to intimidate the ladies."

"Sorry. I never liked to see that. I don't understand why men think they need to overpower the women on the court."

"I have a theory," she said with a laugh.

I looked at her and immediately understood. "Point made."

"So, were you good before you quit playing?"

I didn't want to sound like I was bragging, but I wanted to be honest with her. "I was decent. I won a couple gold medals in men's doubles and mixed doubles before I stopped playing. I was going to move up to 4.5," I shrugged. I think she understood. "But I'm sure I'm rusty now. I might come out and play a little before I move."

"Moving? Why are you moving? Work? You look too young to be retired."

"I'll take that as a compliment. I am actually retired. My wife and I both had businesses that we sold when she got sick, and fortunately it allowed me to retire young. What about you?"

"Oh, I married a rich man and then got divorced," she laughed. I didn't know what to say to that, so I said nothing. One thing about pickleball, whether it's good or bad (sometimes I'm not so sure which), is the social aspect. Within minutes of meeting people, you hear all about their aches and pains and such, and you find yourself sharing with them as well.

"Are you Jewish?" she asked out of the blue. I looked at her, obviously confused. "The star of David," she said, pointing at the gold star around my neck.

"Ah. Yes, I am," I answered as I touched it. I could tell she wanted an explanation and since I was used to the question, I went on to explain, "My wife, Stephanie, was Jewish and wanted me to convert. She gave me this when I finished converting. I wasn't much of a Christian, so I did. It made her parents very happy. Are you Jewish?"

"I am. I have to say, I haven't met too many black Jews," she said and before I could answer, she continued, "Not that it's a bad thing or anything."

"My friends and my parents might beg to disagree. When I converted, the standard line was 'you don't have it hard enough as a black man, you want to make it tougher by being a black Jew?' They weren't wrong. But it seemed like the thing to do at the time."

"You're a hoot," she laughed again. She had a deep infectious laugh. It had been quite some time since I interacted with a woman outside of care givers and doctors, and I found myself enjoying it.

"How did you meet your wife?" Joanne asked.

"College. We dated and got serious. Her parents eventually warmed up to their daughter dating a black man when she told them I was going to convert."

"Sounds like typical Jewish parents. My husband was already a Jew, but my parents hated him. I guess they saw what took me a few years to see. Now I'm happier than I've ever been." She paused and I could see she regretted the last comment. "I'm sorry. Marriage would have been great with the right guy."

We were interrupted by a commotion on the court where Robert was playing. He and another man were at the net arguing about something and it was getting more and more heated. We couldn't pick up everything that was being said, other than a few loud curse words. I hadn't seen Robert in over a year, but I recognized the pattern. He was about to explode. Sure enough, he stepped back and threw his paddle down hard on the ground. It bounced up and over the net, hitting his opponent in the face. The man's hands flew up to his nose and he went down hard. He sat there holding his nose, silent. Most of us would have been dismayed and remorseful by our actions and the damage done, but not Robert. His opponent pulled his hand away from his nose, exposing a fistful of blood. Robert seemed undaunted and yelled at the guy to get up and not be a baby. The man held up his hand to show Robert the blood and said something unintelligible, red spittle dribbling down his chin.

Robert turned and bolted. Before anyone could say anything else to him, he was out the gate, grabbing his equipment bag at a full run.

"Holy shit. Did you see that?" I asked Joanne.

"Oh my god. What the hell is wrong with that guy?"

By now, people were helping the injured man up and applying towels to his nose. He was staggering a bit as they helped him over to the bench area. He was dazed but seemed to be recovering. Then he got angry.

"Where is that shithead?" he asked.

"Gone," I told him, "He ran off toward the parking lot."

"I think he broke my nose."

Someone told him he should call the police and file a complaint, while someone else said it looked like an accident to them. A tall man in a tennis outfit came over and handed the man a business card. I was guessing he was an attorney.

I had seen enough for one day. This wasn't the first altercation I had seen on the courts over the years when I played, but it was probably the bloodiest. Arguments were common, and sometimes they resulted in a shoving match, but no punches were usually exchanged. I've seen guys toss paddles over a fence, into the net, and even seen hard balls hit at people with the intent to intimidate or even hit them, but generally speaking, people stay civilized at the pickleball courts. Short tempers seemed to come with intense competition.

"Joanne, I think I'm going to head home. I've got a big pup that is probably wondering when I'm going to get home and take him for a walk."

"OK. It was nice to meet you, Al. Will you be coming back out here to play?"

"I'm not sure. Butch and I are moving soon."

"Butch?"

"My 80-pound bundle of fur."

"Oh. I would love to meet him sometime. I love dogs."

Was she coming on to me? It had been so long since I dated anyone but Stephanie, I wasn't sure how to read the clues. When she offered me her phone number, all doubt was removed.

"Are you coming back out here tomorrow?" I asked her, hoping she would say yes. "I don't live that far away, maybe I'll come back and bring Butch, so you can meet him."

"I would love that," she said with a big smile, and held out her hand.

As I left, Joanne was running on to a court to play with some ladies. They were all giggling like little girls, and I was feeling a little guilty. Stephanie had been gone for over six months, but it still didn't feel right to be flirting. I was ready to get back out into the world, but I wasn't sure if I was ready for a relationship. Then I scolded myself for even thinking that, after one chance meeting at a pickleball court, this was anything more than just meeting a new friend.

12

My home, the house that Stephanie and I bought at the height of our careers, was only about a ten-minute walk from the Gates Tennis Center. Stephanie had gone into the real estate business right after we graduated and was hugely successful, having started and built one of the more prestigious real estate brokerage firms in the Denver area. She found the house for us before it came on the market, and although it was considered a fixer upper, it was in a great neighborhood and she convinced me it would not only be a great investment, but it would be a wonderful home to raise our future kids in. Sadly, cancer had derailed that plan. Now as I walked up to it, all I could see was this huge family home that was just too big and lonely for a guy and his dog.

I opened the door and there was Butch, as if he could hear me coming, with a disapproving look on his face. Clearly the message was: I had been gone too long.

"Sorry buddy, I didn't mean to be gone that long." As I leashed him up, I tried to explain to him about the fight at the pickleball courts. He was unimpressed. Butch was Stephanie's dog. He worshiped her and tolerated me until she passed away, and then his love for me grew. I guess when he realized she wasn't coming back and I was all he had, he warmed up to me. Now we are best buddies, but he still thinks he needs to put me in my place from time to time. And he isn't wrong. Thanks to him, I hadn't hidden out in the house all day, every day the past six months.

A few weeks ago, I had talked it over with Butch and we came to an agreement that it was time to sell the house and leave Denver. I talked and he listened and when I said, "Let's leave," he didn't disagree. The deal was struck, and for me, the key was to move to a place where I wasn't known and didn't have a ton of memories. The only other requirements I had were warm weather (i.e., no snow), and plenty of opportunity to play pickleball year-round. As it turns out, finding a place with no pickleball drama should have been on the list as well.

Butch and I wandered down the street and headed toward Pulaski Park, which had a nice dog park area. It was a favorite destination for Stephanie and Butch as he could run with other dogs, and she could relax without worrying about him getting into any trouble. It was also close enough that the walk wouldn't put too much strain on Stephanie. When we arrived, I opened the gate and released Butch to run wild with the other pups. I found a bench to sit and watch.

"Al," I heard my name called and turned to see Derrick Green, an old acquaintance from the neighborhood. "How you doing?" he said, as he let his dog, Mickey, loose to run with the pack.

"Good, Derrick, what about you?"

"Alright, I guess. This and that hurts, but at my age it could be a lot worse."

Derrick lived down the street from us and was in his early 70's. Ever since I've known him, he's complained about something hurting.

"But I've finally decided to take up pickleball. Mary convinced me I should play. She took me out there a few days ago and started to teach me." Mary was another neighbor of ours and a devoted pickleball player.

"Good for you, Derrick. I'm sure you'll love it."

"I already do. She told me you used to play at Gates all the time and stopped," he paused, and I thought that I knew what he was going to say, but he surprised me. "She said that you were one of the better players out there."

"I was decent, but then I've been an athlete all my life and it came naturally for me."

"I also heard you were going to sell your house and move."

Wow. News sure does travel fast.

14

"Yep. Officially on the market next week."

"Well, we will be sorry to see you go. Where are you headed?"

"Little Arizona town by the Mexican border called Rio Viejo."

"Geez, Al. Are you crazy? All you hear about are the coyotes and illegal aliens and drug cartels kidnapping people. I don't think it's safe."

I wanted to say, *Quit watching Fox News*, but instead I said, "I think a lot of the news about the border is overblown." Then as a joke I added, "Can't live forever."

"Humph," he grunted. "I'm just saying."

"I'll be careful, but thanks for the warning."

"Why there? I never heard of the place."

I wanted to leave it on a positive note, so I said, "The weather there is extraordinary. No snow and it rarely gets below 40. Even the summers aren't too bad. It's not hot like Phoenix and you won't believe the prices on real estate. For what I can sell my house for here, I can probably buy a bigger house there for less than a quarter of the money."

"That would be nice I suppose, but I don't need the money. I think I'll stay right here."

Good, I thought, because I wasn't inviting him to join me. I decided not to tell him any of the other benefits to living in Southern Arizona.

"When does all this take place?"

"Soon. I already have a place rented down there, just trying to decide what day to leave. Then I'll just pack up a U-Haul and go. Not going to wait till the house sells."

15

"I bet it sells fast. Well, good luck to you, Al," he said as he signaled for Mickey to join him. They left, and Butch and I followed a few minutes later.

"Butch, are you scared about moving to Arizona?"

He turned his head as he often does when he's trying to understand what I'm saying.

"I promise you'll love it."

Pickleball Tip # 1 – Have Fun

Pickleball is fun. It is supposed to be fun, anyway. Yes, it is great exercise for people of all ages, and it is a great way to get out of the house and get some sun and clean air, but it is also a great way to meet people and socialize. Many players get competitive and join tournaments and leagues, but even the lower skill level players participate in them. One thing you will notice around pickleball courts is all the laughter and joking. People are having a great time. They laugh and cheer at both good and bad shots. It is said that pickleball is the fastest growing sport in America, if not the world. As anyone can tell you, it is an easy sport to learn and achieve a modicum of proficiency at. The court is smaller than a tennis court, and it doesn't require as much training or athletic skill as tennis in order to get good enough to have some fun.

It isn't uncommon for a newbie to get hooked within a few minutes of play.

Chapter *2*

The following day, Butch and I rose early. We had a quick breakfast and were out the door heading for the pickleball courts at the Gates Tennis facility. I didn't bring my equipment, so I wasn't going to play, but I had promised to bring Butch by the courts so Joanne could meet him, and I was anxious to see her again, even though I wasn't interested in a relationship so soon after losing Stephanie. It was nice to have someone new to talk to.

A normal ten-to-fifteen-minute walk to Gates turned into thirty, because Butch had to sniff and pee on everything along the way. Even so, when we arrived, I was disappointed not to see Joanne. I decided that I would wait. A few people from my old playing days were around and came up to say hello and meet Butch. He put on a charm show and was reveling in the attention. Right in the middle of his performance, the police showed up. I watched as they went around to various people questioning them and then it was my turn.

"Sir," a tall white officer approached me, "I understand from some of the people here that you were here during the altercation yesterday."

"Yes, I was, but I really don't have any idea what happened."

"Can I get your name and contact information?" he asked, while taking notes on a little pad. I complied politely. The officer continued, "Can you tell me what you saw?"

"I saw a guy named Robert arguing with someone and then he tossed his paddle, and it bounced up and hit the guy he was arguing with in the face."

"You know Robert?"

"Not really. I mean, I played here a year ago and he played a lot."

"Do you know his last name or where he lives?"

"I do not."

"Was there anything you saw before Robert threw the paddle that might have precipitated Robert's reaction?"

"No. I heard some arguing and looked up at them just as Robert threw the paddle. Is the fellow who got hit pressing charges?"

"Yes, he is. Thanks for your time." He walked off to talk with some other players.

Joanne arrived while I was talking to the officer.

"Hi, Al. What was that about?"

"Remember the fight yesterday? Well, I guess the guy with the broken nose is pressing charges, but no one seems to know anything about Robert. Do you know anything about him?"

"No. I've seen him out here, but I never played with him. And if I did, I don't think I would want to get on the wrong side of Robert. He's kind of scary." She bent over to pet Butch. "So, this is your little companion."

I couldn't argue her logic. From my recollection of Robert, I could see how he could intimidate someone. I can't say with any authority, but unless he's changed, he did appear to have a short fuse.

"Butch, say hi to Joanne."

Butch lifted his paw and waved to her.

"He's adorable. So, are you here to play?"

"No. I just came by with Butch so you could meet him." After I said it, I felt like a school kid trying to impress a pretty girl.

"I'm so glad you did," she said with a huge warm smile.

We chatted for a while. I knew she wanted to play and was thrilled that she delayed playing to talk with me.

"So, tell me about this little town you are planning to move to."

"Rio Viejo. It's a small town by the border that dated back to the 1700's. It's quiet and I think they have one stop light, if my memory serves me. It's been a few years since I was there, and we only stayed one night. I remember there were a lot of artists and art galleries."

"Sounds nice," she said.

"You say that, but you don't sound convinced."

"I like a big town with lots to do."

"Well, they have world-class bird watching," I laughed.

"Well, shut the door and turn out the lights," she said sarcastically, and laughed.

"OK. It does sound a bit boring," I agreed, "I'm not actually a bird watcher, but it is very pretty there. There's a nice river running through the area and a resort with a nice golf course."

"Do you play golf?"

"I used to. In fact, there aren't too many sports I don't play or at least used to play at one time or another. But now I mostly just play pickleball, and they have some great courts."

"So, the big attraction for you is…?"

I thought about how much I wanted to share with her. "I'm ready to leave Denver and try something new. I grew up here, met and married my

20

wife here. We both started and ran successful businesses in the area. A lot of history here."

"I'm going to guess you feel like there are too many sad memories here?"

I nodded. "Lots of good and sad memories. Lots of friends here from when we were a couple, and I just don't feel like being the odd guy out. So Butch and I will head south and start something new."

"When do you leave?"

"A couple days. I found a rental online near the courts that should be perfect for us. I rented it for six months. I figure that will be enough time to decide if we want to stay longer or move on."

"Sounds exciting."

"You ever think about leaving Denver?" As soon as I asked, I worried she might think I was asking her to join me. I wasn't. I hardly knew her. I held my breath.

"Not really. I love it here. I ski, and I just love the action here. Plus, I have a lot of friends here and now I have pickleball. But I'd love to come down some time and see it."

We agreed to keep in touch and exchanged phone numbers and email accounts. I felt a pang of guilt in my gut. Was it too soon? After Stephanie died, I vowed I was done with relationships.

Joanne excused herself and took the opportunity to join some of her girlfriends for a game, while I watched. They were all about the same skill level, 3.0+. What they lacked in skill, they made up in enthusiasm. Next to them was a group of guys that looked to be much better. Possibly 3.5 to 4.0 level. They were intense but still seemed to be having fun. They finished their game and rather than leave the court, they stood around drinking water and discussing the game.

21

The waiting rack for their court had 4 paddles up next. The owners of the paddles grabbed them and headed for the court, expecting the previous players to leave. As they reached the court, the players there informed the newcomers that they were going to have to wait out another game before playing.

"We're up next," said one of the men, strutting onto the court.

"After we finish."

"No. That isn't how it works here."

"I don't fucking care how it works here," screamed one of the other men. "We're playing another game and you can either wait or find another court."

"Bullshit."

"Yeah, exactly. Bullshit. Get off the court," said the man, marching up to get in the face of the newcomer.

More insults and cussing ensued. Neither group looked like they were going to back down. I knew that local rules dictated that it was four on and four off if there was anyone waiting to play. But I told myself I wasn't getting involved, and I wasn't the only one that didn't step up. A crowd of spectators grew around me, grumbling and commenting, but no one was willing to step on the court and mediate the argument. I was convinced it was about to explode into a full-on brawl.

"Gentlemen, and I use that term lightly in your cases," said the cop that had interviewed me a few minutes earlier, "I'm going to tell you one time and one time only. Settle this now, peacefully, or I'm going to ban all of you from playing here."

"You can't do that," argued one of the original players.

"Try me. In fact, I'm going to change that order and I'm telling you." He paused and pointed to the loudmouth that had challenged him, "pack your things up and go home or I'll drag you in on a nuisance offense."

The man started to object, but one of his friends pulled him aside and whispered what I assume was good advice, as the man calmed down, grabbed his things, and stormed off, muttering to himself. Crisis averted for now.

This kind of thing was happening more and more on courts all across the country. I had seen a little of it a year ago, but as the popularity of the sport had exploded the last year or two, the competition for court time had become a problem. As the level of play improved, other problems surfaced as well. The better players only wanted to play better players and seemed less interested in helping newbies develop their games.

I turned to someone standing next me, "Is this happening a lot here these days?"

"You must be new here," he said. "There's a fight here almost every day now. Either someone gets their panties in a bind over getting hit with a ball or they are arguing over court time. It's getting like high school all over again."

"It's mostly the guys," said an older woman. "They need to grow up."

"I used to play here a year ago and I don't remember all this drama."

"Too many new players and not enough courts. And if that isn't bad enough, some people that live near the courts are complaining about the noise," said the first man.

"But these men want to hog the courts and if a lady gets on the court with them, they try to hit her with hard shots just to scare her off," added the woman, "I'm sick of them. That cop should haul them all away. Just last week, a friend of mine got hit in the face by a slam from one of those guys."

23

"Is she OK?" I asked.

"She will be, but I wish they would all drop dead."

This was making my plan to leave the area feel more like the right decision. It's not like it was perfect before, but fighting and arguing on the courts wasn't a daily occurrence. When I played with Stephanie, we did encounter a few players we preferred not to play with, but that was usually because of constant bad calls or poor sportsmanship. I rarely saw anyone actually fight. Would it be better in Rio Viejo? Yes, I told myself. It had to be. Denver was just too big, which to me meant more crowded and therefore more people with short tempers fighting over court time.

Butch and I left the courts, and when we got home, I packed the U-Haul. I told him we were leaving in the morning.

At five the next morning, I woke Butch up and asked him, "Butch, are you excited?"

He didn't respond, but I coaxed him into the passenger seat of my Jeep Cherokee with a few tasty treats. Normally he took the back seat, but it was loaded with crap and there was no room for him to stretch out. He looked at me and tried to get comfortable, which was no small feat for a dog his size.

The plan was to drive to a Motel 6 outside of Albuquerque, New Mexico the first day, with a pit stop about halfway, followed by another seven-hour leg the next day. When we reached the motel that first night out of Denver, Butch was thrilled to get out of the car. I'm sure he would have preferred to stay at the motel forever, rather than continue our journey. It took more treats to get him back in the car for the last leg of the trip.

"Trust me, dude, you're going to love it. No leash laws in Rio Viejo. There's a nice trail and river by the house, and I'll get you some rattlesnake avoidance training, so you won't have to worry about them." He raised an eyelid when I said training, as that usually was accompanied by treats.

"And don't worry about the marauding illegal aliens people talk about. It's all a big lie."

We arrived around two in the afternoon and Butch literally flew out of the car. There was a lock box on the house with the keys inside and a binder with restaurant menus and instructions about the house. It was a neat ranch-style home with lots of southwestern art scattered around. It was located on a small cul-de-sac with a brick wall enclosing the backyard. I checked for snakes first, then let Butch run around while I unpacked the U-Haul. When I finished, which didn't take too long since we were traveling relatively light, I told Butch to hang out while I drove to the market to grab some food. He looked at me with pleading eyes that said, *Either take me with you or bring me a burger with no pickles*. I decided he would prefer a burger.

He quickly forgave me for leaving him behind and forcing him into this big move when I returned with the burgers and a six pack of Tecate Light. We ate our burgers while watching some show about amazing dog tricks on TV.

Pickleball Tip # 2 – Scoring

The game starts with the serving team serving at 0-0-2. That means each team has zero points and the server is the number 2 server. The serve goes cross-court and must not land in the kitchen (more on this later) or touch the lines of the kitchen. If it does touch the kitchen, it is a fault and it is side out and the other team takes over the serve. Points are only awarded when the serving team wins a rally. Normally both players on a team get to serve except on the first serve of the game. After the side out the other team now serves at 0-0-1 (the 1 being the first server of the other team). If they score, the server moves to the other side and serves to the other player, again cross-court. Now it would be 1-0-1. If the serving team loses this point, then the second server takes over and now the score is 1-0-2.

Games go to 11 – win by 2.

Chapter 3

I woke up from a fitful sleep, wondering where I was. I had been having trouble sleeping since my wife passed away, and although marijuana seemed to help, it wasn't perfect. I either took too much or too little. If I took too much, I tended to wake up feeling drugged and if I took too little, I had trouble falling asleep or staying asleep. Regardless, I still woke up 3-4 times a night and usually had trouble falling back to sleep. Between the beer, a joint, and a marijuana gummy, it was clear I had had too much. I felt like I did the morning after a few too many shots of tequila. An all too often occurrence the past year. I swear Butch was shaking his head at me while I stumbled over to the bathroom sink and washed my face in cold water.

Butch, however, was in his same dude-like mood. The first few weeks and months after my wife and his best friend passed, Butch would wander around the house looking for her and moaning. He would often sit by the front door staring at it, I assume expecting her to come through there any minute. I think on some level he blamed me for her disappearance, since the last time he saw her, I was taking her to the hospital. But as time wore on, he cozied up to me and we were buddies again. Maybe he figured I was all he had now, and he had better take care of me.

I considered getting back into bed and trying to sleep off my inebriation, but there was Butch, sitting on the bed, staring at me with a mixed expression of anticipation and annoyance. His rule was that I could sleep as long as I needed, but if the sun was up then I should be up as well. Another rule was that if he could confirm that I was awake (i.e., my eyes were open), then it was time for me to get up and pay attention to his needs. That usually resulted in him talking to me (moaning), licking my face (which either meant he was glad to see I survived the night, or my face was dirty), or pawing at me. When you're an eighty-pound dog, one of these methods is sure to work.

I stumbled my way over to the sliding glass door that opened to the backyard patio and let him out. He immediately set to sniffing and peeing on everything in sight. Satisfied that I had done my duty for Butch, I padded into the kitchen and put a pot of coffee up to brew. The sun was just barely above the horizon, and it looked like a typical clear day in Southern Arizona. After a cup of coffee and some prepackaged Danish product I had brought with us from Denver, I was rewarded with a nice little sugar rush and ready for an inaugural day at the pickleball courts. Admittedly, I had a bit of trepidation in anticipation of meeting a new group of players. Would I be up to their standards? After a long layoff, I had my doubts and insecurities about how I would fit in with this new crowd. I knew I would be rusty, but on another level, I figured it would come back to me quickly and I just needed some people to play with to get the rust off my game. But pride and ego can be nasty companions, and I wanted to make an impression early on that I was a decent player and a welcome addition to the group. I also wasn't sure about socializing with new people. I hadn't done much of that the past year. Normally, or I should say, before I lost my wife, I was a fairly friendly and outgoing person, but now I did have a lot of baggage and didn't really want to share it. Pickleball people can be too social, if there is such a thing as being too social.

Generally speaking, I don't mind not having lots of friends, at least not this past year, but I did want to be accepted. It seems every pickleball court across the country has its "home rules" and individual "mores" and you don't want to be the one to buck them. At least not on your first day, and I was anxious to get my first day with new people behind me.

Butch finished his business and came in for a bowl of gravy-infused kibble. If it wasn't mixed with a little warm water and stirred properly, he would just stare at me until I got it right. And if he was being stubborn, he wouldn't touch it until I sprinkled shredded cheese or some other tasty ingredient on top. I got it right the first try this morning and he gobbled it down in about two seconds, then went to get his leash, informing me it was time for a proper walk. I complied.

Although I was antsy to get to the courts and meet the local competition, I also knew better than to cut Butch's walk short. He relished his walks and sniffs, and took the whole thing very seriously. Any deviation from that routine would be met with scorn and punishment. He had a great memory and held a grudge, sometimes for hours. I would pay the price for any indiscretion on my part with the stink eye, accompanied by moans and groans, except when he would purposely ignore me. Not sure which was worse, since neither were pleasant and the only way to get back in his good graces after such a faux pas was through treats and a make-up walk. A long make-up-walk at that. No doubt the make-up treats accounted for a portion of his eighty pounds. So, we walked, and pickleball had to wait.

We leashed up and wandered out the door and were greeted by a warm sunny sky, even though it was only 7 am. We made our way to the Anza trail that followed along the Santa Cruz River, although in my mind it looked more like a creek. Butch was enjoying all the new and fascinating sniffs when he spotted a couple of javelinas walking across the trail. I gripped the leash a little tighter in anticipation of Butch lunging at them. They casually glanced at us and seemed utterly unconcerned, as if they knew we posed no threat to them. I suppose if Butch was off leash, he might have changed their minds on that, but I had no desire to see who would win that fight. If you haven't encountered javelinas in your life, then you are missing out. They look like hairy, unkempt wild pigs. I actually think they are kind of cute, particularly the young ones, but I'm told if threatened they can be quite fearsome, and you would do best to steer clear of them.

Rio Viejo was in many ways like a lot of towns in Southern Arizona. They had very few lawns but an abundance of rocks and cacti. Butch was fond of doing his business on grass, but he would have to learn that dirt and pebbles would do just as well. Picking up after him without disposing of a handful of rocks was going to be a skill I would need to learn. Another big difference between Rio Viejo and our neighborhood in Denver was sidewalks. Rio Viejo didn't have that many, and where they did, they were only on one side of the street. This created a challenge, having to cross back and forth from one street to another. I was also a bit shocked to learn that Rio Viejo had been designated a "dark sky" town, which meant that in the residential areas there were no street lamps, and the lights in front of houses had to be dim and point down. Great for seeing stars in the night sky, but not so wonderful when you are walking at night and want to avoid stepping on a rattle snake or a tarantula, not to mention the bobcats and javelinas I had been told wandered the streets after dark. We were used to well-lit streets in Denver and not having to worry about encountering wildlife in the neighborhood. I could appreciate the stars, but given a choice, I'd opt for streetlights. I made a mental note to invest in some new flashlights so I could spot undesirable critters, but also for picking up after Butch, which could be quite challenging in the dark. Oh, and bats. They came out at night as well, and I can tell you that having them swoop around your head in the dark is creepy.

After about thirty minutes, we made our way back to the house and I suited up for pickleball. My outfit consisted of an elbow brace, that I hoped would prevent a recurrence of tennis elbow, and knee braces on both knees because I had damaged them over the years from being a weekend warrior, playing too much basketball and tennis. Even though it had been a year since playing sports of any kind, I wore the supports and braces out of habit. I finished off with a healthy schemer of sun block on my face and arms. Yes, black people do need sunscreen.

It was only April, and the temperature gauge was already topping seventy-five by nine am, with a daytime high expected to be in the mid-nineties. I was going to have to adjust to this new normal, which meant most of the players would be done playing by noon if they wanted to survive the heat. Feeling the heat rising by the minute, it occurred to me that Butch and I would need to get up earlier to get our walk done, to avoid the risk of burning his paws on the hot pavement. The house we were renting was only about ten minutes by bike to the courts and twenty-to-thirty minutes by foot. An easy trek, with no major hills to climb and no traffic to contend with. I had brought an old mountain bike with me from Denver, so I swung my sports bag over my shoulders and mounted my bike.

Somehow, this little town near the Mexican border had a fairly active pickleball community. Probably because of the advanced age of the residents and the growing popularity of pickleball with the older generation. At least, that is what I read on a website called *Places to Play*, and on Facebook. If choosing a place to live that is pickleball friendly seems odd to you, then you haven't been infected with the pickleball virus. My theory is that it's only a matter of time and you will. The great thing about renting a house was that if I didn't like the pickleball community, I could easily pack up and move to another location.

Rio Viejo wasn't a wealthy town, and neither was the county it's located in, so funds for pickleball courts were limited. I had read that the determined players in Rio Viejo, undaunted by the lack of government support, had passed the hat to raise the funds necessary to make up the difference for maintenance and construction costs that the county couldn't afford. To their credit, the locals had put together six well-appointed and sharp looking pickleball courts. Two of the courts had lines painted for both pickleball and tennis, but as I would later learn, the tennis players had

31

all switched to pickleball, moved away, or currently played over on the courts at the golf resort. In Denver, there was always a fight between the pickleball players and the tennis players for courts. Tennis players felt encroached upon and resented the drive to make tennis courts into pickleball courts. But tennis is hard on old bodies, and pickleball is easier in many ways, especially for older people, so pickleball continued to grow because the city council was mostly run by people of an older age. If you follow pickleball news, you know that lots of heated arguments take place daily around the country, with incidents of violence and vandalism on the upswing. I read about some courts in New York that were going to be shut down because the players appropriated them from children's playgrounds and the parents went ballistic. So, it was just as well that the local tennis players here in Rio Viejo had found somewhere else to play.

As I neared the courts, I could hear the ping of balls against paddles and loud, raucous laughter. Those are the typical sounds you hear from pickleball courts. Hard to believe anyone could object to pickleball, but in many areas where the courts are too close to homes, it is creating quite a bit of friction between neighbors. If I'm being honest, I have to admit I wouldn't want to listen to pickleball all day long, so I prefer to live a few minutes away from the action.

By the time I rolled onto the field next to the courts and dismounted from my bike, there were already about thirty people there. All the courts were occupied, and games were in full swing, with a few people milling about waiting for an open court. Along the fence next to the courts were a mishmash of beach and lounge chairs, shaded by some very mature oak or mesquite trees. They even had a couple of picnic benches and tables covered with water bottles and pickleball equipment bags.

The courts in Rio Viejo were segmented into three sets of two, and on the fences near each set of courts was a paddle rack that could hold up to twelve paddles. The racks determined who would play next on each court. If you wanted to get in a game, you put your paddle in the rack and waited your turn. The courts were all numbered and I quickly learned (you could actually tell by the level of play) that courts 1 and 2 were for beginners, 3 and 4 were for intermediate play, and 5 and 6 were for the advanced players. From what I've heard, this is typical of a lot of courts around the country. If you want to play at a certain level, you put your paddle in the rack alongside that court. Another interesting thing that I noticed was that the amount of fun players were having on the court seemed to be directly related to their skill level. If fun is measured by the level of laughter and joking, then the folks on courts 1- 4 were having the most fun. There was much less laughter and camaraderie on courts 5 and 6. The better players appeared to be very serious and competitive, to the point of not having fun at all. I wasn't too surprised. I've known competitive players who would let a pickleball loss, or even just a bad shot, ruin the rest of their day. Personally, I love the competition and I definitely play to win, but I'm more interested in playing well and having a good time. Maybe I'm an anomaly.

My plan was to sit for a few minutes before trying to get in a game. I wanted to see the level of competition on each court and decide where I would fit in best for my first game. I ignored the paddle racks, and I just held my paddle on my lap and watched. A year ago, I would not have hesitated to put my paddle in the advanced rack and jump right in against the better players, but as I mentioned before, I had been away from the game for a year and was out of practice, out of shape, and uncertain how fast things would come back to me. There were a few players waiting their turn to play, but no one really paid much attention to me, which I was okay with. All the courts were full and I tried to keep my eye on all the games. I guess I looked a bit out of place, because two of the players coming off the beginner court came over and introduced themselves to me.

"Hi, I'm Sheila," said a tall woman with blonde hair and a huge smile. "You look lost."

"I'm new here," I responded, "I'm Al." We did a little fist bump, the norm since COVID struck the world.

Her partner was much shorter, with gray hair and coke bottle glasses. She held up her paddle to wave at me, "Hi, I'm Laura. I'm new to the game too."

"Oh, I've played before," I corrected her, "but I'm new to town and haven't played in a year." I had been watching them on the court and Sheila was a decent player, but Laura was clearly a beginner.

"Well," said Sheila, "get your paddle and get out there. We're a very friendly and forgiving group. You and I can take on Rory and Jack."

There were two paddles in the rack that I assumed belonged to Rory and Jack. They said hello but acted a little put off by me. I think they wanted a competitive game and figured that since I was new, I wouldn't be much competition. We stepped out on the court.

"We already played a game, so we're warmed up," said Jack.

"I'd like to hit a few shots just to warm up. It's been about a year or so since I hit a ball," I told them. I could tell Rory was raring to go, but he indulged me anyway.

I hit a few easy dinks as we chatted, giving basic introductions. I learned that Jack Swenson was the resident janitor, so to speak. He had moved to Rio Viejo from Ohio a year ago in search of warmer weather in the winter. His introduction to pickleball happened just before leaving Ohio. He was an amiable guy, probably in his late 60's or early 70's, who showed up every day, earlier than everyone else. If the courts were wet, or were covered in leaves and dirt, he got his electric powered leaf blower out and cleaned them. He also notified everyone via text on some phone app that they all had as to the weather and the court conditions. And if that wasn't enough, he also brought a cooler full of water bottles and ice to share.

Sheila Smythe, was a sixty-five-year-old divorcee who had moved down from Tucson a few years previously, to escape the big city and work on her watercolor art. She made sure to tell me Smythe was spelled with a Y. She sold her work in one of the local galleries and had supported herself with her art ever since her husband left her for a younger woman. She had been a tennis player at one time in her life but now was devoted only to pickleball. Even though she was on the beginner court, she was far from a beginner.

Rory Townsend was a recently retired attorney from Canada. He had started coming to Rio Viejo a few years ago as a snowbird. Except for trips back to Canada for government sponsored health care, he was now a full-time Rio Viejo resident. He had an intense air about him. He allowed me to warm up but seemed bored by it.

My game came back to me quickly. I wasn't as sharp as I had been in the past, but I was hitting balls back with ease and control, with only a few hitting the net and a few dinks going longer than I wanted. On the whole, I was feeling comfortable out there.

"You look like you can play the game," said Rory, as we dinked back and forth, "I can tell you aren't a beginner."

"I thought I might need to give you some pointers," said Sheila, "but I can see that won't be necessary."

"You might need to go easy on us," added Jack.

I laughed, "I haven't played in a year, so don't worry about me. You guys will have to go easy on me."

I asked why they were on the beginner courts rather than the more advanced. Jack made it a point to tell me he had more fun playing on the beginner and intermediate courts, because the people on the advanced courts weren't as much fun. He said they were too serious and didn't like to play with anyone below their level. He also made it clear that he liked playing with the ladies more than with the guys. I quickly learned he was single and suspected he was a bit of a flirt. He complimented Sheila every chance he got. Not that it wasn't warranted, she was a good player, as well as an attractive woman.

The game started and it was the consummate friendly pickleball game, nobody taking it too seriously. Just what I was looking for in my first time back on the courts. Then it changed. Rory started hitting harder drives at both me and Sheila. He generally had no soft game to speak of, so if he missed a drive, it either went in the net or flew long. When he did manage to keep it low, I was able to take the pace off and frustrate him. Sheila, however, was not so skilled at dealing with bangers. She got hit twice, once in the gut and the other in her butt, as she tried to turn away from a slam. When he did manage a dink, it was a mishit. On the other hand, his partner Jack rarely hit the ball hard. He was all about finesse and he was careful not to hit Sheila. Jack's game was about waiting for his opponent to make a mistake. I'm not sure if that was by design, or he just lacked confidence in hitting hard.

Sheila wasn't a bad player and was able to dink on occasion, but she had no power, so her drives weren't too effective. Her shots weren't necessarily planned, and she lacked any strategy, but she was having a ball out there. She was fun to play with. Never took anything too seriously and was open to getting help. She was even good natured about getting hit, but I was a little miffed at Rory for clearly over-hitting at her.

The game progressed nicely, with Sheila and I ahead 9 to 4. I was quickly getting back into my comfort zone out there but tried not to be overzealous. I wanted to win for Sheila, but I wanted to keep it close. Then Rory hit a ball to Sheila that looked clearly out to me. Sheila called it out and Rory had a fit.

"That ball was clearly in," he yelled.

"I saw it out," replied Sheila.

"Well, you're wrong. Get new glasses."

I stood there quietly not sure what to do. I saw it as out and wanted to support my partner, but I sure didn't want an argument on my first day out there.

Sheila turned to me and asked me what I thought.

"I saw it out, but I was out of position. The rules say it's your call."

"I don't care what the rules say. The ball was in," screamed Rory.

If the ball was out, it would have been side out to Rory and Jack. Rory walked back to the baseline and prepared to serve.

"If it's my call, why is he serving?" she asked me.

I walked over to her and told her to let it go. It wasn't worth a fight. She grumbled something about Rory being an asshole but took my advice and stepped back to return the next serve. After that I stepped up my game a little, and Sheila and I ended up winning 11 to 5. She was thrilled, but Rory? Not so much. We tapped paddles at the net, and everyone said good game, but I could tell Rory didn't mean it. It was clear he had a temper and didn't like to lose to a woman.

As we walked off the court, I patted Sheila on the back and congratulated her on a great game. I wanted to offer Jack and Rory some kind words, but even though they could all use some advice to improve their games, I kept my mouth shut. I've made the mistake in the past of offering unsolicited advice and I was determined not to do it again. Certainly not with people I had just met. I was eager to make friends in my new town. If they wanted advice from me, they were going to have to ask for it. Rory stormed off the court, still grumbling.

The three of us came off the court and sat down, drinking water and discussing many things: the game, pickleball in general, dogs, even the weather. It was a very friendly and talkative group, which made me feel right at home. As we chatted, a group of ladies that Sheila said called themselves the Casual Ladies Club went onto the court we had just vacated. We watched them play until one of the ladies heard her phone ring and excused herself.

The other ladies paused briefly, as the woman screamed into the phone, "I told you I was playing pickleball today, we can discuss it when I get home." She disconnected the call and went back onto the court.

I turned to Sheila and made a questioning face.

"Her husband always interrupts her when she comes to play. I think he's a bit senile," she laughed.

"Aren't we all," joked Jack, more as a statement than a question.

The ladies resumed play and were having a ball. They were almost as good as Sheila and took absolutely nothing seriously. They laughed and cheered at good shots and bad shots. If there had been a fun meter out there, these ladies would have been off the scale.

I was enjoying chatting with the other players and feeling pretty good. They were acting like we were old friends and I felt accepted in the group. There was some talk about my skill level and how I got so good. I was careful to compliment everyone on their games rather than focus on mine. I hadn't been this talkative or friendly with strangers since Stephanie died, so this felt both odd and good to me at the same time. One of the things I have always liked about pickleball is how friendly and welcoming everyone is. I was enjoying getting to know everyone, but what I really wanted was to get back out on the court for another game.

As if Jack could read my mind, he suggested I should get in a game on the intermediate courts, rather than with all the beginners. I guess it was obvious that I wasn't going to get much of a challenge on the beginner courts. I took his advice and put my paddle in the appropriate rack and waited my turn. I watched the players on court 3 and it was clear they were better than Sheila and the Casual Ladies. I thought both Jack and Rory probably belonged on the intermediate courts as well. It was a game of mixed doubles, and they showed some skill at dinking, but play didn't last more than four or five hits before someone made a mistake. The players appeared to range in age from forty to sixty, but then I'm not a great judge of peoples ages. Watching the game, I decided that they weren't quite as good as the competition I was used to, but it would still be a little more challenging than the beginner courts.

A tall man with gray hair poking out of the sides of a Panama hat came over and put his paddle in the rack next to mine. "Take on the winners?" he asked me.

"I would love to," I said putting out my hand for a fist pump, "I'm Al."

"Hi, Hal. I'm William."

"No. I'm Al," I repeated.

"What did he say?" said William, turning to Sheila and Jack.

"He said Al. His name is Al," said Sheila, shaking her head with a frown.

"Nice to meet you, pal," he said holding out his fist to bump hands with me. A few people laughed. "You new in town? I don't think I've seen you before."

Since I was the only black guy out there, I had to chuckle to myself. I had seen other black folks in town. Maybe they played out here from time to time?

Sheila stepped over and whispered, "He's hard of hearing, in case you didn't figure that out, and half the time he forgets to wear his hearing aid. Drives us crazy, but he's nice though, and I guess we are all getting old and losing our hearing a little."

"What?" I said and smiled. I knew it was a dumb joke, but sometimes you just have to go with the moment.

Sheila smiled. "Oh, you are going to fit right in here."

"What brings you here?" asked William.

"Pickleball," I replied, knowing full well that wasn't what he meant.

He shook his head with a sardonic smile. "I mean, Rio Viejo."

I leaned closer to William and raised my voice so he could hear me, then shared an abbreviated version of my move to Rio Viejo. I realized I was going to have to go through this a bunch of times before I had met the entire crew. I was already tired of the story and ready to make up a new one just to keep it interesting. I did stuff like that in the past and my wife would roll her eyes and apologize for me. How I wished I could still annoy her.

"And you?" I asked, "What brought you here?"

"I got lost driving around Tucson one day and ended up here and decided to stay."

"Really?" I said, looking to see if he was joking. He just smiled.

Sheila jumped in and rescued me. "You can't believe half of what Willie says. He wouldn't know how to tell the truth on the witness stand if his life depended on it."

"I was a comedian in a previous life," he added.

"No, you weren't. You were a judge in a civil court."

"Same thing. I had everyone on the edge of their seats. If they didn't laugh at my jokes, I held them in contempt of court."

Glancing around the courts I noticed, and not for the first time, that pickleball brings out an eclectic crowd. I believe that just about anyone from any profession can be found out on the courts. There is no dress code and it's evident that style is in the eyes of the beholder. The ladies are typically more stylish than the men, with floral leggings or bright tennis skirts and tops that usually match. The men, on the other hand, are all over the place. I can just hear their wives or girlfriends telling them before they leave the house, "Are you really going to wear that?" On more than one occasion, Stephanie had me change my clothes before wandering out to the courts. Sometimes you can't tell if a guy is headed to the beach, a safari, or a sporting event. I've even seen guys wearing Bermuda shorts or cargo pants, and one guy used to wear a pith helmet. Color coordination is typically an accident with most of the men out there. I usually just grab the first shorts and t-shirt in the pile. Sometimes they go together, evidently sometimes they don't.

A court opened up and William enlisted me as his partner. We were taking on a couple of men named Tom Martin and Stuart Layton. Apparently, they had been winning against anyone and everyone on the intermediate courts. I had a glimpse of their game from a distance, and they looked like decent players. They came off their last game bragging that they couldn't be beat. They announced that they were 3 and 0 as a team and the games hadn't even been close. It was all good-natured bragging, but they had laid down the challenge. I expected that they were familiar with William's game, but mine would be a mystery to them.

After a few shots, they realized their best strategy was to target William. He was slow, his backhand was a liability, and he had no clue how to play as a team. Tom and Stuart made a good team, each knowing the other's strengths and weaknesses, and they did a good job covering for each other. Their strategy after a few points was to freeze me out and focus on William. It became quickly obvious to me that if I wanted to hit any balls and have a chance of winning, I was going to have to cover most of the court and try to protect my partner. So, I did. As good as they were, they weren't good enough to prevent me from poaching and taking over

41

points. The more I poached, the more they tried difficult angle shots that sailed wide, more often than not. William didn't seem upset by my poaching, as opposed to some players who think the court is divided in half and you should stay on your side. I sensed that William wanted to win, even if that meant he would hit fewer balls. He let me know I could take any shot I wanted. I played hard, and my aggressive court coverage and shot selection confused and frustrated Tom and Stuart. They started making error after error in an effort to freeze me out. William was ecstatic when we took the final point and won 11-9. To their credit, Tom and Stuart were good sports about their loss, even if William was over the top with his celebration. I surmised he didn't win too many games.

"Nice game, you clearly are not a beginner," said Tom, as we tapped paddles at center court.

"Thanks," I said, "I'm a little rusty, but it's coming back to me quickly."

"If that's rusty, I hate to see you at the top of your game," he laughed, loudly. I could tell he was someone you could easily become friends with.

"Get any better and the Royals will recruit you to their court," said Stuart as he pointed over to courts 5 and 6. I could tell he did not mean it to be a compliment to these so-called Royals.

"You don't play with them?" I asked. What I should have asked was, "What the hell is a Royal?", but I didn't. I figured I'd find out soon enough, and I wasn't wrong.

"We are fill-in's when they need us. Either they come over here and bless us with their presence or, if they need a player, they might come over and ask one of us to join them," said Tom, sarcastically, "They're an annoying bunch of SOB's."

I cringed. It seemed people were people and pickleball drama was everywhere, although I had never heard the term "Royals" in reference to any players.

Just then I heard some yelling on the far court where these supposed Royals were playing.

"The ball was in," someone screamed.

"It was out and it's my call anyway."

"You always call balls out when it suits you," screamed one of them, "You need a vision exam!"

Calling questionable balls out is a common point of contention at pickleball courts. Court etiquette says the team closest to the ball has the sole discretion to call the ball in or out. If in doubt, the proper call is to call it in. Arguing about a call from thirty or forty feet away is bad form. Questioning someone's integrity about their calls is also in bad form. It is also one of the most common reasons for arguments on the court and I'd just witnessed it twice in one day.

Sadly, the argument got louder and more heated. A few curse words were thrown back and forth.

"They get pretty serious over there, do they?" I said to Tom and Stuart.

"Assholes," said Stuart, "Everything is so damn serious to them. They think because they are better players than most of us that they can do or say anything they want."

"You guys are pretty good though. Do you think they are that much better?" I asked.

"In their minds mostly," said Rory who had joined the conversation. I had to laugh to myself, since just a few minutes ago Rory was arguing a line call. "Sometimes, even if they need a fourth, they choose to do drills instead of allowing any of us to play with them. They do put on clinics for

43

us lowly peons though. The clinics are free, but they are so condescending that it's almost painful. I don't think you would learn anything from them. In fact, from what I see you could teach the class better than them."

Looking to change the subject, Tom asked why I was rusty.

"I used to play a lot, until about a year ago." I didn't want to get too emotional, but I also didn't want to sound mysterious, so I quickly said my wife was sick and that before she passed, I took time off to be with her. I got the usual expressions of sorrow one gets in these situations. Even that short version almost brought me to tears, so I quickly changed the subject back to pickleball. "I was a pretty decent player at one time and hope to get back to my old level. You guys are good and a hell of a lot of fun to play with. Thanks for letting me join you."

Tom wasn't done putting down the Royals though. "Last time I tried to play with them, I put my paddle on the rack and when it was my turn to go out on the court, they stopped me, saying they were training for a tournament and wanted another game by themselves. They each have their partners and when a tournament is coming up, they only want to play with their partners. We can challenge them, but they don't like splitting up. They also don't think we give them enough competition. I haven't tried to play with them since."

Tom wasn't shy about his scorn for them. The other players nodded agreement and said they had experienced that at least once themselves. A few even complained about getting unsolicited coaching from them that they claimed was questionable. The game on court 5 ended with a few more nasty barbs flying. Everyone clammed up or changed the subject, as the so-called Royals came off the court to towel off and get drinks. They were patting themselves on the back and complimenting each other on their great play. Except the two players who were still arguing about a line call.

"You always call balls out that were clearly in."

44

"Eddie, you are so full of shit. The ball was out, and you shouldn't argue."

"Fuck off, Brian," said Eddie, as he stormed away and sat down on one of the beach chairs a few feet away. He took a drink from his water bottle, shaking his head and muttering something to himself.

It was briefly quiet and awkward, until a brunette in an immaculate tennis outfit, who looked to be in her fifties, came over to introduce herself to me.

"Hi, I'm Nancy," she said with a huge smile, showing off the whitest teeth I have ever seen. "Are you new here?" she asked. Not one to state the obvious, was she? I had a feeling she knew the name and skill level of every player in town, but if I've learned anything from Butch, it's how to keep my mouth shut.

So, I smiled and answered, with no trace of sarcasm. "I am new here. I'm Al. I just moved here from Denver."

"Cool. I'm always curious how people discover Rio Viejo. I've been here for years. Grew up in Phoenix. What brought you here?" she asked.

"My wife and I passed through here a few years ago on our way to San Carlos. I thought it looked nice."

"Does your wife play, too?"

"She did. She passed away last year." I hoped that would end the discussion. She frowned and said she was sorry but didn't question me any further about it.

Another fellow, maybe about fifty years-old and very fit, strutted over to meet me. And I mean strutted, as if he was important and he was going to look the part. He was dressed in a tennis outfit right out of GQ, with blonde, wavy hair peeking out of the sides of a baseball cap that said, "Pickle Much?"

45

"I'm Nathan," he said, holding out his fist for a fist bump and putting his arm around Nancy. I guessed he did that to make it known to the newcomer that he and Nancy were an item. "I'm the resident pickleball ambassador, president of the local pickleball club, and I teach pickleball." Before I could get a word in, he went into what I can only imagine was a rehearsed sales pitch, "Private lessons are $20 per hour per person for a group of four or eight, and I teach a group beginners class on Friday mornings for free if you would like to attend. Private lessons for a single are $50 an hour. I also rep two of the top lines of paddles and can hook you up." He smiled, and just like Nancy, he had pearly white teeth. I wondered if the two of them bought the same teeth whitening system.

I smiled back politely, "Thanks. I already have a paddle and I'm not looking for lessons right now." He looked briefly disappointed, so I quickly added, "but thanks for the offer. I'll keep that in mind."

He nodded but wasn't about to give up just yet. "I've taught most of the players here and we've won lots of team medals. Rio Viejo has one of the best records in league and tournament play. I'm sure I can help you with your game when you are ready." He emphasized "are ready".

His speech over, he disengaged from Nancy and strutted off to sit with Brian and Eddie, who were still arguing, just not as loudly as before. I could hear Nathan bragging about his last game and victory. He then launched into a coaching session, giving strategy advice to whoever would listen. I made a mental note to watch him play the next time he was on the court, and if I got the chance, I wanted to get on the court with him and see just how good he was.

"He's very good," said Nancy, possibly reading my mind.

"Thanks," I said awkwardly, and nodded.

She must have sensed my skepticism, so she added, "and he really is a good teacher and the best player here."

46

I smiled again. I guessed that in addition to being his girlfriend, she was also his marketing manager.

"Since you're new here, maybe you should start over on courts 1 and 2 and see how that goes."

I guess she hadn't noticed that I had already played some games on courts 1 and 3. I was far from a beginner but not so arrogant that I didn't think a good coach could help my game. Still, her demeanor was off-putting. I smiled anyway. I try not to be too judgmental of people I've just met, but I have to admit, she and Nathan were annoying. The immediate vibe they gave out was that they were superior to everyone around them, but I was willing to attribute part of my first impression of them to the comments made about them by the other players. I knew better than to let someone influence my opinion of others, but hey, no one is perfect. But I held my tongue. No sense making enemies on my first day at the court. I hoped that my first impression would be wrong once I got to know them.

"Thanks," I said, still smiling, "I'm just happy to be playing again. The folks over on court 1 already got me in a game and I got one in on court 3, as well."

She raised her eyebrows. "Oh, I missed it."

Nathan had been listening in and wandered back over to us.

"Oh, how did you do?" he asked, in what I took to be a condescending tone.

"He plays quite well, actually," chimed in William, who must have turned his hearing aid up to hear the conversation. Then he added in snide voice, "I'm sure he could beat your ass."

That remark elicited a few giggles from Tom and Stuart and caught the attention of some others standing nearby. I kept my mouth shut. I didn't know Nathan's game yet and didn't want to get into some kind of pissing match with him. For all I knew, he could have been a 5.0, and I was still rusty.

Nathan gave William a dirty look and walked away. He was clearly insulted that William thought anyone here could beat him.

Nancy acted like the exchange hadn't taken place.

"Oh, by the way, since you are new here, I'm a real estate agent, and if you decide to buy a home, I would love to help you." She grabbed her bag off the bench and rifled through it until she pulled out a business card and handed it to me. There was a picture of her, dressed to the nines in front of a fancy home, which I assumed was hers. As if she read my mind, she said, "That's my office-slash-home. Feel free to stop by any time. This is a great place to live, and I've helped most of the players here get situated."

"Not me," quipped William, clearly as annoyed with Nancy as he was with Nathan.

Another awkward silence followed, which Jack ended by saying, "I would use you Nancy, but I'm not looking to buy." I learned very quickly that Jack was always looking to calm things down. A peacemaker, if you will. Nancy smiled.

"Thanks," I said. "I'm not ready to commit to buying a home here yet, but if I do, I will certainly come to you for help."

"Cool," she said, "Oh, and we have a club called the Rio Viejo Pickleball Club. Dues are $200 a year. You can pay me if you want."

"Dues? Aren't these public courts?"

"Yes, but we do lots of things the county won't pay for. If you are a member, you can reserve courts and you get to join our chat text group that we use to keep in touch with each other."

"Oh."

"Or you can donate $5 a day, if you don't want a yearly membership."

"Oh."

With that, she walked over to Nathan, who was clearly fuming over William's remarks and whining something to a little guy that looked like he had a permanent frown on his face. I sat there with Tom, William, Rory, and Jack, and a few ladies who had just finished up on court 1.

Pickleball Tip # 3 – Hit Volleys Down

Most volley firefights continue because the players are hitting the ball chest high. Rather than always hitting at full power, take some pace off and hit down at your opponents' feet. This will cause your opponent to either hit a half-volley off their shoelaces up into your kill zone or into the net. In some cases, your opponent will over-hit that ball, sending it flying out of the court.

Chapter 4

"Piss-ants," snarled William, loud enough that Nathan could hear. People who have trouble hearing tend to speak louder than they need to. Nathan gave William the evil eye. Fortunately, Nathan didn't have any evil powers, or William might have burst into flames.

"They aren't getting any money from me. Damn thieves are what they are. I didn't vote for them and I'm not joining their stupid club and you don't have to, either."

"I see," I said hesitantly. The two hundred wasn't a problem for me, but I wanted to know more about the situation before I coughed it up. When I looked on *Places to Play* it didn't say anything about a private club.

Nathan was still in discussion with the short man with the scowl on his face.

"Who is the fellow Nathan is talking to?" I asked. "Why does he look so upset?"

"That's Little E," William informed me, "He thinks he's better than he is and he's never happy."

"Little E?" I asked, although in retrospect I suppose it was obvious, as Little E couldn't have been more than five-foot-five or five-foot-six inches tall.

"His name is actually Ethelwolf."

I scratched my head. I was confused and it must have showed.

"He's from England and his parents named him after some nobleman, I think. He doesn't like being called Ethel and we don't like saying Ethelwolf, so we call him Little E."

"He's not from England, he's from New York," said Rory, shaking his head.

"Who's from New York?" asked William.

"Get a fucking hearing aid, you old coot," said Jack jokingly.

"I hear just fine. You people need to learn to enunciate."

"Um, does Ethelwolf like being called Little E?" I asked.

"Who cares what that little piss-ant wants?" said William, "I'll call him whatever I want to call him."

I turned to Tom. "What do you call him?"

"E to his face and Little E behind his back."

I suppose that made sense if you were in a Groucho Marx movie. All I could think was, *What the fuck have I gotten myself into?*

"Nobody cares what you call him. Nobody likes him," said Rory.

I decided I would wait for him to introduce himself to me to find out what he wanted to be called. "I see," I responded.

"By the way, he always looks like that," said Jack. "He says he loves the game, but he isn't a very happy guy on the court."

A short, bouncy redhead came dancing over to me and asked if I would join them on court 2. Their fourth had to leave and they needed another player.

"I saw you playing before and you looked pretty good, and fun too. I'm Peggy."

"Hi. I'm Al." I looked around and no one else was asking me to play. Maybe she was just being nice to the new guy, but I was thrilled and said yes. I would have preferred another game on court 3, but I wasn't about to turn her down. I have trouble saying no anyway. She seemed pleased that I had accepted her invitation and off we went. I was her partner, and our opponents were some ladies named Laura and Melanie. All of them seemed of equal skill (above beginner and good enough to have fun), but Laura seemed a bit more serious than the others, which, given the amount of joking and laughter, wasn't much. She wasn't all that good but seemed to think she was and was constantly berating herself on shots she missed that she thought she should have made. Shots that obviously weren't in her repertoire to begin with. She was also quick to dish advice to the other players on the court. She even gave me some advice after I missed a shot. I took it good-naturedly.

We played a very friendly and, I must say, enjoyable game. I felt no pressure to prove myself to the ladies, as they just wanted to have fun and celebrate when they got a shot past me. I was careful not to hit the ball hard at them. There was no chance of them handling a ball hit right at them. It would just be bad sportsmanship. I also made sure I didn't hog the court and take shots from my partner. I was a perfect gentleman.

Peggy didn't seem to think winning was the point of playing. She was all about the fun. My goal was to win friends and feel accepted in my new community, not to impress anyone with my skill. It was easily the most laughter I had engaged in over the last year. It felt good.

I came off the court to get some water and in the back of my mind hoped to get in a game on the intermediate courts. There were 3 paddles on the rack, and I dropped mine into the fourth slot. The new game turned out to be more competitive, as I had hoped it would be. I was teamed up with a Hispanic girl named Sandra, who had some decent shots that I guessed came from a background in tennis. She hit the ball well but was still struggling, as many ex-tennis players do (you can always spot them), with

53

some of the nuances of dinking and hitting angles, which are more important in pickleball than tennis.

On the other side of the court was Cary and his wife, Mary. No joke. Cary was a banger. I mean the guy hit every ball he could, as hard as he could. He didn't care if it was a short shot, a long shot, at a man, or at a woman. He just hit hard, and he often hit people. When the balls didn't sail long or into the net, his shots were tough to handle. I could see how he might intimidate a lot of players.

Mary, on the other hand, didn't hit hard but was great at keeping the ball in play. She could block balls and even hit a decent dink shot. She probably got good at blocking balls practicing with Cary. They didn't employ any strategy that I could see, but they played well and were a lot of fun to play with. As with the other games that day, I just tried to be competitive without overdoing it. I restrained from poaching and just tried to keep the ball in play as long as I could. Sandra and I won the game 11 to 5, but there were some great rallies and no shortage of laughter.

After the game we all sat down for a water break and once again I got the third degree. Why was I there? What did I do before I came there? Was I retired? I looked too young to retire. Where did I learn to play and how long had I played? On and on. I barely could finish one answer before being bombarded with another. It was exhausting but gratifying that all these people wanted to get to know me. I tried to ask about the other players, but I wasn't too successful, as they were more interested in learning about the new guy. There was, however, a consensus about the players who dominated courts 5 and 6, and it wasn't positive. During the grilling, I kept trying to watch the players on the advanced courts. I wanted to see if they were as good as they thought they were, and of course I wanted to know how good Nathan was, and if I could compete with him.

After watching a few exchanges, I came to the conclusion that, although Nathan was the best player out there, he wasn't that great and certainly not as good as he acted. He had some skill, I could give him that, but he didn't show a lot of strategic knowledge and his power shots would have been derided as wimpy by my old group in Denver. He may have considered himself a 4.0 or 4.5 in this group, and he certainly had the most skill of the players here that I had seen so far, but if he played against the top players in Denver, he would have a tough time.

Ethelwolf, E, or Little E was a true 3.5 but would probably lose to most 3.5s he encountered. He was slower on the court than Nathan but actually had a better than average block shot that won him a lot of points, so long as they were hit right at him. He did well against the bangers here, but up against some of the monster bangers I saw in Denver, Ethelwolf would be target practice. The fact that he was slow didn't matter much as no one here really hit the open court and made him run. Nancy could dink okay and hit a decent, albeit soft, drive, but she had a habit of hitting backhands awkwardly that resulted in numerous pop-ups and put-a-ways. Even though she could dink, she couldn't force mistakes with aggressive dinking, so she relied on the lack of patience of her opponents when she got into a dinking battle.

I concluded that I could play with them. I tried not to be too egotistical, but I was fairly confident I could outplay them. That is, if they ever asked me on their court. And from the impression I got from Tom and the others, I would have to be invited to play with them. As I watched and answered questions about my past, the term Royals came up again and again. People were careful not to use that term in front of them but weren't shy about saying it to me. I learned that the Royals ruled the courts, and you didn't want to cross them, lest you be shunned. There was no love lost for the Royals, but that was on the down low. I wondered if there was a list somewhere with all of the members' names, but I didn't ask. I tried to create a mental list by watching who played on the Royal designated court and who was mentioned in the other players' snide comments. Some names kept coming up: Jane, Nathan, Nancy, Anna, Ethelwolf, Molly, Anne, and

Brian. It didn't appear that skill alone got you Royal designation. According to William, you could get accepted by being a kiss up. I was having trouble absorbing all the names coming at me at one time and then putting faces to the names. Name tags would have been nice.

The game on court 5 ended and the players came off the court. I have to admit, they mingled like Royalty. I could see why the other players weren't that thrilled with them. I thought back to high school and the cliques that were so prevalent that made the experience a living hell for so many kids. But for gods' sake, we were adults now, bordering on old age. Wasn't it time we hung all that up? The Royals even took their break as a group and when finished, headed back out as a group, even though there were two paddles in the rack that belonged to Julio and Jesus, two young Hispanic men that were waiting to play.

"We'll take on the winners," said Julio with a slight Spanish accent.

I thought nothing of that, as that is the protocol on courts all across the country.

Nathan turned to them and shook them off, saying, "We're going to play another game first and then you can have the court. We're training for a tournament and need to practice together." Without waiting for any discussion, as if it mattered, the four Royals, consisting of Nathan, Nancy, Ethelwolf and Jane, marched back onto the court and began playing.

I could see that Julio and Jesus were not happy, but they backed down and returned to the bench. Julio tossed his paddle onto the picnic bench and said something in Spanish that either meant dick or fuckhead. My Spanish wasn't that good, but the sentiment was understood.

"Pendejos," agreed Jesus nodding.

By now a little group was forming and they had witnessed the snub.

"What the hell," Rory grumbled, "I thought that this was open play."

Milton, a player I had seen on the intermediate courts but who clearly had the skills to play above that level, said, "Not for the Royals." He said the word with obvious scorn.

"Happens all the time," said William, "You get used to it. You shouldn't let them do that to you, Julio."

I was amazed at how many people joined in the grumbling, but no one really challenged their authority. From what I could gather, the Royals consisted of a core group of about eight players, with another two or three, depending on who you talked to, of Royal wannabes. I had to think the Royals knew what everyone thought of them, but it didn't seem to matter. Most of the snide remarks and grumbling seemed to take place out of earshot of any Royals.

There had been no vote giving them authority to decide court designations, club tournaments, club dues for maintenance and balls, and just about anything else that came up in regard to pickleball. If you didn't meet their approval, you would not be asked to play with them, unless they were desperate for a player. Generally speaking, to play on courts 5 or 6 you had to be rated by none other than Nathan. Everyone seemed to defer to his expertise and authority. It still wasn't clear to me why though.

I was starting to doubt my decision to move to Rio Viejo. I was in need of new people and scenery, but I wanted tranquility, not constant squabbling and bad feelings. I could have stayed in Denver for that. Before I had left pickleball to take care of my wife, there had already been fighting on the courts. The better players wanted to dominate the court time, and the newbies, or maybe I should say the less competitive players, just wanted equal court time. Then there were the arguments over line calls. Some players always called anything close out, which started numerous arguments. On top of all that, there were the players that couldn't resist intentionally hitting someone with a ball, sometimes so hard that it left a mark. In one case, a woman was hit so hard in the face that it caused serious eye damage. She needed surgery and never returned to the courts again. Somehow, I had managed to stay clear of all the drama in Denver. Maybe just because I was relatively easy-going. I rarely disputed a call and would only hit hard against the better players who could take it as much as they dished it out. Jokingly, I was called "Mr. Geniality". The pickleball community in Denver was also so big you could easily avoid playing with assholes. In Rio Viejo, with only 6 courts and a small community, you either went along or didn't play. It appeared that I would have to be careful in my new environment to steer clear of the drama. I would respect the Royal pecking order if that's what it took to remain neutral.

I will admit from what I had seen so far, the Royals looked like the better players, but not by much. Certainly not enough to justify the kind of elite attitude they demonstrated. The complaints against them were understandable, but I wasn't sure why people weren't willing to directly call them out on their behavior. My guess was, human nature being what it is, no one really wanted to be confrontational. So, they put up with the abuse. I vowed to myself to try to steer clear of the squabbles. If I needed to complain about someone's on-court behavior, I would save it for Butch. He was a good listener, for the most part, and had yet to take someone else's side over mine.

Julio and Jesus gave up trying to get in a game against any Royals and instead played a couple games against me and Tom. The two of them were younger than us, I would guess they were in their late thirties, and had the speed and stamina you would expect from young men. They were fast and hit the ball hard and were clearly good athletes with good skills, but they hadn't quite yet learned the fine art of dinking. We beat them both times, but the games were close. They were fun to play with and they were gracious losers. I think they would have beaten Nathan and any Royal he picked as his partner. I told them I would love to play with them anytime and that with some work on their dinking game they would be tough to

58

beat. They expressed some interest in coming out some time and just drilling to hone their dinking skills.

When we came off the court, people were already starting to pack up. Most people were done for the day and were heading home, but a few said they were going to go to a local taco bar for (what else?) tacos and beer. Nancy invited me to come along so that I could get to know everyone a little better. I really didn't want to go, and used Butch being home alone as an excuse. She kept insisting to the point of being rude, so when Tom said he would go with me, I relented and agreed to join them for a quick drink. It seemed odd to me, after all the grumbling and complaints about the Royals, that anyone not designated a Royal would want to tag along. But the group was about 50-50.

Pickleball Tip # 4 – Shorten Your Back Swing

Tennis players come into pickleball with a desire to pound ground-strokes, and they tend to take the paddle back too far. This is particularly bad when trying to control dinks. Learn to shorten the back swing and get ready quicker and easier for the ball that comes back.

Chapter 5

The taco bar was a little hole in the wall called Taco Tim's. With only enough seating for about twenty people, the pickleball group took up half the place. It was clean and had a short menu on a chalk board above the cashier. The prices looked reasonable. I decided to have a beef taco and a Tecate. Being so close to the border, I was surprised the taco was more like Taco Bell than any traditional taco I had ever had, but it was edible, and the beer was cold. The owner came out to say hi to Nancy and Nathan. He might have even comped them a beer. Royalty has its rewards.

The Royals, consisting of Nathan, Nancy, Brian, Little E and Jane, sat at the head of the table as a group, while Tom, Cary, Mary, William, and I sat at the other end. Tom whispered to me that he was surprised to see Little E there, as he rarely socialized with anyone away from the pickleball court.

"He thinks he's in a different social class than the rest of us, but I think all the Royals feel that way."

And it did sort of feel that way. The Royals mostly engaged with each other. We did the same at our end of the table. After a while, Nancy turned to me. Maybe she felt bad that I was being left out of their conversation.

"So, what brought you to Rio Viejo?" she said with a big smile. I started to retell my story, one I thought I had already explained to her, but I was quickly learning that Nancy had the attention span of a six-month-old puppy. Maybe she really wasn't interested, or something Little E was saying to Nathan caught her attention, but she turned away before I could finish. I didn't mind the fact that she didn't really care about getting to know me, but I was annoyed, nonetheless. If you ask me a question, at least have the decency to hear my answer. I mumbled to myself to chill, and I did.

Nathan was giving a pickleball strategy lesson to Jane and Little E, using a napkin to draw on. Jane was fascinated by whatever Nathan was drawing, but Little E seemed to be in disagreement about the advice Nathan was giving. I tried to eavesdrop, but all I could hear was Nathan saying that he had been to a clinic a year ago and this is what the pro told him. Brian was trying to interrupt Nathan, saying the game had changed in a year. That old advice was no longer valid. He wasn't wrong about that. Pickleball was evolving quickly. Shots they used to discourage you from trying were now commonplace. The game was now faster and more aggressive.

When they bored of strategy lessons from Nathan, the Royals turned to our group and started harping on the importance of tournaments and league play. I could tell Tom wasn't interested and quite frankly, neither was I, and we tried to politely say no. They were relentless, though. In their minds, if you wanted to fully get immersed in pickleball, you had to participate in these events. They made it sound like Rio Viejo's reputation depended on it, and we would be letting them down if we didn't help the team win more medals.

"I have plenty of medals," I whispered to Tom, "I'm not interested in getting more of them. I'd be happy to donate mine if they need them."

Tom laughed. "I played in one and I was too stressed. Winning is so important to them."

"Who's winning what?" said William, "What are you guys talking about?"

"Nancy wants you to be her partner in a tournament," joked Tom.

"Hell, I wouldn't play with her. She's always bossing me around."

We just laughed some more. I glanced at Nancy and she didn't look amused.

"Seriously," said Nathan, raising his voice so everyone could hear, "We need you guys to step up and join the team. We need more players in the 3.0 category, and I'll make sure you do well. We can start training next week. I'll personally run the training camp. Al, I hear you're pretty good. You could lead the 3.0 team."

Tom turned to me so Nathan couldn't hear. "Count me out."

Personally, I have no problem with tournaments and leagues and things. People like a little team spirit, and of course tournaments challenge you to be a better player. But here I was, the new guy in town, and I already felt the pressure to join, and I didn't want to join anything. I could only assume the regulars felt this pressure daily, until they relented and agreed to participate, although I doubted Tom and William would be persuaded. Would I get ostracized if I didn't join in?

"I'll have to think about it," I said, hoping that would end the discussion.

"Come on, Al. We could use you," said Jane, "I saw you play a little and I would be happy to do some practice drills with you." I think she might have winked at me.

"Careful, Al. I think Jane is making a move on you," whispered Tom.

"What? No," I replied, a little nervously. I wasn't ready to jump back into the dating pool, and although Jane was cute, I really wasn't interested. "I hope not."

I turned back to Nathan and Jane. "I need to pass for now. I'm just getting settled in and I really can't be leaving Butch home alone that much. But thanks for the offer."

63

But Nancy and Nathan weren't so easy to dissuade and didn't seem prepared to take no for an answer.

"Al," said Nancy, between sips of beer, "You really need to join the team. We saw you playing on court 3 and you are a decent player." I wondered if this was a way to establish her dominance, as she played on the advanced courts. It was condescending, especially since I didn't think she had actually watched me play. Then she added, "I think you could help the 3.0 team." Even though I was rusty, I was thinking I could take her apart on the venerable court 5. But again, I held my tongue and didn't share with her my true feelings. Even if I wasn't feeling humble, I was going to act like it.

"Well, I don't know. I haven't been playing much and I'm a bit rusty. Besides, I really need to consider what's best for Butch."

"Who's Butch?" interrupted Little E.

"My dog."

"Really?" said Little E with a snicker, "You can't play because of a dog?"

Now I had reason not to like Little E. "Butch and I are inseparable. He's more than a dog to me. I can't do that to him. This whole move has been stressful for him."

"Oh, he'll be fine," said Little E, unwilling to let it go.

I wanted to say, *Who asked you, you little cretin?* but instead I said, "You don't know Butch, Ethelwolf. He's not the type of dog you want to be on the outs with. He holds a grudge."

That got some laughs and some nods. Clearly there were some dog lovers in the bunch who understood where I was coming from. Just not Little E.

The guy named Brian, who had been playing with the Royals but wasn't quite as good as them, offered his two cents. "Ah, come on. The 3.0 team could use another player. Just leave Butch a big bowl of food. He'll be okay. He's just a dog, for god's sake."

I wanted to tell him to shut the fuck up. Was I ever going to hear the end of this? I instantly took a disliking to Brian and was sure Butch would back me up on that. And not just because of the dog comment. Brian was one of those guys that thought he was funnier than he really was and, if his jokes were any indication, was a terrible human being. He had been telling jokes at the table that weren't funny and showed a lack of compassion for people in general, but specifically for anyone of color. Either he didn't think the jokes were out of line or didn't think I could hear them. Even his jokes about women were off-putting, but none of the ladies at his end of the table objected. I wanted to call him out a number of times, but once again, I bit my tongue. The Royals seemed to like him, and I guessed that was because he was a Royal suck up. I vowed to myself that if I ever got on the court against him, I would plaster him with a body shot or two to shut him up.

I pushed back again for what I hoped would be the last time, "Thanks, guys, but I'll have to pass. I haven't played in tournaments in a long time and I'm not sure my heart is in it. I'm just out here for some fun and exercise. Besides, I'm a better player than 3.0 and that just wouldn't be fair."

"League is fun. How do you know how good you are unless you challenge yourself?" asked Nancy.

I wished someone would slap her. I wanted to tell her I've played and won medals at 4.0 and 4.5, but I just sipped my beer.

Cary had been quiet through all of this but suddenly jumped in. "Al, maybe you could stop by and practice with the 3.5 team and help us improve? I could use some help, and you know the game better than me."

Nathan didn't look too pleased that Cary was asking for help from the newcomer, but he didn't say anything.

"We are all coming back to the court at four today," said Cary, "Come out if you can."

"Are you going to join any of this?" I asked Tom.

He shook his head and whispered, "No. I can't stand the Royals and have no desire to spend that much time with them, but I might practice with Cary."

I nodded. I might be able to do that.

I stood up. "I better go and check on Butch and make sure he isn't destroying the house." I turned to Cary, "I'll see if I can make it to your practice, Cary."

Well, if things weren't strange already, they were about to take a major leap. Two men, probably in their late fifties or early sixties, walked up to our table and started talking, or I should say, speaking aggressively, to Nathan and Nancy.

"You people need to find another place to play your stupid game. The noise is outrageous, and we are tired of you taking over our courts."

"You have two courts by the resort. You don't need these anymore," answered Nancy in a mild-mannered tone that I assume she thought would placate these guys.

"We lost two courts to you idiots and two isn't enough for us. And besides, you guys make so much damn noise; I can't take it anymore," replied one of the men.

"Then move to another house," replied Nathan, without even looking at the men.

"We have been living in that house for ten years. Long before you assholes decided to invade."

"Well, we're here now. Deal with it 'cause we aren't going anywhere. There are more pickleball players than tennis players, so you don't need any more courts. In fact, the way pickleball is growing we might just get the county to build us more courts," laughed Nathan.

"Over my dead body you will," responded the second man.

"We should be able to all get along," said Jane.

The men laughed. "We're going to get you assholes driven out of town," said the first man, as the two of them marched out the door.

"What was that all about?" I asked Tom.

"Some of our courts used to be tennis courts, and they resent us taking them for pickleball. The tall guy is named Roger and the shorter guy is Richard. They live in the neighborhood closest to the courts and claim we make too much noise. They've even stolen the net straps to annoy us. They are trying to convince the county to shut us down, saying we are a nuisance."

"We've been fighting with them for months about this. They aren't happy that the council is ignoring them. Screw them," snarled Brian.

I had heard about this kind of fight taking place around the country. We were lucky at our Denver courts, as they weren't too close to any homes, and they had already been abandoned by the dwindling tennis crowd. In pickleball, it is easy to learn how to play well enough to have fun, so the number of pickleball players keeps growing while tennis seems to stagnate or even dwindle in popularity. I had read about noise complaints and fights between the two groups but hadn't really experienced it for myself.

"Is there a compromise we can reach that would make them happy?" I asked.

"Don't bother trying," quipped Little E, "You won't make them happy so don't bother trying. I agree with Brian, screw them."

With that, I said my goodbyes and returned home, mostly in good spirits. My first day of pickleball had gone well, even if I had developed a major dislike for a number of people there. Hearing the argument between the pickleballers and the tennis players wasn't too thrilling, but I suspected if it was a real problem the county could build a couple more courts nearby. There certainly was room to fit them in. Not sure about the noise though. In some places, I had heard of restrictions on time of use. You couldn't play before 7 am or after 8 pm. The good news was, I had been accepted immediately into the group and even found a couple of people that I liked. Sadly, like in most social groups, there were a few obnoxious people that were not so likable. In this case they were called the Royals.

Butch did make it clear that he was not impressed with my prolonged absence. He didn't get off the couch to greet me as he usually did and instead sat on the couch and glared at me disapprovingly. I tried to explain to him about why I was gone so long, but he showed no interest in hearing about all the new people I had met. I went to the cupboard and took out his favorite cookies and offered him one. He grudgingly took it and gobbled it down, then stared at me until I gave him a second cookie. Then he was happy, and we were best buds again.

Pickleball Tip # 5 – Learn To Dink

The dink is critical to successful pickleball. It is a soft shot that should land inside the kitchen (the area between the net and the NVZ line) and, if executed properly, be difficult for your opponent to attack. The dink is not meant to be a put away shot. Be patient while dinking and look for a chance to speed up the exchange and attack.

To hit a dink, position yourself just outside the kitchen line, with your knees slightly bent, allowing you to move left or right with just a shifting of your feet. Don't take a big back swing. Keep the ball in front of you and hit with a soft follow through, just lifting the ball a few inches above the net, with the intent to have it drop just inside the kitchen line. After a successful dink, hold your position at the line. Stay low, and if the ball comes to you and you can take it before it bounces, do so. Move your dinks from side to side so your opponent doesn't get too comfortable.

Chapter 6

Tuesday, day two of my time in Rio Viejo, had me up early and raring to go. I wanted to be on the courts a little earlier and see if I could get some more games in with the better players. I had also heard that there were quite a few players that preferred the Tuesday group, and I was eager to meet them. During my wife's illness, and for the year after she passed, I had avoided meeting any new people, other than doctors and nurses. I just didn't have the interest or energy for that kind of thing. But with the passage of time, I realized that I did miss human interaction. After yesterday's encounter, it was apparent to me that I'd even settle for bad human interaction. I felt like a little kid again, off to school after summer vacation, ready for new friends and new adventures. As this was my second day however, I was over my first day jitters.

I took Butch for an exceptionally long walk in the hopes of wearing him out and not having a repeat of yesterday's stink eye treatment. Being as he was my only true friend, I didn't want to upset him, if at all possible. He could be moody and easy to annoy, and I wanted to keep his stress level to a minimum. He marked his territory numerous times and ate a few things of dubious origin off the trail that I wasn't quite fast enough with the leash to prevent. I could have tried to take them from him, but at eighty pounds, getting anything out of his mouth was an exercise in futility, and possibly dangerous as well. If it was something he considered a tasty find or treasure, my best bet was to hope it didn't get him sick. When out on a walk with Butch you needed to be paying close attention to things coming up on the trail. On more than one occasion, strictly by accident, of course, he almost dislocated my shoulder by tugging too hard when he wanted to go in a different direction than I had planned, and it was usually in search of some forbidden fruit.

Once I had Butch back at the home-site with a nice treat as his reward for doing his business, I hastily dressed for pickleball and rushed to the courts. By the time I arrived there the courts were packed, with maybe fifteen to twenty people waiting to play. Clearly, Tuesday mornings were popular. As expected, at least half the of the people were new to me, which was good and bad. There was definitely a limit to how many new names I could learn, but it also meant that there were more players I could play with without having to spend too much time with the Royals, although part of me was itching to take them down a notch or two.

Courts 5 and 6 were full, but with no one waiting on the sidelines to play on them. Maybe the word was out that those courts were reserved for royalty. Longer lines were waiting for openings at the intermediate and beginner courts. I watched the action on the advanced courts and wasn't at all intimidated. Their games were intense and the play decent but still nothing that would intimidate a 3.5 or higher. There was much less joy on those courts though. Nathan and his court jesters just didn't seem to have as much fun as everyone else out there. I finally decided it was time for me to challenge the Royals to a game. I set my paddle in the appropriate rack and sat down to wait.

Rory and another gentleman came over to chat with me. They had their paddles in the intermediate rack and were also waiting for a game.

"Al, I want to introduce you to Dr. David Baird. He's our resident pickleball doctor."

We traded fist bumps.

"Nice to meet you doctor."

"Please call me David. I've been retired for a couple of years."

"We call him Dr. David just to remind him that he is our resident doctor, and we expect free advice from time to time."

David laughed. "Rory says you're a pretty good pickleball player."

"I'm working on getting my game back after a long layoff," I answered, trying to be humble.

"If he's this good after some time away from the game, I can't wait to see how good he is when he gets his game back," exclaimed Rory. "Don't let him kid you. He can beat anybody out here."

I think I might have blushed a little.

"Are you thinking of getting in a game with the Royals?" Rory said, with a smirk.

"I think I'd like to try."

Dr. David chimed in, "Maybe they will invite you to play with them. We know they don't think our skills are up to their standards, so we don't even try anymore."

"That doesn't seem fair," I said. "I've seen Rory play and I've seen a few of their games. I think he could compete with them."

"Not about competition really. Although, they are trying to get everyone ranked so they can officially designate the courts as beginner, intermediate, and advanced. But really, it's because I had a run in with them a while back, and since then they just won't play with me."

I wanted to know more about the run in, but decided it was best not to get too involved in any drama. "What about you, David, do you ever play with them?"

"No," he answered quickly. "I'm in good shape because I exercise a lot, but I'm still learning the game. I've got a way to go."

"I heard that Nathan gives free clinics."

72

"I've been to them, and they are somewhat helpful, but he saves the important advice and training for his paying customers. Even so, word is the private lessons aren't really that much better."

"Why do they get to use the courts for private lessons? These are county courts, right?" I asked.

"Yes, they are county property," said Rory. "But the Royals created a committee and made rules that they like. They claim they have the blessing of the county commissioner."

"Rules?" I asked with a quizzical look.

"The Royals," snarled some lady I had never seen before, "formed a club and announced the results to us peons. They voted for officers, and then informed us about the rules of usage and dues. By the way, my name is Samantha," she held out a fist and I bumped mine against hers.

"I take it you don't play with them?"

"I did at one time, but they think they are too good for me now. Pickleball is serious business to them. If you don't go to clinics and tournaments constantly, you aren't worth their time. I love the game too, but geez, I also have a life away from pickleball."

The joke about pickleball is that it is addicting, and any life outside of the game becomes irrelevant. I'd met many people that lived and breathed the game 24/7. They would go into withdrawals if, for any reason, they couldn't play for more than three or four days in a row. I've seen players shoveling snow and mopping water puddles, so they didn't have to go a day without playing. I've even seen players wearing parkas when the temperature was below freezing.

"Besides that, we're more fun to play with, aren't we?" asked Dr. David.

"I think so," she responded, smiling. "Smiles and laughter on courts 5 and 6 are kind of rare."

"I've noticed that." There was a time I had taken the game too seriously, as well. I hated to lose and drilled constantly in an effort to get better, and I played with a group that was that way as well. Games were intense in that group. Winning and losing was a big deal. Then I got a jolt of reality about what was really important in my life. There are a lot of top-notch players that I have met that have figured out how to be really good and still have fun. They don't destroy weaker players on the court and aren't devastated if they lose a game. They enjoy the game as much as anyone and willingly share their knowledge of the game with beginners and intermediates, asking nothing in return for their time. I love playing with those kinds of people, because they are fun to play with, while still being extremely challenging.

I noticed two men walking toward us in a determined manner and as they approached, I recognized them as Roger and Richard, the tennis players from the encounter at Taco Tim's the day before. As they neared, I could see scowls on their faces. These were not happy people.

"Oh great," said Samantha, as the men got closer. "Jerks approaching."

"Ready to get yelled at?" asked Rory.

"They come here often?" I asked.

"Once a week or so to harass us," said Dr. David. "I know them from an exercise class we all take. Hi Roger, hi Richard," he said in a cordial voice, with a friendly smile.

"David," answered Roger, as he nodded but didn't return the smile. "You still part of this group?"

"It's a great game with a lot of great people. You should try playing sometime. I think you would like it."

"Not going to happen," he growled back. "I'd just as soon see the game go away."

"Get over it, guys. Haven't you heard that pickleball is the fastest growing sport in America?" offered Rory.

"It's a joke," answered Richard. "It's not a real sport. Take up tennis or golf."

I stayed quiet. I had plenty I wanted to say but let the regulars deal with them without my help.

"You can enjoy all three," said Samantha.

"You guys are a waste of time. You think you can take over any paved surface for your silly game. You make too much noise, and you make me sick."

Samantha giggled a little and shook her head. "OK."

I watched the two men stomp off and march from court-to-court scowling at people, but no one spoke to them. I'm not sure what they thought they could accomplish with that. No one acted intimidated by them. The pickleballers had experienced this behavior often and had come to the conclusion it was best to just ignore them.

By now, I was getting antsy to play. I wanted to get in a game, but it seemed like the games on 5 and 6 were taking forever. I tried to listen to the score, but they called it quietly. If I had been more comfortable with everyone, I would have asked the score, but instead I waited impatiently.

"You might be waiting a long time," said Rory.

I must have looked confused.

"When they don't want to give up a court, they will reset the score when you aren't paying attention."

75

"Really?" I was getting annoyed. I wanted to get in a game, and I wanted a game with the Royals to see just how good they were against someone that could challenge them. I was starting to understand firsthand why people didn't like them. I hadn't wanted my opinion to be based just on gossip, but now I was experiencing a snub by them, and I didn't like it one bit. It's not that they were such great players and didn't want to lower their standards by letting me play with them. No, they were just rude. I admit I'm not the greatest player of all time, but I've played a lot and watched a lot of pros play. I can tell great pickleball when I see it. The players on the Royal courts may have been better than most of the players in Rio Viejo, but they were not great and had no business shutting anyone out. I knew a lot of players that would pickle (11-0) this group.

I'm generally a very mellow guy and don't take too much seriously. I'm even less serious about little things since losing Stephanie, but I had to admit my blood was beginning to boil as I waited my turn to play. I was about to say something to the Royals, when Samantha approached me and asked me to join her, Rory, and Dr. David for a game. I considered saying no. I wanted my chance to take the Royals down off their self-constructed pedestal, and the sooner the better. But I have trouble saying no, so I accepted the invitation to play with them. I glanced back toward the Royals, but it didn't look like they were going to finish their game anytime soon. I'm sure they didn't see me sneer at them as I followed the group over to court 3.

Apparently, the accepted court etiquette in the pickleball world didn't apply to the Royals. In most courts I've seen, if four people are waiting for a court, then the players coming off do so as a group, allowing the four waiting players to take the court. In some cases, a court might be designated as a challenge court, allowing two waiting players to challenge the winners that had just played. Usually, it is bad form to allow challenge courts if the courts are crowded. Even if a challenge court is appropriate, some local rules dictate the winning team split up, so that there isn't a dynasty taking place.

I took the court with Samantha as my partner, facing off against Rory and Dr. David. I didn't want to be a jerk with this group, so I was careful not to try to overpower anyone, and I refrained from giving any advice, although they all had some glaring weak spots that could have been improved with some help. If I had an easy put-away, I tried to hit it a little softer and with a little less angle, in an effort to keep the points going and the game fun for everyone. My mantra was placement, placement, placement, and don't hit too hard. Dr. David and Samantha could hit both soft and hard, but Rory was an all-out banger. If he could get a full swing he did; if he couldn't, well, he tried to hit hard anyway. I didn't mind him targeting me with hard shots to my gut, but I didn't appreciate him banging balls at Samantha's chest or head. I wanted to comment, but Samantha was good natured about it.

"That's Rory's game," she shared with me. "He never tries to slow it down. Maybe later you'll teach me how to deal with bangers."

"I'd be happy to," I replied.

The trouble with bangers like Rory is that they get positive reinforcement when they hit the rare passing shot that stays in or hits their opponent. But when they get up against a better player that isn't intimidated by pace and knows how to block those shots for winners, they have no strategy to stay in the game. Statistically, bangers with no control or finesse hit the ball in the net or past the baseline more often than they hit it in. The best players have control over the hard and soft aspects of the game. They can bang as hard as anyone, but they are also patient and know when to bang and when to dink.

The game was spirited and fun. The three of them were a joy to play with. Even Rory with his constant banging. Samantha got hit twice and joked that she would have marks on her chest but wasn't going to pull up her shirt to show us. Somebody watching from the sideline kept yelling at Rory to hit harder. And he tried. It cracked me up that each time it went in the net or sailed long, he looked at his paddle, as if it was the paddle's fault that he had missed the shot. At one point he asked us to measure the height of the net, because there was no way he was hitting the net so often unless it was too high. I went over to the net and pushed it lower and asked if it looked right now. He laughed and told me to stand there and keep it low.

Samantha was a great partner and had no problem letting me poach or take any ball I wanted, but she wanted to win. Taking on two men was a source of pride for her, and she was happy to win any way we could.

Dr. David was scary. At times, he ran around the court like a chicken without a head. He fell a couple of times but popped back up. He had trouble controlling his movements on the court and didn't know when to back off a shot and let his partner take it. He ran into Rory and almost knocked him down. They argued a little but got over it quickly. I vowed that if I played with David as my partner, I would give him a wide berth. I've been hit by a paddle, and I can tell you it hurts like hell.

We were hot into the middle of a long rally when we heard shouting and screaming coming from court 5. The Royals. We stopped play to see what was going on. It wasn't the normal pickleball yelling and laughing, or even a heated argument over a call. It sounded more like terror. A group of people were gathered around someone on the ground. The rest of the courts had gone silent, as everyone was either watching what was going on or rushing over to get a better look. From where I stood, I couldn't see who was on the ground.

"Looks like someone has fallen," I said.

"Can you see who it is?" asked Rory. "I hope it's Nathan."

David and Samantha had medical backgrounds, so they rushed over to see if they could help, with Rory and me following.

I've seen my share of injuries on the court. I've never wished ill on anyone and was taken aback by Rory's comment. I knew he hated Nathan, but wishing him an injury was out of line. Pickleball is a great sport and has become popular with all age groups. But it used to be considered a sport for seniors, sometimes referred to as "old people's tennis", and as such, the frequency of injuries is astounding. In areas where pickleball is popular, emergency rooms have reported an increase in visits from people over fifty with injuries they attribute to pickleball. Orthopedic specialists have noticed a huge increase in business because of pickleball injuries requiring surgery and rehab. Go to any court and you'll see the latest in sport braces on knees and elbows. Talk is always about who hurts where and why.

So, my first thought was someone sprained an ankle, or maybe even fell and broke a wrist. People joke about having defibrillators and people trained in CPR handy, but I've yet to see any heart attacks on the court. I wasn't too concerned as we made our way over to the fallen player. I hate to admit that the fact that it was on the Royal courts, the ones I should have been playing on, made me a little less sympathetic. A sprained ankle might teach them a little humility. As we got closer, I saw that the body sprawled out on the court was Nathan's.

When we reached the crowd that was circled around Nathan, I could hear people murmuring that his condition looked serious. Someone even said he was turning blue, which is not something that happens with a sprain. Someone else said they thought they heard a gunshot before he went down, but I hadn't heard it. Arizona certainly had no shortage of guns, but I had never read about any gun violence issues in Rio Viejo.

Nancy was standing off to the side and looked to be in shock. "Oh my god, oh my god," she kept repeating. "He said he was feeling a little off while we were playing, but I didn't think anything about it."

Nathan appeared to be around sixty, and most players over fifty complain of "feeling a little off" sometimes. Nobody pays any attention to that; none of us are getting any younger. A typical joke among older players when asked how they are doing is to say, "Vertical" or, "Any day you wake up is a good day".

Jane was standing by Nancy, with her arm around her.

"He's going to be okay. Don't worry."

Brian and Little E were standing apart from the group, talking. I came up to them and asked if they knew what was going on.

"He was sweating like a pig just before we started the game," said Little E. "I didn't think it was a big deal."

"He kept rubbing his stomach or his chest. I thought he had heartburn. Maybe he's having a heart attack?" suggested Brian.

By now, Samantha and Dr. David and someone named Rick, who I learned later was a paramedic, were taking turns giving Nathan CPR. I couldn't see much more than his body lying flat on his back.

Rio Viejo was a small town and did not have a hospital or an emergency room, but it did have a firehouse extension with paramedics. Someone had already called them, and I could hear sirens in the distance. The closest hospital was about thirty minutes away, so the paramedics needed to stabilize him enough for the drive.

Rick was urging everyone to back up and give them room to try to help Nathan. He looked in control, like he had done this a million times, but he also looked worried. When everyone backed off a little, I could see Nathan's face, and it did indeed look blue. I'm not a doctor, but I thought that meant he wasn't breathing.

When the paramedics arrived, they pulled up as close as they could to the court and ran toward us. Within seconds, they had a respirator over

Nathan's face and were putting him on a gurney. They spoke to David, Samantha, and Rick as they wheeled Nathan to the ambulance, then sped off.

The paramedics didn't speak to the rest of us, so we had no clue what Nathan might have suffered, but it was clear it wasn't a sprained ankle or knee. Nancy and Jane raced to the parking lot and jumped in Nancy's car, followed by Rick and Dr. David. The rest of us just stood there, quietly stunned.

As everyone started to recover, tales of this or that person having gone down with a broken ankle or a broken wrist were shared, as if this was a normal thing and Nathan would be just fine. But anyone who saw his face knew it was not just some normal sports injury. I wasn't going to be the one to tell them this was really bad. But there were some who did, like William, who shared a story he'd read of someone on a pickleball court suffering a fatal heart attack. Sheila told him to shut up.

"Nathan's young. He's going to be just fine," she tried to assure anyone willing to listen.

"Did he have a history of heart problems?" asked Jack.

"He never mentioned any problems that I heard of," replied Brian.

"Sometimes you just don't know 'til it's too late," added Rory. "I remember reading about some young pro basketball player dropping dead of a heart attack a few years back."

"I remember that, but I think I remember he was also doing cocaine," said Tom.

"Did Nathan do cocaine?" I asked.

No one wanted to answer. Either he did and they didn't want to admit they knew, or they had no clue. Everyone said they didn't think he smoked cigarettes but might have indulged in marijuana from time to time.

"Nathan was healthy," said Molly. "He played pickleball almost every day, and on top of that, he ran two to five miles several times a week. It's hard to believe it was a heart attack."

"Stroke?" suggested Jack. "I've heard of healthy people dropping dead with no warning because of a stroke or maybe an aneurysm?"

I'd seen plenty of injuries on the courts in Denver, including broken bones, sprains, ruptured Achilles tendons, a few eye injuries from shots to the face, and even a few bruises from errant paddles. All part of the game. When that happened, everyone would mill about for a few minutes and commiserate with each other and the injured party, but then we would resume play as if nothing had happened out of the ordinary. Accidents happen, it's just one of those things, but the game goes on. But this had the air of something much more serious. I don't remember ever seeing anyone suffer from a heart attack, and certainly I'd never seen a stroke victim or aneurysm, but I could tell this was not an ordinary injury.

We could hear the ambulance siren getting fainter and fainter in the distance. Still, no one got back on the court to play. When something like that happens, it's hard to just go back to doing what you were doing. Samantha seemed unwilling to speculate on what it might have been that struck down Nathan.

Rory said he was sure that Nathan had stopped breathing and he didn't think the CPR had done any good. Reading between the lines, I thought that Rory was saying Nathan had died. Peggy screamed at Rory to stop talking negatively and pray for Nathan. She was convinced he was going to be okay and didn't want to hear anything to the contrary.

Pickleball Tip # 6 – Get Your Serves In

You can't win a point if you don't get your serve in, so take your time. Get into a routine that you can practice and repeat each time you serve. Don't rush the service motion. If you have trouble with the drop serve, try letting it bounce to give yourself more time. Once you have mastered getting the serve in with consistency and confidence, then you can start to develop a more offensive serve.

When you can hit the serve in over 90% of the time, experiment trying to aim for wide serves or your opponent's weakness, probably a deep serve to their backhand. You might even want to try slicing the ball or hitting topspin serves to try to give your opponent a more difficult ball to return. Another key to a good serve is to hit it deep, so your opponent has to back pedal and delay their charge to the no volley zone (NVZ). After you serve the ball, remember to stay back on the baseline until you see what kind of service return is coming to you. If you charge to the net, or even step in a few feet, a good opponent will target their return deep, so it lands at your feet, forcing you to back pedal or lean back and hit off balance.

Chapter 7

The courts cleared out quickly after Nathan was carted away in the ambulance. We were all unaware as to Nathan's status and no one wanted to seem so heartless as to continue playing under those circumstances. There was speculation about his condition, but since no one really knew, the group disbanded with a few hugs and tears and Peggy imploring everyone to pray. I've never been a big proponent of thoughts and prayers; I've never found them to be effective, but I don't try to dissuade anyone else from using them. Personally, I had plenty of thoughts and prayers during my wife's illness. If they really worked, she would have survived.

I rode my bike home alone and was immediately greeted at the front door by Butch. Either he could hear or smell me coming, or he just knew it was time for me to return. I've read that dogs have some innate relationship with time. For all I knew, he was sitting by the door the entire time I was gone. In any event, he gave me a nice kiss and sat down patiently to listen to my story of what happened on the courts. I often discussed major issues of the day and other serious matters with him, and he had shown to be a good listener as long as the story didn't drag on too long. I must have been guilty of the latter that day, as he soon lost interest and started to dose off, as indicated by some loud snoring. It's also entirely possible that he remembered the name Nathan as someone I was not too keen on, so he had no interest in his well-being. Even though I didn't think much of Nathan, I didn't wish him any harm and I'm sure neither did Butch, but that didn't mean he wanted to hear me drone on about the details of Nathan collapsing on the court. When the snoring got too loud, I got the message and stopped talking about Nathan. I changed the subject to taking a walk and Butch woke right up.

There was nothing Butch or I could do for Nathan, so we proceeded to go about our day. For Butch, that meant naps, walks, and treats. For me, that meant providing all that for Butch, with personal breaks for me to eat, surf the web, and read. The suddenness of Nathan's collapse got me thinking about what would happen to Butch if something were to happen to me. All of my oldest friends were in Denver; they couldn't be called on to watch Butch in an emergency. Worse still, if I had an accident, who would even know? I had no real friends in Rio Viejo yet and no one in the pickleball group even knew my phone number or what house we were renting. I looked over at Butch and had a slight anxiety attack. Visions of him starving to death waiting for me to return made me shudder.

"Butch, we're going to find someone to take care of you if something happens to me," I said, holding his face. He stared back at me. I didn't want him to panic, but I explained to him that, even though I felt perfectly fine, I had to make sure he would be taken care of. I had read an article once about some old lady who died alone at home with just her cats. No one came by the house for days, and by then the cats were starving and dying of thirst. This would not be Butch's fate. I grabbed Butch's leash, put my phone in my pocket, and we headed out the door. We were on a mission.

The house we were renting was on a street with about twenty other homes, spaced generously apart and landscaped with rocks and various cacti, of which I could only identify Barrel and Saguaro. I wasn't too keen on the fact that there were probably ten types of snakes and hundreds of scorpions living in the area, but so far, we had not encountered any. I assumed it was only a matter of time. The house we were living in was only a few yards from the trail's head and probably home to more snakes and other dangerous creatures than the rest of the neighborhood. Butch, at least to my knowledge, had no fear of snakes (although he aced the rattlesnake avoidance training), spiders, or scorpions, and would have been happy to be let off leash to explore the woods or sniff under and behind every rock or cactus. I, however, have an intense fear of snakes and scorpions, so I held Butch on a short leash.

We left the house and stayed in the middle of the concrete path to the street. The trail was quite popular in the mornings with hikers and bird watchers, but it was usually quiet later in the day. Our goal was to meet people, so we chose to walk to town via the streets and not the trail. Unfortunately, there were no neighbors out and about. It was already warming up, but I wouldn't have thought it was too hot for people to be out and about. Maybe Butch and I looked shady, and people were avoiding running into us?

We eventually found our way to the local market, Bebidos Y Cosas. It took us over thirty minutes to reach the market and would have taken longer if I had allowed Butch to smell everything along the way that looked interesting to him. It was hot and I started to sweat. I had brought Butch's water bottle but not one for myself, so I was anxious to reach the market and get a drink. Walking an eighty-pound dog with a bit of a stubborn streak is not exactly a leisurely stroll in the park; it's work. We encountered exactly one person along the way, on the other side of the street, and he didn't look like he wanted to chat with us. I guess he wasn't a dog person. It was a rather eerie feeling, walking along deserted streets in the middle of the day. When we finally made it to the market, I was relieved to see other live humans, confirming that the apocalypse had not occurred.

Now that we had arrived at the store, I realized my plan had a serious flaw. I couldn't take Butch into the store with me, although I'm sure he would have been more than happy to enter. He didn't look like a service dog, and he didn't have a vest designating him as one. Although I didn't know the rules regarding dogs in stores in Rio Viejo, I assumed it wasn't allowed. Not to mention the fact that the aisles in the store were narrow, and trying to control Butch with so many distractions would have been a costly disaster. I either had to find someone to stand with him outside while I went inside or tie him to the bike rack. With no one around that I knew, I settled on tying him to the bike rack. Butch isn't the type of dog people steal and I wasn't worried about him hurting anyone. One thing Butch had learned was sit and stay. The longest I had tested him on it was thirty minutes, but I had no doubt my boy would stay longer if need be. I set down his water bottle, which doubled as a bowl, and told him that if he behaved while I was in the market, he would get a huge treat as a reward. I had no doubt he understood every word, as he dropped into a sitting position and prepared to wait for me.

The store was small. No one did their weekly shopping there, but lots of people stopped in for odds and ends, and it served as a kind of community meeting place. They also had a great deli section with prepared salads and sandwiches. It wasn't the cheapest place to shop, but you couldn't beat the convenience.

Once inside the store, I wandered around, looking at the selection of items and, of course, the small array of dog treats. My plan was to grab a bag of chips and a beer for me, and some meaty dog treats for Butch, then sit outside on the shaded patio and wait to meet someone that we could befriend and trust in case of an emergency. Truthfully, I figured if we stayed long enough, someone I had met at pickleball would eventually wander by. By the door, there was a bulletin board with dozens of business cards tacked up on it. I grabbed one for a dog sitter.

When I walked back outside, I found Butch surrounded by adults and children. While I failed to meet anyone inside the store, Butch was outside holding court. Kids were begging their parents to let them pet him, but their parents were cautious. Butch was good with kids and was being adorable. He knew a few tricks and knew humans, especially kids, loved to see him perform. He didn't disappoint them and was loving the attention; he was in dog heaven. Normally, I have to treat him to perform a trick, but here he was showing off everything he knew for nothing more than laughs and giggles. I stood there and watched in amazement. He noticed me watching and I swear he winked at me before doing his next trick.

"He's so cute," said a little girl, "Can I take a picture with him? What's his name?" And she wasn't the only one peppering me with questions when they realized he was with me. If I had known he was this talented, I would have put him to work earning his keep. Maybe he could have his own TikTok or Instagram page. As a successful pup influencer, he could afford to buy his own cookies.

"Yes," I managed a smile, "Butch seems to be enjoying all the attention." I opened the bag of dog treats and handed them out to the kids. "Give him one of these and he'll be your friend for life."

Butch took the treats from the kids, careful not to nip their fingers. With each treat given, he held out his paw, as if to say "thank you" before turning his attention to the next kid. He even gave a few brave kids a kiss on the cheek. What a ham.

"Hey there," said a voice from behind me. I turned around and saw a man I knew I had met before, but for the life of me I couldn't remember his name. He noticed my difficulty and bailed me out. "It's Tom, and this is my wife, Leslie. We met on the pickleball court."

"Yes, yes, of course I remember you," I smiled. "Sorry, I'm bad with names, especially when I have to learn twenty of them in one day."

"No problem," he said good-naturedly. "You're Al, right?" He was already one up on me.

"Yep, I'm Al. This is Butch, my trusty companion and ham." I shook hands with both of them, while Butch held out his paw. Tom and Leslie took turns shaking his paw and laughing their heads off.

"We were just sitting here having a beer and watching the show Butch was putting on. He's so sweet," said Leslie, as she patted Butch on the head. She saw the beer in my hand, "Would you like to join us over there in the shade?" She pointed to the patio area that had a few tables and chairs, mostly empty.

"Yeah, come join us. We're waiting for Celeste and her husband. I think you might have met Celeste at the courts."

I didn't have to think long. "I'd love to, thanks. Is Butch allowed in that area?"

"Absolutely," said Leslie, with a grin. "If you can pull him away from all his fans."

The throng of Butch admirers shaking his paw and taking selfies with him was thinning out now, so I untied his leash from the bike rack and joined Tom and Leslie at their table.

"Tom told me there was a newbie at the courts, but he didn't tell me anything about you. So, tell us about yourself," said Leslie.

I opened my beer and took a drink. "What would you like to know?"

"The usual, of course. Where do you come from? What brought you here? Do you still work? You look too young to be retired."

"I sold my business a while back. I was a stockbroker-slash-investment consultant. Now I just do a little day trading, to keep my hand in the business and make some income."

"You must be pretty good. We're both retired, but maybe you can give us some investment advice some time?"

"I'd be happy to."

"Are you married? Or is that too personal?" asked Leslie.

"It's OK. It's just me and Butch now, since I lost my wife." I hesitated but decided to bare all, the short version anyway. "We're from Denver. After my wife died last year, Butch and I decided to start fresh in a new place."

"Oh my. I'm so sorry," said Leslie. "That had to be hard. What happened, if I may ask?"

"Cervical cancer," I managed to say without bursting into tears, which was rare. "Pretty sudden and not much the doctors could do." Looking to change the subject, I said, "How long have you guys been here?"

"We got here a few months ago, so we are pretty new ourselves," said Tom. "Moved here from Seattle. I think most of the people in this town are from somewhere else. We got tired of the misty rain all the time and decided to try desert living."

"And how do you like it?"

"Hotter than we realized, but so far so good," said Leslie, "Tom loves the golf and pickleball here, so maybe we'll stay 'til we die."

As soon as she said the word die, I could tell she was sorry. I let it go. Tom sensed it too and changed the subject. "Well, Butch is sure a hit."

"Yea, he's a piece of work. I can barely get him to sit for me, but then I see he's showing off for all the ladies."

They laughed. "Well, he's very cute. If you ever need anyone to watch him, call us. We love dogs," said Leslie. I was ecstatic. Were they reading my mind?

Before I could respond, another couple strolled up to the table and said hello.

Leslie introduced everyone. "This is Celeste and Martin," she said, then pointed to me. "This is Al, he's new here."

I did recognize Celeste from the courts earlier, but as with most of the people out there, I had not played with her yet. She had wandered back and forth between the intermediate and beginner courts and seemed to be very popular. I had not seen Martin at the courts, so I didn't know if he was a player or not.

"I saw you on the court," I said to Celeste, "You play pretty well." I actually hadn't seen her play, but you can never go wrong complimenting someone on their game – even if it is only partially true. I'm not opposed to earning cheap points when meeting new people.

"And who is this?" asked Martin in what sounded like a Spanish accent, as he bent over to lavish Butch with pets to his head. "Aren't you sweet."

Butch didn't say anything, but I could tell he quickly took a liking to Martin.

"He's my trusty companion and a consummate ladies' man. Butch, wave to Martin." Butch raised a paw and waved, then laid down and rolled on his back so Martin could pet his tummy. Oohs and ahhs came from everyone. I smiled and rolled my eyes. Pretty sure Butch winked at me again.

Since everyone was being so nice to me and Butch, and because I wanted to fit in quickly, I offered to buy the next round of drinks. After some resistance, they all conceded. Martin went for some kind of IPA, while Tom and I ordered Mexican beer. The ladies asked for premade margaritas in small bottles and I got another chew treat for Butch. I would have taken a shot of tequila along with my beer, but I didn't, for two reasons. One, I didn't want to look like a lush by taking a shot of tequila this early in the day, and two, the only little airplane bottles of tequila were Cuervo and, being a tequila snob, I have to draw the line somewhere. Cheap tequila only belongs in a margarita or a tequila sunrise, and maybe not even then.

More small talk ensued about me and Butch and how we ended up in southern Arizona. Since Tom and Leslie had already heard the story, I abbreviated it for Celeste and Martin. They were a delightful couple, as were Tom and Leslie, and I was feeling pretty good about our new home. Best of all, I now had someone to watch Butch if something came up. Thoughts of Nathan dropping on the pickleball court came to mind.

"So, what do you think about the pickleball community here," I asked.

Leslie rolled her eyes. "Oh, here it comes. All the drama."

"Leslie has heard all the complaining," said Tom, "and she's tired of it."

"Yes, I have and I am. It's like high school all over again. These people are like kids. You have the popular group and the jocks and," Leslie paused and rolled her eyes, "there's always a little snipping going on."

Celeste spoke up, "Leslie and Martin don't play, but they get the gossip about everyone from Tom and me."

"Have you met the Royals?" asked Martin.

"I've met a couple of them. They look like decent players."

"They are," agreed Tom, "Too bad they are such assholes."

It didn't take a rocket scientist to see the animosity. None of the Royals were here and no one was holding back. "It seems like a lot of people feel that way," I noted.

"From what Celeste tells me," said Martin, "most everyone feels that way about them, except the Royals themselves and the wannabes."

I had to laugh a little. Déjà vu. Every pickleball court I've ever played at or heard about seemed to have its elite players. At one time, some people in Denver might have thought that about me. These are the guys and gals who are a step or two ahead of everyone else on the court and generally don't want to waste their time playing with anyone of a lower ability level. They want to win, and many keep track of their wins and loses each day. For the most part, they are good people who are just better at the game than most everyone else and don't intend to be mean; they just want to play with players that will challenge them and make them better. Then there are the players with over inflated egos that just think they are better than everyone else and don't care what anyone thinks about them. I've seen it in every sport I've played.

Pickleball might be a little more unique than other sports, in that it lends itself to beginners wanting equal playing time with the better players. Unfortunately, there aren't enough courts to meet the growing demand, although this is changing rapidly. So the different skill levels have to compete for court time, each thinking they deserve the courts more. Beginners want to play with better players in order to learn the game and improve, and more advanced players want to play with people who will challenge them so that they can continue to improve. So, they clash. But don't get me wrong, there are a ton of really excellent players that will get on the court with anyone and often give advice and help to beginners and intermediates. But the Royals in Rio Viejo seemed to flaunt their perceived superiority, and it had clearly become quite obnoxious to the other players.

"They are full of themselves," said Tom, snapping me out of my thoughts.

"How so?" I had already heard many of the complaints about the Royals but couldn't resist hearing more. I guess Butch knew where this was going, because he let out a loud sigh and closed his eyes.

"Where do I start?" said Tom.

"They run everything to do with pickleball here," added Celeste. "The clinic, the dues, the rules. It's not as bad now that we have more courts, but when we only had two courts it got rather contentious. Even now, when it gets really crowded on the beginner and intermediate courts, they won't let us on the advanced ones."

Tom interrupted Celeste. "You would think they invented the game and built the courts with their own hands. I feel like we are just there for their benefit. Fodder for their league and tournament practice and when they are short a player, they bless us with an invitation to play. But without us peons, they don't have enough dues to keep the courts nice."

"The city doesn't pay to take care of the courts?" I asked.

"Our little city and county are relatively poor. We are lucky to have what we have," replied Tom. "Honestly though, they don't want to be bothered. They still aren't really sure about this pickleball phenomena, and they think it is a fad that will die down, so they don't want to spend much money or effort on it. Plus, Nancy and Nathan have friends on the council, and I don't think the council wants to go against them."

"There are more of you that aren't Royals, though. Why do Nancy and Nathan carry more weight?"

"Nancy is the top selling real estate agent in the county. She does fund raisers and donates a lot of money to the council," explained Tom.

"Ah," I groaned.

I had seen this before. City councils strapped for cash and trying to keep everyone happy, but mostly committed to making sure the big donors were pleased. It's hard to make everyone happy, so they focus on the quid pro quo.

"You're a pretty good player, Tom. I don't understand why they don't want you playing with them."

"I did play with them at first, when we just had two courts, but as the number of players grew, they didn't appreciate me calling them out on their attitudes. Plus, I don't play league and tournaments and have no desire to. To the Royals, it's all about bringing home the hardware so they can brag. Because I made some snide remarks about their obsession with all that, they have snubbed me from playing with them."

"How so?"

"Oh, rather than invite me to play with them, like they used to, they started using the excuse that they are getting ready for a tournament and need practice time with their partners. It's the same old excuse they always use when they don't want to play with someone."

Martin jumped in. "I don't play, and rarely go out to the courts, but from what I've seen and heard, they run things in a way that benefits them. Celeste has come home on numerous occasions with stories about how they were rude to someone. I get tired of hearing about it, and although they are nice to me, I have to admit it taints my opinion of them when I see them."

"You run into them a lot?" I asked.

"Small town," he answered. "I work at the golf course, and they always plan these little social events, and I go to give Celeste moral support. And the food at the gatherings isn't bad either," he laughed. "After a drink or two, they don't seem as obnoxious."

"If these weren't the only pickleball courts in town, a bunch of us wouldn't play there," added Celeste.

The table got silent as everyone turned their attention to their drinks.

"Tell me about Roger and Richard. They seem fairly antagonistic toward the pickleball group," I said, breaking the silence.

"They are harmless," said Tom. "They came out a couple times to play when we first started our group but got snooty, saying that it wasn't really a sport. Not like tennis, which they think is the best sport next to golf. They stopped playing, and when our group started to grow, they started complaining about the noise. I think they nearly had heart attacks when we went from two courts to six."

Personally, I like the sound of pickleball, but I had to admit I wouldn't want to live so close that I heard it all the time. I imagined it would get annoying.

"The county actually sent some people out to determine if the noise was a nuisance to the near-by homes and they concluded that it wasn't all that bad. After that, they essentially wiped their hands of the whole affair."

I made a note to stand over by the homes someday and hear for myself.

Tom continued, "Roger and Richard suspect Nathan twisted the arms of the council to get them to roll over for us. I don't like Nathan, but I have to admit he did a lot for the local pickleball scene."

"I kind of like Nathan," said Leslie.

"Oh, you just think he's a hunk," said her husband Tom, shaking his head and rolling his eyes.

She blushed. "Well, he is, and you know it. But I think he's fun. He says funny things all the time."

"Fun?" said Tom, "He's annoying and thinks he knows everything. He thinks he's the best player on the court, and if his head was any bigger, it would burst. You know he has to buy hats that are specially made to fit his big head."

"Oh, stop it," said Leslie, elbowing Tom.

"No really. He can't shop for hats off the shelf," he said with a big laugh and took a chug off his beer.

"Don't you think he's the best player here?" asked Celeste.

"He might be," admitted Tom. "Or maybe Craig."

I hadn't met anyone named Craig and I certainly hadn't seen anyone that much better than Nathan. "Who's Craig?" I asked.

"Craig is a young guy, maybe your age, that used to play here quite a bit. He's a stockbroker or day trader or something. I'm not sure I really know the difference," answered Tom. "He was a pretty good player. Used to beat everyone here."

"What happened to him?"

"He took some huge loses in the market and kind of disappeared."

"He and Nathan didn't get along. Not sure why, but I know Nathan didn't like getting beat by him," said Celeste. "I remember the two of them had some words on the court a few months ago."

"I liked playing with Craig. He's not annoying like Nathan and Little E. You will like him if you get a chance to meet him. I think the two of you would easily be the best players here," said Tom. "Nathan is one of those people who if they make a bad shot blames it on the paddle or the wind. They never give credit to their opponent. Craig, on the other hand, never blamed anyone or made excuses the few times he screwed up. He just moved on to the next point."

Tom was starting to get heated. "Nathan also thinks he needs to know what everyone on every court is doing. He stops play to give advice, and comments constantly on stuff that's going on in other games. When I did play with him, he would act bored, looking around the other courts. It feels like he thinks he's doing you a favor by playing with you. Then he runs off to a tournament and brags about the medals he wins. Thing is, he's a sandbagger. He always brags about being a 4.0 or higher and then he enters tournaments as a 3.5, just so he can win easily."

He lifted his beer bottle and took a drink before continuing. "Stuart and I beat him and Little E one day, and instead of congratulating us, he said he played badly because of the sun in his eyes. He doesn't take losing well."

"Does he lose very often?" I asked.

"No, I admit he does win most of the time, but that's more because the competition here is a little weak. Not because he's so great. And besides that, he's a nut and thinks everything is a conspiracy. Don't ever get into a political conversation with him when he's been drinking. Not a pleasant experience."

I decided not to probe that line of discussion any further. I've learned the hard way not to bother with conspiracy nuts, and I wasn't ready to get political with this new group, so I let the information pass without comment.

"Um, guys," said Celeste, "You know he was taken off the court in an ambulance this morning. Maybe we shouldn't speak ill of him right now. I actually hope he's OK."

"Maybe we will have some peace and quiet at the courts until he returns," suggested Tom, without a hint of concern.

She was right about not talking trash about someone who is having health issues, but I wasn't so sure that Tom was right about Nathan returning. I'm not normally a pessimist but I didn't think Nathan would be returning anytime soon. The blue color on his face had looked rather serious to me. I decided not to voice my feelings on that matter, so instead I asked, "Does anyone know what happened to him? Is he OK?"

"No news yet that I've heard," said Celeste.

"Well, I hope he's okay." And I meant it. I liked Tom and didn't want to criticize him for his feelings about Nathan, but I also didn't wish for any harm to come to Nathan. I didn't really know him, and based on what I was learning, I probably didn't want to, but there is a tribal thing about pickleball players, as well as compassion for others that I like to think I have. Plus, losing Stephanie taught me that life is short, and you don't want to waste time hating on others.

It seemed everyone was done dissing on Nathan. I could tell that Martin and Leslie were tired of talking about pickleball in general but despite their best efforts, the conversation kept drifting back in one form or another. For the most part, they were good natured about it. I can talk about pickleball for hours, but I also wanted to know more about Rio Viejo. They were kind enough to share with me the best places for food and live music - what little there was in a small town like Rio Viejo - and even a little about local politics. Turned out, it was a mostly blue county, but with a few very vocal people who tended to be red. I reminded myself that nowhere was perfect, but with a sizable group of pickleballers and a generally blue population, I could be happy there. I was given a rundown on a few of the personalities at the courts, who to avoid why and when. Like Nathan when he's been drinking, or William when he didn't have his hearing aid turned up. It was gossipy, but it brought me up to speed pretty quickly. They told me about how Nancy and Nathan were an off and on thing, but currently on. Periodically, she would throw him out over some issue or another, usually having to do with his drinking problem and the resulting abuse. Apparently, he was a mean drunk. Whenever they were on the outs, their presence at the pickleball courts would be awkward for everyone.

Our table was situated in such a way that we had a clear view of the entrance to the market, and it seemed that everyone that came in or out knew at least one person in our little group. My four table mates were rather popular. The market and its outdoor patio were almost an official town meeting place. Just about everyone in town went there at least once or twice a month. It was the closest place to shop for food without having to drive to Nogales, which was over twenty miles away. The prices were a little high and their selection a little light, but that didn't seem to matter.

I spotted Rick, the pickleball paramedic, and Dr. David about to enter the store.

"Isn't that Rick and Dr. David?" I asked, pointing at the two men.

Tom stood up and called out to them. "Rick, David, over here," he said, and waved to them to come join us. They detoured away from the entrance and walked over to our table slowly. They didn't look very happy, in fact they looked totally dejected.

"Hey guys," said Rick, as he stood by our table. He didn't wait for us to ask about Nathans' status. "I've got some bad news about Nathan." I noticed his eyes were red.

"Is he OK?" asked Leslie.

"No." He struggled to say more.

Dr. David bailed him out and said, "Unfortunately, he died on the way to the hospital."

There was a chorus of "oh my god" and "no, that is horrible" around the table.

My beer didn't taste so good anymore. I set it down. I hardly knew Nathan and sadly had participated in some nasty gossip about him. I didn't feel good about that. Going on first impressions and the rumor mill, I probably wouldn't have liked him, but I was still bowled over by the news. Having lost my wife recently, I always took news of someone dying pretty hard. Especially those who died relatively young. I suspected that Tom and Martin weren't feeling too good about themselves either, having just dissed the guy.

"That is terrible," said Martin, and I think he was sincere. Martin seemed like decent a fellow and although he didn't like Nathan, I doubt he would have wished him any harm. Tom nodded. He absolutely didn't like Nathan but looked equally shocked by the news.

"Any idea what happened?" Celeste asked the question that was on all our minds. I have found older people, which I am fast becoming, obsess over the cause of death of people from their age group.

"I'm sure the hospital will do some more tests, but from what I saw and what I know, it looked to be cardiac arrest," said Rick. "Unfortunately, I've seen a few cases, working as a paramedic."

Dr. David nodded.

"Does that mean he had a heart attack?" asked Leslie.

"I think so," answered Rick.

"Wow. Did he have a history of heart problems?" I asked.

"I've known Nathan for two or three years," said Celeste. "He ran around the courts like a kid."

"You can never know these things for sure unless you do lots of tests," shared Dr. David, "I wasn't his doctor, and he never mentioned any issues to me, but sometimes heart problems don't reveal themselves until something like this happens. In my practice, I saw a few young athletes in their prime who suddenly dropped dead of an aneurysm or enlarged heart."

Once again, I thought about what would happen to Butch if I were suddenly out of the picture.

"I need to get some things, then I'm going over to see Nancy and sit with her. She's in shock, as you can imagine," said Rick. "Jane is with her now."

"Yeah, I better get going too," said Dr. David.

I had lost my taste for beer and conversation. "I should go too," I said, as I patted Butch on the head. "You ready to go?" He immediately stood up, indicating he was done with socializing. We all said our goodbyes and wandered off in different directions. Butch and I trudged home quietly, me deep in thought, and Butch happy to smell and pee on everything in sight.

Pickleball Tip # 7– Avoid Injuries

Never just walk out on the court and start playing. Warm up before play. Stretch your arms and do leg lunges to avoid common muscle tears, strained calves, or worse yet, a torn Achilles tendon. Spend at least five minutes hitting various shots ranging from dinks to drops and even some baseline drives. Hit a few volleys from both the kitchen line and the transition zone. You'll play better and avoid injuries. During play, make sure to properly hydrate.

During a match, remember that you can't reach every ball. Sometimes you just have to acknowledge a good shot by your opponent and let it go, rather than going too far and possibly diving or running into a fence to save a ball. Remember the mantra, "No ball is worth a fall."

Another way to avoid injuries is to communicate with your partner. Before a game starts, discuss who will take shots down the middle in different situations, so that you aren't colliding in the center of the court and possibly hitting each other with your paddles.

And lastly, if you have an easy put-away slam, don't aim for your opponent's face.

Chapter 8

Butch and I spent the next few days exploring our new town, meeting new people and even a few dogs that Butch decided weren't total jerks. He loved people in general, but he was picky about other dogs.

We consciously avoided the pickleball courts in deference to the death of Nathan. I assumed since he was the lead Royal, resident pickleball teacher, and local expert, everyone else would refrain from playing. I was still new to the scene and didn't want to appear callous if in fact anyone was out there. If anyone was playing, I wasn't sure I wanted to know who they were. Butch concurred. As far as he was concerned, I probably shouldn't play pickleball ever again. He liked having me around and liked the extra-long, more frequent walks. More walks meant more adoring fans and, inevitably, more treats.

On the sixth day after Nathan's death and first day after the funeral, which I did not attend, I ventured back to the courts. I figured five or six days was enough to show respect, and I was itching to resume my pickleball comeback. I arrived at the courts at eight in the morning, after an abbreviated walk with Butch, about which he was not pleased. I was surprised to see at least twenty people already there, with games at full speed. Others were arriving at the same time as I did. It seemed I wasn't the only one who thought it had been long enough to show some respect to Nathan. At that time of year, mornings were nice and cool, and you wanted to get your vigorous exercise in well before noon, when the temperatures could reach eighty or ninety. I had been told that the more serious players arrived at six-thirty or seven. If it was going to get this crowded by eight o'clock, I was going to have to get Butch out for his walk a little earlier.

No matter where you go to play, I find that pickleballers are a dedicated lot. I've seen games played when it was raining and I've even seen people try to play in twenty or thirty mile per hour winds. You can even buy glow in the dark balls. I draw the line at wet and windy, and I don't like playing when I can see my breath.

I waved to a few people I knew and put my paddle in the rack in front of the intermediate courts, then did some stretching exercises while I waited for my turn to play. The advanced courts were full of players I had met, as well as a few faces I had never seen. I wasn't that surprised that the Royals had returned, although I thought they might give it at least a week after Nathan's passing. Someone had posted a banner in honor of Nathan, with a sharpie hanging from the fence next to it. There were a number of signatures and condolences addressed to Nancy. To my great surprise, Nancy was also out there playing. Evidently, the game must go on.

While I was stretching, Tom arrived and placed his paddle next to mine on the rack. We exchanged pleasantries.

"Been a few days," he said.

"Butch and I spent a few days hanging out and exploring the neighborhood. Have you been playing?"

"No. Leslie didn't think it would be good form to show. This is my first day back out. I did play some golf with Martin, though. Do you play?"

"I did play a few years ago but haven't played in a while. I brought my clubs with me, though, so I might go out and hit a few buckets and see about getting back into it. The problem is, it takes four to five hours to play a round and I hate leaving Butch alone for that long."

"Yeah. I hear ya. You want to take on the winners?"

"Sounds like a plan," I replied, eager to get on the court. There were two players that I hadn't seen before. They both looked to be younger than me and quite athletic. Watching them, I could see they were very good players. I wondered if they played with the Royals. From what I could see so far, they were clearly the best players out on the courts that day. They won the match they were playing eleven to five, and it wasn't as close as the score would indicate. They came off the court to get a drink.

Tom spoke up. "Nice game. You guys new here?

"We are just here for a few days. We're staying at the resort. I'm Giovani and this is my soon-to-be brother in-law, Leo."

"I'm Tom and this is Al." We exchanged fist bumps. "Wedding at the resort?"

"You guessed it," said Leo, with a huge smile.

"Can we challenge you guys to a game?" asked Tom.

"Absolutely," they replied in unison.

We went out on the court, and Tom and I warmed up, hitting a few dinks, drives and volleys until we felt ready. We started slow, losing the first 2 points easily, but we did get a feel for Leo and Giovani's strengths and weaknesses. Giovanni was a banger. He hit everything hard, even his opponents. If he could dink, he didn't show it. Maybe he was just testing to see if we could handle the heat. His backhand was adequate, but he clearly tried to avoid having to hit it. When he did hit a backhand, he tried to over hit it, but he lacked control. Leo, on the other hand, was just the opposite. He was an excellent dinker from both the backhand and the forehand side but had a tendency to get impatient and panic if the rally lasted too long. Invariably, after six or seven dinks, he would go for an ill-advised speed-up and either hit the net or send it sailing out.

Tom and I both played well and were able to take advantage of their weaknesses and soon had turned the score in our favor. It was a spirited, fun match, with Tom and I prevailing over them eleven to five. No one was waiting for the court, so we decided to switch sides and play it back again. The result was about the same.

105

"You guys are better than everyone else out here," said Giovanni. "We would love another crack at you, but we have to get back to the wedding party. Rehearsal dinner tonight."

"Anytime," I replied. "Good luck and congratulations on the marriage."

Leo and Giovanni headed off, and I removed my shirt that was soaking wet and grabbed another one from my bag.

"Are you Jewish?" asked Tom.

I looked at him, obviously confused.

"The Chai necklace," said Tom, pointing to my chest. I had forgotten I was wearing it. Stephanie had given it to me when I finished converting, but I didn't wear it all the time until she passed away.

"Yes. My wife gave it to me. Are you Jewish?"

"No, but I have a couple friends who are. I know it means "to life". I hope you didn't mind me asking, but you don't see a lot of black Jews." He seemed concerned that I might be offended.

"No problem." I wanted to set my new friend's mind at ease. "I converted when we married, but there is actually a whole tribe of Jews from Africa. I don't know a lot about my ancestors, but there are rumors that we were Jewish at one time."

"Wow. Fascinating."

I put my shirt on, covering the symbol. I'm not shy about being Jewish, but I learned from my relationship with Stephanie that there is a lot of antisemitism. It's one thing to be proud of the heritage, it's another to invite hatred. Outright bigots won't hide their feelings about race, but closet bigots will. Being Jewish with no one knowing you're a Jew means you overhear things you wouldn't hear if they knew. I've heard the common tropes about being cheap, hook-nosed, controlling, etc., and sometimes I choose to confront them and other times I bite my tongue.

106

When I was in business, I couldn't hide the fact that I was black, but I could hide the fact that I was a Jew. I'm not proud of it, but it is what it is.

"We have a couple other Jews who play here."

Odd thing to say, but I let it pass.

William came over to chat with us, and I prepared myself to start yelling.

"You two should go take on the Royals." He was pretty loud, and I was sure it was overheard by Brian. Tom grimaced. He didn't like the Royals, but I guessed he didn't like confrontations either. William didn't get a response, so he continued on. "You guys made pretty short work of those two newcomers, and they were good. I think you could beat the Royals easily."

"Oh thanks," I replied, "but we just got lucky."

"Lucky my ass. I'd pay you to beat the royal piss-ants."

An awkward silence followed. Rory arrived and joined the conversation. "You two play well together. I think it would be fun to watch you take them on, but good luck getting in a game over there."

"You have to be invited to play with them," Tom reminded me, "and no way do they want to play against you and lose."

"Oh, I see," I said. Now I was starting to feel a little feisty. At times, Stephanie used to call me a troublemaker. "But these public courts with open play? What would happen if we just put our paddles up and challenged the winners?"

"That depends on the Royals," said Jack, joining in. "I appreciate playing with guys like you; the only way to get better is to play better people. Go on and challenge them." I think Jack was feeling a little feisty as well.

A new player I had never met was coming on the court with Dr. David. He looked quite a bit younger than the geriatric crowd. He was fit and didn't have knee or elbow braces. He held his hand out to do a fist bump with me. "Hi, I'm Eddie, you must be the new guy I heard about."

"Yes, I guess I am. I'm Al."

"Well, I heard you were pretty good. Better than Nathan."

I didn't want to speak ill of the guy, so I said, "Sorry to say, I never got a chance to play with Nathan. I heard he was very good."

"He was OK. He ran the clinics here, but I really didn't learn that much from him. He mostly liked to hear himself talk, and he liked to show off rather than teach."

Yikes, I thought, not sure how to respond. I guess you could talk bad about the dead if they were one of the Royals, and the other Royals weren't there to defend his honor. It was quite clear to me that the Royals had created a lot of resentment among the "lesser" players.

Eddie decided he wanted to take me and Tom on. He enlisted another player, an Asian man who looked to be in his early fifties, I had never seen before but that he seemed to know. The man introduced himself as Phil. He was one of the few non-white, non-Mexicans I'd seen since moving to town. He probably felt as out of place there as I did. He was tall and athletic, and during a brief warm up he proved to be a decent player, with a good command of drives, volleys, and dinks. I was looking forward to the match.

Eddie was probably the youngest player on the court, maybe thirty, and he was fast. A Hispanic man, he worked for a produce company in Mexico, importing strawberries, melons, and avocados. That explained the huge flat of strawberries sitting on a bench nearby, which I learned was a fairly common occurrence. He was very friendly, always smiling, and had a great attitude. Eddie was still learning the game, but what he lacked in strict

108

pickleball skills he made up for with his speed and athleticism. It didn't hurt that he was a good tennis player.

Phil was the better player of the two, hitting some wickedly hard drives and not afraid to go at an opponent's body. Tom was having trouble with the pace that Phil was hitting and popped a few up for easy slams. One shot that I didn't have time to set up for hit me square in the chest. It hurt and would no doubt leave a mark. Phil apologized profusely, but I smiled and assured him it was part of the game and our fault for popping it up. Tom also felt bad for setting me up like that, but since I was sure Phil meant no harm, I let it slide. I joked that I had been thinking about getting a pickleball tattoo on my chest, and he had just saved me a trip to the tattoo parlor and a bunch of money. I've tagged a few people in my day as well and hopefully they didn't think I was out to harm them either.

It was easily the most competitive game I had been in since arriving in Rio Viejo. Phil and Eddie were good enough to hit most of the balls at Tom, and if I wanted some action, I was going to need to poach a few balls. The points were exciting and the score close.

Some of the Royals had joined the group watching us play, and we were giving them something worth watching. People were hooting and hollering at good shots and teasing us when we hit unforced errors. It was all good until the Royals started giving advice. It was unsolicited and mostly poor advice, but worse still, it was annoying. They were interrupting the flow of the game by calling out to Eddie, Phil, and even Tom. I guess they felt they didn't know me enough to try to give me advice. Court etiquette generally demands advice be given after a game, not during it. No one told them to shut up, but I was getting close to saying something. I bit my tongue, which by now was getting tired of being bitten, as I was the new guy and didn't want to sound rude.

Tom and I held on to win eleven to nine, but not without a hard-fought battle. I didn't play my best, but between Tom and I we had just enough weapons and strategy to hold Phil and Eddie off. I learned that the speed of both Phil and Eddie was so fast that no point was really over until it bounced twice. We tapped paddles at mid-court and congratulated each other on a good game.

"Nice game," said Eddie, then in a whisper added, "Could those fuckers over there just shut the fuck up? No one asked them for their damn advice or opinions." Then he said a few words in Spanish that I didn't understand. I vowed to learn some key phrases.

"It was pretty rude," I quietly agreed, not wanting the Royals to hear me.

"They are always like that," replied Phil. "No one knows as much about the game as they do," he added, with a definite note of sarcasm. "You should have been here when Nathan was around. It was barely tolerable." Once again, I learned that Nathan had few real fans.

I grabbed my water bottle and took a large drink, then sat down to rest. Playing against the young, athletic legs of Eddie and Phil after my long layoff was harder than I had imagined. I vowed to get in better shape.

Little E came over to where I was sitting. "Hi, I'm Ethelwolf, Vice President of the Pickleball Club. You can call me E." Odd, since we had met not long ago at Taco Tim's, and he had tried to recruit me for league play. I didn't want to make him feel bad for forgetting me so soon, but it was especially weird since I was the only black guy that I had seen on the courts since I got there. Maybe there were other brothers that played on different days than I did? I gently informed him we had met at Taco Tim's.

"Oh. Yes, I remember," he said, unconvincingly. "I guess with all the trauma of losing Nathan I forgot." Nice excuse, but he didn't seem all that traumatized to me. What I really thought was that he was too self-involved to think about me or anyone else. I wasn't sure why he felt the need to tell me he was the Vice President. Maybe it was an important position here in Rio Viejo? Was I being too judgmental?

I smiled. "That's OK. I'm Al."

"Nathan was our President, you know."

"I had heard that." I didn't care.

"I think that would make me President now."

"Hmm." Again, I didn't care. Not sure what else to say, so I took another drink of water.

"I saw you playing just now," he said. "You look like you've played before. You're quite good."

My memory wasn't perfect, but I did remember telling people at Tim's that I had played before. Maybe he wasn't listening. Instead of reminding him, I nodded and said, "I used to play a lot and took some time off, so I'm a bit rusty right now."

The other Royals he had been playing with came over to join the conversation. I wasn't sure if I should be honored or intimidated. Maybe with Nathan's passing they needed a new player to join the Royals? I hoped that Tom would come to my rescue. He did not.

"Hi, Al," said Nancy. Even in mourning, which I assumed she was, she was immaculate in her appearance and quite likely the most fashionable person on the courts. She was wearing a fancy, colorful tennis outfit that probably cost more than my entire wardrobe. To her credit, she at least remembered my name.

"Sorry about what happened to Nathan," I said.

"I used to date Nathan and help him with the clinics," she answered with a sad face.

"I had heard that. This has to be rough for you." I was doing my best to be sympathetic. I knew all too well what it was like to lose someone you love.

"It was quite a shock for sure, but he died doing what he loved. He was one of the founders of the pickleball club here and was responsible for teaching most of the people here the game."

"Wow," I sighed. "I saw him play and he looked pretty good."

"It just doesn't make any sense. He had no history of heart problems. None in his family. He was so healthy." She started to tear up.

"These things happen. At our age nothing is guaranteed. We could be hit by a bus tomorrow and that would be the end of that," said Jack rejoining the group.

I hate that phrase. Stephanie heard a lot of comments about being hit by a bus when she had cancer. When it came back the second time, she tried to joke that the bus did hit her the first time, but since it didn't kill her, the driver was backing up to see if he could finish the job. She always tried to lighten the mood.

Jane walked up to comfort Nancy. Because of her tall skinny build and stringy blonde hair, I couldn't help but be reminded of the scarecrow in the Wizard of Oz. She said, "Jack takes care of the courts for us. He's always the first guy out here and blows the courts clean when they are full of leaves."

I had already heard that but didn't say so. "That's awesome you do that, Jack. These are great courts here and I'm looking forward to being a part of the group. Let me know if I can help you sometime."

"It is a great group. Won't be the same without Nathan," said Nancy, wiping tears off her face. "I'm really going to miss him."

"Yeah, it is sad," I agreed, not sure what else to say.

Brian, the fourth in their group, came off the court and nodded in my direction. I couldn't tell if he was trying to be cool or just disinterested in our conversation. He sat down by his bag and took out his phone. He started scrolling through what I assumed were important messages, based on his facial expression. There was a time when I was a stockbroker that I was glued to my phone too. Now I do some day trading, but I'm not obsessed with it, and I don't get messages and calls all day since I sold my firm.

"I saw you playing out there," said Jane, drawing my attention away from Brian. "You're pretty good. Have you been playing long?" Maybe it was something in the water, or being in the southern Arizona sun too much, but she seemed to have the same malady of forgetting things quickly as Little E. I distinctly remembered saying all this when she was sitting near me at Taco Tim's. But I decided not to be too judgmental and once again repeated my story.

"About five or six years I think, and before that I was a tennis player, so I have a good foundation with racket sports. But I've been away from the game for a while." I wasn't going to explain why unless she asked and thankfully, she didn't. "But it seems like it is coming back to me." I noticed she either she didn't care to hear my answer or had the attention span of a child, as she keep looking around the courts.

"You should join us over on court 5," she said. *Ah-ha*, I thought. They are recruiting for a replacement for Nathan.

I guess that meant I passed the Royal muster, at least in her eyes. I had watched her play a few minutes the last time I was at the courts and what she lacked in skill she made up for with her competitiveness. I mean serious competitiveness. She was clearly an ex-tennis player and, like most of us, she had a huge back swing and liked to drive balls from the baseline and try to pass her opponents. I remembered that she didn't exhibit a lot of finesse or strategy, but given the level of competition here, her aggressive nature put her toward the top of the heap. She could benefit from some advice, and from what I saw of her drive to win she would probably welcome it, but I vowed she wasn't going to get any advice from me unless she asked for it. It's easy to be an expert from the sidelines, but most of the time the advice given isn't appreciated. I had no desire to come across as any kind of expert.

From the looks I was getting, and the body language from Tom and some of the others milling about, it was obvious they were annoyed by the intrusion of the Royals and how they had come to dominate the conversation. The Royals didn't seem to care, however, or they were so caught up in themselves they didn't notice.

Eddie, who was openly showing disdain for them, turned to me and said, "Why don't you and Tom take on Ethelwolf and Brian. I think that would be a good game." I thought I noticed a little gleam in his eye. He wanted to watch someone take them down.

Nancy seemed to bristle at this. "We were going to play another game," she paused ever so briefly, "if that's OK?" It sounded more like a statement than a request. "You know we are training for a tournament."

Eddie waved that off. "Plenty of time for that. I want to see the new guy and Tom go against Brian and Ethelwolf," he said, adamantly. He seemed intent on pissing off Nancy. It was working.

"Well, we really want another game," she pleaded.

"Plenty of time for that," repeated Eddie. "Go on, you guys. Take them on."

"Works for me," said Tom, eagerly. I could tell he was enjoying seeing Nancy fume.

"I'm OK with that," said Ethelwolf. "What do you think Brian? Should we take on these guys?" He looked confident.

Brian looked up from his phone disinterestedly. "Sure. Whatever." I decided right then that I would make Brian pay attention early in the game.

Nancy started to object again but was interrupted by Jane. "That's OK with me, I could sit out a game."

Nancy sighed but didn't say another word. She sat down with her water bottle and frowned. I recognized that look. My mother used the same one with my father when she didn't get her way. She didn't even try to hide her displeasure, but no one seemed to care. I wouldn't have been surprised to see smoke coming out of her ears, like in a cartoon.

Although both Brian and Ethelwolf were Royals, I sensed some animosity between them. In fact, I didn't really see a lot of camaraderie between any of the Royals. The few games I had watched showed spotty teamwork and rather than supportive encouragement, the banter between Royals seemed more biting than helpful. Brian and Ethelwolf took the court and acted disinterested, as if it was going to be an easy win for them. They were going to teach us interlopers a lesson.

Even before the opening serve, I could tell Tom had something to prove. I knew from earlier comments that he didn't care for these people, and it went deeper than just having been snubbed by them in the past. If there was any doubt, Tom laid it to rest immediately.

"Let's beat the shit out of these assholes," he whispered to me.

I, on the other hand, was new to town and had no ax to grind with anyone and wanted to keep it that way, but I wasn't going to let them beat us. Not if I could help it. I was going to do whatever it took to impress Tom and the people watching from the sidelines. The more Ethelwolf and Brian acted nonchalant about the match, the more I was determined to make it a lopsided victory for us. I'm not proud to admit this, but I told myself to hit one of them early in the game to establish our dominance. When I say hit, I mean a gut shot or at their legs. I had no intention of hitting either of them in the head and causing any injuries. I've known a few headhunters and I had no intention of being tagged as one.

As we warmed up, the crowd grew larger, as people wandered over from the other courts. I had no doubt they were hoping to see a Royal take-down. I thought I even heard a few bets being wagered.

Little E and Brian started slow, probably due to their arrogance. They had little doubt anyone there could be a threat to their dominance.

They were wrong.

Tom and I were focused and in sync with each other from the first serve. We were quickly up five to zero and the audience wasn't quiet about it. They were razzing Little E and Brian and it was obvious the two of them weren't pleased about it, or the score.

"Can we have a little quiet over there?" demanded Little E. "You people are distracting us."

That only made it worse.

Every attempt by Brian or Little E to match our intensity or superior play put them deeper in the hole. Soon down eight to zero, Brian called time out. The two of them huddled to discuss strategy and after a minute or two, they came back from their meeting looking intense, maybe even angry. Up to now the rallies had been short. Brian and Ethelwolf were either making stupid, unforced errors or just getting plain outgunned. I think they were embarrassed at the beating they were taking in front of the crowd. What they thought of as their crowd. But instead of support, they were getting mocked. Jane and Nancy tried to root them on and encourage them, but it wasn't much help. They called another time out at ten to zero, hoping to freeze us and initiate a major comeback. I told Tom I had no desire to pickle them in front of everyone. Although he disagreed with me at first, he relented, and we let them win a couple of points.

"You guys are done," said Brian, trying to sound convincing. "We're serious now."

Tom shot me a look that said, *No more.* I nodded in agreement.

On the next point, Brian hit a soft dink that stayed too high and went too far, giving Tom an easy slam that hit Little E in the chest. E glared at him but didn't say anything.

Tom took the ball back to the baseline to serve. He called the score, ten to two, loud enough for everyone watching to hear. His serve went deep to Brian's backhand, eliciting a weak return that just cleared the kitchen line. I teed off on it hitting a deep drive to Brian who was still back at the baseline. He stabbed at it, and it came back to me for an easy volley with too much angle for Little E to put a paddle on. Game over.

Coming to center court for the paddle tap, Little E and Brian were already blaming each other for the loss. We tapped paddles and exchanged the obligatory "good game" comments, but I could tell that Brian and Little E didn't mean it. Truthfully, they hadn't played all that badly. They were just outperformed. I've been there. Sometimes you just get beat by a better team.

Brian came off the court complaining that they hadn't had time to warm up. They had been sitting too long and were stiff. The sun was in their eyes. The people watching were distracting him. The call he took on his phone was still bothering him. He had every excuse I had ever heard.

I shrugged, but Tom was a little more brutal. He gave me a high five and teased Little E about losing.

"We were just getting going at the end. We took two quick points and if we had more time, it would be a different outcome," boasted Brian. "In fact, I want a rematch."

On the one hand, I can appreciate the bad feeling after a loss when you think you didn't play your best and it had nothing to do the skill of the

117

opponents. You want to get back on the court as quickly as possible to try to avenge and redeem yourself. However, that wasn't the case here. These guys were outmatched from the start, and they would have lost playing their best pickleball. They thought they had earned the two points they got, but Tom and I had relaxed our game on purpose. Getting pickled is not a good feeling, and this being rec play with nothing more at stake than bragging rights, I just didn't want to do that to them, no matter how annoying they were.

I was more than happy to give them the opportunity for redemption, but I knew that Nancy was still seething. She didn't want to watch; she wanted to play. She and Jane had their paddles in the rack and wanted their turn on the court. Wherever I've played, proper etiquette said we should either split up the winners and allow two new people on the court or take on the challengers. I had no desire to be the guy bucking the local rules, even if the Royals often bent the rules to suit their desires.

"Let's go," said Little E, heading for the court. "Rematch, switch sides."

"There are people waiting to play." I pointed at Nancy and Jane. "We can wait."

"I don't care," grumbled Brian. "They can just wait. I want a rematch, this time with no distractions."

I still hesitated, but Tom said with a smirk, "No problem. The result will be the same."

Nancy wasn't going down without a fight. She was up and steaming and started to step onto the court. "We want a chance to play them."

Brian wasn't about to give in. He had been beaten soundly, even humiliated, in front of the crowd and wanted revenge. "You can play the winner of this game." He nodded to Little E. "Come on E."

All I could think was, "The king is dead, long live the king."

I wasn't sure if the fight was over and looked at the ladies to see if they were going to give in. They were clearly angry, Nancy more so than Jane, and Nancy was not shy about showing it. I thought I saw Nancy mouth the words, "Fuck you, Brian".

Tom was clearly enjoying the exchange of "pleasantries", having been on the receiving end on more than one occasion. He grinned at me. "They pull that shit on me and others so many times I can't even count. Pay back is a bitch."

I thought Nancy and Jane could have heard Tom, but if they did, they didn't show it. But Nancy wasn't quite ready to back down just yet. "I really think we should get to play against them," she pleaded, as she headed toward the court and motioned for Jane to follow. "We could do better than you guys did."

"We're going to play a rematch," barked Brian, as he edged by her. With his back to her he said, "You can play us after we put them in their place." He marched onto the court and took the opposite side from the one they had just lost on. "Switch sides." There was no wind or sun creating an advantage for one side or the other, but I figured it was Brian's way of saying there was. Just another excuse for losing.

A few of the spectators spoke up. "We want to see them play again." It was as if they were sending Nancy a message to sit down and shut up. No doubt because they had experienced the same treatment at one time or another and thought she should taste a bit of her own medicine. Nancy was clearly angry and stormed back to the benches.

I waited for her to blurt out "Well, I never!" but she didn't. Instead, she mumbled between clenched teeth, "Fine, but Jane and I have winners."

I was surprised she backed down. Nancy struck me as someone who had to get her own way. Clearly, the Royals were not a tight knit group, and it was obvious there was going to be a power struggle between her and

119

Brian. With Nancy backing down to a few scattered giggles, Tom and I entered the court. It was hard not to show any emotion, but I think I managed.

Tom handed me the ball to serve first, but I said we should let them start. He laughed and said, "Let's take it to them again." He wanted a repeat of the score from the previous game and he wasted no time setting up the opportunity. He was playing harder and meaner and went for blood on any and every point he could. Short lobs were crushed, volleys were hit crisply, and dinks were perfect. I kept the ball in play and Tom hit with no mercy. He tagged them each multiple times. Their meager attempts to retaliate were either hitting the net or sailing long. They were clearly angry and rattled and blaming each other. Tom was looking for the pickle we could have had in the first game. The game ended quickly at eleven to one.

We met at the net and tapped our paddles together and once again said good game, but it felt even less cordial than it had after our first game. Little E and Brian were upset, and they weren't shy about showing it. They stormed off the court, mumbling something, but I didn't pick it up. The audience was thrilled with the drubbing they had witnessed and weren't holding back. This only seemed to infuriate Brian and Little E even more.

Rory might have been the most vocal and cruel. He laid it on thick and no amount of excuses by Little E and Brian could stem the flow. They had been soundly beaten and a little of the shine was taken off the Royal armor. They were not only beatable, but they weren't good sports about it. Even Jack, the friendliest guy on the court, couldn't help but comment how one-sided the games were. He said it without any emotion, but I could tell he thought the outcome was deserved. I tried to play it down, but Tom wasn't having any of it. Normally an easy-going guy, he reveled in their defeat and made it clear he wanted them to feel the humiliation of their loss. They had dished out enough insults to others in the past, that whatever they were getting now was well-earned.

We drank some water, and after a brief rest, we went back on the court to play against Jane and Nancy. The game was not nearly as intense, and Tom and I relaxed a bit to allow for longer and more frequent rallies. Neither Tom nor I went for hard body shots, even though that resulted in some unforced errors and some points for our opponents. Not only was the game a little closer than it was against Brian and Little E, but it was also more fun. Tom no longer played as though he had something to prove, and although Jane and Nancy might have been annoying Royals, they weren't as obnoxious as the men in losing. We allowed the game to be closer, but we still won eleven to five and followed up by a second game at eleven to six. Staying closer to us in the score gave Jane and Nancy a moral victory over Brian and Little E, which they made sure did not go unnoticed by anyone, especially Brian and Little E.

I declined any more games with the excuse that I had to return home to Butch. It was uncomfortable at the courts with the Royals griping at each other. Brian and Little E were still arguing about each other's mistakes and who was most to blame for their lopsided losses. They went back out on the court against Jane and Nancy, looking determined to prove they were better players.

Pickleball is a game that should be fun and social. Few of us are ever going to go pro, but to see the intensity of some of the Royals, you would have thought it was life and death. I had met a few people like that before; they only walked away happy if they won, no matter how well they played.

I returned home to find Butch greeting me with a wagging tail and treating me to a slobbery kiss. "Butch, you should have seen it. We beat the crap out of the Royals, and they didn't like it one bit." I may have played it low-key at the courts, but I was going to brag to Butch. He stared at me, which encouraged me to go on, as I was sure he didn't believe me. So, I continued, "Really Butch, they couldn't compete with us, and they were sniping at each other like dogs fighting over a stick." His ears perked up. I don't think he liked the dog reference and I immediately apologized. "No

121

offense, buddy. You know I love you." I went over and hugged him. He barely responded. "You think it's time for a walk, don't you?"

That got his attention. He marched over to the door expectantly and waited for me to leash him up.

"OK. Let's go for a walk."

I leashed him up and we headed out the door toward the trail. Within five minutes we ran into Melanie and her two off-leash Australian Shepherds. They were both friendly and well-mannered dogs, and they immediately ran up to say hi to Butch. He's a ladies' man, both two and four-legged.

"Hi, Al," Melanie said as she approached. "I saw you and Tom take apart the Royals today."

"We were lucky," I replied, not really believing my answer.

"No. You crushed them all and it was fun to see. They need to be taken down a notch. You know Nathan was the best player, but I think you're better. It's so sad that he died like that. It would have been fun to watch you play against him."

"Even though I didn't know him, I'm sorry he passed away. It was so sudden." I wasn't sure what else to say.

"Nancy said she thinks something is wrong."

"Dying so young is pretty tragic. I guess you never know when your heart will go out." *Or if you might develop cancer*, I thought to myself.

"Nancy can't believe he died of heart failure."

"I understand. It can be hard to accept something so unexpected."

"No, I mean she doesn't believe it. She thinks someone killed him."

"What?" I exclaimed. "Who would do that? Why? Didn't the paramedics say it was heart failure?

"All I know is she was talking to a few people, saying it didn't make any sense and she wants someone to look into it."

"What about the police?"

"She said they didn't think there was any evidence of wrongdoing and that it was what it looked like. A heart attack."

"What else could it have been?"

"This is where it gets strange. Do you know Anna from Pickleball?"

"Vaguely. I think I've heard the name but I haven't played with her."

"First off you need to know that I have a powerful hearing aid and can turn it up so I can hear conversations from as much as fifteen feet away even if the voices are low. Well, during one of Nancy and Nathan's breakups about three months ago, I overheard Nancy complain to Anna that Nathan was a jerk and had cheated on her. So, Anna, who is from Mexico, told Nancy about these witches that lived in the mountains near La Paz. She said that the witches there created a brew from some local plants that women could give to their cheating husbands to get some revenge and teach them a lesson. In small doses, it causes paralysis, and in large doses, it can cause death that would look like a heart attack."

"Huh. That is crazy. Is that really true?"

Melanie shrugged.

"Are you suggesting that Nancy killed Nathan using this brew?

"Oh no, of course not. Nancy is too nice and besides, they were back together again soon after that conversation. I don't think she would want to kill him, but rumor has it he had lots of affairs. I wouldn't be surprised if one of the husbands of the women he cheated with wanted some revenge."

She may not have wanted to kill him, but I wondered if Nancy might have tried to spike his drink with this magic brew in order to teach him a lesson and accidentally gave him too much.

"Well, if it was poison, I would think the coroner would have discovered it," I theorized.

"Maybe not. I think it might be something they have to test for specifically, and they wouldn't know to do that."

"Hmm. Have you gone to the police with this information?"

"No, of course not. I don't want to get involved."

Yet there she was, spreading rumors about people and their possible motives. With that hearing aid, I wondered what other stories she had heard. I wasn't too keen on getting involved in gossip, but I had to know more.

"Who else was around when Anna told Nancy about the witches?"

"Oh. My memory isn't that good, but I think most of the Royals were there."

So, if Nancy was right, and Melanie heard what she thought she heard, then someone might have killed Nathan and made it look like a heart attack. I began thinking I had dropped into a modern-day Agatha Christie novel, and I wasn't thrilled about it. I liked reading murder mysteries; not playing a role in one. I told myself that as soon as I got home, I would look up witches' brews from Mexico.

"You're sure about all this?" I asked.

"I'm just telling you what Nancy believes and what I heard Anna say."

Wonderful, I thought, as Butch and I walked away. It didn't make much sense, though. If either Anna or Nancy was serious about this brew thing, why would they discuss it openly? No, if someone did kill Nathan with this brew, it probably wasn't Anna or Nancy.

"Oh, by the way," said Melanie, before Butch and I could leave. "Nathan has had affairs with Anna, Jane, Molly, and Anne. I think he also had a few with some local ladies that don't play pickleball."

Geez, I thought. The guy was a real Don Juan. I wondered if he had been with Melanie too, but I didn't ask.

"Does Nancy know about all of them?"

"Oh, everyone knows," she giggled. "Not too many secrets in a small town. But he wasn't the only one. Brian and Nancy had a fling during one of Nancy and Nathan's separations. Nathan took it out on Brian for a while, but they seemed to have made up."

I shook my head as my jaw dropped. What was this place? I had moved into a damn soap opera.

"Lots of drama here," said Melanie with a laugh, as she trotted off with her pups.

Butch and I walked away, questioning our move to Rio Viejo. I tried asking Stephanie what she thought and if she had any theories, but I got no answer, so I asked Butch. "What do you think, Butch? Is that the craziest thing you ever heard?" He just lifted his leg and peed on a bush. "Yeah, I agree."

Pickleball Tip # 8– Return Of Serve

First order of business is to get your service return in. In fact, it may be the most important shot in the game. If you miss it, the other team gets a point. If you hit it short, the serving team gets an easy path to the kitchen and can take control of the point.

Once you have some consistency getting the service return back, work on hitting your returns deep. Stand behind the baseline, especially against people who hit hard and deep serves. Give yourself time to set up and step into the return, rather than getting caught having to hit off your back foot or short hopping a ball. Once you master that, you can start to aim for the server's weakness, usually the backhand. Ideally, this keeps the server back on his heels, allowing you an easy path to the kitchen and control of the point.

Chapter 9

The following day, I decided I would head out to the courts early and get some practice against the wall by myself. I had given Butch a quick, abbreviated walk and afterward, as I went out the front door, he jumped up on the couch and let out a loud sigh, as if to tell me he was not pleased with me. I apologized and told him I would be back soon. He closed his eyes and went to sleep without giving me another thought.

When I arrived, Jack was already there, using a leaf blower to clear the courts of debris. He told me he had already sent out a text message to many of the local players, announcing that the courts were clean, and the weather was perfect for pickleball. "They should be here any minute," he said.

"That is awesome, man," I said. "Do you really do this every day?"

"I do. If you give me your cell phone number, I can add you to my list and keep you informed of court conditions."

Why not? I thought.

I gave him my number and asked, "How long have you been doing this?"

"I moved here about a year ago. After my divorce, I thought this would be a great place to live. I learned pickleball when I got here and loved it."

I was impressed. He was not a bad player, considering he'd only been playing a year.

"Retired?"

"I am, but I do some pet and house sitting on the side to help with my bills. Lots of people here need my services and I'm pretty booked up."

"Wow. Good for you." I filed away the info on pet sitting for future reference, not that I went anywhere without Butch. Still, you never knew.

Jack moved off to clear another court and I started my stretching and warm-ups. When I finished, I walked over to the practice wall and did some drills, practicing dinks and volleys. I was getting in a nice groove, when I noticed two people ride up on mountain bikes. I recognized one as Samantha, the retired doctor I had recently met and played with. She called out to me to come meet her husband.

"Hi, Al. This is my husband, Joe."

We did the fist bump that had become the norm since COVID. "Do you play?" I asked.

"No. I just rode over with Samantha. I wanted to meet the new guy in town."

"Ah. I'm guessing that would be me."

"Unless someone else has just arrived here. I'm a retired detective. I guess my old habits die hard."

"Old habits?" I asked.

"I like to know a little something about the people my wife hangs out with."

Was that because I was black or Jewish? Or did this guy have a dossier on everyone that played here? I was starting to feel a little strange. My mind conjured up the image of a policeman harassing a stranger, wanting to know what he was doing in town. Kind of like in a Rambo movie. I wasn't anything like Rambo, except I was a bit scruffy looking, and although I'm not ripped like him, I am pretty fit. But just like Rambo, I wasn't looking to make trouble, unless beating the locals at pickleball was troublesome. I hoped there was no law against that.

"I just moved here to get out of the cold and start over in a new place."

I don't know why I volunteered any information. If he had come up to me like anyone else here and asked me about myself, I wouldn't have felt like it was odd. But the fact that he introduced himself right off the bat as a detective gave me the willies. Even worse, I couldn't stop talking, as he just stared at me. I'd never actually been interrogated by the police, but I imagined this was what it must feel like. If I thought he could take a joke, I would have said it wasn't me who killed Scarlet in the study with the fireplace poker.

"My wife died last year, and I thought I needed to get away." Why did I say get away? It sounded ominous and a tad guilty. He probably thought I had killed her.

"I'm sorry," he said with a sad face. "How did she die, if you don't mind me asking?"

Ah ha, I was right. He probably suspected me of killing my wife and thought I might have had something to do with Nathan's death. New guy comes to town and someone drops dead. My paranoia was running wild. I looked away and then back again quickly. Worried that I was looking guilty of something, I made sure to make eye contact.

"Cancer," I answered.

"Oh geez. Sorry to hear that."

I wasn't sure he believed me. He was looking at me suspiciously. Hell, I would have too, and I wasn't an ex-cop. Why was I acting so weird?

"Yeah. Cancer sucks." I wanted to change the subject. "So, why don't you play? Your wife is very good."

"I tried it, but it just wasn't my thing. Samantha likes it though, and she said you were really good."

I smiled. Partly because I liked the compliment and partly because I felt I had successfully changed the subject.

He continued, "I like to ride bikes and motorcycles and I play a little golf. That stuff is enough for me. How about you? What do you do besides terrorize the pickleball courts? Maybe you'd like to go for a ride sometime?"

I knew it. He wanted to know more about me. Persistent, like Colombo. *Still doesn't believe my wife died from cancer*, I thought. No doubt he had some connections that could do background checks. That thought finally calmed me down. I didn't kill my wife and I didn't have a shady background. I'd never even had a speeding ticket. So, a background check of me would prove that I was a law-abiding citizen. I relaxed.

"I play a little golf. Not quite as good at it as I am at pickleball, though. I used to ride a mountain bike in the mountains near Denver, but now that Butch and I moved here, I just ride around town."

"Butch?" he asked.

"My dog."

"I love dogs," he said, smiling. "I'd love to meet him. What kind of dog is he?"

"Just a big ole mutt. He's very lovable."

"I'm sure he is."

"I want to get in a game," said Samantha, interrupting the interrogation.

"Yeah, me too. Let's warm up a little," I said, eagerly.

"OK. You guys go play, I'll just ride around a bit and come back for you in a while. I'd like to see the new guy play." He started toward his bike, as I went to grab my stuff. "Oh, by the way," he called back to me, "I understand you were here when Nathan died on the court?"

"I was. I was over on another court and didn't see him go down. They say it was a heart attack." Again, I felt like I was under a bright light and the cops were grilling me.

"Samantha said that she heard Nancy say she didn't think it was a heart attack. She thinks that Nathan was too healthy for that."

I walked back toward Joe. "I heard about that from Melanie. Something about witches and poison from Baja or something. I guess Anna mentioned it. I think she's from Mexico. I wasn't there when she said it, though." I wanted to say, *That's all I know, please don't ask me any more questions. Talk to Anna.* I was really getting paranoid again. I wanted to tell him to leave me alone, but I thought it best to just stop talking.

"Yeah, Samantha told me about that conversation. Just curious if you heard anything else?"

"No. It's pretty wild if it's true. I hope it isn't. I would hate to think someone here would do something like that. Wouldn't poison show up on an autopsy, though?"

"Maybe. If they did one and knew enough to look for that, but small towns like this don't always do full autopsies. I doubt they even did one at all. I'm going to look into it though."

"But they would do one if they suspected something, right?"

"Maybe." He stared at me with intense green eyes that made me really nervous. "You're from Denver, right?"

"Yes." I racked my brain. Did I tell him I was from Denver earlier or had he already checked me out? Samantha must have told him.

"Lots of murders in Denver."

131

"Huh?"

"My experience is that there are murderers everywhere. Given the right circumstances, anyone can become a murderer."

What the fuck? This guy was creepy.

"Oh? I guess. I just didn't think stuff like that would happen in a small town like this." I was expecting him to ask me if I'd ever been to Mexico. If he did, I would have really freaked out.

"Yep. Well, you guys go have a good game," he said, with an obviously fake smile. "I'll be back in a little while. Nice meeting you, Al." And off he rode.

Jeez. As I walked on the court for a game with Rory, Samantha, and Dr. David, I couldn't help thinking I was in the Twilight zone, or maybe a Murder She Wrote episode. Stephanie had spent a lot of hours in the chemo chair, and we passed the time watching old shows. She loved detective dramas. She probably would have enjoyed the intrigue in Rio Viejo.

Maybe I shouldn't have been, but I was haunted by Joe's questions. As a black man in a predominantly white town, I think I was justified in those feelings. I was entirely distracted, and the game should have been a lopsided victory for me and my partner, but I kept missing easy shots. Generally, I don't make a lot of unforced errors, but in that game, I was having trouble with dinks, drives, and volleys. I was even missing easy overheads and put-aways. Somehow Samantha and I were still able to eke out a win, but it wasn't pretty. My mind was elsewhere. I was shaken up by the combination of Joe giving me the third degree and the very real possibility that someone in town was a murderer. Which was worse? I hate to sound like a victim, but history shows it's easy to blame the black man, or the Jew, or the newcomer, and I was all three. I told myself I was over thinking it. I tried to replay the conversation with Joe and tell myself I was overreacting, but was I? Was he just being inquisitive, as would be the nature of a retired detective regarding people who interacted with his wife? I was also trying to tell myself that the story of witches and poisons from Baja Mexico was just a bunch of old people letting their imaginations run wild. I mean really. These people were bored and probably just looking for some excitement. Wasn't pickleball enough?

Playing against Rory was an adventure. The best way to describe his style was frenetic. He was all over the court, running side to side and front to back. He'd jump for balls that were going out, and if you weren't careful as his partner, he'd knock you down chasing a ball he had no chance of reaching and should have let you take. Or he might hit you with his paddle on some wild swing. He could hit soft, I'd seen him do it in warms ups, but in a game he rarely did. I seriously feared for his life, as well as anyone near him, when I saw him play. Halfway through the match he ran to the sideline for a ball, a ball he had no chance of reaching. His momentum took him into the net that separated the two courts. The net, and the posts that held the net, were no match for a one-hundred-and-seventy-pound man running at full speed. Rory and the netting tumbled to the ground in a tangled mess. I feared we would be calling the paramedics again.

He was slow getting up, mostly because he was still caught up in the net. We rushed over to help him untangle. He was shaken up but assured us that he was okay. A sore wrist and a damaged ego and maybe a bruise here or there, but he would live to play another day. As we returned the net structure to its original position, Rory continued to assure us that he was fine and wanted to continue the game. Then his watch started to beep, and I could see the watch face had turned bright red and was flashing.

"I better call in or they'll be sending an EMT out," he said, blushing.

"What the hell is that all about?" I asked. I had never seen anything like it.

"Medical alert watch," said Karen, who had been on the adjacent court and was helping to fix the netting. "I have one, too. It knows that he fell

133

down and it notified a medical alert company. If he doesn't call in quickly, it sends out a notice to the local EMT, as well as his emergency contact person."

"Wow. That's quite a gadget. I should have one of those, so I can get help when I trip over my own tongue," I joked.

No one laughed. I guess they didn't appreciate my self-deprecating humor.

By this time, Rory was talking into his Dick Tracy watch, telling the agency he was alright; it was just a fall on the pickleball court. Given the average age of pickleballers, and the fact that they account for a large percentage of emergency room visits near pickleball courts, I imagined I would be seeing a lot more of these gadgets on the court. The funny thing is, when I was young and saw a Dick Tracy comic with him talking into his watch, I thought it was cool and wanted one. Now, not so much. Besides, if I got one now who would they call? Butch? He's smart, but he still hasn't learned to answer the phone.

After the emergency interruption, we resumed the game. It was agreed that Samantha and I did win the point just before Rory hit the ground. Just because someone falls doesn't mean the point is over.

Samantha and I managed to eke out a win against Dr. David and Rory, mostly because Samantha was able to keep the ball in play and I hit enough decent balls at Rory to expose his weaknesses. I was not proud of my performance. I'd much rather play well and lose to better players, than play poorly and win against much weaker players.

It didn't help matters that I could overhear Anna telling stories to Jack about the witches in the mountains of Baja California and the way they controlled their men through various potions. How did she know so much? They were still talking about Nathan when they took the court to challenge me and Samantha. I promised Samantha I could and would play better this game, and I did. We made short work of them and won the game eleven to five. Thankfully, there was no talk of witches and poisons during the match. Besides, Anna was just spreading crazy rumors, right? Nathan died from a heart attack.

As was common when there wasn't a crowd waiting, the winners stayed on until they lost, or got tired and needed a break. Samantha and I weren't tired and didn't need a break, so we took on Jesus and Stuart, who had placed their paddles on the fence during our match against Anna and Jack. As Anna and Jack left the court, they resumed their discussion about poisons and witches, but I tried to block it out. I still believed it was an "old witches' tale". Sorry for the pun.

Stuart was a sixty-year-old computer expert, who had recently retired and moved to town a year previously. He said he had finally made the commitment to stay in Rio Viejo and was going to buy some real estate. Since he was a pickleballer, he was going to have Nancy represent him. Stuart was a tennis player, from the look of his strokes. He had the fundamentals down and a decent form for tennis, but that meant he liked to bang from the baseline and had almost no dinking ability. Jesus was Mexican, with dual citizenship in Mexico and the US. He mentioned he was an attorney for the avocado growers of Mexico and didn't say much more than that. He was friendly, but tight-lipped about his personal life. His English was pretty good, with an occasional pause to find the right word. He told me that he spent half his time in Mexico, and he was happy to report that pickleball in Mexico was growing almost as fast as it was in the US. He looked young, maybe late thirties or early forties, handsome and athletic. From the way the ladies looked at and talked about him, I have to say, I was envious. His movement on the court led me to guess he was a great soccer player, as well. Even though he said he was new to pickleball, I could tell he was going to be tough once he picked up more dinking skills and strategy. Another six months and he would likely be the best player in town.

The game was close. I was getting better the more I played and the less I thought about Nathan's death and Anna's witch stories. I was moving well and able to anticipate the shots that Stuart and Jesus were going for, as they tended to telegraph their intentions. It was obvious they were keying in on Samantha with hard body shots, which allowed me to read their next shots and poach many of them for easy winners. I edged closer to Samantha to pinch off the court and force them to try difficult, low percentage shots, and for the most part it worked. Even though she played well, they were successful in intimidating her. We barely held on to win thirteen to eleven in a fun, spirited game. At center court, we tapped paddles, and I congratulated them on a well-played game, hiding my frustration that they targeted Samantha so much. Players will often target the weaker player, and I have to admit it can be a great strategy to win games.

We came off the court and took a water break. The Arizona sun was starting to beat down hard on us and we were sweating profusely. Fortunately, the courts had some chairs and tables situated under a few old mesquite trees, offering some great shade. With a slight breeze, it felt good. Players were sitting around either regaling each other with verbal replays of great shots or sharing stories about their various aches and pains that came with old age. I'd been told people over sixty love to talk about the realities of getting old, and now I was seeing firsthand that it was no joke. I heard every type of malady that awaited me. Everyone had a bad elbow or trick knee or fear of carcinoma (a few even showed off surgery scars). Some stories were funny, and some were sad, and, unfortunately, some were just gross. I also heard stories about everyone's past lives and professions. Most of which I would soon forget, as I was still having trouble putting names to faces. The more I know about someone the more likely I am to remember their name, so I tried to ask a lot of questions. I've also learned that if you ask questions about people, they will think highly of you, so it would also help me make a good impression. I loved avocados and Mexico, so I tried to pepper Jesus with questions about both, but he didn't seem all that interested in talking about either. I couldn't tell if he didn't want to talk about them because it bored him, or if it was because his new passion was pickleball and all he wanted to know was what he had to do to get better. Since I had proven myself to be a skilled player, he kept asking me for tips. Once in a while, he would talk in Spanish with Anna or Julio, a Mexican fellow from Sonora that imported furniture to the states, but my Spanish was too rudimentary to understand more than a word here or there.

I was starting to forget all about my conversation with Joe and feel comfortable again. Samantha told me that she and Joe were from Philadelphia, where she had a career as a surgeon, while Joe had been a homicide detective until he took a bullet from a perp he was trying to arrest. He retired a few months after he recovered. They decided it was too cold much of the year in Philadelphia and decided to take up seasonal residence in southern Arizona. They kept a small condo in Philadelphia and would go there when the heat was too oppressive, usually in June or July, and return in the fall. They both had nice pensions and were quite comfortable in their home by the golf resort. They were considering moving to Rio Viejo full time.

Just then Joe rolled up on his expensive looking street bike, a bit sweaty from his ride, and joined us on one of the benches.

"How were the games?" he asked, as he took a large gulp of water from the bottle on his bike.

"Awesome," answered his wife. "I played with Al, and we won." It was clear she had quite a competitive streak in her and she really got a kick out of winning. I think competing against and beating men is a particular source of joy for many women players.

"Samantha played great," I added, wanting to give her as much credit for the win as I could.

That pleased her even more. We chatted about everything but Nathan, which pleased me immensely. I was starting to take a liking to Joe. He was intense, not surprising for a detective, I suppose, but he was likable and interesting. He played golf, rode bikes, fished, and loved tequila. He talked extensively about fly fishing, a subject I knew next to nothing about but found fascinating. The only time I had heard so much about fly fishing was in the movie *A River Runs Through It*. We were hitting it off.

Samantha was quite knowledgeable about the history of pickleball and its recent rise in popularity. She talked about the rapid growth in popularity of pickleball within the geriatric crowd and how the need, or should I say demand, for orthopedic surgeons had exploded. She had a trick knee she blamed on pickleball but wasn't about to quit playing. She wore braces on both knees. Trouble was, all these old people wanted to run around and play like they were still in their thirties. I'd seen people in their eighties, and even a couple in their nineties, who were passionate about the game, but when people that age fall, stuff breaks. These are people who haven't been that athletic for some time, so falls are common and can be catastrophic.

Anna and Stuart got out of their chairs and headed out to the court to take on Julio and Dr. David. Samantha and I decided to continue to rest and cool down, so we watched their game from the sideline. It was looking like a fun and evenly matched game. Suddenly, without warning, Anna went down on the court. I didn't see what caused her to trip; the shot she went for didn't look overly challenging. She just toppled over. Samantha jumped up and ran to the court to try to help, saying that it looked like her knee had given out. Since Samantha had experience with trick knees, I figured she would know. I followed, expecting to help carry Anna off the court and take her to the closest medical facility.

By the time we reached her side, Anna was unresponsive, and Dr. David was screaming for someone to call 911. Samantha tried to take her pulse and shook her head when she couldn't find one. Joe had already called 911 and was keeping other people, back telling them to give her air. Dr. David and Samantha took turns giving CPR, but by the time the fire department arrived with their paramedic it was too late. Anna had died, and to those of us watching in horror, it seemed like déjà vu.

Within moments, the rumors and theories started to fly. Two ladies started arguing; one screamed that it was COVID and that we should all stay clear, and the other was telling her to shut up. The COVID theorist was trying to say that the COVID vaccine could cause spontaneous heart attacks without any previous symptoms, while another lady yelled back at her that COVID was a hoax put out by "Big Pharma" and the Democrats to get us all to take vaccines that had a control chip inserted in them. A few people tried to offer their opinions as to why both theories were baseless, but neither lady was willing to hear an alternate viewpoint. I was about to interject myself into the conversation to tell them both about the latest medical studies, but I was too slow. Dr. David had already jumped in and was explaining the science to them. He tried to be logical and patient with them, but when they both turned on him, calling him names and cussing at him, I thanked him silently for saving me from getting embroiled in their argument. However, judging by the body language of those listening, it was clear that some people were scared and moving farther apart. I could only surmise that they were already convinced it was some kind of communicable disease and distance and masks were the only salvation. I saw a number of people grab hand sanitizers and just about take a bath with them. I didn't believe it was COVID, the flu, or one of the other respiratory illnesses spreading around, but on the other hand, I was concerned. The argument didn't end with any consensus, but at least they stopped yelling. Fortunately, looks can't kill.

Joe acted like the consummate detective and immediately took control of the situation. His call for help wasn't just for the paramedics, he had also called the police. He immediately instructed everyone not to touch anything and made it clear that no one should leave. His tone was adamant, and no one argued with him. He screamed out to those still sitting around the tables and chairs where her belongings were that no one was to touch Anna's things, especially her water. It didn't take me long to realize that Joe suspected foul play and his first concern, given the rumor about witches' poison, was that her water could have been spiked. I hadn't given that much thought to it before, but now I wondered if my water could be suspect too? I had been drinking from my bottle just before Anna went down, so I started to worry. I even felt a little faint. Did the water taste odd? I thought maybe it did, and I wasn't the only one. When Joe instructed everyone to leave Anna's water bottle untouched, a slight panic spread through the crowd.

Stuart was freaking out and screaming, as were a few of the ladies. I saw Julio grab his paddle and pack and slip away, even though Joe had told everyone to stay put until the sheriff arrived. I thought it odd but decided not to speak up. Either no one else noticed him leaving or they decided not to say anything either. Jack stayed incredibly calm and told everyone to do the same. But no one was calm, including me, as I once again rethought the wisdom of my move to this little southern Arizona town.

Pickleball Tip # 9 – Get To The Kitchen, Also Called The No Volley Zone (NVZ)

If you are on the receiving team, try to hit the service return deep, and possibly even slow and high, giving yourself time to join your partner at the NVZ and put yourself in a position to control the point. If you are the serving team, learn the 3rd shot drop, a slow-moving shot that drops in the kitchen in front of the receiving team. A drop shot falling into the kitchen in front of your opponent should be un-attackable and will give you and your partner time to safely come in to the NVZ. Be prepared to hit more than one shot to make it all the way in. Once everyone is at their position at the NVZ, hit dinks, aggressive or defensive, in order to force a mistake. Cross court dinks can clear the net at the lowest point and travel the greatest distance giving you more margin of error. Ideally, your opponent will falter and either hit a shot in the net or a pop-up that you or your partner can put away. If you are the server and the service returner does not follow the shot in, make sure to hit back to them to either keep them back or if they are rushing the net aim at their feet as they approach.

Chapter 10

When the paramedics arrived a few minutes later, Joe was in full control and cleared a path for them to get to Anna. Rick, our resident pickleball-playing paramedic, was with them. He took over administering CPR from Samantha, but Anna couldn't be revived. Her heart had stopped and nothing they did could change that. Dr. David was consoling Samantha, telling her they had done all they could for her, and the paramedics concurred. I heard someone ask if anyone knew the phone number for Anna's husband.

Joe introduced himself to the paramedics as a former homicide detective and said he was very suspicious about Anna's death because another player had died in much the same way a week earlier. He informed them that he had already called the sheriff and they shouldn't move the body until he arrived. They agreed and covered her body.

Sheriff Raul Martinez and his two deputies arrived from Nogales about twenty minutes after Joe had made the call. They came in with their sirens blaring and pulled up as close to the court as they could. I couldn't be sure, but I thought only Julio had left. Everyone else had calmed down a bit. I think everyone was too shocked to do anything but heed Joe's instructions to stay put, as he told us the Sheriff would want to talk to everyone before we left. Joe clearly suspected foul play and at that point, I had to admit, I didn't think he was being paranoid. I still hadn't taken another drink from my water bottle, but I wasn't feeling faint anymore. I felt a little foolish, actually.

As I watched Joe flash his old detective badge in front of the Sheriff, I decided to make a mental note of everyone there, and I even took a few surreptitious snapshots with my phone. I felt a little like a spy, but I didn't want to trust my memory if questions came up later. I was careful not to let anyone see what I was doing. I still didn't know everyone that played there, but I had met, or at least seen, most of the faces around me. Jane was huddling together with her Royal friends and wannabes and the rest of us were gathered off to the other side. Anna had been one of the Royals; was it a coincidence that both dead players were part of that group? I kept the thought to myself. As I checked who was in attendance, one notable person was missing: Nancy. From what I'd seen, and what I'd been told, she was always at the courts that time of day. She and Nathan practically owned the place, and were self-proclaimed, if not official, pickleball ambassadors.

Stuart stood by me as we watched the Sheriff talk to the paramedics and Joe, while the deputies cordoned off the area and made sure that we all stood by waiting for further instructions. There were the expected comments about her health and how shocking all this was. Thankfully, there were no off-color jokes. The mood was quite somber. Players shared stories about how nice Anna was, even though she was a Royal. Jack had opened up the cooler that he always brought to the court and was handing out bottles of water and consoling everyone. The only reason I accepted one was because it was still unopened and therefore could not have been tampered with. Not that I suspected anyone in particular, but my paranoia was still with me. I overheard a few people expressing personal fears about their safety. I wondered if the other Royals made the connection I did and if they were feeling especially vulnerable? A few people made calls to tell someone they would be detained for who knew how long until the Sheriff released us.

"I don't see Nancy here," I said to Stuart.

"That's right. I didn't see her here today. I'm supposed to meet with her later to discuss some property I'm considering buying. As our club leader, she should know about this. I think she and Anna were close friends too."

"You think you should call her?" I said, more as a suggestion than a question.

"Yeah. Good idea." He stepped away from me and dialed up Nancy's cell. I glanced back and forth between him and the Sheriff, not sure what else to do. I was worried about Butch being alone too long, but I had no way to call him and explain what was going on. Samantha was still sobbing as she came over and stood next to me.

"This is just so horrible," she whispered, a tear frozen on her cheek. "I really liked her."

"She seemed very nice to me," I agreed.

"What is going on here?" she asked as she wiped her eyes.

"I don't even know what to think," I replied. I considered leaving it at that, but instead I added, "Especially with her comments about that witch poison thing from Mexico. And her dropping like that, just like Nathan. Could they both be heart attacks?"

"I don't know. Seems rather unlikely, but so does the whole poison thing. Joe has been doing a little research about that, you know? Ever since Anna started talking about it."

"What did he learn?"

"It's not an old wives' tale. There really is a poison they use down there."

Melanie had joined us and heard Samantha. "I knew it. Anna was right and they killed her to shut her up."

"Who?" I asked.

144

"The killers," she said. "Obviously."

"Who do you think they are?" asked Samantha.

"I don't know, but I'm scared," she whispered, looking around at the people milling about.

Stuart returned and stood by us. "I tried Nancy's cell and no answer. I tried a half dozen times. I left a message for her to call me."

I didn't think much of that, since I'm not a great one for answering my phone and sometimes have trouble even finding where I left it. But hearing Stuart's comment made me wish Butch had a phone, so I could call him to tell him I would be late and not to worry. I remembered reading about some gadgets you can get that allow you to watch and even talk to your pets when you aren't home. I made a mental note to order one. Don't judge me. Butch is my best buddy, and he gets worried.

"Maybe she's just busy," I suggested. "I often misplace my phone or don't answer if I'm doing something important."

"No," replied Stuart. "Nancy is glued to her phone. If it isn't pickleball related, its business. She's never far from her phone." He waved to Jane to come over to us. "Jane and Nancy are also tied at the hip because of pickleball. Partners and co-ambassadors. She'll know where she is. In fact, we call the two of them…" He looked around and whispered, "Jancy." He seemed a bit embarrassed saying it. I was going to have a hard time not calling either of them Jancy from then on.

Jane walked over and joined our group.

"I've been trying to call Nancy," Stuart told her. "Have you talked to her?"

Jane shook her head. "I tried calling her too. No answer. We were supposed to play today 'cause she and I are training for a tournament. It's not like her to not show up and not call."

145

"Maybe she isn't feeling well and is sleeping late. We should go to her house when we get released." Stuart nodded toward the Sheriff. "When do you think they'll let us go?"

"My husband is an ex-detective, and he says that when something like this happens, the police want to interview everyone as soon as possible, so they don't forget anything important," said Samantha. "They're not going to release us until they talk to all of us."

Made sense to me. Even in the best of situations, people's recollections of events get cloudy, but with all these old people, I could imagine how difficult it would be if they waited to interview us. These were people who forgot the score between points, how were they going to remember what they saw a few hours ago?

"Crap," replied Stuart. "We could be here awhile."

I considered what that meant. I had nothing I could share, other than repeating rumors I had heard from Melanie and others about what Anna had said. I never spoke directly with her about the witches and poisons; until Samantha said that Joe had researched and confirmed it, I wasn't even sure that I believed it. I barely knew Anna, and try as I might, I couldn't remember seeing anybody doing anything suspicious before she went down. My anxiety over Butch being alone grew. If I was detained for hours, he'd be pissed off. He rarely had accidents in the house; in fact, he'd had none since he was a puppy. But how long could he hold it in?

The other thought that came to mind was about Nancy. I'm not a conspiracy nut case and I don't generally come to outrageous conclusions, but two deaths in a week, both apparent heart attacks by relatively healthy people, albeit older, with someone talking about poisons from Mexico? Not a big stretch of the imagination to think that Nancy's absence and these two unusual deaths were related.

I looked at the benches and tables where everyone kept their bags and water bottles while playing. Most everyone had a bottle with their name on it, but there were also single use bottles everywhere. If it was poison, were any of these also tainted? I looked at my water bottle with understandable suspicion. Cramps be damned, I wasn't about to drink from my bottle again until I had thoroughly cleaned it. Hell, I might just toss it out to be safe. I wondered if the police would test our bottles? I once read in a novel that a clever detective never believes in coincidences. Still, there was no actual evidence so far that anyone was poisoned.

The Sheriff came over to address the group, with Joe beside him.

"Everyone, I am Sheriff Raul Martinez from Nogales and many of you know Joe Rivers here." He nodded at Joe. "He's an ex-homicide detective and he has agreed to help me in this investigation. Because of the similarities between Anna's death and the one last week, there is some concern by Joe and myself that they could be connected. I don't want anyone jumping to conclusions, but we feel we need to take a closer look. We are not accusing anyone of anything, but we want to talk to each of you today, while everything is fresh in your minds. We are going to set up an area over there," he said, pointing to a shaded picnic table set away from the others under a mesquite tree, "and talk to each of you individually to find out what you know and what you might have seen. As we interview each of you, you will be released to go home."

There were a lot of murmurs and grumbling among the group.

"What if we didn't see anything?" asked Stuart.

"Then you won't have much to share, but we will still need your statement before we let you go home. We can start with you, sir. Please step over there and have a seat." Stuart followed the sheriff over to the table and sat down. They were sitting far enough away that we couldn't hear what they were saying. I wished I had been the one to speak up so I could have gone first.

147

While the Sheriff and Joe did their interviews, the deputies finished taking pictures and collecting Anna's things in plastic bags. They loaded the evidence into a squad car, while the paramedics placed Anna's lifeless body onto a stretcher and wheeled her over to the ambulance. Watching all this unfold in front of me was surreal. I had seen Nathan get carted off last week but that was different. At least at the time we didn't think it was foul play. Now I really felt like I was a character in a movie or at the very least a spectator on set, watching a movie being made. If it weren't for the dead body that people suspected had been murdered, I would have thought it was an interesting experience. I preferred seeing this kind of thing on TV, where I could stay detached, eating popcorn and drinking a beer while, of course, criticizing the TV cops for being incompetent and not seeing the obvious, or for uttering nonsensical dialogue.

While we waited our turn to be interviewed or interrogated by the sheriff, we sat together as a group on some benches and chairs in a shady area, but not so close that we could overhear the sheriff talking to our friends. Although I did wonder if Melanie, with her super strong hearing aid, was picking up anything. A deputy sat with us to make sure we didn't leave, and maybe to make sure we didn't start talking about what happened and possibly influence each other. But we were all chatting, so I guess that was allowed. The deputy mostly kept quiet, only answering a basic question or two. The answer always being, "Just sit tight and the sheriff will get to you soon."

I sat there quietly, taking in as much as I could, and even though I had nothing to fear, I was nervous about what I would tell the sheriff when my turn came. I had nothing to share. I was going to tell him that I didn't do it, whatever it was. I was new to town and didn't know anyone well enough to want to kill them. I didn't even know anyone well enough to know if they were capable of killing, unless killing someone because of an argument on the pickleball court counted as a reasonable motive to kill. If it was, then just about everyone that played here, except me, had a motive to kill Nathan. I wasn't sure what motives anyone had for killing Anna.

I thought about what I had observed. Was any of it important enough to tell the Sheriff? I supposed that Julio running off quickly was a bit suspicious. And Nancy not being at the courts she helped build and was normally at every day seemed suspicious too, didn't it? I wondered if I said all that, would I just be drawing attention to myself? I've always had a deep fear of being accused of something I didn't do and going to jail for it. Growing up black in a predominantly white community meant I was always going to be the first suspect. I've even imagined myself in a cell on death row for a crime I didn't commit. We've all read stories about that kind of thing, so it's not so odd to have that fear. I couldn't risk getting taken "downtown" for questioning and leaving Butch all alone. I told myself to be careful what I said. Sometimes innocent people do look guilty.

Dark thoughts just kept running through my brain. I shook my head and tried to stop my mind from going there and instead focus on the people around me. They were all talking about Anna. Did anyone see anything suspicious? Did anyone know why someone would hurt Anna? Was Anna healthy? Could all this be an overreaction by Joe that he somehow transferred to the Sheriff? I could tell the way people were looking at each other that they knew, or at least assumed, that if she was murdered, it was by one of us. I could imagine them turning on each other at any moment. It had to be one of us. How else could Anna have been poisoned? That is if, in fact, she was poisoned.

"Well," I interjected, "if she was poisoned, it is entirely possible that someone spiked her water bottle before she came to the courts."

Everyone stared at me, and I immediately wished I had kept my mouth shut.

Someone blurted out that they thought she was fighting with her husband. That was quickly shot down by someone saying they knew that

149

Anna and her husband were very much in love, and he wasn't capable of murder. But hadn't Melanie said that Anna cheated on her husband with Nathan? I wanted to say, *Are you sure about that?* but I bit my tongue.

"Where's Julio?" someone asked.

"He was here playing with us and now he's gone," Samantha answered.

"That's not right. He was told to stick around like the rest of us."

"No, I think he left before the Sheriff arrived," I said. I had no idea why he left, but I was aware that all too often the immigrant is the first to be accused and I wanted to defend him.

The conversation continued for a while, although our numbers began to dwindle as the Sheriff called each person in turn for their interview. Suddenly, as if she had just woken up, Melanie piped in with her story about the witches in Mexico. I guess not everyone had heard the story before. If true, it didn't shed any light on who did it, but it got everyone thinking about how it might have been done. Melanie struck me as someone who liked to gossip and come to quick conclusions about people. I wondered if it was her car in the parking lot with the bumper sticker about closing the border and building a wall.

I was growing more impatient by the minute, wondering when my turn to meet with the Sheriff would come. My suspicious mind thought it was no accident that I was going to be interviewed last. I needed to learn not to see racism in everything around me, but old habits die hard. I wanted him to pick me sooner so I could get it over with and go home to Butch, but I also didn't want to appear nervous or anxious, so I tried to be patient. Finally, my turn came. I wasn't last, but close to it.

Joe called me over and I sat down next to him, with the Sheriff across from me. They both had notebooks they were writing in. Not like on TV, where the investigators keep everything in their heads. I didn't see any tape recorders.

"For the record, can you state your name, address and contact phone number?" asked the Sheriff. I did as asked. "How well did you know Anna?"

"Not that well, really. We had just met," I explained. "I'm new in town and we only met a few days ago here at the courts."

"What about Nathan? How well did you know him?"

"Even less. I just met him a couple days before he died."

"I see," he answered, as he took some notes.

He asked me where I came from and why I was there and I answered truthfully, giving him the same story that I had given all my new acquaintances over the last week. Again, he jotted notes as I spoke, but he looked up frequently and stared at me intently. Joe watched and listened with a serious look on his face that gave nothing away.

The Sheriff asked if I saw anyone give any drinks or food to Anna. Then he asked the same about Nathan.

"I didn't notice anything," I answered, as I wracked my brain trying to remember anything that might be helpful.

"Do you know if Anna or Nathan had any enemies? Can you think of anyone that would want to harm either of them?"

"No, sir," I lied. "I'm new here." I didn't want to say people thought Nathan was a jerk and hated him, but I didn't think that would be a motive for murder anyway. And I sure didn't want to be the one to mention the names of people that had spoken badly about Nathan. "As far as I could tell, both Nathan and Anna were well-liked." Joe rolled his eyes. He knew I was lying about that but didn't correct me.

"Have you seen or heard about any fights that either of them were involved in?"

"No. Anna was very sweet. I can't imagine anyone fighting with her."

"And Nathan?"

I hesitated. "I think he had a lot of friends here."

"But?"

"He might have been a little arrogant about his pickleball skills, but I can't imagine anyone murdering him over that."

"We've been told a lot of people didn't like Nathan," said the Sheriff. "You didn't notice any of that?"

I looked at Joe. He sat there with no expression that I could read, but I wondered if he had told the Sheriff that his wife was one of the people that hated Nathan.

"Do you know someone named Roger?"

"There was a guy named Roger that came by the courts the day Nathan died. I think he lives in the houses over there." I pointed to some homes a few hundred yards away. Their backyards bordered an open field between the homes and the courts.

The Sheriff nodded. "Was he alone?"

"No. I think the guy with him was named Richard and I think he lives over there too. They were complaining about the noise from the courts, and they were arguing with Nathan and Nancy about that."

"Did they make any threats toward Nathan or Anna?"

"If they did, I didn't hear it," I answered, truthfully.

"Yes. That lines up with what some others have told us."

"I really don't have anything else to add," I said, hoping the interview was over.

"Almost done. Have you heard about the witches from the highlands in Baja Mexico?"

"Only recently," I answered. Clearly someone he already interviewed told him about the witches' brew. Or maybe it was Joe? "I think Anna told some people about that, but I had never heard about it before." I wanted to ask him questions of my own but thought it wouldn't be wise. I also wanted to admit that my first impression of Nathan wasn't flattering, but again I held my tongue. Lots of people had a low opinion of Nathan, but I couldn't imagine being annoyed with a guy would cause you to poison him. But even if someone did hate him enough to kill him, why kill Anna the same way? Maybe it was all a big mistake. Something in the water they both drank? Maybe they only planned on killing Nathan, and Anna was a mistake? My mind was spinning, and I had trouble paying attention to the Sheriff. I wondered if the Sheriff and Joe had all the same thoughts I had.

There was an awkward pause, and I knew I should keep quiet, but I couldn't. "Sir, I don't know anyone who would want to kill either of them, and other than some intense competition on the courts, I don't think either of them had any enemies here. I can't imagine anyone I've met here is capable of murder."

Both Joe and the Sheriff stared at me. There was another long pause, and I wasn't sure if I should say anything to fill the void. This time I resisted the urge.

"Did you know that Nathan had a drunk driving record?" asked Joe.

"No," I answered. "I don't really know much about him."

"It was in Canada. He killed some kids a few years ago. He also had a DUI here in Arizona about a year ago."

I shrugged. I didn't know what to say, so I stayed quiet.

"No one ever mentioned that to you?"

153

"Um, no."

"Have you ever been to Canada?"

"No." That seemed like an odd question.

"Did you know that when Nathan got drunk, he would get angry and belligerent?" asked Joe. Obviously, he knew Nathan's history better than I did.

"No. I've never seen him drunk. Look guys, I'm new here and I've never even had a drink with him." I wondered if I had just lied? Did a beer at Taco Tim's with a group after pickleball count as drinking with Nathan? And what did that have to do with Anna's death?

"Did you know that Nancy and Nathan were an item?" asked the Sheriff.

"Sure. Everybody knows that."

"Did you know they fought from time to time?" he asked.

"I'd heard that, but it seemed like gossip. From what I saw, the two looked very happy together."

"Did you know anything about Nathan and Anna having an affair?" asked the Sheriff.

"Again, I thought it was just gossip."

"Did Anna and Nancy get along?"

"I really don't know more than what I've seen here at the courts. They seemed friendly here."

"Do you know why Nancy isn't here today?"

"No."

"OK. I think we have enough from you at this time. As this is an ongoing investigation, I want to ask you not to leave town until we have finished it." The Sheriff handed me his card. "If you think of anything else that might be helpful, please call me."

I got up and stood for a second. I wasn't sure what the proper protocol was. Do I offer to shake his hand? I didn't. I grabbed my things and rushed home without a word to Tom, who was the last person there. I was already on my bike riding out when he sat down for his interview.

When I got home, Butch was sitting by the door, giving me a very disapproving stink eye as I entered. I'm sure if he didn't need to go out, he probably would have been in my room sulking.

"Sorry I'm late, buddy." I grabbed his leash and hooked him up. "Let's go for a walk." And we were out the door a minute later.

The best way to get Butch to forgive you for an indiscretion that had pissed him off was to shower him with treats or distract him with a walk. I chose the walk. Seconds after leaving the house, it was clear he had forgotten his anger at me for delaying his walk, as he was busy peeing on any cactus in his reach and identifying any and all things worth sniffing.

We went up and down each street and I gave him ample time to sniff and pee as he desired. I was determined to wear him out. About a mile from our place, we spotted Joe and Samantha sitting on a bench in front of a house I assumed was theirs. They were in deep conversation, but when they noticed us, they waved us over.

"Hi guys," I said, as Butch and I approached them. "Is this your house?"

"Yep," said Samantha.

Obviously, Joe had completed his pickleball interviews and returned home.

"Come up and have a drink with us. Do you like margaritas?" said Samantha.

It was already getting hot and as the saying goes, it's five o'clock somewhere, so I didn't consider the offer for very long. "Sure. If it has tequila in it, I'll drink it."

Samantha scooted inside to make me a drink while Butch and I settled in across from Joe. There was a dog dish by their bench and Joe filled it with water from the hose.

"We're dog lovers," he said. "Our two mutts are in the back playing. Does Butch like other dogs?"

"Butch is friendly with everyone as long as he gets most of the attention," I informed him.

"Great. We'll have to let them meet up and play. You are quite a way from your house," he observed.

"You know where we live?" I asked, surprised and a bit confused.

"Al, I think I told you, I'm an ex-detective and some things die hard."

I did remember him saying he like to check up on everyone Samantha played with, but I still felt creeped out and a bit paranoid that he knew where we lived. My lack of a good poker face must have revealed my thoughts.

"I can see you're surprised, maybe even worried about that. But don't be. I just think you can't be too careful these days, and with a little effort you can learn all sorts of things about people. And let's face it, with my career and connections it's easier than you can imagine to do so." He let that sink in for a few seconds. "By the way, I found out enough about you to know that you are an OK guy."

I wanted to ask if he also knew what kind of underwear I wore, but thought it was too soon for my demented humor. It was also no surprise to me that he learned I have a clean record. I've never even had a speeding ticket.

"Thanks, Butch seems to think I'm a good guy."

He gave a half smile and nodded. Samantha rejoined us and brought me a large margarita on the rocks. I tasted it and was immediately impressed.

"That's very good," I said. "A lot of people make their margaritas too sweet, and you can't tell there's any tequila in it."

"Thank you," she said, beaming. "We love tequila too and often just sip it straight, but on a hot day like this, a margarita really hits the spot."

I fell in love right then. Not really, but it moved them up the ladder on my admiration scale. We made a little small talk, briefly chatting about the town and the neighborhood, but we all knew we would eventually discuss the intrigue taking place on the pickleball courts. I decided I would break the ice.

"What do you think happened to Anna and Nathan?" I asked.

Joe stared at me briefly and scratched his chin.

"Well, for one thing, I don't think you had anything to do with their deaths."

"No, I didn't," I said, but I was relieved to hear him say it. It felt good to hear that I wasn't a suspect, at least as far as Joe was concerned. I suppose he could have been lying to me, but it didn't feel like it.

He went on. "One reason I don't think you had anything to do with it is lack of motive. You just got here a day or two before Nathan died. Based on your history, I don't see any connections between you and Nathan or Anna. Although unconfirmed at this point, I think Anna's story about poison has a ring of truth to it. I did some research and there are poisons in Mexico that can mimic a heart attack and unless tested for specifically, wouldn't show up on a typical autopsy."

"Are they testing Anna for that?" I asked.

"They are going to. They didn't test Nathan, but they may exhume his body and test him for it, as well."

"Is it possible that they both just had heart attacks?"

He looked at me. "I don't believe in coincidences like that. I'm sure you have already learned that Nathan had lots of enemies here."

"Well, I had heard he wasn't all that popular, but I haven't heard anyone talk like he was an enemy. I mean, he was annoying, but lots of people are annoying and they don't get murdered. And besides, everyone seemed to like Anna."

"She was popular," agreed Samantha. "Did you know that Anna and Nathan had a brief little affair?"

"I wasn't sure if that was just a rumor."

"It was short lived, and then Nathan got back together with Nancy and Anna got back together with her husband."

"Did her husband know?" I asked, wanting to learn more about what Joe and Samantha already knew.

"Everyone knew," said Samantha with a giggle. "Small town."

It was not the first time someone told me that small towns don't keep secrets very secret. I wondered just how possible it was that Anna's husband might be the killer, looking to get revenge on both her and Nathan? Joe was a detective, so he had to have already considered that, but I asked anyway.

"Do you think Anna's husband had anything to do with it?"

"We were just discussing that when you came by. What if Anna's husband poisoned Nathan and then wanted to punish Anna for the affair, but killed her by mistake? We understand a small dose causes paralysis, but

158

too much can be fatal. Or maybe, Anna killed Nathan by accident," surmised Samantha, while Joe just watched my reaction.

"If she had an affair with Nathan, why hurt him?" I asked.

"She was mad that Nathan told some people about the affair. So, she might have decided to punish him."

I didn't buy that theory. If she did that to Nathan, then who poisoned her? I didn't think she would accidentally poison herself too. I supposed it was possible she killed Nathan, either on purpose or accident, and her husband figured out what happened and killed her.

"Was Anna's husband even at the courts during either of the deaths?"

"Not that we know of," answered Joe, "but the Sheriff is heading over to their house to inform him of her death and, of course, interview him."

"I just can't see Anna doing this and then telling people at the court about this strange witches' brew. I would think that she would act clueless," I said, shaking my head and taking another sip of the margarita.

"Murderers can be tricky," said Joe. "But it's also possible she told her husband about the poison, and he did it without her knowing."

That theory made the most sense to me. Jealous husband gets revenge on his wife and her lover. My mind was reeling, as it usually does in times of stress, fear, and anxiety. Here I was, sitting on the porch of a retired homicide detective, theorizing about murder motives. I had no business being there, as I didn't have a clue what I was talking about, except for things I had seen in the movies or in the murder mysteries I'd read. But I couldn't stop myself from throwing out another possible explanation.

"What if there is no connection between the two. What if the murderer wanted to kill either Nathan or Anna and used the murder of the other to create a red herring? In other words, one of the murders is a red herring, a fake, to set the investigation off in the wrong direction." I was starting to get into this whole amateur detective thing. Maybe I was just getting a little buzz off the margarita. It was on the strong side.

Joe smiled. "Not bad for an amateur."

I think I blushed.

Joe went on, "At this point we want to consider all possibilities. There may be some other connections between Anna and Nathan that we don't know about. The toxicology report will be in soon enough. It's still possible that Nathan had a heart attack. It's also possible that Anna had one too and there is no crime here."

I tried to read Joe's expression when he said that, and my take was that he didn't really believe this was all just an odd coincidence. But if it was, I wouldn't have to worry about the water in my water bottle being tainted anymore. I wouldn't have to be paranoid that I was in close proximity to a murderer. However, I had a hard time believing this was a case of two random heart attacks in the span of a week, in two people who had recently had an affair. The witches' brew story might have seemed fantastical, but in this case, it sure would tie it all together.

"I don't believe you think they died of heart attacks, though," I said. "When Anna went down, your first thought wasn't heart attack, or you wouldn't have shut the area down and called the police. You think there is a connection."

He nodded and cracked a half smile. "As I said before, I don't like coincidences. The odds that two seemingly healthy people would die the same way, a week apart, at the same location, doesn't seem plausible to me. The fact that they were also involved in an affair throws up a red flag, too. In my career, I have seen too many affairs end up as murder cases. Furthermore, Nathan has a checkered past."

160

I, like most people, never turn away from gossip and didn't want Joe to stop there. "Yeah, the Sheriff mentioned that. He killed some kids?" I encouraged him to continue.

"Nathan used to live in Canada and turns out he had quite a drinking problem. Two DUIs, with one resulting in the death of two kids and permanent disability of a third. That only got him a year in jail, somehow. Based on the police reports, he also had a history of domestic abuse and bar fights. First marriage ended in a nasty divorce, with his wife accusing him of abuse. Hard to tell from our interviews if he really had any serious enemies here, but he did have a DUI last year that resulted in him losing his license and spending thirty days in jail."

"Wow. Not exactly an example of an outstanding citizen," I said. "No injuries to anyone from his DUI here?"

"Not unless you count destroying a stop sign as an injury. He was trying to elude the police when he hit a stop sign, before sliding into a ditch. I'm still looking to see if he had any other legal battles here or in Canada that might have involved a disgruntled business partner, but so far nothing. He's had some odd jobs like car sales and phone sales but nothing that would get him in any real trouble."

I thought about some of the stories I'd read where the mob killed someone who stiffed them. "What about gambling debts? Maybe he got in some trouble that way."

"If he did, we don't know about it, and I'm sure the local bookies aren't going to volunteer anything."

"How does Anna fit in?" I asked.

"She has a clean past, from what I can tell. She's here legally. She was born in Mexico and got US citizenship at a young age. No record of any legal problems. I don't have access to records in Mexico, but maybe the husband will be able to shed some light on that for the Sheriff."

161

"Curious if she's been to the mountains in Baja?" I asked, although I didn't know that the plant was exclusive to that area. It might have grown in Sonora too. Maybe Nancy thought they were having another affair and decided to poison the two of them. It didn't seem that far-fetched to me. Jealousy can mess you up. I drank my margarita and kept that theory to myself. Maybe she avoided the courts that day to set up an alibi when Anna died. Of course, then there would be the question of how and when she could have spiked Anna's drink. And how did she get the poison? Could she and Anna have been in cahoots in killing Nathan, but then Nancy decided to kill Anna to eliminate any loose ends? I started thinking that maybe I could have a new career as a detective, or maybe just a mystery writer.

Samantha was about to get us refills on the margaritas, when we saw Stuart roll up in front of the house in a stylish golf cart that looked like a mini-Cadillac. He set the parking brake and jumped out of the cart, then jogged up to the porch. He looked troubled.

"I just stopped by Nancy's house and no one was home, even though her car is there," he exclaimed, while trying to catch his breath.

"Did you try calling her?" asked Samantha. "Maybe she's out on a bike ride."

He rolled his eyes. "Like ten times, and I left five messages. I could actually hear her phone ringing in the house. I thought about going inside but was afraid I might frighten her. With all the stuff going on, there was no way I wanted to barge in uninvited."

"Smart move," said Joe.

"We were supposed to have a meeting today to talk about some real estate I want to buy. It's not like her to just not show up for a commitment."

"Given what has been going on lately, I think we should call the Sheriff and have him go into the house and see if anything is wrong," said Joe.

We all nodded in quiet agreement, as Joe called the Sheriff.

Pickleball Tip # 10– How To Deal With Bangers

Many players, especially ex-tennis players, like to hit the ball hard at any and every occasion. We jokingly call them bangers. It can be tough to handle balls hit hard at your gut when you are at the non-volley zone line. Bangers are counting on intimidating you into a mistake. First thing is to learn to identify when an opponent is about to hit a hard drive at you. Look at their back swing - are they taking a huge back swing in preparation of hitting the ball? Learn their tendencies - Do they often hit hard in certain situations? Or all the time?

When you think you are about to be targeted by a banger, get set, stop moving, loosen your grip a little on the paddle, and prepare to just block the ball back. If they are about to hit the shot from mid court to the no volley zone, look at the position of the ball. If it is lower than the net cord at impact, assume the ball will have an upward trajectory. In that case, the ball will likely sail out. Learn to dodge those balls and win the point on their mistake. A good motto to employ is, "If its head or shoulder high, let it fly". If it's coming at your mid-section, set yourself in a good stance with your paddle out front and just block it back. Don't swing. If they are driving from the baseline, don't get too intimidated. By the time the ball reaches you at the NVZ, it won't be traveling that fast. Either block it back to keep them at the baseline or hit a soft dink into the kitchen, forcing them to charge the net to save the point. Typically, they will pop the next one up for an easy put-away.

Chapter 11

By the time the Sheriff received the call from Joe, he was nearly back to Nogales, but he told Joe he would meet him at Nancy's house. Stuart gave Joe the address and he relayed that to the Sheriff. Part of me thought this was an over-reaction. We had no proof anything was wrong, but I guess given the circumstances, it made sense to be overly cautious.

Nancy lived on a quiet street between Joe's house and the pickleball courts. It was a high-end neighborhood with huge lots, long driveways, and mature trees. If anything had happened at her house, it was possible that no neighbor was close enough to hear anything.

Butch and I decided to tag along and hitched a ride on Stuart's golf cart. Butch sat perched between me and Stuart, his head turned into the wind and a huge grin on his face. As far as he was concerned, there was no emergency, just a wonderful new experience.

We got there after Joe and Samantha had already arrived. They were circling the house and, I assume, looking for anything suspicious. The Sheriff was still en route. Nancy's car was in her driveway. I've mentioned that I've seen hundreds of detective movies, and the detective always touches the hood of the car to see if it's hot, indicating it had recently been driven. So, I ran my hand on the hood. Cold. We tried the doorbell a few times and knocked on the door. No answer. Stuart called her cell phone a few more times and still got no answer.

"We looked in the windows and couldn't see anything or anyone," said Joe. "Don't touch anything," he instructed us. "Let's just wait for the Sheriff to get here."

I walked Butch over to an old mesquite tree with a swing hanging down. He sniffed around and did his business. An older gentleman, probably in his 70's, came out of a house across the street and approached me.

"Nice dog," he said. "Are you waiting for Nancy?"

"I am. She didn't show up for pickleball today. Have you seen her?" I asked.

"Hmm. Not today. I saw her yesterday though. Is something wrong?"

"I don't know."

"Those your friends?" he said, pointing at Joe, Samantha, and Stuart.

"Yes."

"Hmm," he said again. "She gets a lot of visitors because she sells real estate, and this is her office."

"Yep. I heard that."

"You looking to buy around here?"

"No. Just concerned about her well-being."

"OK." And he just walked away without another word.

The Sheriff arrived a few minutes later with his lights flashing. Joe met him at his car as he was getting out. They spoke for a few minutes with a lot of pointing and gesturing. A second squad car pulled up and two deputies piled out and stood with the Sheriff and Joe. Then they approached us on the porch.

"Folks, we'll take it from here," said Sheriff Martinez. "I'd like everyone to step off the porch and wait in the driveway." We followed his instructions and waited by the cars while a few other neighbors came out of their homes to see what was going on. We explained the situation and asked them if they had seen anyone come or go. They had not. If it hadn't been for the flashing lights on the police cruisers, they wouldn't have known anything was amiss.

The Sheriff mimicked our earlier attempts to knock on the door and circle the premises. He found the same thing we did: nothing. The Sheriff asked Stuart for Nancy's phone number and tried that as well. Still no answer. He got her voice mail and left a message. Satisfied that something wasn't right, the Sheriff went back to his squad car and opened the trunk. He pulled out a lock pin gun and inserted it into the front door keyhole. He pulled the trigger a couple of times and the door opened. I had wondered if those things were real or just an imaginary gadget mystery writers used. The Sheriff pushed the door open, calling out her name a few times. He and the deputies entered cautiously, hands on the guns in their holsters. We watched silently as they entered. A few minutes later, the Sheriff appeared at the door, shaking his head and motioning to Joe to join him. They spoke quickly, then the Sheriff went back to his squad car and used the radio, while Joe rejoined those waiting by the cars.

"Nancy's inside on the floor," said Joe. He paused, then added, "She's dead."

"Oh my god," cried Samantha. "What happened?"

Butch moaned as if he knew what was going on. He could read emotions.

"The Sheriff isn't sure yet, but he thinks she was strangled. He said there were marks on her neck, but that's all he knows right now. They're going to seal off the area and get the crime scene people in."

Within a few minutes, we could hear the paramedics siren in the distance. I had seen and heard enough and wanted to leave, but Joe stopped me. "No one should leave until the sheriff comes back out."

"But I don't know anything. I've been at the courts with you guys all morning."

"He thinks she has been dead for a while. Maybe since last night or early this morning."

I didn't ask how he knew that, but the image of a stiff body came into my head and it creeped me out. At this point, I wanted to take Butch, pack our things, and hit the road for some other place to live. This move was proving to be a disaster. I wanted to ask Stephanie for advice, as she always knew what was best in strange and uncomfortable situations, but I refrained. I figured Stuart, Joe, and Samantha would think I'd lost my mind if they heard me, and everyone knows dead people can't hear you unless you speak out loud.

The deputies were already placing crime scene tape around all the doors to cordon off the area when the ambulance arrived. The group of neighbors had grown and were gathered across the street. The paramedics jumped out of the ambulance and wheeled a gurney to the front porch, where they were led into the house by one of the deputies. One of the deputies came over to Joe, handed him gloves and paper booties, and told him to join the Sheriff in the house. We all watched this unfold, while the neighbors mumbled about what they had or had not seen. The consensus was that nobody had seen or heard anything suspicious.

Nogales didn't have their own crime scene investigators, so about a half hour later a team from Tucson arrived. Three men and a lady emerged from a van, quickly and quietly donned white jump suits and gloves, then entered the home. A couple minutes later, Joe came out the front door and joined our group of onlookers. He informed us that they would be looking for fingerprints and gathering DNA from the scene. If he knew anything else, he didn't share it with us. I could see camera flashes coming from the living room area, where I presumed Nancy was found. After about an hour, we were all sweltering in the afternoon heat. One of the neighbors brought over some cold, unopened bottles of water to share with us and a bowl to fill with water for Butch. Another neighbor brought over some folding chairs and set them up under a large cottonwood tree. If it hadn't been a tragedy, it would have felt like any other neighborhood gathering. Kids were playing with Butch, and adults were gossiping and sharing theories about what might have happened. None of the neighbors were pickleballers and they were unaware that just a couple hours earlier, Anna had dropped dead on the courts. A couple people did note that it was odd that Nancy died so soon after Nathan.

While the crime scene technicians were still busy inside, the Sheriff exited the house with his deputies. He signaled Joe to join him on the porch and after a brief chat, Joe came back over to us.

"Al, the sheriff would like to meet with you first, if you don't mind." said Joe. "Samantha, can you watch Butch while Al and the Sheriff talk?"

She nodded and I handed her his leash. Butch watched me get up and follow Joe and fortunately didn't object, although he didn't look pleased. He may not have understood everything going on, but he could read emotions pretty well, and he knew something was wrong. He sighed and laid down in the shade but never took his eyes off me as I joined the Sheriff and Joe on the porch.

"Al, I need to ask you some more questions."

"OK," I answered, "but I don't know any more than I told you earlier."

"Let me decide that please," he replied curtly. I nodded.

"How well do you know, I mean, how well did you know Nancy?"

"Not well at all, sir."

"Where were you last night and early this morning?"

Oh, shit, I thought. He fucking suspects me after all. Why not? I'm the new guy in town and the murders started just after I got here.

169

"I was home with Butch."

"Just you two? No one else?"

"No. I live alone. I went to bed after watching some TV, and then took him for a walk this morning before going to play pickleball."

"Pickleball," he said, disdainfully. "I think I'm getting tired of pickleball players. Tell me again how you knew Nathan."

"I didn't really. We just met a few days before he died. The same time I met Nancy. On the pickleball courts."

"And Anna?"

"Same thing. I met her on the courts." Did he really think I would have a different answer to the same questions he had asked a couple hours ago?

"You live near here?"

I thought it was a dumb question. It's a fucking small town. Everyone lives nearby. But I held my sarcasm in check and answered. "Maybe a mile away. I rent a home on Third Street." I could see where he was going, but I had no clue what to say or do to convince him I had nothing to do with all this. Yes, I did live close enough to walk here.

"Would you be willing to submit to a DNA test and fingerprints?"

"Do I need a lawyer?" I asked, nervously.

He frowned a little and shrugged. "Do you have some reason to believe you do? Have you ever been in Nancy's house?"

He didn't really answer my question, but I answered his second one anyway.

"I've never been in this house before and I didn't even know Nancy lived here."

170

He nodded with a little smile. "Then you shouldn't be worried about getting fingerprinted or giving us a DNA sample."

I didn't know if that was true or not. I had always believed if you were innocent, you had nothing to fear. But I was black man, and I knew better. They had no reason to suspect me. I was new in town and didn't know anyone 'til a week ago. Did he think I was some kind of hit man, hired to kill the three most prominent pickleball players in town? That made no sense. But I had watched enough police dramas to know that when you were getting questioned by the police you should always get a lawyer. What if they took my fingerprints and framed me? I was getting nervous. I looked at Joe, who was sitting nearby watching the proceedings.

"Joe, I think you know I had nothing to do with all this." But did he? He just met me, and even if he said he looked into my past, what did he really know?

Joe finally came to my defense. "Sheriff, I think you are making Al pretty uncomfortable here."

"I'm going to be doing the same to all the pickleball players. One or more of them is involved and I intend to find out who they are. No one is getting singled out here."

I was no expert, but I thought his conclusion made no sense. Unlike the others, Nancy wasn't killed on the pickleball court. Her death may or may not be related to the others.

"Just the same, I think I should get some legal advice," I interjected.

"So, are you saying you won't voluntarily submit DNA or fingerprints?"

Oh fuck. This was sounding terrible.

"For now," I said.

"Do you have a lawyer?"

"No. I just moved here and didn't think I needed one on retainer or anything."

"OK, let's say we put that on hold for now. Let me ask you some other questions."

"Okay," I said, reluctantly.

"Is there anyone that you can think of that would want to harm Nancy, Nathan, or Anna?"

"Look, as I've said before, I don't know anyone here that well. But honestly, I don't think most of the players liked Nathan or Nancy very much. They called them 'The Royals' and it wasn't a compliment."

"Why is that?"

"They were rude and inconsiderate to the other players, so a lot of the other players resented them."

"Give me a list of who you think hates them," said the sheriff, as he prepared to write the names.

"Just about everyone talked behind their backs."

"Including you?"

"Sure, I thought they, um... well, they were annoying," I admitted, "but I've seen that behavior on other courts I've played on. It's kind of the nature of pickleball and competition. But I don't think their behavior was egregious enough to justify murder."

The Sheriff raised his eyebrows. "What would justify murder?

"Nothing. I didn't mean anyone deserves to be murdered under any circumstances."

"You'd be surprised to know all the reasons why people commit murder," interjected Joe. As a homicide detective in a big town, I imagined he'd seen just about every motive during his career.

The Sheriff handed me a pad of paper and a pen and said, "Could you just give me a list of names that you know didn't like Nathan, Nancy, or Anna?" After I took the pad and pen, I realized I probably just gave him DNA and fingerprints. Was he really that diabolical? I realized it too late and decided not to make a scene. Instead, I started to write down everyone I had met. Since I literally wrote down the names of everyone, I didn't feel like I was singling out anyone in particular. I even included Joe and Samantha on the list. It was a test of my memory, and I wrote down every name I could remember. It took me a few minutes, and I felt the watchful eye of the Sheriff as I wrote.

When I finally finished, I handed the list to the Sheriff. He did not look amused.

"That's a long list. Are you saying everybody hated them?"

"I don't know if everybody hated them. These are all the people that discussed them with me and openly criticized them at one time or another."

"I don't see your dog's name on the list," he said, sarcastically.

"Butch loves everyone," I replied with a straight face.

"This is serious Al," he chastised me. "This list is not much help."

"Sheriff," said Joe, "my wife plays out there too, as you know, and she says that most every player has had a run-in at one time or another with Nathan and Nancy. They could be very annoying and selective about who they played with. But the thing is, Anna wasn't like them. She was really nice and well-liked."

I was grateful to Joe for stepping in and helping me. He was right. No one ever said anything disparaging about Anna. She wasn't the greatest player out there, but she was decent and friendly. But she was a Royal, or at least a wannabe. The other Royals accepted her, from what I had seen. Was I the only one that had made the connection that all three of the victims had been Royals? I kept my mouth shut. The Sheriff would have to figure that out himself. It did concern me that Anna and Nathan died by poisoning, and Nancy didn't.

Finally, the sheriff had had enough of me.

"I'll let you go, for now. We'll be in touch about the DNA and finger printing. I suggest you talk with an attorney in the meantime."

I rushed down the steps, angry and frustrated. I grabbed Butch and hurried home without saying more than a "thank you" to Samantha for watching him. We could have waited for Stuart to have his interview and get a ride from him, but I wanted out of there as quickly as possible, and I didn't mind a long walk home.

"Dude," I said to Butch, "we might want to consider moving. This town is fucked up." He lifted his leg and watered a barrel cactus. I took that to mean, *Whatever you say.*

Pickleball Tip # 11 - Returning Lobs

Many of the injuries experienced on the pickleball court are from improper form or movement to a ball – especially the lob. One of the most common mistakes is going back for a lob or overhead using the wrong form. Unfortunately, many beginners and intermediates back pedal, finding themselves tripping over their own feet and landing on their wrist, or in some cases, banging their head on the court.

Proper technique is to turn and run back or sidestep, until you are under or behind the ball and can get into position to hit a proper overhead slam. If you are right-handed, point at the ball with your left hand, while bringing your paddle behind your back, so you can hit down and through the ball.

If you can't take the ball as an overhead slam, retreat so you can come in with the ball alongside you. Try to hit a baseline drop that lands softly in the kitchen, giving you time to re-approach the NVZ or throw up a lob of your own, and prepare for the next shot.

Chapter 12

Butch and I awoke the following morning, still shook up over the prior day's turn of events. I had had four, five, or maybe six shots of Don Julio, before falling asleep watching a murder mystery on PBS. I was feeling it now. It was bad enough that three people in this little town had seemingly been murdered, but now the Sheriff actually thought I was a credible suspect. Maybe he didn't really suspect me, but with each shot of tequila I convinced myself that he did.

What could make him think it was me?

More importantly, for me at this point, was what could I do about it? I had never been to Nancy's house. I hadn't touched any water bottles but my own and I had no grudge against any one. Giving DNA and fingerprints might seem logical, but somewhere in my head I had visions of someone manipulating evidence to frame me. Why would the sheriff do that though? Solving a murder quickly always sounds like good motivation for the authorities, but that would also mean he had the wrong guy. But that shit still happens, right? Or was I being paranoid? My quick answer was yes, I was being paranoid, but with good reason.

I asked Stephanie what she thought I should do. Do I need an attorney? She had always had great instincts and I always welcomed her advice. I waited for an answer. I asked again, this time out loud. Butch stared at me. No lightning bolts. Her voice didn't pop into my head. No images in the mirror. Either I was asking wrong, or this shit didn't work in real life. I was on my own. Butch was no help.

I decided to call Tom and Leslie and Martin and Celeste to see if they could drop by. I figured they might have some advice, or at the very least, the name of a local attorney. They all agreed to stop by after lunch. In the meantime, I considered my options and the one that kept popping up was pack my bags and leave. The Sheriff might not like it and it might make me look even more suspicious, but no law said I had to stick around and become the scapegoat.

Something that had not occurred to me until then was the possibility that Tom or Martin could be the killer just as much as anyone else. Neither of them liked Nathan or Nancy, and Martin had expressed his dislike for pickleball. For all I knew, I had just invited the killer into my home to ask advice on what to do next.

My head was still pounding from the tequila, and my paranoia wasn't helping matters. I took two Advil and considered washing them down with more tequila, but Butch gave me a look that said, D*on't do it*. He went to the front door and grabbed his leash, then dropped it at my feet.

"I get it buddy. Let's go for a walk." He wagged his tail in agreement, clearly proud of himself for communicating his desires effectively. I leashed him up and locked all the doors and windows before we left. We had plenty of time before the gang was coming over, so I decided to make it a long walk, but I made sure to take a less popular route so we were less likely to run into anyone.

I reconstructed the reasons for my anxiety. Did I actually have anything to worry about? The Sheriff was just trying to do his job. If he was any good, he wouldn't jump to conclusions, and there was no evidence that could possibly implicate me. I was letting my overactive imagination run amok. Granted, I had no iron clad alibi for any of the murders, but then I suspected a lot of other people didn't either. I also had no motive to kill anyone. But others did.

By the time we returned from our walk, I was exhausted. Not from the walk itself, but from trying to think through all the possible motives and suspects. Butch, on the other hand, didn't have a care in the world, except to show me that his food dish was empty, and I was being remiss in not filling it up. Clearly his need for food outweighed his duty as an emotional support companion. He scarfed down a full bowl of dog food and stared at me until I gave him a Dentabone. Oral hygiene is very important to Butch. While he cleaned his teeth, the doorbell rang, and in a move that is so un-Butch-like, he dropped the bone and ran to the door, barking. As soon as he saw who it was, he calmed down. They say you should trust the instincts of dogs. Based on that, I figured none of my visitors were killers.

"Thanks for coming over," I said, as I ushered them in and directed them onto the living room couch and love seat. I dragged a chair in from the kitchen for myself. Butch went from one person to the other to greet them and receive his obligatory hugs and kisses. When he was satisfied, he went back to his Dentabone and laid down while he finished cleaning his teeth.

I barely let them get settled before I informed them of my situation.

"I think I need an attorney."

"Um, you know that none of us are, or ever were, attorneys," said Martin.

"I know. I was hoping you could suggest someone."

"What's going on? What kind of attorney do you need?" asked Tom.

I explained my encounter with the Sheriff. They had heard through the Rio Viejo pickleball grapevine (which was even faster than Facebook) about Nancy's murder but had no idea I had been put through the wringer. Evidently, Joe or the Sheriff hadn't interrogated them yet.

"I've always had a fear of being accused of something I didn't do," I explained.

178

"Have you ever been accused of something you didn't do?" asked Celeste.

I nodded. "Yes. Maybe it's just that I'm black, but I've had my share of unfounded accusations growing up. I wasn't exactly the perfect kid, but it was all minor stuff that most kids get involved in. But when something bad happened, I got questioned."

I could see the concern in their faces.

"No. I never got arrested and I never did anything worse than minor shoplifting or smoking pot. But because of being accused a few times, I've always had this fear of getting blamed for something I didn't do. So, with the intensity of the Sheriff's questions, I'm feeling nervous. You guys have probably never heard of Bob Jackson, have you?"

They all shook their heads.

"Well, when I was living in Denver a few years ago, this guy, Bob Jackson, had a popular radio show where he helped people fight shady contractors. They called him the Consumer Champion. Then the contractors started dying, and the entire city turned on Bob. It was brutal. They accused him of murder. Later, it was discovered that he wasn't the killer, but by then his reputation was ruined. I've seen how rumors and bad police work can destroy someone, so I'm a bit paranoid."

"What happened to him?" asked Martin.

"Don't know for sure, but he never came back on the air."

"But the Sheriff didn't actually accuse you of anything, did he?" asked Leslie.

"No, but it sure feels awkward when I'm getting questioned by him. Now he wants my DNA and fingerprints. Has he asked any of you for that?"

They all said no.

179

"So, you see my point?"

"Well, I would hope that the Sheriff is honest and wouldn't do something like that," said Celeste.

"Me too, but I just panicked. At this point, I think I should talk to an attorney to make sure I don't get railroaded."

"We have a couple people we know from pickleball who are ex-attorneys, but I don't know any criminal defense lawyers who are still practicing," said Tom. "Rory was an attorney at one time, but I don't know what kind."

"I don't know if I would go to Rory," said Celeste. "He has anger issues. I've seen him explode on the court over little things."

"But you just need advice right now, don't you?" asked Martin.

"Can they force you to give DNA without charging you?" asked Leslie.

"I don't really know. I've never been in trouble before and all I know about the law is what I see on TV." I was starting to wonder if I could get any legitimate advice from my friends. "I didn't do anything, and I've never been in Nancy's home, so there is no reasonable way my DNA could be there. I just don't know what to do."

"That sucks," said Tom. "All this sucks. What the fuck is going on here? Who would kill all these people and why?"

"I sure don't know. I just got here. I'm the new guy. I was hoping you guys might have some theories." They all looked clueless, so I decided to tell them about the connection that I noticed about all the victims. "They were all Royals."

"What?" asked Martin.

I couldn't believe no one had seen the pattern. "Am I the only one that sees the connection? They were all Royals."

180

Tom made a funny face and said, "I don't think Anna was really a Royal."

"Oh, I see your point though," said Celeste. "She's been hanging out with them more and more and they let her play with them, even though they snubbed most of us."

"She was never as rude as the rest of them," said Tom, defending her.

"Maybe not, but she really wanted in," replied Celeste.

"Well, I didn't know any of them that well, but from what I've seen, I would have thought she was one of them," I said.

"I could see how you might think that," agreed Tom.

"Do you think someone is going after the Royals?" asked Martin.

"It's crossed my mind," I admitted, "A lot."

"Have you said that to the Sheriff?" asked Celeste.

"I thought about mentioning it to the Sheriff, but I decided that it was best to keep my mouth shut. You guys are the first people I've voiced my opinion to. Maybe that was a mistake."

"Maybe you should bring it up with Joe," suggested Leslie who had been staying mostly quiet.

I had thought about telling Joe, but I wasn't sure how sincere Joe was about not suspecting me. In all the detective stories I've read, the detective pretends to not suspect the culprit, in order to trick him into letting down his guard and making a mistake. Okay, so this wasn't a story, but still. Since I'd never been involved in a real-life murder mystery, I had to rely on my fictional expertise.

"It's nuts," said Leslie. "I can't believe anyone would kill over a game."

"You need to spend more time around the courts then," said Tom. "It can get pretty nasty out there at times."

"Still. Murder? You people need help," she proclaimed sarcastically.

"I can't disagree," stated Martin. "Although, I've seen people toss a perfectly good set of golf clubs in the lake after a bad shot."

"I don't know who's behind all this, or why, but I'm not sure I want to go near the courts right now, and I'm sure as hell locking my doors and windows tonight," Leslie said with a shudder. "At least you have Butch here to protect you."

"What about me?" asked Tom. "You don't think I can protect you?"

Leslie looked at him and shrugged. "I can barely get you to kill a spider, and a few weeks ago when I told you to kill a scorpion, you nearly had a heart attack."

"Great," he said sarcastically. "See what I put up with?"

"You guys all heard about what Anna was saying before she died, right?" I asked.

"About the Mexican witches and poison?" asked Martin.

"Yea. What do you think? Were Anna and Nathan poisoned? And if they were, why did someone strangle Nancy?" I had lots of questions with no answers, and I'm not sure if I really believed anyone in the room could help.

"Maybe Nancy knew who it was and was killed to shut her up," said Leslie.

"You watch too many crime shows," said Tom.

"OK, Mr. detective," she answered with a snarl, "What do you think is going on?"

182

Tom thought for a moment, and then, as if a light went off in his head, he said, "Well if it is a poison from Mexico, does that implicate one or more of our Mexican friends?"

Silence followed and I was glad when Martin spoke up. "Let's not be too hasty in suspecting one of our Mexican neighbors just because they are Mexican. Even if they find out it was poison and it was from Mexico that doesn't prove any of them are involved. Anyone could easily have gone to Mexico to get it. In fact, half the people in our group go there for cheap medicine or dental work."

"Guys, I'm sorry to dump this on you. I just need to get an attorney to help me right now, so I don't do anything that gets me in trouble, and I didn't know who else to turn to."

"Wait a minute," said Leslie suddenly, "Wasn't Joseph some kind of attorney before he retired and became an artist?"

"I thought Joe was a detective," I asked.

"Different person," said Celeste. "You probably haven't met Joseph yet. He doesn't play that often."

"That's right," agreed Tom. "I think he might have been a DA or something before he retired."

"Great. I'll talk to him. Do you have a number?"

Celeste pulled out her phone and scrolled through the screens until she had his number. I wrote it down and told myself to call him as soon as possible.

"Well, don't say all this in front of Lauren," said Celeste.

"I don't think I've met her," I said.

"Oh, you would remember her if you did," added Tom, "She's a nut and believes any conspiracy she hears. If she hears the Sheriff is suspecting you, she'll say she saw you go in Nancy's house. She'll be spreading rumors that you were seen tampering with Nathan's water bottle."

I shook my head in disbelief. What the fuck little town had I dropped into? It was starting to feel more and more like an episode of *The Twilight Zone*. I wouldn't be surprised if Rod Sterling knocked at the door or came out of the back room with an explanation of how things can easily get twisted. Spooked didn't really describe my feelings, and as if things couldn't get worse, Butch jumped up and ran to the door barking. We all just about jumped out of our skins. No one had knocked at the door, but Butch was going crazy. Then the doorbell rang. I fully expected to see Rod Sterling when I opened the door, but it was Joe. I'm not sure if that was any less spooky.

"Hi," I said, with a surprised look on my face. I was somewhat relieved to see that Joe was alone. No Sheriff.

"Can I come in?" he asked.

I hesitated. "Um, I guess. I have some people here."

"That's OK. I'm not going to say anything confidential."

I opened the door and guided him into my little living room. Everyone knew him, so I didn't bother with introductions.

"Hey guys," he said smiling. "Crazy shit going on, huh?"

No one said anything, but they all nodded.

"Listen, I wanted to stop by and talk to you after your talk with the Sheriff. I know that was pretty intense. He's never really had an investigation like this before. Murders in small towns aren't usually complicated, so he's a bit out of his league. He's agreed to bring me on as a paid consultant to help him with the investigation, since my experience as a homicide detective goes back quite a few years."

"I suppose that's a good thing," I said, though it came out sounding more as a question than a statement.

"It is. He's also agreed to back off of you for now. He agreed he might have been a bit out of line. I told him we should wait to get the lab results from the crime scene guys before we start fingerprinting anyone. It's still possible that Anna and Nathan died of natural causes and that Nancy's death is totally unrelated. I don't think you need an attorney right now. Once the lab results are in and logged, that will prevent any perceived shenanigans that I could tell you were worried about."

I must have sighed out loud because everyone was staring at me.

"Yeah, thanks," I finally managed. "I did have my concerns. So, after the lab results are back, you'll want me and everyone else here to come in and submit fingerprints and DNA?" I wanted to make it clear that everyone needed to be considered a suspect and submit to this procedure, not just me.

"I think that makes sense," he agreed, but I'm not so sure he did.

"What happens now?" asked Tom.

"I interview everyone that had any contact with any of the victims again. See if I can't narrow the field a bit and if I'm lucky, figure out a possible motive."

"Any ideas?" asked Martin.

"Not really. As you all know, Nathan wasn't really popular, and even Nancy had her issues with the group, but from what I can gather no one had any issues with Anna. Even still, it's just hard to believe that anyone would murder someone over pickleball, but I can tell you over my career as a detective I've seen all kinds of weird motives for murder. The most common ones are love, lust, loathing, and loot, but I've even seen murders based on the day of the week, internet passwords, lost tickets to a concert, and of course revenge."

Then Joe just had to show his deep-down enmity for pickleball. "As fanatical as you guys all are – I mean pickleball players in general - I would not be surprised at anything."

The pickleballers in the room moaned and gave him the stink eye.

"Present company excluded, of course," he added quickly.

I can't say I disagreed with the statement that pickleballers are fanatics. We are and sometimes we go over the top. I'd seen arguments turn into fist fights over line calls, forgetting the score, not calling out the score, court assignments, yellow outfits that make seeing the ball difficult, trash talking, not trash talking, and hitting someone with the ball; you name it, it's happened. No court? No problem. They'll take tape or chalk and mark a court on a tennis court or even a driveway. There is no limit to the extent these people (myself included) will go to play. There are some people who can barely walk because of age or injury, but somehow find the energy and ability to play a few games. For the most part it is fun and amusing, but it can get serious. And if these murders were pickleball related, deadly serious.

"What do we do in the meantime while we wait for these lab results?" I asked, hoping he wouldn't say to not leave town.

He smiled. "Don't leave town," he replied, as if he could read my mind. "Sorry. Just joking. Unless you were already planning on leaving town, then don't."

"Well, honestly, given what's going on, it did cross my mind. It's not like I want to be next on the list," I said nervously.

"Any reason why someone would want to hurt you?"

"No. At least, I don't think so." Although, I'm quite sure if you had asked our recently deceased players if they thought they were targets of a homicidal maniac, they would have said no as well. "But then we don't really know why someone killed Nathan, Anna and Nancy."

186

"We haven't even confirmed they were all murdered yet. Listen, I'm pretty good at what I do, and I think I'll have some good ideas in a few days. I don't think this is random, but it could be. If it isn't random, then there is something tying all these people together and after some digging it should become apparent. It does seem that were all, as some of you dubbed them, Royals, but that doesn't mean that is the motive."

"But it doesn't mean it isn't the reason either," I added, proud of my deductive reasoning.

"Actually, was Anna really a Royal?" asked Joe.

Tom was quick to answer, "She hung out with them a lot, both on and off the courts. She practiced with them and really wanted to be included. She wasn't really rude and overbearing like them, but on the other hand, she never stood up for anyone they snubbed."

I knew that Tom had felt that personal insult on more than one occasion. I was too new to the scene to have witnessed it much, or been the brunt of it, but then I was a better player than the Royals, so they probably would have welcomed me into the click, if I wanted to join, which I did not.

"Everything is on the table right now. They are all certainly connected by pickleball, but then they are all connected because they live here too. Don't worry though, I'll find the connection and the motive. Killers almost always make mistakes and get caught, and I had a pretty good track record during my career. Any help you guys can give will be greatly appreciated. Just keep your eyes and ears open for anything you think might help me."

"And don't drink the water," I joked. No one laughed except Martin. I think he has a dark sense of humor like I do.

Joe left us sitting in my living room.

Finally, Leslie broke the silence. "So, what now? We just go back to normal until the next body is found? Uh-uh. Not me. I'm not going near anyone in that group out there and I don't think you guys should either. Tom, you can skip pickleball until this is over."

It sounded like an order, not a suggestion.

"I suppose you're right," he agreed reluctantly. "At least for a few days," he hedged.

"I'm serious Tom. There is some crazy fuck out there killing people and I have no intention of becoming a widow because you can't stay away from that stupid game."

"What if, as Joe said, the connection is something unrelated to pickleball?" I asked.

"Then if they have a beef with us, they'll have to come to our house to get us," she responded forcefully. "And I'm packing."

"Leaving town?" I asked, a bit concerned that two of the few people I had become friendly with and liked might be leaving.

"No silly," she said, "I have a gun and I know how to use it."

Oh. I was a bit stunned. I had never owned a gun but wondered if I should change that? I heard that Arizona was an open carry state. Whatever that meant.

I guess she could see the concern on my face. "Don't worry, Al, I'm not one of these second amendment crazies who thinks we should all have assault rifles. I believe in the second amendment, don't get me wrong, but I don't believe it should apply to any type of weapon. I've had guns since I was a kid and my parents taught me how to be a responsible gun owner, but if someone were to break into our house or try to kill one of us, they will learn very quickly that I'm not some easy mark."

Tom nodded in agreement. I wondered if she had a gun in her purse?

"You mean like they killed Nancy in her home?" asked Celeste. "It wasn't some crazy person breaking into random homes. Whoever did all this is someone we all know. I'm sure Nancy wasn't feeling threatened by the person. She probably let him or her in."

"Well, speak for yourself on that," I said. "I don't know anyone that well. Remember I'm the new guy."

"That means you haven't been here long enough to make any enemies," suggested Martin. I think he was only half kidding. He turned to Butch, who seemed uninterested in the conversation, "You'll protect Al, won't you?"

Butch rolled onto his back so Martin could rub his tummy.

"I suppose he might try to protect me, unless the killer brought treats," I joked.

"Can you all agree to take a few days off from pickleball?" asked Leslie.

"I really don't think we are all in danger," said Tom.

"Seriously," said Leslie, "You don't know what the motive is, or who's at risk. You just can't stand to miss a few days of pickleball. You're addicted. I'm going to stand my ground on this. At least let things die down a bit before returning."

We all stared at her, clearly shocked by her choice of words. She realized her faux pas.

"OK, sorry. I didn't mean to say die down."

"Guys, thanks for coming over and talking about this. I think I'll hold off on calling the attorney for now and wait to see what the autopsy report says."

What more could be said at that point? Crazy theories leading to more paranoia. I had no plans to play pickleball again for a while anyway, and wondered if anyone else would, or would they abide by Leslie's admonition not to play? Did it even matter? As Martin said, I haven't been there long enough to make any enemies. I couldn't see any reason for anyone to barge into my home and strangle or poison me, and besides, I had Butch. I doubt any would-be killer wanted to go up against him. As for the others, well, they had each other, and in Leslie's case, a gun. They didn't seem like the type of people to have enemies either.

Pickleball Tip # 12 – Going For An Impossibly Difficult Low Percentage Shot

Everyone wants to hit an outright winner. The shot that the opponent can't reach and can't return gets everyone animated. The urge to hit the line with a passing shot is huge and the reward is extremely satisfying. The problem is, it's a low percentage shot that more often than not will sail wide and out of bounds. Hitting that shot may bring the crowd to their feet with cheers but the pros know better. Rather than go for a shot with a very low margin for error the pros keep the ball in play waiting for an attackable ball. One they can hit a high percentage of the time either for a winner, or to put their opponent out of position, opening up an even easier shot for a winner. Players with skills less than a pro would be wise to emulate this, especially since their ability to hit a ball within a few inches of their intended target is questionable.

Chapter 13

Butch and I didn't sleep well that night. In my case, I couldn't stop thinking about the murder spree taking place in my new town, whether it was because they were Royals or some other nefarious reason. I know for a fact Butch had no such concerns. But he was annoyed with me and all my tossing and turning. I know this because each time I moved and resettled he groaned at me. And not the groan he lets out when I rub his ears or tummy. No, this was clearly telling me to lay still and let a guy get some sleep.

I would have been more than happy to forget the past events and sleep soundly through the night, but each time I dosed off I was plagued with one nightmare after another. I was either the victim or the perp and neither was a pleasant experience. In one dream, I was handcuffed and shoved unceremoniously into the back of the Sheriff's squad car, while my pickleball friends cheered and tossed tomatoes at me. In another dream, I confronted the killer with my suspicions and realized too late that he had spiked my drink and was now telling me how I was about to pass out and die. Why I would tell the killer I suspected him is anybody's guess. Certainly not very bright, but in my defense, I had been drinking tequila and smoking some pot to try to get to sleep in the first place. I'm sure either of those could have produced some interesting dreams, but coupled together with the threat of a homicidal maniac on the loose, it was a sure recipe for the bizarre.

It was still dark out when I finally gave up on sleeping and got out of bed. Butch reluctantly got up and followed me into the kitchen. I brewed some coffee and turned on the news, but it was too depressing. Everything was breaking news. The Chinese were spying on us, Russia was attacking Ukraine, the Israelis and Palestinians were killing each other, and the Republicans and Democrats couldn't agree on anything. I found a rerun of Jeopardy and got depressed when I couldn't get even one answer right. So, I turned off the TV and got my paddle out and started to bounce balls off the wall until the sun came up. Butch got bored and went back to sleep on the couch.

I looked over at Butch. "Dude, we need to take a walk, and we need to really reconsider living in this town." If you were to ask Butch his advice, it would always be that a good walk solves all problems. His ears perked up when he heard the word "walk" coupled with "take". He sat up and looked at me with his big brown eyes, as if to tell me a walk was a brilliant idea. I leashed him up and started to sing the Clash Song *Should I Stay or Should I Go*.

Butch just stared at me.

"I mean, help me out, Butch. Seriously, what should we do? This town doesn't have much going for it if I can't play pickleball, not to mention the looming threat of who is next in line for the murderer."

I interpreted the look on Butch's face to mean, *I never wanted to move here in the first place, but now you ask me?*

"I know you were perfectly happy in Denver, but what should we do now?" He licked my hand. Just in case Stephanie was listening, I decided to ask her opinion. "Steph, was this all a big mistake? Help me out here."

Crickets. So, no help.

We left the house and I checked to make sure I locked the doors. Twice. Couldn't be too careful in these circumstances. We walked and Butch sniffed, pooped, and peed, while I thought. I had no planned route in mind when we left the house, and because it was still early and there was a chill in the air, we didn't see another soul. I was lost in thought when I realized we were in front of Nancy's house. It was not my intent, or maybe it was? There was yellow crime scene tape and some kind of notice on the front door that I didn't bother to go read. Unlike yesterday, her neighbors weren't outside watching the police and crime scene team. It was quiet and deserted. Just as well. I had no desire to talk to any of them. Butch wanted to stop and do some business on her property, but I wouldn't let him stop. I even made a point not to stare at her house as we passed by.

We walked aimlessly for another thirty minutes, and as I've said before, it was a small town, so if you walked long enough and made enough turns, you'd pass by just about everyone's home. Our circuitous route brought us by a small mobile home park. It looked like a nice, well-tended neighborhood, with its own pool and kids' playground. Sitting on the wooden porch attached to a silver double-wide was Jack Swenson, our pickleball buddy and court maintenance man. On any other day at this time, I would have expected to find Jack cleaning the courts in preparation for a day of fun. Not that day. If Jack wasn't on the courts, then I suspected the rest of the group wouldn't be either. Three players deaths should take a toll on attendance. I wondered how long it would take for everyone to trickle back out to play.

Jack was sitting in a rocker, sipping a drink, when he noticed Butch and I walking by. I didn't have a lot to say to him, or to anyone else for that matter, and if I had noticed him earlier, I would have steered Butch away. But I was daydreaming until it was too late. He spotted us first and was waving and calling us over. Not wanting to be rude I acknowledged him and led Butch over to his porch. The joys of small-town living, I guess.

He greeted us with a big smile. "Who's your furry friend?"

"This is Butch." I turned to Butch and said, "Butch, say hello to Jack."

Butch raised his paw and waved it. It was a trick I had taught him while Stephanie was bed ridden, that always brought a smile to her face. Jack was evidently impressed and came down to shake hands with Butch. Butch was

194

always happy to greet someone new and held out his paw for Jack to shake it.

"That is incredible," he laughed. "I love it, what else can you do?" He kneeled down. Always the ham, Butch laid down and rolled over, looking to me to see if that had earned him a reward. I always carried a pocket of dog trail mix for these situations and handed a couple pieces to Jack to give to Butch.

Jack fed them to him and patted him on the head. "Aren't you something else?"

Butch did have a way with people. I wondered if I had made a mistake not introducing him to the Sheriff. Everyone likes dogs, don't they? I doubted a serial killer could be a dog lover, but then what do I know.

"So, I guess this is where you live, Jack?"

"Yeah, just a rental I have had for the last year or so. It's cheap and comfortable, and as you can tell, pretty close to the pickleball courts. Can I get you a hot chocolate or coffee or something?"

"No, we're just on our walk and I really shouldn't stay long. We've been out for quite a while. I take it you and everybody else are not playing pickleball today?"

"No, I don't think that would be very respectful. Do you?"

I shook my head. Of course not. Why did I even ask?

"What do you think is going on? You seem to know everyone here quite well. Were Nancy and Nathan really hated that much?"

"Well, I don't know if they were exactly hated by everyone, but I'm going to be honest with you, I'm not sure if anyone really liked either of them. Sure, they were good players and helped get all this going, but they really weren't that pleasant to be around. I told the Sheriff when he interviewed me that just about everybody here felt the same way."

195

I thought the same, but then I didn't know everyone that played here yet. And even with that, I would think just disliking someone wouldn't be enough to justify murder.

"I mean, from what I saw they weren't that bad. Did something happen here that I don't know about that would really drive someone to murder them?"

"Listen, Al, you seem like a nice guy. Maybe a little naive though. Everybody has a past and not always a good one. I've overheard people say things about Nathan that weren't too flattering. I don't think they thought he was such a nice person, and neither was Nancy. I personally didn't have anything against either of them, but I heard that Nathan and Little E had some business dealings in Canada or Florida, I can't remember which. I also think I heard he had a drunk driving conviction after an accident. In fact, I think he might have served some time in prison for that."

"I didn't know about any of that," I said, even though I had heard some of it.

He nodded and continued, "We also have quite a few people here from south of the border and I think some of them might have some shady dealings going on."

"Shady?" I asked. "How so?" I was hoping that this wasn't going to turn into a racist rant about Mexicans. "You don't think one of them is behind this, do you?"

"Possibly," he answered, deliberately. "Hard to say, but I think there may be some cartel ties."

I had heard things like this about Mexicans in Arizona from my friends in Denver before we left. It made me uncomfortable then and was putting me on edge now. Why do people think all Mexicans must have some ties with a cartel? Do they also think all Italians are part of the Mafia or the

Jews have a space laser? I held my tongue. I was getting quite adept at keeping my thoughts to myself.

Maybe he could tell my concern. "I'm just saying that someone should investigate their backgrounds."

"What about Anna? I can't believe she had a questionable past."

"Don't be so sure about her, either. Before Nathan died, she was the one talking about Mexican witches and witches' brews. I don't know much about her past, but she was from Mexico and had lots of relatives there, and she had an affair with Nathan and who knows who else? I heard a rumor that Jesus has some ties to the cartel. I'm just saying that not everyone here is as innocent as you might think."

If you live long enough, I guess we all have some things in our past. "You honestly think this has something to do with cartels?"

"Al, I'm just an old guy trying to play a little pickleball down here. I hear things, and I really haven't done any research to figure out if any of it's true or not."

But he clearly wasn't opposed to spreading those rumors.

"Have you told Joe or the Sheriff about your theories?"

"I mentioned some of it to the Sheriff, but not Joe. I will if he asks me. I heard that the Sheriff gave you a hard time. Isn't it just like some small-town Sheriff to suspect the new guy, or is it just because you're black?"

I guess he noticed.

"I don't know," I answered, not wanting this to be about racism. I wanted to change the subject, but I couldn't get a word in. Jack enthusiastically shared the local gossip and rumors he'd picked up during his time there. I learned he had moved from Chicago to get out of the wind and cold. He'd picked up pickleball when he got to Rio Viejo and was actually a decent player. He had stories about everyone. Some rather sordid

197

and others just unflattering. I wondered if he was keeping notes. His memory was exceptional. Maybe he had a super hearing aid like Melanie and listened in on everyone. It was interesting to hear this all coming from the quiet guy that cleaned the courts and everyone seemed to like.

"It's almost as if they think because I'm old," said Jack, who looked like he was around 80 or had maybe just led a hard life, "that I can't hear what's going on around me, or they just don't care. I do use a hearing aid, but I got to tell you, when you turn up the volume you hear all sorts of shit."

"Really? Like what?" I responded.

"Well, I don't know what you've already heard, but Nathan was a heavy drinker with a history of DUIs. He also had a short temper and liked to fight. If that's not enough, he was a conspiracy theorist too. Nancy was also a big drinker, and although not a conspiracy nut, she would defend Nathan to the death, even though rumor had it that Nathan had beaten her up a few times and threatened to kill her. She suspected, with good reason, that Nathan often cheated on her, and she even caught him a few times. Even Jane, Nancy's regular doubles partner, apparently had eyes for Nathan and may or may not have rolled in bed with him. According to popular belief, Jane knew about the alleged abuse, but that didn't stop her from going after Nathan. Did Nancy think that Jane was competition? I don't think it was possible for her not to know, so maybe she just chose to pretend she didn't."

According to Jack, Ethelwolf, or "Little E", was an egotistical jerk and not at all liked, by just about anyone. He had evidently made a small fortune in Florida land deals before moving to Arizona. He and Brian were involved in some deals together, and one of those deals landed Little E some prison time while Brian skated free. They were both originally from Canada. Why or how they both ended up in Rio Viejo was a mystery to

Jack. I thought, it didn't take an expert to see the tension between the two of them.

"Anna was sweet," continued Jack. "Maybe too sweet. Rumor had it that she had slept with Nathan, Brian, and Jesus. When she wasn't playing pickleball, she worked part-time at a shop that specialized in Mexican artwork."

Jack seemed to be enjoy sharing all his stories. He kept going.

"Molly doesn't seem to have a sordid past, at least not that I have heard, but did you know that she is gay?" he asked me.

"No, but that's not a problem, is it?"

"Not to me, but it is to some people. Too bad, though."

"Why is it too bad?" I asked.

"Because she's cute, and that's one less girl for us."

"Are you interested in dating her?"

"I could be, but she clearly isn't interested in me. But I've heard she swings both ways so maybe I'm not feminine enough for her. She is quite a tiger on the court, though, and I think she wants to be a Royal. I even think she had designs on Nancy. I'm betting her and Jane went at it a few times."

I was tongue tied by this time. I wondered what he said about Blacks behind my back and Black Jews on top of that. My opinion of Jack went downhill fast. He was giving me a headache. I wanted to escape. This was more information than I could handle, and his attitude was more than I could stomach, but he wasn't done yet.

"Anne is an up-and-comer on the court and recently broke into the Royals and is openly dating Brian. I'm not sure if she knows about Brian cheating on her with Anna, but if she knows, she's acting like she doesn't. There's a lot of hanky-panky going on in our little town."

199

"What about you, Jack?" I said, but I didn't think he caught my sarcasm or disgust.

"Oh, I just dream about that stuff now. I talk a good game, but in reality, I had prostate issues and can't get it up anymore."

TMI. Boy, was I sorry I asked, but all I said was, "Well that sucks. We should probably get going."

But Jack continued before I could extricate myself.

"So, next we have Larry. He comes and goes a lot between the US and Mexico. He and Jesus can often be seen chatting in Spanish off to the side where they can't be heard. I think they're gay too. My Spanish isn't that good, but if I had to guess they're cartel players and up to no good."

It seemed like Jack thought anyone that was Mexican, or went regularly to Mexico, was a cartel member.

"Then there is William, who at seventy-five still sees himself as a ladies' man and is always flirting, mostly with Nancy. It's kind of annoying to me. He was a gynecologist until he retired a few years ago. I told him about my issues, and he offered me some Viagra, but I turned him down. He told me it was working for him, but I still said no. Now Tom, he's a cool guy, but he doesn't talk much about his past. He's a Vietnam vet who was wounded in action and moved here a couple years ago. You've seen him play. He's pretty good, and if you ask me, I don't know why the Royals don't want him to play more with them. He's good friends with Martin, who's a Spaniard, and you have to be careful around Spaniards, you know?" I didn't, but I didn't want to ask. "But Martin doesn't play pickleball, so who cares? I think they play a lot of golf together. Even though Martin doesn't play, I don't think he's fond of the Royals. Probably because Tom hates them."

I wanted to throttle him, but instead I asked, "What's your story, Jack?"

200

He hesitated, as if he was thinking of a good answer, then finally said, "You know, I've been a lot of places and done a lot of things. So many, I don't think I can say one place I'm actually from. I'll probably stay here another year and then try someplace new. With pickleball, of course, now that I'm addicted."

"Military?" I asked.

"No. I just like to try new places."

I nodded. I hadn't lived in a lot of places myself, but I'd traveled a bit and always enjoyed seeing new places and how things were different. But I did it as a tourist, which is not the same experience as living somewhere. I wanted to leave but had a couple more questions for Jack before I could go.

"So, Jack, you know all these people, do you have any idea who might be behind these deaths?"

"It's a mystery to me. I mean, I see a lot of people who didn't like them but being annoying doesn't seem like a good reason to kill someone. On the other hand, I saw some postings online about people getting so angry on the courts that they got into fights."

This wasn't news to me. I remember one time a guy got so mad at his partner that he went over and whacked him over the head with his paddle. He hit him so hard the paddle broke, which probably was a good thing, or the guy might have had a concussion. Another time, I saw two guys go at it at the net because they couldn't agree on the score and accused each other of cheating. A lot of people forget scores, but these two guys almost came to blows, and probably would have if someone had not intervened. Most of the time, people are fairly friendly on the pickleball court, but there are some people who either have anger issues or are so competitive that they will do anything to win.

"So, you don't have a theory as to who is behind all this?"

"No, not really, but I'm going to watch my back, just in case," he answered. "You should probably do the same."

"Everyone seems to like you, Jack, so I can't imagine anyone hurting you."

"Life is strange, but I go out of my way to make friends with everyone."

I figured that if Jack didn't have a clue who the killer was, considering he talked to everyone, listened in on everyone's conversations, and had gossip on everyone, then what chance did I have of figuring it out? It was time to get the hell out of there. Jack had just said more to me than I'd heard him say in all the times I'd seen him at the courts. I was surprised that once you got him talking, you couldn't get him to stop. He was still droning on about some people, but I had zoned out trying to think of a polite way to leave. And by leave, I meant packing our stuff and hitting the road. If Joe and the Sheriff had not made it clear that I should not leave town, I would've done just that.

Finally, I interrupted Jack's stories, saying, "Jack, uh, I think that Butch and I better be moving along before it gets too hot for him out here. I guess I'll see you on the courts in a few days."

"Yeah, yeah, you don't want to burn his paws. I'll see you out there," he said. "You and Butch take care and stay safe."

We left Jack sitting on his porch and headed home. I didn't look back, but I could feel his eyes boring into the back of my head, and it was creepy. The guy I had thought was the most polite and quiet person on the courts was actually a small-minded gossip, just waiting to spread the juicy stuff on everyone he knew. He was now the second person I'd met with these super hearing devices, and it was a bit unsettling. I wondered if that made him a target for the killer. Assuming the killer knew that Jack had so much dirt on everyone.

Pickleball Tip # 13 – When To Reset

A lot of times you find yourself in trouble and need to give yourself a chance to get back in the point. It might be because your opponent pulled you off the court wide or hit you a quick ball at your feet and you don't have time to set up properly, or you might have been pushed back to the transition zone or even the baseline.

When that happens, try to hit a reset shot, rather than trying to put extreme pace on it or going for a shot with a low margin for error.

Slow down the point with an unattackable dink or drop shot. Basically, it's a slow ball back into the kitchen, that gives you time to get yourself back in position. Usually, it is best to go down the middle, unless they took you so wide you have a shot at an ATP. Trying to hit a drive while out of position gives your opponents a perfect put-away in the area you just vacated, and you'll be surprised at how quickly it comes back for a winner.

Chapter 14

My head was reeling from all the information Jack had on everyone. I had no idea how much of it was true and how much of it was common knowledge. From what I had seen, Jack certainly wasn't the only one out there that liked to gossip, but I wondered how much these gossips had shared with Joe and the Sheriff. I was torn as to what, if any of it, I should tell them myself. Was it all true? Would it really help with the investigation? Was it my place to share unverified gossip? Was it given to me in confidence, and would that even matter? This was about murder. For all I knew about Jack, he could have been some conspiracy nut case and I would have been like the people on the internet that I hate, who spread lies and rumors like they are the truth. If I believed Jack, then everyone in town had a motive to kill the recently departed. If I did alert the authorities without verifying the information and it turned out to be baseless, then I might as well move now, because I would be damaging the reputation of those people, as well as turning them into suspects. On the other hand, what if all that stuff was true and the information would really help in the investigation?

What to do?

I decided to try to verify some of the information Jack had given me before I passed it along to the Sheriff or Joe. Since I wanted to do this quickly and knew only a few people well enough, that meant calling Tom and Martin back over for help. If they could collaborate Jack's stories, then I would feel comfortable passing them along. If Joe and the Sheriff already knew all of this, it wouldn't matter. If they didn't know, it might help steer the investigation in the right direction. Tom and Martin had been there for some time. They knew all the players and would know what were idle rumors and what was real. I had already concluded in my mind that they were safe, as in, they weren't the killers. Jack hadn't told me any stories about them, and he seemed to know something about everyone. If they had any dark secrets, they were pretty good at keeping them hidden.

By the time Butch and I returned back to the house, my mind was made up. I called Tom and Martin back for another consultation and asked them to come alone. Not that I didn't trust their wives, but I wanted this to be a guy thing. Don't ask me why. They both agreed, even though they didn't know exactly what they were agreeing to. They arrived together fifteen minutes later.

Butch greeted them at the door and showered them with affection as if he was a love- starved child. He ran back and forth between them and even brought out his squeaky toys to show off. I led them to the living room, and it was a full ten minutes before Butch settled down and let us talk without interruption.

"Guys, thanks for coming over like this on such short notice, again," I told them. "I seem to be calling on you quite a bit." They both smiled and said they were happy to help out. It was almost noon, and it was heating up outside, so I offered them cold beers. "You might need a drink when I tell you what I just heard."

"Sounds ominous," said Tom.

"Possibly gossip, but I want your opinion." They both nodded in agreement.

"Tecate okay with you guys?" I asked, hoping they would say yes, since it was either that or shots of tequila.

"I won't turn that down," replied Martin.

I scooted off to the kitchen and came back with three bottles of Tecate and passed them around.

"What's up, Al?" asked Martin, as he took a beer from me and opened it. "You sounded pretty serious on the phone."

I went on to explain the conversation I had just had with Jack. I recounted the details as best as I could, considering my bad memory and the volume of information Jack had shared. The short version being that just about everyone in town had a sketchy history and most of them had a reason to kill one or all of the victims.

Except me, of course.

"So, you are telling us that Jack has been spying on all of us all this time?" asked Tom, as he took a draw off his beer. "But he didn't say anything about me or Martin?"

I hesitated, and finally said, "Not much, really, except that you were a Vietnam vet and got wounded over there and that you hate the Royals. And Martin, well, Jack doesn't trust any foreigners, as he put it, so I guess that would include you. He never actually accused either of you, but..."

"I might be from Spain, but I've been in the US for most of my life and I don't even play pickleball. So why would I be a suspect?"

"Your wife plays. Maybe she transferred her hate of them to you and you acted on that?"

"And I'm a foreigner who can't be trusted?"

"Exactly. Well, in his eyes anyway. Although he didn't say it, I'm sure he thinks I have a motive to kill because I'm black and they were all white. Who knows what he really thinks."

"And what? Because I'm a vet I have deep-seeded issues that translate into violence? PTSD?"

206

I shrugged.

"Is he telling all this to the Sheriff?" asked Tom.

"He said he hasn't yet, but I'm sure he will at some point."

"What about Jack? Maybe he's the killer and trying to throw smoke at other people? Or Joe? His wife plays and he often says he hates the game." suggested Martin, clearly getting annoyed.

"I was wondering if I should tell Joe or the Sheriff all this stuff?" I asked.

"Look," said Tom, "no one really likes the Royals. They're rude and annoying, but if we killed people that were rude and annoying, there wouldn't be a lot of people left standing. Certainly, the pickleball courts would lose a few players."

Martin and I nodded.

"So, is all that stuff true?" I asked. "If it isn't, I sure don't want to spread it around, and quite frankly, I'm not sure I want to be spreading it around even if it is true. Just because someone has some shady business dealings or is from Mexico it doesn't make them a killer. Although it seems jilted lovers have been known to kill."

"I'm not out there much and Celeste doesn't tell me everything she hears. What about you, Tom, have you heard all of this?" asked Martin.

"Hey, I just go out there to play pickleball. I don't ask questions about everybody's history, but from time to time I do notice some tension that doesn't seem to be related to the games."

"Like what?" I asked.

"Brian and Little E are always arguing on and off the court. They don't seem to like each other that much. I didn't know about all the affairs, but now that I think about it, I guess some people have acted kind of strange around each other. Nobody's hitting on me though. Should I be insulted?"

I thought about that comment. I was pretty sure that Jane was flirting with me on more than one occasion.

Tom continued, "There was one particularly bad fight we all knew about between Nancy and Nathan. It was brutal and spilled out onto the courts. They wanted us all to take sides and I think some people did. I didn't care much for either of them, and I couldn't care less who was screwing who, or why. As to cartels," he shrugged, "seems that gringos suspect all Mexicans if they are at all successful, but I haven't noticed anything that would indicate anybody here has any connection to a cartel."

I'd certainly experienced that kind of not-so-subtle racism.

"So," said Martin, "if I understand you correctly, you are afraid to go to the Sheriff or Joe and bring this up, in case Jack made it all up?"

"Precisely. If Jack tells them then it's on his head, but if I say it and it gets out that I spread all that junk around, then I might as well leave town now. Everyone would hate me. On the other hand, if I don't say anything and Jack keeps quiet, and that shit is true..." I didn't finish the thought. Instead, I took a long draw off my beer.

"How can we help?" asked Tom.

I shook my head. "I don't have a fucking clue, actually. What would you guys do?"

"I'd tell Joe," answered Tom.

"But then Joe goes and confronts Jack and Jack will know that I told him all that."

"And you are worried Jack will become an enemy?" asked Martin.

"It crossed my mind."

"Does he scare you?"

"Well," I thought for a moment, "not really. What is he, like eighty years old or something? I can't see him hurting me, but I don't want to be ostracized either. He seems to have a lot of friends here. I would hate to put him on the spot. He seems like a nice guy. Maybe a bit creepy, given that he seems to have a dossier on everyone."

"Or a vivid imagination," added Martin.

"Or that," I agreed.

"I don't think we are going to be much help," admitted Martin. "So, what are you going to do?"

I rubbed my face. "Shit, I just don't know. This is all so fucking surreal. I've never been so close to this many murders and I haven't heard this much gossip since high school."

"Welcome to Rio Viejo and the retirement crowd. You think this is a lot of gossip, just wait. After you've been here a little longer, all the gossips will be sharing with you. They just don't know you well enough yet," said Tom laughing. "You said you haven't been around this many murders. Does that mean you've been around some murders?"

"I grew up in the Denver. We certainly had our share of gang violence, and quite a few accidental drug overdoses, but no one I personally knew was ever murdered. I've never been questioned as a possible suspect or witness to a murder."

"Good to know," laughed Martin. "Sorry, I didn't mean to laugh. There are dead people here, and possibly someone we know is responsible."

Yeah, back to reality.

"So, do you think anyone Jack was talking about could be a murderer?"

Martin ran his hand through his receding gray hair. "No. I'm sorry, I don't. Yes, they have some anger issues, but if I had to bet on anyone actually being a murderer, I would say no. I've been around these people for a long time. None of them ever seemed angry or violent enough to commit murder."

I was the only guy that was new to town that no one really knew. I didn't remind him.

"Are we really sure there were three murders?" asked Tom. "I mean, isn't it possible that Nathan and Anna died from heart attacks?"

"Yes," I admitted, "but that would still leave Nancy. Remember, Joe said she was strangled. I don't want to scare you guys, but I don't buy it being a coincidence that three people all died suddenly, within a week of each other. I think they were murdered and there is a connection. It may seem trivial to think it's because they were all Royals, but give me another theory."

No one offered one.

"If this is, in fact, related to pickleball, then I don't think it's over," I said, taking a huge drink.

"I can't believe this is about pickleball," said Martin. "Nobody takes it that seriously."

I told them that I had seen and heard lots of stories about fanatical players and even witnessed some violence on the court, but nothing so permanent as murder. I wanted to believe this wasn't related to our wonderful game, so that we could get back to playing and having a good time.

"Well, if it is about being a Royal, then all I can say is, I'm glad I never joined their team," said Tom. "I would have guessed most murders are about revenge or jealousy."

"Really?" I asked. I had no clue what the most common motive for murder was, especially multiple ones that weren't part of a mass shooting. I made a mental note to Google that.

"Yes," Tom continued. "Like Joe said, lust, unrequited love, jealousy."

"If that's true, then I'm safe. I haven't slept with anyone here," I proclaimed.

They laughed.

"You know that really has a ring of truth to it," stated Martin.

"What?" I replied. "That I haven't had sex since coming here?"

"I'll take your word for that, but what I meant was that it's been like a soap opera here lately. People sleeping around and cheating on each other. Jack isn't wrong about that," said Martin.

I stared at the two of them.

Almost in unison they replied, "But not us."

"So, it's just a coincidence that the people murdered were Royals, and what really doomed them was a triangle of sex?"

"I think that might be the case," said Tom.

"Then we are all safe," I declared. We tapped our beer bottles and took a drink.

"But," I added, as I went to the kitchen to grab more beers, "I'm staying clear of the Royals, just in case. I'm not taking any chances."

I handed them each another beer.

"Back to the question you asked when we got here. What are you going to do with all this knowledge?" asked Martin.

Was it knowledge or just a bunch of rumors? I had no answer, and getting advice from Tom and Martin was proving to be a waste of time.

"Fuck if I know," I finally said. "You guys weren't as helpful as I had hoped, but thanks for listening."

"What do you mean? I thought we just solved the case," joked Tom.

"Solved?" I made a face. "All we did was come to a weak conclusion that we don't think it's pickleball related, and I'm still not so sure about that, but we don't have a theory who the killer is."

"I think someone should share all the information you got from Jack with Joe," said Martin. "I'll volunteer to do it. Al, I know you are hesitant, and I play some golf with him. I can drop a bunch of hints that I've overheard this stuff. It won't get tied to you or Jack. If he did already hear it from Jack, then it will sound more credible. Also, since I'm not a pickleball player, I don't have to worry about spreading rumors about the players and getting ostracized."

That worked for me. I didn't want to get tagged as being the source of these stories, as that might get back to the group, or Jack in particular. If it was about sex and relationships, then the information could help Joe focus his investigation.

We all agreed that would be the plan. Tom and I also agreed to steer clear of the courts for a few more days, until, hopefully, something was resolved.

Pickleball Tip # 14– Deception

Don't always hit the same shot in certain situations.

Practice being unpredictable. Although the 3rd shot drop can be an ideal strategy, if you do it every time, your opponents will be ready for it. Just to keep them on their toes, try hitting a drive at them once in a while. Sometimes go down the line and sometimes go cross-court. If the return is short and your opponents are at the kitchen, you might even try an offensive lob.

In a dink battle, don't always hit cross court or down the line. Change it up. Move them around. Learn to hit balls that are unpredictable, while still staying in your comfort zone.

Chapter 15

Butch and I decided to lay low for a few more days. That meant no pickleball and staying away from anyone related to pickleball. Butch liked to socialize, but if I was willing to forgo pickleball, he could do without his adoring fans for a few days, especially if it meant keeping me safe. Butch was a team player. We limited our trips out of the house to walks, and only when we thought there would be fewer people out that we might run into. I even had groceries delivered for fear of running into pickleball folks at the market. We made sure our walks didn't go anywhere near the pickleball courts. I wasn't sure if anyone would be there anyway, either out of fear of being the next murder victim, or of looking insensitive. I was having some pickleball withdrawal though. Pickleball is addicting. If you've played, you understand, and if you haven't, you will soon find out. Someone you know will get the pickleball bug. I'm not so insensitive that the killings didn't bother me, they did, but I still missed the game.

However, that didn't mean I couldn't hit some balls.

The house we were renting had a fairly good size living room with a large white wall and wood floors. I removed all the pictures and moved the furniture to one side, clearing off enough space that I could use the wall to practice against. Butch was intrigued at first by my new game but quickly grew tired of running back and forth trying to catch the ball out of the air. He caught a few and would return them to me, but then he decided to just take the ball, lie down, and chew it. I had a bag full of balls, so I allowed him to destroy one. The wall did get scuffed up, but I convinced myself that a can of paint and a paintbrush would be a small price to pay to keep me occupied.

There was a funeral service for Nancy that, because I didn't want to stand out as a possible next target for the killer, I decided not to attend. In the movies, the killer always attends the funerals of his victims, either looking for his next target or just relishing the sadness he's created. If I could have attended incognito so I could scan the crowd, I would have, but being the only black man in a group of white people made that impossible.

Anna had been "shipped" back to Magdalena, Mexico, where she had been born and still had a large family. From Rio Viejo, Magdalena was a relatively short distance over the border. It was said to be a relatively safe drive, but I skipped her funeral for the same reason I'd skipped Nathan and Nancy's. I found out later that a few of her Hispanic friends from Rio Viejo attended, but most of the other pickleball players stayed away. Maybe they were uncomfortable driving in Mexico, or they just didn't feel that close to Anna. Or maybe they were playing it safe, like me.

I learned about all the services and other goings on in Rio Viejo from Tom and Martin, who stopped by from time to time during my self-imposed isolation. I did not see Joe during this period, but he evidently felt close enough to Martin to share how the investigation was going and Martin shared the information with Tom and me.

There had been no arrests made, but Joe had been busy with his online research, as well as interviews with the numerous players and acquaintances of the deceased. He was now well aware of the rumors, reputations, and connections the Royals had with each other and the pickleball community. One piece of good news was that there had been no new deaths in the past two weeks, and people were starting to trickle back onto the courts. I guess they either felt it was now safe to play, or there had been ample time for everyone to grieve. Either the killer was gone, or he had completed his task, whatever it was.

215

Joe made it abundantly clear that he didn't think it was over. He was sure it was one killer, or possibly two acting together, as evidenced by the toxicology report he shared with Martin. Both Anna and Nancy had the same poison in their system, even though Nancy had actually been killed by strangulation. They had exhumed Nathan's body to ascertain if he had been poisoned as well, and they were still waiting for the results, but Joe and the Sheriff were convinced it would show the same toxin. With a little digging, Joe learned that the poison was in fact the same poison that Anna had talked about before her death. It was a brew commonly used by "witches," the shaman or medicine women who lived in the hill towns and villages of Sonora and Baja California. The brew was used to incapacitate the victim, usually a man who was caught cheating, so that the woman could inflict some punishment on him while he was unable to defend himself. It rarely resulted in death because the makers knew just how much should be ingested to cause paralysis. But in larger doses, it could cause heart failure and death. It was colorless and odorless, and the victim would have no clue it had been placed in their drink until they started to lose control of their bodily functions. This alone could cause enough embarrassment to deter them from future infidelity or other abuse, but in some cases, the woman might tattoo the husband or boyfriend in some way. The symptoms came on quickly, and there was no known cure. You just had to give it time to wear off. If you didn't die first, of course. Anna was given such a large dose that she never had a chance. Most likely Nathan was, too. The report showed only a small amount in Nancy's system, which would not have caused immediate death. Presumably, the killer resorted to finishing the job by strangulation.

Joe admitted he was having trouble with motive, though. He believed the stories tying the victims together because of their "Royal" status but had trouble concluding that was enough to drive someone to murder. As a homicide detective, he had seen just about every motive possible, but not pickleball. He was more interested in learning about the victims' histories and any activities, outside of pickleball, that they were all involved in. He

216

had gone back and re-interviewed everyone hoping to discover some drug cartel ties, but other than rumors and suspicions about the Mexicans in town, he couldn't pin that theory down. Then he considered the love triangles. He'd seen enough murders by jilted lovers over the years to think that theory had more credibility, but so far, he couldn't come up with anything concrete.

When he sat down with Jack a second time, he grilled him on the various rumors that were circulating, but Jack was less than helpful. He claimed his memory was faulty; either he was purposely hiding stuff, or he truly was ignorant of what Joe asked him about. Joe thought it might be out of fear. A few of the other interviewees were also afraid to say too much. So, Joe did his own background checks using his old police contacts and internet sources. He learned that quite a few of the characters at the courts had some seedy and dubious histories.

According to Martin, Joe and the Sheriff were stymied but pleased that there had been a break in the killings. As the investigation dragged on with no new deaths, they wondered whether that was because the killer, or killers, had completed whatever vendetta they had against the three victims, or because no one was playing pickleball, so there was no more drama at the courts. Better yet, maybe the culprit had left town.

Tom said that people were getting antsy to play and were feeling like the threat was over. Much like people did during COVID. They either got tired of being afraid or felt the danger had passed. Even without an arrest, people throughout Rio Viejo were feeling safe again. The town, which for two weeks had resembled a ghost town, with people hunkering down and staying home, was alive again, with people filling the restaurants and shops.

I have to admit that I was feeling calmer as well. I had no idea if the killer was just lying in wait, or if he had left town, having accomplished his goal. Maybe the killer really was from Mexico and had returned home to

217

wait until the police gave up trying to solve the case. I had been slightly outraged when people automatically suspected one of the Mexicans as being responsible for the killings, but now I had to admit it might be so. Or was the killer lulling us into a false sense of security? I mean, the poison was confirmed to be from Mexico, so was it unreasonable to think the killer was from Mexico, too? At some level, we are all biased and racist and too quick to judge, aren't we? Stephanie and I used to talk about prejudice all the time before she died. She, as a Jew, and I, as a black man, always wondered how people who have been the victim of racism and prejudice can also be racist. Her Jewish ancestors were accused of all sorts of outrageous crimes, as are black people today, and yet we are still capable of bigotry against others. She was the least racist person I had ever known, and I had grown to be a better person because of her, but she admitted she had her own set of biases.

Pickleball Tip # 15 Study Your Opponent And Know Your Teammate

Too many players walk out onto the court and have no clue about the strengths and weaknesses of their opponents or partners. Before the first serve, talk to your partner to find out what their best shot is and what their weakest shot is. If your teammate has a better backhand than forehand, make sure you give them room and let them fully extend on those shots. If they have a glaring weakness, discuss the best way to cover them on that shot.

Talk to your partner about your opponents. If one of you knows their tendencies and weaknesses, discuss how to exploit that. It's always a good idea to have a strategy, and to make sure you and your partner are on the same page.

Chapter 16

As two weeks of relative calm stretched into three, I decided it was time to return to normalcy. I thought, as did others, the killer or killers were done and gone. Whatever their reason for killing was, it had been accomplished. It felt like it was safe again and I was itching to play. I think even Butch was ready to have me out of the house. He enjoyed the numerous walks, but I think he was tired of me trying to teach him silly and meaningless dog tricks. He liked the treats that went with training, but he hated to have to work for them and I believe he thought learning to roll over and do the military crawl was demeaning. But the worst thing about me not playing was the constant complaining; my whining and griping was driving Butch crazy. Even the number of walks I made him take was over the top.

"Sorry, Butch," I said, in my most consoling voice. "If you don't want another walk, I understand." We had already been on two, and it was now noon and getting hot. "You stay here, and I'll go out by myself." He stared at me for a moment, then went over to the couch, letting out a loud sigh as if to tell me, *Finally, you get it. Now get the hell out of here and let me nap.*

I grabbed a cold water bottle from the refrigerator and left him without another word. As I left, I had no destination in mind for my walk, but as if by hypnosis, I was drawn to the courts. I'd always shown some signs of ADD, or what some had called "mind-wandering", and as I walked alone my thoughts covered a myriad of topics, ranging from the local climate to world politics and, of course, the wisdom of my move to Rio Viejo. Not surprising, since I really hadn't factored in a murder spree in my relocation plans. The thought of packing my bags and leaving crossed my mind for the umpteenth time. *Screw the lease*, I thought. *I can afford to lose the money.*

Even though part of me thought the murders were over and it was safe, I still had a nagging need to try to figure out what had happened, why it happened, and who was the perpetrator. No one had been eliminated as a possible suspect, so that left a huge list to work with. This is where I could have used Stephanie's help. She was always better at keeping track of all the possible suspects in the murder mysteries we watched together, and she always picked the culprit long before I did. But I had finally come to the realization that I was on my own.

I went over the possibilities in my head.

First was Rory. Rory hated the Royals, didn't hide it, and seemed to have some serious anger issues. Wouldn't it take someone with anger issues to commit murder? I vowed to stay clear of him, assuming he was still in town, which I didn't know, since I had been holed up for so long.

Second was Brian. He also seemed to be an angry guy and quite possibly jealous, and not just about Nancy. I don't think he appreciated playing second fiddle to Nathan.

Little E was an interesting possibility. Oftentimes, it's the quiet one that is behind the crime. Little E was certainly quiet, and he had issues with a few people, mostly Brian, which didn't help since Brian wasn't murdered. But still, there was something about Little E that wasn't right, and he had done prison time, too. Not that prison time means you're a killer or anything, but...

Suddenly, I heard a familiar and wonderful sound.

Ping, ping, ping. Followed by laughter. A lot of laughter at that, which is very common for pickleball, no matter where you play, although on courts that had just experienced murder it seemed a bit odd. I was still at least a quarter of a mile away from the courts, but those sounds carry well.

221

Hence the reason why courts around the country were getting a lot of complaints, especially from residents who found themselves living close to courts that were once tennis courts. For many people, living by a tennis court was a plus, like living near a golf course. Hitting tennis balls with a string racket doesn't make the loud pinging sound of a pickleball hitting a carbon-faced pickleball paddle, and due to the fact that tennis isn't quite as social or as easy to learn as pickleball, the players are generally more serious about their games and there isn't as much yelling or laughter on the court. That, by the way, is also one of the reasons that pickleball is so popular and growing so rapidly.

I wasn't sure what the socially accepted grief period was after a death, let alone after three murders, but clearly here in Rio Viejo, it had passed. It was possible that, because pickleball is so addicting, that social norms were suspended, or it could be that these people just weren't all that upset over losing three of their top players. In any event, as I approached, I could see quite a crowd playing – both new and old faces. I didn't have my paddle, and I was glad I didn't, or I might have joined in. Even though I didn't know the recently deceased well, I thought a few more days without pickleball was appropriate. I did, however, sit down and watch the games taking place.

On the "Royals" court, Little E, Jane, Molly, and Brian were going at it. They were banging away at each other and arguing about calls, as if nothing had changed. Watching with me was Joseph, a decent player and, in a past life, an attorney, who now spent his time playing pickleball or painting landscapes, and Rory, the ex-attorney with serious anger issues. I thought about asking Joseph about my potential legal issues but decided to hold off for now.

We all exchanged fist bumps.

"Are you going to play?" Rory asked me.

"No, I didn't bring my equipment. I just went out for a walk and ended up here. I'll be back out in a few days, I think. Have you been playing?" I asked him.

"I started playing again a few days ago," he replied.

"I have a spare paddle you can borrow," offered Joseph.

"Thanks for the offer, but I think I'll just watch today," I answered. Truth be told, I really wanted to get back out there and almost accepted Joseph's offer. But I stuck with my decision to wait.

"Are you guys going to take on the winners?"

"Joseph and I tried to get in a game with them a little while ago and the shitheads turned us down. Said they were doing a little round robin and didn't want to break up the rhythm."

I frowned and shook my head. "I thought it's open play?" As soon as I said it, I was sorry, as I already knew the answer. Maybe I was trying to stir the pot? If the courts were full and people were waiting, then it should have been four on and four off. I guess even with three Royals dead, the royal attitude lived on. As Rory complained about the Royals, I couldn't escape the thought that I might be sitting next to a killer and this latest snub might trigger a new murder. I gripped my water bottle a little tighter.

But Rory was right, they were being shitheads, and that was all he needed to fire him up. For the next five minutes, he went on a rant, and no one could stop him or calm him down. He rattled off every insult he could think of to describe the Royals, and I must say, he had some I had never heard before, and this is coming from an old gym rat who played basketball with people from every corner of Denver. He didn't stop with insults, though. He commented on every mistake or rude behavior the Royals exhibited. The more he said, the louder he got, and I think he was going out of his way to make sure the Royals heard everything. Rory was clearly enjoying himself, even as his anger grew. He seemed determined to get everything off his chest, and it didn't matter that the Royals had finished their game and were now coming over to get water. Jane and Molly were visibly uncomfortable with Rory and made an effort to steer clear of him and the ruckus he was creating. They settled onto the benches farthest away from him, but not so far that they couldn't hear what he was saying.

There were some new faces in the crowd, and they had a look of shear horror as Rory continued his tirade. I wondered if they were clutching their water bottles close to them as well? Clearly, a few of them had had enough and were collecting their equipment and heading off to the parking lot. Little E and Brian, however, weren't rattled, in fact, quite the opposite. They marched up to Rory and stood there glaring down at him. Not wanting to look up at them, he stood up and smirked.

"You got something to say to us, say it to our faces!" shouted Little E, which surprised me, because he was said to be a soft talker and generally non-confrontational.

Rory laughed. "I will, you shitty, egotistical piece of shit. You and Brian think you are so fucking important and can dictate what goes on around here. I'm sick of it and sick of you."

"Fuck you, Rory," yelled Brian, leaning closer to him.

"I'll fuck you up," responded Rory, with a little spit flying from his lips to Brian's face. "You and your asshole Royals can take a flying fuck. Why don't you all just curl up and die like Nathan. No one will miss you."

There was an audible gasp from a few of the ladies watching the confrontation unfold. I have to admit, even I thought mentioning Nathan's death like that was a bit over the top.

By now, they were in each other's faces and there was no need to yell, but that didn't stop either of them. Players on the courts stopped playing to get a glimpse of what was going on. With spittle flying everywhere, all I could think about was COVID. Would this qualify as a super spreader

224

event? I stepped back, just in case. I also didn't want to catch a wild punch that I was sure was about to be thrown.

Jack came running over from his game on court 1 with a few ladies. He tried to break things up.

"Come on, guys. We're all friends here. Calm down before someone says something they are sorry for later."

Too late for that, I thought.

"Oh, Rory has made it quite clear how he feels," said Little E, "and I couldn't care less about him. He's a little puke with nothing good to say."

"Little?" laughed Rory. "You're a goddamned little fucking dwarf with a Bonaparte complex."

Little E turned bright red. I'm sure it was an insult he experienced quite a bit growing up. He was almost a foot shorter than Rory.

"Fuck you, Rory," he bellowed back, his fist tightening around his paddle. I've seen fights start in the gym with less of an insult.

"Come on, guys. Calm down," pleaded Jack, with his arms outstretched. "Let's all shake hands and make up."

Brian laughed. "I wouldn't shake his hand if you paid me. Fucking neanderthal probably wipes his butt with his bare hand."

That was it. Rory balled his hand into a fist and threw a punch at Brian faster than a hard hit pickleball. I had anticipated something like this and saw it coming before Brian did. The punch landed squarely on the side of his face, knocking his glasses off and sending him to the ground. Little E sprang into action and charged at Rory. Jack tried to block Little E, but was too slow and missed, leaving a clear path. Little E plowed into Rory, while Jack stumbled and fell to the ground, scraping his hands and drawing blood. Little E had to be fifty pounds lighter than Rory, but with surprising speed, he had caught Rory by surprise. Rory went down like an unsuspecting quarterback blindsided by a linebacker. Little E fell down on top of him, driving Rory's head into the dirt. Then he followed up with some punches, but he was so close they didn't look very effective.

Rory, the bigger man, easily shoved Little E off of him and came up swinging and kicking, landing a couple of kicks on Little E, who let out a shrill scream. Rory wasn't satisfied though, as he kept landing punches and kicks on a helpless Little E. He was swinging wildly, arms flailing around like a helicopter. Clearly, Rory was not an accomplished fighter. I was staying back, not wanting to take a wild shot to my face, but Jack regained his composure and, lifting himself off the ground, tried to corral Brian. He was rewarded with a wild whack to the side of his head, and he went down hard; I thought he might be knocked out.

Brian was now getting off the ground, shaking his head from the sucker punch he had taken. He looked a little dizzy. The rest of us just watched the melee, too shocked at the chaos to do anything. Brian shook his head, spraying blood from his nose on anyone standing too close, got his bearings, and made a charge at Rory. Rory, who was still swinging wildly like he was swatting at a swarm of bees, got lucky and landed another punch on Brian's face. But Brian continued forward into Rory, wrapping his arms around him, and effectively halting the barrage of punches. They fell to the ground in each other's arms and rolled around in the dirt.

Finally, Tom jumped into action and grabbed Rory by the collar, pulling him away from Brian. By now, the rest of us had decided to step in, and we created a wall between Rory, Brian, and Little E. The separation seemed to work. The fighters were either too tired to continue, or had realized how crazy they were acting, and they looked like they were going to calm down.

A few of the ladies lit into the fighters, calling them names and expressing their displeasure with what they had just witnessed. By now, all the courts were empty, with everyone congregating around the fighters.

226

Celeste had been on one of the far courts when the fight started. She had joined the group now and was yelling at the men.

"You guys need to cut it out. You're acting like a bunch of school kids." A few others joined in with much harsher words.

"He started it," whined Little E to Celeste.

"Really?" she said, sarcastically. She looked from Rory to Little E and back again. "Children!"

"Yeah? So what? These shits had it coming. You know it," Rory said, hoping to get some agreement from someone in the crowd. "They've been annoying the rest of us since the courts went up. But I, for one, even if no one else here will admit it, am tired of it. You guys don't own the place. You fucking think you are so special." He was getting worked up again and I was worried the fight might continue. "You pretend to be such great players, but you aren't even that good." After that, he seemed to calm down some, as he brushed the dirt off his body.

From what I'd seen since moving there, he was right; the Royals weren't quite as good as they thought they were. They might have won most of the time against the local competition, but they didn't dominate. Regardless of their prowess, it didn't give them the right to be snobs and monopolize court time.

The Royals' behavior wasn't necessarily unique, though. Disagreements on court time are common. Players tend to want to play someone better than them and hate to have to play down. I once heard a woman at the courts in Denver say, "We all start as cucumbers before becoming decent picklers." Okay, maybe that was too cute, or a bad analogy, but the point is we all started somewhere and weren't very good at first. Players typically gravitate to players at the same level or if they are lucky, higher. That's how we all improve. I had seen arguments before about court etiquette and snobby players, but this was the first time I had seen it come to blows. Usually, it ended with people calling each other jerks and walking off in disgust. Maybe some profanity laced in. But then this was also the first time I had experienced murder at a pickleball court, and I suppose emotions and tempers run high in such circumstances.

Staring at the group while they continued to shout insults at each other, I couldn't help but ask myself, *Is one of these people a killer?* Rory was sure acting like one. I wasn't about to take sides in that fight. It could also easily have been Little E or Brian. They all had anger issues. During the fight, I had lost sight of my water bottle. I decided to toss the water out and disinfect it when I got home. You can't be too careful in these situations.

Where was Joe when we needed him? I looked around but didn't see Samantha either. It looked like things were calming down, so I started to relax and sat back on the bench, thinking the fight was over. Jack had gone over to the huge cooler he always brought to the court, pulled out an ice bag, and applied it to the bruise on his cheek that was already swelling up. He also handed out some water bottles to the fighters as he did his best to calm everyone down. I have to give him credit, he stayed calm during the fight and didn't seem too concerned about the beating he took. I would have been furious.

Rory came over, sat down next to me, and let out a big sigh. "I just hate those motherfuckers. I wish they would all drop dead." I didn't respond. My wish was that I had stayed home that morning and missed the whole affair. But then, if wishes came true, Stephanie would have still been alive and we would have still been in Denver.

After a few minutes of relative calm, I asked Rory if he was OK. He nodded and took a drink from the water bottle Jack had given him. Even though I suspected Rory of being the killer, I watched him carefully to see if the water Jack gave him was tainted. When he didn't keel over, I breathed a sigh of relief.

No one took sides, and just about everyone dished out criticism to all the participants in the fight. One lady I had never met decided to lecture all three men.

"You people should be ashamed of yourselves. Pickleball is supposed to be fun. I'm disgusted right now. You should all be banned from playing here."

I could tell a few people wanted to agree but were clearly intimidated, so they kept their feelings to themselves. A few people left, while others started to wander back to the courts to play.

Brian walked over to us, still shaken up. He was wiping the blood off his nose and straightening his bent glasses. I was concerned he wanted another piece of Rory. "I should fucking sue your ass for this," he said, as he held up his broken glasses. "And you're lucky I don't have you arrested for breaking my nose."

"Your nose isn't broken, you wimp," replied Rory. He took a bill from his pants and tossed it on the ground, adding, "And here's ten dollars for some new glasses."

"They cost a lot more than that, you cheapskate."

Rory laughed. "They look like dime store glasses to me."

Peggy, the fiery redhead who, according to gossip, had a thing for Brian and was a borderline alcoholic, marched over to Rory and started yelling at him about his behavior. Rory just laughed again and held up a hand, letting her know he wasn't listening. Which only infuriated her more.

"You think you are so special, Rory. Well, I know you are just an ambulance-chasing shyster lawyer. By the way, Nancy told me before she died what a dick you are."

"Did Nancy also tell you that her boyfriend Nathan was convicted of manslaughter in Canada, and I got him off with a light sentence?"

"She told me you ripped him off on legal fees."

"That bitch didn't know shit. That dick Nathan died owing me thousands. He never fucking paid his bills, and I wasn't the only one he stiffed."

This was news about Nathan I didn't know. Not only did he have a manslaughter conviction, but he hadn't paid the attorney who represented him. I hate to speak ill of the dead, but now I had more reason to dislike him, aside from being an arrogant Royal. I turned to Tom with a questioning look to see if he knew any of this. He shrugged, as if to say it was new to him, too. I got up and walked over to Tom, not wanting to be near Rory and Brian if things escalated again, and it felt like they might.

"Did you know that stuff about Nathan?" I whispered to Tom.

He whispered back that all he knew was that Nathan and Rory had some history together, going back to their days in Montreal. He thought they had been friends at one time in their past, but something had happened. Before Nathan's death, they had barely tolerated each other. He couldn't shed any other light on the dispute.

"I never got too close to either of them. I found them both to be intolerable." He frowned and dropped his voice even lower. "Honestly, if all the Royals moved away, I wouldn't be upset, and that goes for Rory, too."

Then the argument started heating up again.

"Well, that is just like the dick you are," snarled Brian. "Talking bad about Nathan when he isn't here to defend himself."

"The guy was a useless pathetic drunk and killed some kids in a car crash. My guess is you're just like him, and that's why you're defending him now. You stink at pickleball, and you just kiss up to those fucks so you can play and hang out with them like a sad little mutt. You probably sucked Nathan's dick, too."

230

Rory started to laugh again and didn't notice Brian lunging at him, knocking him off the bench and onto his back in the dirt. The fight was back on, and this time it was looking to be more violent. Tom and I sprang into action and tried to separate the two, but Brian was on top of Rory throwing punches before we could reach them. I tried to grab Brian by his shirt to pull him away, but it was like wrestling a giant octopus, with arms flying all over the place. I took a wild punch in the jaw from Rory, intended for Brian, that stunned me and set me back on my heels. Tom also tried to grab Brian but couldn't hold on and fell down next to me. With Tom and I on the ground, Brian was free to unleash another barrage to Rory's face and stomach. The sound of fist to face was alarming, and even more scary was a solid shot to Rory's stomach that clearly winded him. He doubled over, struggling to catch his breath. I regained my footing and came at Brian again like a linebacker, knocking him back a few feet. He hit the ground hard and looked back up at me. If looks could kill, as they say.

Out of the corner of my eye, I saw Joe riding up on his bicycle. Seeing the melee, he rode to within a few feet of us, coming to a screeching stop, while simultaneously dismounting the bicycle. I was impressed with his skill. He jumped into the fracas just as Little E prepared to attack Rory, even though Rory was down on his knees still trying to catch his breath. Joe stepped in front of Little E, blocking him from doing more damage to Rory. Joe was an intimidating presence, standing at least a foot taller than Little E, and Little E quickly backed off. Joe stood there like a teacher breaking up a school yard fight.

"What's going on here?" he demanded.

William, who probably hadn't heard half of what had gone down, was first to speak up. "Brian and E were fighting with Rory and Tom and Al tried to break it up."

"Rory started it," said Jane.

Rory had finally regained his breath enough to speak. "Stay out of it, bitch."

Accusations went back and forth, and by now, no one had a clear idea how the fight actually started. Tom and I had seen it all but remained silent.

Finally, Joe had heard enough and yelled over the crowd, "Everyone shut up. The next guy to throw a punch spends the night in jail."

"You're not a cop here," screamed Brian. "Mind your own business."

"No, I'm not a cop anymore, but I'm helping the sheriff with the investigation. We can either end this now, or I can kick your ass into tomorrow. Maybe I should just let the Sheriff lock the three of you up for assault and public fighting."

Brian snarled but didn't say another word.

"He started it," yelled Rory, pointing at Brian.

"Did I not make myself clear?" said Joe, raising his voice again. "I don't fucking care who started the fight. It ends now. You guys are amazing. There is a god damned murder investigation going on and you guys are fighting over who has the biggest dick."

"That wasn't what it was about," said Little E.

Joe rolled his eyes and shook his head. "Enough. Clean yourselves up and get out of here. I mean it. If I hear about you guys fighting again, I'll ask the Sheriff to shut down the courts as a public nuisance and put a lock on the gates."

That brought out a number of complaints from people saying this was between the fighters and no one else needed to be punished. Reminded me of when I was a kid, and rather than try to figure out who was at fault, our parents punished both of us. It wasn't fair then either, but I wasn't going to bring that up.

"Really?" Joe responded. "You people are pathetic. We have three people dead, these yahoos fighting, and all you care about is your precious pickleball?"

But the crowd wasn't ready to let them go. Someone shouted, "Ban them from the courts. We weren't involved."

Joe shook his head. He didn't care for pickleball and never had. He hated that his wife was so involved in the game and wasn't shy about expressing his opinion. "I personally don't care if they tear down the courts and build a garden."

That brought out a bunch of grumbles and complaints. I groaned but had no desire to argue with Joe.

Joe turned to Brian, Little E and Rory, "I'm not going to bother asking you idiots to kiss and make up. I don't care if you ever bury the hatchet, but I am going to tell you to get your stuff and go home," he paused to see if they were going to heed his advice. When they didn't make a move he shouted, "NOW!"

More grumbling, but I could see no one wanted to challenge Joe. He looked like he could handle himself in a fight and wouldn't take no for answer.

Pickleball Tip # 16 – When To Attack

Create openings to attack the ball by moving your opponent around and keeping them from getting comfortable, rather than trying to attack a ball below the net that will either hit the net or sail wide or long. The object of this is to force your opponent to hit a weak drive, a pop-up volley, or a dink, giving you an opportunity from the NVZ line to hit down on the ball, either at their feet, or at an angle they can't reach.

Hitting to the weaker player is one way to gain the advantage. Know your opponent's weakness and aim for it. For example, the backhand. Many players will have trouble hitting a backhand drop from the baseline or hitting a dink without popping it up for an easy put-away. Generally, hitting a ball low to your opponent's feet will also generate a pop up, as many players have trouble with short hops.

When you are at the NVZ line and your opponent hits you a weak shot that you can hit with force in a downward motion, don't waste the opportunity by letting the ball get lower, forcing you to hit a defensive block, and giving them another chance to take back control of the point.

Chapter 17

Brian, Little E, and Rory were the first to leave, but within a few minutes other people started to follow them to the parking lot. There was more grumbling, but I couldn't tell if they were more upset with Joe or the fighters. Joe hadn't told everyone to leave, just the brawlers, but I guess no one was in the mood to play anymore. Jack was packing up his supplies and asked me if I wanted a ride home. I declined.

Joe walked over to me and asked me if I had driven to the courts.

"No, I walked. I wasn't going to play today. I just wanted to see what was going on and if people had started to return to the courts yet."

"I'll walk back with you, if you don't mind," he said, as he bent over to pick up his bike.

"Sure."

"The pickleball players were back here a few days ago," he informed me, shaking his head with disgust. "Pickleball players are just so fanatical. I don't understand it."

"Including your wife?" I joked.

"Yeah, including Samantha," he laughed. "That's all she talks about these days. She would have been here today if she wasn't getting her hair done. I am so tired of hearing about pickleball. Who did this or who did that. Who slighted whom or who hit who with a ball. And if she isn't playing, she's watching videos on YouTube on how to play better. Now she is even thinking of going to clinics and tournaments."

"It's addicting," I admitted.

"I wish it had never been invented. And who names a sport after a dog?"

"Actually, it was named after the left-over oarsmen on a crew team. It's called the pickle boat."

"Huh? I thought it was named after a dog."

"The dog story is a good one, but wrong," I corrected him.

"Who cares? Dumb name, dumb sport."

"So, you aren't a fan?"

"Brilliant deduction, Holmes," he said with a grin. "I guess I've made my dislike of pickleball pretty clear."

I thought so, but I wasn't going to hold it against him.

"You have to admit, it's great exercise," I managed to say, in defense of the sport. "For me, especially after I lost my wife last year, it has been very helpful."

"Sorry about that. That had to be rough."

"Yeah," I said, trying not to look or sound too gloomy. "Still is, but I'm doing better, thanks."

Our route took us through the parking lot. As we approached, we saw a number of people still milling about. Jane and Molly were talking with Brian and Little E. I was worried the fight had resumed, but I didn't see Rory anywhere. Brian was upset and waving his arms around again. We headed their way, and when they noticed us, they waved us over.

"Something wrong?" asked Joe.

"Yes, there is definitely something fucking wrong," screamed Brian. "Someone slashed my tires."

"Did you see who did it?"

"No. But it had to be Rory."

"You don't know that," said Joe shaking his head.

"Who else would do that?"

I looked around. Across the street, I spotted Roger and Richard sitting in deck chairs, watching us. They looked amused.

"Let's not make any wild accusations," Joe demanded. He turned to a few players who were walking by and asked, "Did any of you see anyone near Brian's car?"

Everyone shook their heads.

"It was Rory, I tell you. He left before me, and when I got here, my tires were flat."

Joe and I walked over to look, and sure enough, two of Brian's tires had huge gouges in them. The only thing that could have caused that was a large knife.

"Did anyone see Rory go near Brian's' car?

No one said they had. I whispered to Joe to look across the street. "Those are the two guys that came over to the courts complaining about us making too much noise."

He nodded. "I know them." He started across the street and told everyone to stay put. Joe spoke with them for a few minutes and returned to us. "They didn't see anyone. Brian, I think you should make a police report and get a tow truck. Stay away from Rory. No one saw him near your car, and I doubt he had time to do this between the time he left and when you got here."

"Bullshit," Brian snarled back.

Joe gave him a stern look and Brian backed down, then took out his cell phone.

Joe turned to me and said, "Let's go."

Once we were out of earshot from Brian and the rest of the group, he said to me, "I think it was Roger and Richard. Obviously, I can't prove anything, so I didn't accuse them, but I made it clear that we were going to keep an eye on them."

"That would have been my guess too. They really hate pickleball." Then another thought occurred to me. "Um, Joe, do you think maybe they were involved in the murders?"

"It's crossed my mind a couple times. This latest episode makes me more suspicious of them, but I've got no evidence yet. We might need to get some DNA and fingerprints from them at some point. I'll also see if the Sheriff wants a formal interview with them."

We walked quietly for a couple of minutes, then I asked Joe, "What do you do for fun?"

"Golf, bike riding, exercise, fishing. If I wasn't retired, I wouldn't have enough time for everything."

For me, it was the other way around. After selling the business and losing my wife, I realized I didn't have much else besides pickleball and Butch in my life. I thought moving would give me a fresh start, but I wasn't so sure that was the right choice anymore.

I still had a brother and his family back in Colorado, but we weren't that close, and they didn't understand why I left town. Especially to live in a place rife with illegal immigrants and drug trafficking, or so they thought.

"So, when you retired, you were a homicide detective?"

"Yep. My last ten years on the Phoenix PD were as a homicide detective. I thought about sticking around and continuing up the ladder, but I was burned out."

"And now here you are again, working on a murder case. Not much of a retirement, but at least this is right up your alley."

"Yep. If the Sheriff didn't want my help, I'd stay out of it, but I can tell you I'd be watching Samantha like a hawk until the killer was found."

"What brought you to Rio Viejo?"

He thought about it for a moment. "It's nice and quiet here. Until this, I don't think they'd had a murder case in ten years. We liked the scenery here, and there's some great fishing nearby, with lots of trails for bike riding and hiking." He paused and thought for a moment, then added, "And on my last case I took a bullet in the gut and Samantha convinced me to hang it up. She didn't want to be a police widow."

"How does she feel about you working this case?"

"Not good, but she loves it here and she loves pickleball, so I need to make it safe for her. The Sheriff is an old friend and hasn't had to deal with this kind of thing before, and he doesn't really have the staff. Hopefully, I can do some digging for him, ask some questions, and then hand it off to him."

"Are we in any danger?"

"Good question. The killer seems to have gone quiet, so that's good, but I don't have any clue as to why. Maybe he's done and left town, or maybe just done. I will share a little with you, but you need to promise to keep it to yourself." He stopped walking and stared at me, with a serious look on his face.

"Sure. Of course," I assured him. "I don't really know a lot of people here yet anyway."

"You might have heard that the lab reports came back. Nancy had traces of the same poison in her that killed Anna and Nathan, but in her case, the cause of death was strangulation."

I had heard this from Martin, but I didn't want to burn that bridge, so I acted like it was news to me.

"Wow."

"You know we exhumed Nathan's body, right?"

"Um. I guess I did hear something about that."

If he was testing me, he didn't let on.

"We did. They all had the same poison in their blood."

"Why strangle Nancy if she was poisoned?"

"It's possible the killer screwed up and didn't give her enough to kill her, only knock her out, so to finish the job he strangled her. Or he always intended to strangle her and used the poison to incapacitate her. We just don't know."

"But you know she was strangled?"

"Absolutely."

Thinking of every crime novel or movie I had ever read, I asked the obvious. "Fingerprints?"

"No. We checked the water bottles, glasses, doorknobs etc. Nothing that shouldn't be there."

"So, the killer is careful." I said. The thought sent chills down my spine.

"Extremely careful and thorough. We also have no prints from the water bottles that Nathan and Anna used on the courts."

"Do you mind me asking questions?" I asked, afraid I was going too far.

"No. Who knows? Maybe one of your questions will trigger something I missed."

We kept walking, and occasionally he waved or said hello to someone he knew.

"So, other than the obvious connection that they were pickleball players living in the same town, is there anything else that Nathan and Anna had in common?" I wondered how much of the rumor mill had made it to Joe.

He laughed. "Well from what I'm learning about Nathan, he was a total shitbag and a ladies' man, with plenty of enemies. He may or may not have had an affair with Anna, as well as his relationship with Nancy."

"But if he cheated on Nancy, I see why Nancy might want to kill Anna, or Anna might want to kill Nancy, but why kill Nathan?" After I asked, I realized that was dumb. The jilted lover kills the cheat and his paramour. "Never mind. But if that's the case, who killed Anna, since Nancy was already dead when Anna collapsed? Another lover in the mix?"

"Sounding like a soap opera here."

I thought it was time to talk about the Royals. "Speaking of soap operas, you know all about the Royals, right?"

"I do. Samantha has complained about them often."

"Motive for murder?" I asked.

"I've seen a lot of dumb reasons people kill, but I have to say I've never seen snobbery as a motive for murder."

"Then what?"

"I don't want to speculate and cast any aspersions on anyone," he said, after a long pause.

"But…" I tried to encourage him to continue.

"I still have lots of questions. Like, have you seen any of the players from Mexico lately?"

"You mean Jesus or Julio?" He nodded. "Um, no, I haven't seen them since this all started."

Then I remembered seeing Jesus bolt from the courts after Anna went down. As far as I knew, he hadn't returned. I could see where this was going. Joe may not have tied a motive to them and the deceased, but they were suspicious in their absence, especially since the poison was found to be of Mexican origin.

"Someone I interviewed said that Jesus was there when Anna went down and left before me or the Sheriff could interview him. Did you know that?"

I fessed up. "Yes, now that you mention it, I do recall seeing him there and might have seen him leave."

"I wish you would have said something earlier," he admonished me.

"Sorry."

"Hmm," he grunted, "I hope you aren't trying to protect anyone."

"Why would I do that?"

"You tell me." He seemed perturbed with me.

"I have no connections to them, or anyone else here, for that matter. I'm not trying to protect anyone. It just slipped my mind."

He grunted again. "Do you know anything about the other Mexicans that play here?"

"I'm sure I know less than you. I've met a few people here and some were from Mexico."

"Okay. Assume I don't know any of these people. Tell me about everyone you know from Mexico."

"There is this guy I remember meeting named Larry who splits his time between Mexico, California, and here, and there's Eddie who lives here, but is an importer of Mexican produce. I think Jesus or maybe Julio is an attorney. I can't remember now. One of them is in produce and the other an attorney." I was getting flustered. "When you meet so many people in a short period of time, it's easy to get them confused."

"Okay, I get it. Have you seen any of them in the past two weeks?"

"No."

Clearly, he was trying to connect one of the Mexicans to the crime. He didn't seem to buy the idea that they were killed because they were Royals.

"Have you seen any drugs at the courts?"

"No. You think this is drug related?"

He just shrugged, but it seemed like he did. Were Anna, Nathan, and Nancy involved in some drug smuggling operation, and I just didn't see it? It was certainly possible that things were going on that I didn't know about. I wasn't sure if this new theory made me feel better or not. Killing someone over a drug deal gone bad seemed more likely to me than killing someone over a pickleball dispute. Although, after the violence that day, I was starting to rethink that conclusion.

"You pickleball people are fanatical, and the intensity of emotions here is over the top, but I'm having a hard time connecting these murders to pickleball. I'm more inclined to believe there is a connection to the Mexican drug trade. The Sheriff does too. He's looking into cartel ties to the area to see if any names come up. Are you sure you haven't noticed any drugs at the court?"

"You mean people buying or using?"

"Either. I'm curious if these people were involved in moving drugs over the border."

Before moving here, my friends had warned me about drugs coming over the border, and they couldn't understand why I would put myself at risk. Had they been right?

"No one has offered to sell me any drugs since I got here, and I can't say that I noticed any kind of shady things going on."

"It's possible these guys were bringing stuff in and transporting it to other parts of the state or country, rather than trying to sell to a bunch of old people," he responded.

I wasn't offended by the age comment, as he was basically right. Most of the players there were old.

I racked my brain to remember what people had told me about the different Mexican players. I remembered that Larry, who played often but wasn't a regular, told everyone he was an artist, but no one had ever seen any of his work. Rumor had it that he also worked for a cartel. I hated to spread unsubstantiated rumors but told Joe what I had heard about him. I also told him about Eddie, who said he worked for an importer of Mexican produce, which made sense, since he brought fruit to the courts to share. But now that I thought about it, it seemed like the perfect cover if you wanted to smuggle drugs into the US.

On the one hand, if you could divorce yourself from the obvious danger, this was all very interesting. I wanted to be helpful but really had nothing else to add. In fact, I thought I may have made things worse by giving Joe more names of people who could have possibly been guilty. The drug angle hadn't come to mind before, but it made more sense than it being pickleball related. It's true I had seen my share of arguments and fights at our Denver courts and had seen a couple since moving here, but they always seemed rather petty, and typically cooled off pretty quickly.

The fight today was about as violent as any I had seen before, but then it turned out these guys had some history outside of pickleball.

We reached my house, and I didn't invite Joe in. I had had my fill of murder mystery intrigue for one day, and I had nothing else to offer. Joe got on his bike and started to ride off, but then circled back.

"Al, do me a favor and keep your eyes and ears open, but don't go questioning people, especially the people we discussed today. If one of these people is involved, I don't want you getting into any danger or possibly scaring off any suspects. Just pay attention and call me." He handed me a card with his name and number on it, though I thought I already had one. I agreed and went in to find Butch sleeping on the couch, with his head on the pillow. He looked up at me when I entered and then went back to sleep.

So, Joe suspected the Mexicans because of possible drug connections and the fact that they weren't anywhere to be seen. I could understand that theory, but up until then I had been leaning toward Rory. He had extreme anger issues and his disdain for all things Royal was disturbing. Today's fight did nothing to dissuade me. But now I had to add Roger and Richard to the mix. Joe and I both suspected them of slashing Brian's tires, so they apparently had no problem with violent acts. Maybe murder, as well? Whoever it was, they were calculating and careful. That didn't sound like Rory, who just seemed angry and impulsive, and there were plenty of others in the group that fit that description as well. I thought if it was the Mexicans and drug cartel related, they would have just shot the targets, none of this witches' brew crap. Or was I getting that from TV? I really had no firsthand knowledge of drug cartel protocol. The killer knew enough not to leave fingerprints behind, though. If I was really considering all possibilities, why couldn't that be Joe? He hated pickleball and Samantha hated the Royals, and if anyone knew how to commit a crime like this without getting noticed, it would be a homicide detective. And then, of course, there were all the love triangles. Could this have just been a case of lust and revenge?

I tried to recall anything and everything from the day that Nathan was murdered. Did I see anyone touch Nathan's water bottle? Did I see Roger and or Richard hanging out? And what about Anna? How did she fit in? I think someone had to have had access to their water bottles in order to poison them, and it almost assuredly had to have happened at the courts. But nothing came to mind. If it happened there, I must have missed it just like everyone else there. The killer was good, and that shattered any sense of security.

Pickleball Tip # 17– Be Ready

It may seem obvious to hear that you should always be in the proper ready position, but so many players are caught flat-footed or with their paddle in the wrong position. The game is infinitely easier if you are in the right place on the court and are prepared for a ball to be hit to you. Being ready can mean different things in different situations.

After hitting a service return, for example, you should move toward the NVZ and do a split step when your opponent is about to hit, so that you aren't moving when the ball comes to you, but you should also make sure your feet are about shoulder width apart, knees slightly bent, with your weight on the balls of your feet. Your paddle should be out in front of you, facing forward, and if you are a righty, the tip should be around 11-12 o'clock. If you are a lefty, it should be around 1 or 2 o'clock. Assume that every shot you make will come back, so don't let yourself or your paddle be out of position.

Chapter 18

I was awakened the following morning by the sensation of someone washing my face. It was Butch, and he was determined to wake me up. I gently pushed him off me and dried my face with the covers. My head felt like it was going to explode. A familiar feeling, but one I hadn't had in a while.

Right after Stephanie passed, I had fallen into a deep depression, and rather than seek help, I decided to self-medicate. Seeing her struggle to fight off cancer was devastating to watch and losing her felt like more than I could handle. It didn't seem fair that I was still around and she wasn't, even though there was nothing I, or anyone else, could do to save her. We were so in love and dependent on each other that it didn't seem possible to live without her. So, I started to drink and smoke pot. Copious amounts of both, by the way. At first it was a couple of shots of tequila, and then it grew to three, then four, then five; all the time adding in a few puffs of pot. That's the thing with alcohol and pot, the more you do, the more you need to ease the pain.

I knew where I was headed, and it didn't matter to me. We didn't have kids and my parents had already passed. Although my brother lived nearby, he had his own life to live and didn't need me as a burden. And besides that, we weren't all that close anyway. I would have continued down that rabbit hole to self-destruction until I killed myself, had it not been for two things. One, I hated the mornings after my binges, and two, Butch. I had promised Stephanie I wouldn't let anything bad happen to him, and I realized that was what I was doing. So, I quit. Well, mostly.

The revelation came one morning when I found myself on the bathroom floor, lying in my own vomit. My head ached and I could barely move. Somehow, I managed to get up, wash my face, and look in the mirror. I had a huge bruise on my forehead, and I looked like shit. As I stared at the stranger in the mirror, I saw Butch in the reflection. He was sitting in the doorway, staring at me with his sad brown eyes and moaning. As I picked up my phone, it dawned on me that I couldn't remember the last two days, which meant Butch hadn't been fed for two days. I don't know if he was worried or just hungry, but it shook me to my core. I couldn't do this to Butch, or the memory of Stephanie.

For the next month, I didn't drink or smoke. I spent my time with Butch getting my life back together. We took walks until he told me he was done, and then I ran until I was back in shape. I even ventured back onto the pickleball courts, and within a week I was competing with the better players. Another nice benefit to drinking less is that when you do drink, it doesn't take much to get a buzz. I'm now what you would call a "cheap date". Two shots and I'm buzzed; three and I'm slightly inebriated. I hadn't had four drinks of anything in one night since that episode. Until Rio Viejo, that is.

I thought I had taken three shots of tequila the night before, but it might have been four or five. I also vaguely remembered beer and pot being involved. I kept some pot handy to help me sleep on occasion. Deep sleep had been elusive since Stephanie died.

To the best of my memory, Joe had walked home with me, and after he left, I grabbed a beer and cooked up a frozen pizza. I shared it – the pizza that is - with Butch, and we watched an old movie about drug lords and cartels. After the second beer, I switched over to tequila and pot. Somehow, I made it from the couch to my bed, where I eventually found myself being washed by Butch.

I cursed myself and vowed that it was just going to be a one-night bender, as I downed a couple of Advil and a huge glass of water. I let Butch out to do his business and filled a bowl with his favorite kibble, then sat down to wait for the pain reliever to kick in. Fortunately, this was nothing like my last foray into a drunken stupor. This time I didn't have a bruise on my face, and there was no vomit anywhere to be seen.

The Advil did the trick. The headache started to subside, and I was suddenly famished. I looked in the refrigerator and there were a couple of pieces of pizza left over. I didn't even bother to heat it up. I took a bite, and it tasted really good. When the phone rang, I had to search for it in the couch cushion.

"Hello?" I said, with a mouthful of food.

"Al, is that you?"

"Yeah, hang on a sec," I said, trying to swallow quickly. "Sorry, I was just having a piece of pizza. Is this Tom?" I still hadn't programmed my phone, so when someone called, I had no advance clue as to who it was.

"Yes indeed," he answered quite quickly. "Pizza for breakfast?"

"Isn't that the breakfast of champions?" I responded with a chuckle.

"I have had my share of pizzas for breakfast." Then he added, "And sometimes with a morning beer."

"I'll have to try that sometime," I answered, as if I had never done such a thing, when in fact I had eaten more than my share of cold pizza and beer for breakfast. "What's up?"

I really hoped he wasn't going to inform me about another murder. He sounded too cheerful for that kind of news.

"Calling to see if you could join us for some pickleball. I've got Stuart and Sam and we could use a good player as a fourth to fill it out." I was immediately honored by this, for two reasons. One, he considered me enough of a friend to invite me, and two, he thought I was a good player. Before I could answer, he added, "Things are a little quiet right now because of the fight yesterday, so we should be able to get a court to ourselves." Keeping a closed group was always tough if there was anyone waiting to play, but if it wasn't busy, it could work.

"Yeah, that would be great. When?"

"How does thirty minutes sound?"

"That should give the Advil plenty of time to work its magic and even a few minutes to take Butch around the block."

"Advil?" he asked. "You OK?"

"A little too much tequila last night, but I'm OK now."

"Did you have a party?" I could sense he might feel hurt at being left out.

"No party, unless you think sitting home alone with a frozen pizza, a bottle of tequila, and Butch is a party."

He laughed. "I get it. Been there and done that. With all the shit around here right now, it's a wonder we all aren't drinking ourselves to death." There was a long pause as we both considered the poison drinks killing people. "Um, that was unintended. Probably not funny."

"It's OK. Fortunately, my poison last night was anejo from Don Julio and it only resulted in a headache."

"Listen, come on over as soon as you can. Bring Butch. He won't get into any trouble over there."

I thought about it. Butch was usually pretty good around people and other dogs. If I tied him to the benches in the shade, I'm sure he would be fine.

"OK. Good idea. We'll start over there in a couple minutes."

I quickly changed into my pickleball clothes, which consisted of baggy blue shorts and a white t-shirt. No one ever accused me of being a fashionista, unlike the ladies who showed up in the latest high fashion tennis skirts or colorful leggings. One of their outfits could pay for my entire pickleball wardrobe. I filled up a couple water bottles, one for me and one for Butch, and tossed them into my shoulder bag. I threw in a water bowl, along with a bag of dog treats, and made my way to the door. As soon as he saw the treats go in the bag, Butch was up and ready to go.

By the time we arrived at the court, the group was waiting for me and already warming up. It was still early and there were only a few players on the other courts. Of course, with the brouhaha the day before, it was anyone's guess how many people would even show up to play. I was pleased that the brawlers weren't there, though it was still early.

I used a carabiner to clip Butch's leash to the bench and placed his water bowl within reach. I handed him a couple of dog treats and hustled over to the court to join the others. I carried my water bottles with me onto the court. We still had no clue who the killer was, and I wasn't taking any chances. I noticed a few unattended water bottles on the bench, and at the risk of sounding paranoid, I told my group that they might not want to leave them unguarded. It didn't take much persuading.

They were ready to start, but allowed me a few minutes to warm up, during which I got some good-natured ribbing about my overindulgence the night before. I guess Tom didn't think he needed to keep that a secret. After a few minutes of warm up, the group got bored and demanded we start the game.

"We've seen you play. You don't need to warm up."

We played a spirited game, with Tom and I beating Sam and Stuart easily. No one was waiting for our court, so we rotated partners and played another game. That time, Sam and I beat Tom and Stuart. They were all good games, but I clearly had the advantage, even with my hangover. But by the time the third game was under way with Stuart as my partner, I was losing focus. I kept glancing over to Butch to make sure he was okay, and I watched the others as they came and went to see if anyone looked suspicious. They all did. The crowd had grown, and all the courts were busy now. Joe showed up with Samantha during our third game and he looked suspicious too, but that might have been because he was suspicious of everyone else. I started missing easy shots and my lack of concentration showed.

After a particularly easy shot that I missed wide by five feet, Tom approached me at the net.

"Something wrong, Al?" he asked. "You don't usually miss those shots."

I shrugged. "Yeah. I'm missing some easy ones." I didn't want to blame my poor play on any excuses as most of us do, but it was clear my mind was elsewhere.

"Effects from the tequila last night?" he asked, trying to give me a valid excuse.

I decided to take it. It seemed better than admitting I was paranoid the killer was there and could be targeting one of us. Glancing at Joe as he watched us play, I thought what a perfect cover that would be for a killer. He certainly would know how to cover up a murder, or murders. He had a dislike for all things pickleball and knew that his wife didn't like Nathan or Nancy. Maybe he was the killer, and he had inserted himself into the investigation to avoid being a suspect himself.

Giving it more thought, I was sure he had been there for each murder. No one paid much attention to him because he wasn't a player, so he could have easily spiked the drinks without anyone noticing. Then, to obfuscate the investigation, he indicates the Mexicans, conveniently absent, as key suspects. He ingratiates himself with me so that if I learn anything useful, or possibly incriminating, he can squelch it quickly. This seemed like an entirely plausible scenario. Granted, I'd seen this same plot in more than one murder mystery, but aren't those stories usually inspired by actual crimes? It was no wonder why I hadn't slept well the night before and couldn't concentrate on the game now. It didn't help that every time I glanced his way, he was staring at me. It's not paranoia if they really are out to get you, right?

We came off the court, and although we wanted to keep rotating partners and continue playing, the courts were all full, so we surrendered the court to a group with their paddles in the rack. I wondered, if the dead Royals had been more considerate about sharing courts, would they still be alive? The group coming on only had three players, so Sam stayed on while Tom, Stuart, and I took a break and sat down with Butch. He was getting bored but was behaving perfectly. A few more treats insured he would continue to behave. Jack came over and sat by me, then started making small talk while giving Butch plenty of his attention.

"I was wondering where Jesus and Julio have been lately," he said.

"I don't know," I replied. "I only know them from playing here." Not only had they conveniently disappeared when the killings started, but the killings had stopped after they left, making me rethink who I should be afraid of.

"Eddie is still gone too, isn't he?"

"I don't know. I haven't seen him," I answered, wondering why Jack was bringing this up. It seemed like he was trying to create some suspicion. Eddie was in the Mexican produce business, so he could have a very logical reason for being away. But on the other hand, his absence and connection to Mexico made him a suspect too. The way Jack and Joe had been quick to lay blame on the Mexicans didn't sit well with me, but I couldn't escape the logic. Was I falling victim to the same kind of bigotry and racism I had experienced in my life? I didn't want to fall into that trap.

"Jack, have you seen any indication of drug use or dealing by any of them?"

He thought for a moment. "No. Can't say that I have."

"And did you ever see Nathan, Anna, or Nancy do drugs?"

"No. What are you getting at?"

"Just that it seems everyone wants to point the finger at our Hispanic friends and assume this is all drug related. Seems too easy and too obvious."

"Hmm," he said.

My mind continued twisting itself in knots. I wanted answers. Joe was still watching me, but after a brief wave in my direction he wandered over to court 1 to watch Samantha play. While I had been playing, Little E, Jane, Molly, and Brian had started to play. I guess they had all recovered from the excitement the day before, but they didn't appear to be getting along really well. I could see some animated discussions taking place and soon it had devolved into yelling. The riffraff, as people like William called us, loved it when the Royals went at each other. I think I even saw William smile when the yelling started. Joe must have heard it too. He came over to stand by us and get a better view.

"Hit me again, E, and I'll make you sorry," yelled Brian.

"It wasn't on purpose, Brian. Lighten up, you pussy."

"Fuck you, Little E. You were aiming for my head."

"If I was aiming at your head, I would have hit it."

"You were aiming for me, but you aren't that good you little shit."

William laughed when Brian called Ethelwolf little. "He hates it when people call him little," he commented. "Just watch, things are about to get interesting."

I was a bit appalled at William's attitude. Instead of being disgusted by the arguing and violence that had taken place, he seemed to be relishing it.

"Come on, you guys, settle down. It's just a game," pleaded Jane. "Haven't we had enough drama out here lately?"

"Tell that to the little dickhead. He's the one head hunting," replied Brian.

"Shut the fuck up, Brian. Didn't you take enough of a hit from Rory?"

"You shut the fuck up. I beat the shit out of Rory, and you don't see him out here today, do you? I can do the same to you."

What I saw yesterday was far from a beat down by Brian over Rory.

"Can we just finish the game?" pleaded Molly.

"No. I'm done pretending Brian is a nice guy, and I'm done playing with him."

Little E started toward the gate to leave.

Brian started laughing and calling him "Chicken Little" and a poor sport. "You were losing anyway. That's why you tried to hit me. And by the way, maybe we should tell everyone how you threw me under the bus on those land projects in Florida. I lost a fortune and almost went to jail because you're a coward and a terrible partner. The whole deal was your idea, and like the little shit that you are, you tried to make me the fall guy."

Little E turned back, his face red as a beet. "That's a fucking lie and you know it. I should sue you for libel and defamation of character."

"Do it. Maybe we should tell everyone how you lost your wife, too. She was cheating on you 'cause you weren't man enough for her."

Brian had barely finished the sentence before Little E was running at him with his paddle in the air. Brian saw him coming and easily dodged the first swing of the paddle, but Little E anticipated that and quickly brought it

256

back around and whacked Brian on the side of the head. We could hear the thud from the benches where we were watching. Jane and Molly stood back, probably afraid to get hit, but the fight was already over. Brian staggered for a moment before dropping to his knees. A little blood appeared on his temple. Little E backed off, appearing shocked at what he had done, but then stood over Brian, taunting him.

Rick, our resident paramedic, was playing on the court next to them, and he ran over to assist Brian. William was laughing and clapping his hands, thrilled and entertained by the fight. Tom, Joe, Stuart, and I rushed onto the court, getting there in time to prevent any more violence.

Brian tried to get up, but Rick convinced him to stay down as he took a look at the wound. It didn't look too serious to me, but Rick wanted to make sure that Brian didn't have a concussion and wouldn't pass out if he stood up too fast. We ushered Little E away from them. He looked a bit stunned.

"Just relax, Brian," said Rick. "How many fingers am I holding up?"

"Two," Brian replied, correctly. I didn't know enough about concussions to know if that was a definitive test or not, but it seemed convincing to me. Another player named Mary came onto the court with Jack. She had some wet wipes, and Jack had a first aid kit and some ice wrapped in a towel. They wiped off the blood and had Brian hold the ice pack to his head. He was already looking better, although clearly still stunned.

"What the hell, Ethelwolf. Are you crazy?" he blurted out when he saw the bloody towel.

Little E wasn't looking shocked anymore. Now he was looking defiant. "I'm sorry I hit you, but you kind of had it coming."

Kind of? I thought. *What does he mean by that?*

That set Brian off. "Are you fucking kidding me? You are out of line and out of control. I didn't deserve this."

"You shouldn't have been talking about me like that," said Little E, in more of a whine than a statement.

"I didn't say anything that wasn't true," replied Brian, still dabbing at his wound with the ice pack.

"OK, guys," said Joe in a stern, commanding voice, "I think you need to cool down. E, I think you should leave right now." He stared at Little E with a face that said, *You don't want to mess with me.* Joe was easily a foot taller and forty pounds heavier than Little E.

Little E started to respond, but then thought better of it. He stormed off the court, grabbed his things, and left, not looking back. No one spoke to him.

Although Tom and Stuart didn't care for either Brian or Little E, they seemed genuinely concerned with the direction things had taken.

William was still amused by the whole event, even though he probably didn't hear a word of the argument. "What are they saying?" he asked. No one answered.

Rick continued to give Brian medical attention until he seemed satisfied that he didn't have a serious injury, then helped him to his feet.

"He's out of control," said Brian.

"You all are," said Joe.

"Doesn't matter," said Rick. "Things have gotten way of hand here. This used to be a great, friendly place to play."

"Are you going to press charges?" asked Jack. That elicited an angry glance from Rick.

Before Brian could respond, Rick spoke up. "I think you'll be OK. It doesn't look too bad, and you won't need any stitches."

"Still," insisted Jack, "that was over the top. You should file an assault charge."

Brian looked at Joe.

"If you want to file an assault charge, you're going to have to call the Sheriff," instructed Joe. "I'm not authorized for that."

"You have plenty of witnesses," offered Jack.

"Maybe I will."

I couldn't argue with that, and the fact that there were so many witnesses wouldn't bode well for Little E. All I could think at this point was, thank goodness no one got poisoned. And then it occurred to me that I had left my water bottle on the bench unattended during the fight. I decided I wasn't going to drink from it, so, with no water, I was done with pickleball for the day. It didn't matter, since I wasn't the only one that had lost their enthusiasm to play. It may not have been as serious as the recent deaths on the court, but seeing someone whacked on the head does tend to damper one's spirit. It didn't feel right to go on laughing and joking around after seeing that go down. The courts were emptying out, and people were already heading home.

Another great day of pickleball ruined.

Brian assured us he was okay and could walk on his own, but we stayed by his side just in case he started to falter. Rick checked the wound and saw that it had already ceased bleeding. Once again, he asked Brian how many fingers he was holding up and was satisfied with the answer. Brian would have a nice bruise on his head, but he would survive.

I was starting to wonder about the whole Royal situation. It appeared that the kingdom was crumbling ever since Nathan and Nancy died. The

Royals didn't seem to like each other any more than the peasants did. Maybe they never had liked each other. With Nathan and Nancy gone, the glue was starting to come undone.

Rick decided to err on the side of caution, so he loaded his bike in the back of Brian's truck and drove him home. Samantha, Joe, Tom, Stuart, William, Jack, and I stood watching.

"A lot of infighting among the Royals," said Jack to no one in particular, as he gathered up his belongings.

"Maybe they'll stay away now and give the rest of us some peace and quiet," said William, with a slight grin. He was enjoying this a little too much for my taste.

"I think Little E has some anger issues," stated Tom. "I've seen him get upset before but never violent like that."

"I'll bet his wife is getting an earful right now," I said.

"He's no longer married, and doesn't have any pets that I know of, so he's probably screaming at the walls," replied Stuart.

"Nobody could stay married to that son of bitch," said William.

"All of you pickleballers need to chill out," said Joe. "This obsession you all have is unnatural and unhealthy. If it were up to me, the courts would be torn out and replaced by a garden or something."

"It isn't that pickleball is bad, Joe," objected Samantha. "It's just some people who are rude and obnoxious. There is no need to punish all of us. They just need to be taught a lesson."

Joe frowned back at her. It was clear he didn't appreciate being corrected by his wife in front of everyone. But he bit his tongue and didn't argue. I imagined Samantha would get an earful when they get home. I wanted to take her side and agree openly, but Joe scared me a bit. Getting on his wrong side could be a mistake I would regret, even if he wasn't the killer, which I still was unsure about. In any event, I thought his relationship with the Sheriff was enough to make pissing him off unwise.

Was I a little paranoid? Overthinking? Probably both.

At this point, the group was breaking up. I untied Butch's leash and headed for the street. Just to be on the safe side, I poured out my water bottles. We didn't get far before I heard my name called.

"Al," Joe called out, "do you have a minute?"

Butch and I stopped for him to catch up to us. Samantha told him she would meet him at the car.

"Have you heard anything new? Anyone saying anything that might be useful?"

"No. Not really. Except what I saw today, and you saw the same thing I did."

"OK. Thanks. Keep an eye and ear out."

"I will, but I'm not sure what to look out for. No new clues from the police investigation?"

"No. No fingerprints or other clues to help us. Have you seen any of the Mexicans back in town?"

I didn't like the way he said it, but I didn't comment on it. "I didn't see them at the courts today, and I don't get out much."

"OK. I thought I saw Julio drive by earlier but wasn't sure if it was him."

They all look alike, right Joe? I thought to myself. "Maybe they don't think it's safe to return yet."

I can't say I'd blame them for feeling unsafe. Given the bias and rush to judgment I was hearing, I was starting to think they had the right idea by staying clear, guilty or not. Joe turned to rejoin Samantha, and Butch and I headed home. We spent the rest of the afternoon trying to learn a new trick – rolling over and playing dead. By the time I gave up, the treats were all gone, and I had made myself dizzy trying to demonstrate what I wanted him to do.

For dinner, we agreed I would run over to Taco Tim's. Tacos for me and a dry cheeseburger for Butch. We settled on a movie we both liked, *Going Home,* and ate our dinner in silence.

Pickleball Tip # 18 – The Lob On Offense

Most people hate to return the lob. They either have trouble retreating or don't know how to hit an overhead. So, when you and your opponent are at the NVZ in a dink contest, throw up the occasional lob and drive them back. Aim it to land on their backhand side, forcing them to retreat. If they are able to reach it, most players will either put up a weak lob back or drive it back with little force. Either should result in an easy put-away, provided you are at the kitchen line waiting.

Chapter 19

Butch and I awoke to a beautiful southern Arizona morning after a surprisingly peaceful night. Sure, yesterday's fight was disturbing, and it had cut into my pickleball time, but I have seen plenty of fights in my days playing basketball, football, baseball, and of course pickleball. At least no one had died, so I didn't lose any sleep over it. Hell, I'd even seen worse fights in the stands at a Broncos/Raiders football game. Laying off the alcohol may have also helped me sleep better.

I took Butch for his obligatory morning walk before breakfast, and we were treated to the sight of a small family of javelinas on the trail. Butch was fascinated by them, but we kept our distance, as we had been warned that the parents would protect their babies from any and all threats, and that they were fearsome fighters. Butch moaned, thinking they would make grand friends, but I insisted we give the pack at least fifteen feet of clearance.

After we returned from the walk, I poured a hefty amount of kibble into Butch's food bowl, then grabbed a banana and granola bar for myself. I washed my granola down with a large glass of orange juice and Butch slurped up half his water, spilling the rest on the floor. By now, Butch knew the routine. He jumped on the couch for his morning nap, and I gathered my things and was out the door, anticipating a rousing day of fun, competitive pickleball. Not too much to ask, as long as there were no deaths or fights.

By the time I arrived, the courts were already bustling with activity. An overnight wind had blown debris over the courts but Jack, as usual, was busy with his gas-powered air blower, cleaning them off. A few games were already in session, and I could hear laughter and the popping sound of pickleballs hitting paddles. I recognized most of the people out there, but as usual, there were a few new faces. Brian and Little E were nowhere in sight. I assumed neither had any appetite for each other, after their fracas yesterday. Maybe they were even a little embarrassed by their behavior? No. I didn't think they were the type to be easily embarrassed. Maybe Little E was, and Brian just had a big bruise and a lingering headache.

One of the Royal courts was occupied with a group I had never seen, and the other had Molly, Jane, Rick, and Stuart. They were laughing and cajoling each other as if nothing had happened yesterday. They finished the game, tapped paddles, and came over to the bench area for a drink.

"Late start, Al?" asked Jane.

"No, I'm just not up as early as you guys," I replied. "I need to get used to playing earlier now that I've moved here."

"You'll learn to appreciate it more once summer sets in," said Molly. "When it gets to be a hundred in the shade, you won't want to be playing out here." She laughed heartily, and it sounded like a cackle. I grinned.

"Where's the rest of your team?" I asked.

"Team?" asked Rick. I wasn't sure if I had gone into uncharted waters. Maybe the Royals didn't really think of themselves as a team.

"Brian and E," I said, managing to stop myself from saying "Little".

"Good question," said Molly. "Normally they are here right after Jack cleans the courts."

That made it sound like Jack was a custodian. It's one thing to do all that he does because he likes to be helpful, but the way she said it, it almost sounded like an obligation. I wondered if Jack would mind? I made a mental note to show up early sometime to help him.

"I stopped by Brian's before I came over this morning, to make sure he was OK," said Rick. "He was fine last night, but I thought I should check on him again just to be sure. He's got an ugly bruise and a slight headache, but he's going to be fine. He said he felt good enough to play today, but he just wasn't in the mood. He should be back tomorrow or the day after. I told him I thought that was prudent, considering the blow he took to his head."

"Nice having a paramedic hanging around our courts," said Stuart, patting Rick on the back. I think I saw a gleam in Rick's eye.

Considering the average age of pickleball players is over fifty, I think every court should have a resident paramedic, and a defibrillator wouldn't be a bad idea either.

"We do have a couple retired doctors, as well," added Rick.

"I've gotten plenty of advice from Dr. David over the years, and between me and the oak tree, it hasn't been all that great," said William, who had just joined the discussion. No one disagreed with him.

"Maybe someone should call Ethelwolf," suggested Molly.

"I've got his number. I'll call him," Jane volunteered, grabbing her cell phone and clicking on a bunch of keys. She stepped away from the group so she could hear him when he answered. We continued chatting about pickleball strategies and equipment while she called.

I asked Rick and Stuart if they would join me on the court and warm me up. I made sure to take my water bottle with me. I stood across from them and practiced dinking to each one of them alternately, then a few harder shots, until I was ready. We needed a fourth to join us and the best player on the sidelines was Jane, so we walked over and asked her to fill out the team.

"Sure, I'd love to. Maybe while I'm playing, someone can keep an eye on my phone? I tried Ethelwolf a dozen times, and he didn't answer," she said, picking up her paddle.

"Did you leave a message?" asked Molly.

"I did. Hopefully he's on his way here now."

No one seemed all that concerned that Little E wasn't on the courts yet, so why was I? I know, I have an overactive imagination and I'm a bit paranoid. In my defense though, I thought there was good reason to be concerned. We'd had three murders in the past three weeks and two brutal fights on the courts in the last few days. The question was, why wasn't everyone more on edge? And being the suspicious sort that I am, I wondered if Little E's absence had anything to do with Brian? I could see it clearly in my mind. Brian, still fuming over the beating he took, confronts Little E at home and exacts his revenge. It was even possible that Brian had killed the others, and Little E was just his latest victim.

Everyone went back on the court and resumed play as if nothing was wrong. Within minutes, they were laughing and joking and teasing each other. I was still distracted, however, but not so much that I didn't remember to keep my water bottle close to me.

I played a distracted, lackluster game, often glancing at the bench area to see if Little E would show up after all. He didn't, but Joe and Samantha rolled up together on their matching mountain bikes. Joe sat down, while Samantha quickly got in a game with a few ladies, and of course, Jack. My guess was Joe was going to accompany Samantha every day until the killer was caught, but I'm sure if he had his way, she wouldn't play at all. We finished what I would call a very unsatisfying game. At least for me, anyway. My opponents were, however, thrilled at beating me. We sat down to rest, drink some water, and discuss the game, when Jane suddenly jumped up.

"There's Brian."

I turned around and, sure enough, Brian was strolling up to the bench area. Jane ran up and hugged him.

"I'm so glad to see you. Are you OK?"

"I'll live, no thanks to E. Where is the little shit?"

"No one knows. He didn't come by or answer his phone," responded Jane.

"Probably afraid to be seen," said Brian.

"Do you think someone should go over and check on E to see if he's OK?" asked Jane.

"I'm the one that got cracked over the head. Not him," snarled Brian.

"And we're glad you're OK, and I'm sure he's sorry."

"I doubt it. Let him stew in it. It would do him some good to be ostracized," Brian growled.

Hard to argue that point. I think if I had gone off the deep end like Little E had, I would want to steer clear of everyone until things simmered down.

"Well, I think we should go over to his house and check on him. Brian, you and he were great friends. Maybe if he apologized, and you told him you weren't holding a grudge, we could get back to normal," suggested Molly. "I know I would feel better if we checked on him."

"Do what you want Molly. I could care less if I never see him again."

"It's just pickleball," said Stuart.

"Bite your tongue," replied Jane.

"All you people take this way too seriously," said Joe, joining the conversation. "I'm thinking of asking the Sheriff to shut this place down for a few weeks, so you can all cool your jets."

A chorus of complaints and grumbles directed at Joe filled the air.

"See what I mean? Even the mention of losing your playing privileges for a short time drives you nuts," Joe countered.

"I don't want to be punished for what E did. It's bad enough I have a lump on my head," whined Brian.

"Joe," said Jane, "I think we all just got too exuberant but that is no reason to shut us down. I'm sure E will be back here shortly and apologize to everyone, especially you, Brian."

Brian grumbled but didn't say anything. A few others expressed agreement with Jane, and to his credit, or maybe just because he was outnumbered, Joe didn't respond.

"I want to check on Ethelwolf," said Molly. I think she might have been one of the few who ever called him by his full name, and it sounded odd to hear it. "We need to let him know we don't hate him. Will someone go with me?"

"I'll go with you, Molly," offered Jane. "Maybe Al will come with us to show that even the new guy doesn't think he's a jerk."

Wait, what? I didn't care for the guy, and although I meant him no harm, I didn't want to waste my time checking in on him. Besides that, after his performance yesterday, I wasn't so sure he wasn't the killer. But, as I have often admitted, I have trouble saying no, especially to women. So, I said yes, I would go with them. Little E didn't live far, but it was too far to walk, so we piled into Molly's SUV, and she shuttled us over there.

It was close by, just like everything in Rio Viejo. We pulled up to a western-style adobe ranch surrounded by cactus and rocks. Typical Rio

Viejo house. He had a cute little metal donkey in the front yard and a bunch of ceramic geckos and lizards hanging from the walls, which I had come to recognize as Southern Arizona home decor. The house looked quiet and deserted.

We got out of the car and waited while Molly marched up to the door and knocked. And knocked again. It was creepy, but she went around peeking in windows, knocking on them, and calling out his name. No response. The garage door was closed and there was no window to look inside. She came back to the car looking concerned.

"He's not home," I said. "Let's go back to the courts and play. I'm sure he's just out running some errands." Hopefully, getting some psychiatric help for those anger issues.

"He would have told me if he had some errands," said Molly, while she rifled through her purse.

This was a small town. Still, I didn't expect everyone would know everyone else's comings and goings. I hoped not anyway. It's not that I had any major secrets or anything, but the idea of everyone knowing everything about me seemed kind of creepy, a feeling I was getting all too often.

Molly found what she was looking for. "Here it is," she said, as she produced a key attached to what looked like a miniature pickleball paddle. "E gave it to me as a present."

"A key to his home?" I asked, thinking there was more to their relationship than we all knew.

"No silly, I've had that for some time. The pickleball paddle key ring," she answered with a giggle.

Jane gave Molly a quizzical look.

"You have a key to his house?" Jane asked.

"We've been dating for a few months now."

"I didn't know that."

"We wanted to keep it on the down low and see where it went, before we told anyone."

"Well, you sly girl," said Jane, with a nudge that almost knocked Molly down. "You sure had all of us fooled. I'm going to want to hear all the details."

I didn't say anything, but I was thinking that Molly, a good-looking woman in her mid-fifties, could do a lot better. She was probably a foot taller than Little E, for one thing. But that was just me being judgmental, and I do try not to be judgmental.

Molly inserted the key and unlocked the door. She walked in slowly, calling out his name as she went. We followed her in. It crossed my mind that we might find Little E with another woman, which was not a sight I wanted to see. All the lights were off, but the TV was on.

"Maybe we should leave," I suggested nervously. I figured if he was with someone, there was still time to leave, and no one would be the wiser.

"That's odd," Molly said.

"What?" I asked, thinking this entire situation was odd.

"His keys are on the key holder." There was a key rack by the garage door with a full set of keys hanging from it. "He would need them to go anywhere." She opened the door to the garage and there was his Jeep. "It's not like him to walk."

Now, in addition to worrying about finding him with another woman, I started to imagine us finding his dead body. We followed Molly into the living room, and I let out a loud sigh when we didn't see him there.

"What?" asked Jane, turning towards me.

"Nothing," I replied.

Everything looked neat and tidy. No sign of any trouble. It was incredibly clean for a bachelor pad and rather well-decorated. It seemed Little E had an eye for interior design. Once again, my bias was taking over, and I fought against making a snide remark.

Leading away from the living room was another hallway that led to the rear of the house and, I assumed, the bedrooms. Molly had turned off the TV and now the place was silent, except for our footsteps. Molly headed straight for the master bedroom while Jane and I looked in the kitchen. Nothing out of order, as far as I could tell.

Then we heard a shrill scream and Molly came running back toward us.

I'm not a coward by any stretch, but that scream sounded like Jamie Lee Curtis in *Halloween*. It sent shivers down my spine. As a testament to my bravery, I stood my ground and didn't go running out the door screaming. I figured she'd either seen a dead body or a giant tarantula, which wouldn't have been at all strange since the area had a million of them. Tarantulas, that is, not dead bodies. I had already encountered my share around town. Instead of panicking, I tried to stay calm.

"What did you see?" I asked her, trying to keep my voice steady.

Rather than answer me, she ran straight into Jane's arms, sobbing uncontrollably. With all the manly willpower I could summon, I slowly approached the bedroom, scanning the walls and ceiling, ready to flee if I spotted a giant spider.

I reached the doorway unscathed and carefully peeked around the corner. Little E was sprawled out on top of his bed, with a pickleball paddle by his head. The paddle was bloody and there was a huge pool of blood staining the top blanket. I looked around quickly to make sure the killer wasn't still there, lurking in the shadows. Satisfied that we were alone, I inched closer to Little E and checked for a pulse. I'm not an expert at these things but I was pretty sure there wasn't one. I fumbled trying to get my cell phone out of my pocket to call 911. Then I called Joe.

Pickleball Tip # 19 – Keep Your Paddle Up And Ready Between Shots

So many people drop the paddle tip down by their side when they are at the NVZ after a shot, or while waiting for their opponent to hit the next shot. This puts them at a great disadvantage. When you are at the NVZ, most quick shots will come waist high or higher, not at your feet. If the next shot comes toward your chest or head, you will have to bring the paddle up quickly to block or strike the next ball. Those extra few milliseconds can be huge, causing a mishit or a popup. Ideally, you should be in the ready position at all times, which means your paddle is up, slightly in front of you. From this position, it is easy to hit a block shot or even a downward slam. If your opponent hits a dink, you will have plenty of time to readjust and reach the ball to hit a dink back to them.

Chapter 20

Not wanting to be anywhere near a dead body, we waited outside on the porch until Joe arrived a few minutes later. I could hear the siren from the paramedics in the distance. Pickleball injuries are common, but I'm sure the paramedics hadn't had this much activity in months.

"Did you touch anything?" Joe asked as he approached us, pulling on some latex gloves. He must have had a box of them in his car. "I called the Sheriff. He's on his way."

Molly was too distraught to talk yet, so I said, "Molly had a key and opened the front door. We followed her in, and I don't think we touched anything, except I did check his wrist for a pulse before I called 911." The ambulance pulled up and turned into the driveway. I waited to continue briefing Joe until the siren was turned off. "Molly found him first and then I went in, which is when I checked his pulse. I don't think she touched anything either, but I haven't actually asked her."

Two paramedics that I had never seen before jumped out of the cab. Joe went over and talked to them for a minute before they opened the back and pulled out a gurney. A fire truck arrived a moment later.

"I'm going inside with them. You guys wait here for me. I'll be right back," said Joe, as he put on some paper booties over his tennis shoes.

We sat down on the porch steps and waited for Joe to return. Jane tried her best to console Molly but didn't have much success. She and E had kept their little affair secret from the pickleball crowd, but I could see by her demeanor that it had been serious. My mind was reeling again. I felt bad for Little E, but I was once again doubting the wisdom of my move to Rio Viejo. Denver had its share of murders, but it was a big city. Rio Viejo now had four murders in less than a month and it was barely a fraction of the size of Denver. Joe interrupted my thoughts as he appeared back on the porch. The paramedics were still inside. He motioned for me to follow him down to the sidewalk, out of earshot of the ladies.

"Has she said anything?" he asked, pointing to the still sobbing Molly.

"No. She's inconsolable. What do you think happened? Did he die from being hit on the head with the paddle?"

"Won't know for sure 'til the crime scene people get here. I'm telling you this, but if I hear that you've told anyone else, I'll fry you." He glared at me, while I tried to imagine what he meant by "fry". I was getting a little tired of his warnings.

"I won't say anything," I promised.

"There's some blood splatter on the floor and wall leading to the master bath. I'm guessing he was hit over the head coming out of the bathroom. Then he must have staggered to the bed and fallen over. No sign of struggle anywhere else in the house."

I replayed what I saw when I went in his room. He wasn't in his pajamas, in fact, he was on top of the bedspread. So, he wasn't asleep when it happened. I hadn't noticed the blood splatter on the wall. I assumed he had to have been hit pretty hard to create that. I did notice the paddle was one of the new Kinetics that Little E used, so it could have been his. I wondered if the killer had poisoned him like he did Nancy; maybe it only incapacitated him, and the killer whacked him to make sure he would die. So, the question was, how did the killer get Little E to drink the poison? I didn't remember seeing a glass with liquid in it, but then I wasn't looking for one either.

Joe was staring at me intently, as if I had been talking to myself out loud. I worried that I had. Lately, I had found myself talking out loud to Stephanie, so it was feasible that, being alone so much, I had started talking out loud to myself.

"What?" I asked.

"That's what I'm wondering," he answered. "You look pretty deep in thought. What about?"

Okay, good. I wasn't thinking out loud. I hesitated, but I wanted to help and didn't want to be a suspect, so I blurted out, "Brian."

"What about Brian?"

"Well, you know. With the fight yesterday between Brian and Little E. Maybe Brian got his revenge?"

"Careful with your accusations," he warned me. "But I will be talking to Brian very soon. Any more theories?"

Why was Joe asking me? He was the trained detective. I had just read detective novels and had never actually solved a murder mystery, unless you counted the game of Clue. Although one year, Stephanie and I hosted a murder party, and I did solve that case.

"Well," I started to surmise, "what if he came over to talk last night, and they got into an argument and Brian hit him on the head with the paddle? I was also wondering if there was any poison involved. Like with Nancy."

"There is a glass with some liquid in it that we will be testing."

I wondered out loud, "Was there a second glass? Was he drinking alone?"

"You thinking of taking up a new career as a detective, Al?"

"No. Just trying to help."

"That's OK. What else are you thinking?"

"What if the killer was just waiting for things to quiet down before he got back to killing Royals? This time he could make it look like Brian was the killer, since they had that terrible fight yesterday. Wait... or maybe Brian was the killer all along? He and Little E clearly had a long-standing feud. He didn't want anyone to suspect him, so he killed the other people, that were not personally connected to him, just to create a smokescreen. Maybe Little E was the intended victim all along?" It sounded like the plot of a million murder mysteries, but that didn't make it impossible.

"Quite an imagination you have. Maybe you should write crime novels."

I thought Joe was probably making fun of me, but I let it slide.

"All I really know is that I'm sorry I ever moved here. I have no clue who is doing all this or why. I'm fucking new here." I was raising my voice, just shy of yelling. "All I know is I fucking sleep with one eye open and watch my water bottle like a hawk."

"Calm down. I was just hoping you might have seen or heard something. We won't know what really happened until the crime scene guys go through the house. I think it's kind of suspicious that just after Brian gets hit in the head by Ethelwolf, Ethelwolf gets attacked in the same way. You obviously considered that, too. But Brian would have to know that the timing of this murder would make him a prime suspect."

I thought of that too, but we've all read stories about stupid criminals. We've all seen the stupid criminal videos on YouTube. Maybe he was guilty and stupid.

"OK. Not a great theory," I admitted. "If this is about being a Royal than Brian, Jane, Molly..." I stopped.

"Yes. They would all be in danger, but...," he paused.

"But what?"

"Listen, Al, I know about the Royal reputation, and it looks like they are being targeted, but I'm not ready to hang my hat on that theory just yet. Too neat and tidy."

"The Mexicans and drugs?" I asked, to see if Joe was back to that.

"Actually, no. I find it suspicious our Mexican friends are missing in action, but now with four murders I don't think this is drug related. Both the Sheriff and I considered that at first, but now it doesn't make sense. I suppose it is possible this latest murder is unrelated to the first three though. I still want to talk to them if they come back, but now I'm convinced something else is going on."

Joe may not have believed that this was pickleball related, but he would be the first to admit he didn't believe in coincidences, and the fact that all the dead people were Royals told me that he was wrong. I didn't believe this was a coincidence, and I didn't believe this had to do with drugs. Someone was killing pickleball players, and I had no intention of becoming their next victim. I vowed that not only would I make sure not to let my water bottle out of my sight ever again, but I was also going to avoid playing with the Royals, just in case. Butch was not going to become an orphan because I moved us to Rio Viejo.

"Take Molly and Jane back to the courts. We can talk to them later, but I'm guessing it will be the same information you gave me. Tell Samantha to go home without me and I'll meet her there later. I think I'll be here awhile. Also, I know you can't control what Jane and Molly tell everyone but keep my theories quiet, if you would." It wasn't a suggestion, though. How many times was he going to tell me the same thing?

"OK." I gathered up Molly and Jane and hustled them over to the car. The Sheriff and the crime scene investigators pulled up to Little E's house just as we were pulling away. Molly was calming down, but still very upset. I offered to drive us back.

"You guys probably will be surprised to learn that Ethelwolf and I were talking about moving in together," said Molly, between sobs. "Maybe even getting married."

Jane gave me a funny look.

"I'm very sorry for your loss, Molly. I know what it's like to lose a loved one," I said, trying to console her. The fact that I didn't much care for Little E had nothing to do with my compassion for someone who lost a partner, or in this case, a soon-to-be partner. I didn't say the loss gets easier over time because, although you figure out how to move on, there is always a hole in your heart. At least, that had been my experience.

"Thanks, Al. I guess you know what it's like."

I nodded, having said all I thought I should say.

After a minute of silence, Molly asked, "Why would anyone harm Ethelwolf? He really was a sweet person." I think I tasted blood on my tongue from biting it.

"None of this makes any sense, Molly," said Jane.

I pulled up into the parking lot in front of the courts. There were a few people leaving, but there were still a few games being played. Jack and Stuart saw us park and walked over to meet us as we made our way back to the bench area.

"Where's Little E?" asked Jack.

As soon as he said it, Molly started to cry again. Jane guided her over to the benches to sit down. When they were settled in, I took Jack and Stuart off to the side to explain what had happened. Tom and William followed.

"He's dead. Joe and the Sheriff are at his house, and they aren't sure yet what happened. I think he's been dead for a few hours."

"Holy shit," said Stuart. "What the fuck?" He was throwing up his hands and pacing around. "I thought all this shit was over. What the fuck is going on?" He was shouting now.

"What did he say?" asked William. I repeated myself a little louder, but unfortunately Molly heard and started crying all over again. Rory and Brian looked like they were having a private discussion, but when they heard me say Little E was dead, they stopped talking and came over to us.

"Little E's dead?" asked Rory.

I nodded.

"How? What happened? Did you see the body?"

"Yes. They don't know for sure, but whoever killed him whacked him on the side of his head with his paddle. There was blood all over the paddle. I don't know if that's what killed him, but it looks like he was hit pretty hard."

Everyone looked at Brian.

"Hey, don't look at me," he protested. "I didn't do it. He hit me; I didn't hit him." Then he began to panic. "Do the police think it was me? Are they coming over here now?" Brian was getting more and more animated.

"Brian, I don't know what they think or what they are going to do next. All I know is what I saw. We knocked on the door and he didn't answer, so Molly, who has a key, let us in. She found the body," I explained, as calmly as I could.

"Did you go over there last night?" Jack asked Brian, somewhat accusingly.

"I told you I had nothing to do with this," screamed Brian, "and I resent you implying anything, Jack. Just keep the fuck out of this. Why don't you ask Rory? They were fighting too, you know."

Jack didn't look convinced. He glanced at Rory.

"Don't start, Jack. I had nothing to do with this."

"What's going on?" whined William. "Someone killed Little E?"

"Keep your voice down, William," said Tom, nodding toward Molly. He guided us a little farther away from her. "I'll explain it to you later."

"You guys believe me, don't you?" pleaded Brian.

I had no clue if Brian or Rory were involved, but given the circumstances, it didn't feel like a big stretch to consider them suspects. I wasn't going to bring that up, though. Both men were volatile, and I wasn't looking to fight with them. Whether they believed it or not, Tom and Stuart tried to settle the two men down by telling them they didn't think either of them had anything to do with it. This calmed Brian down, but Rory was glaring at Brian for bringing his name into it.

Samantha had come off the courts and had joined Jane and Molly. She was offering to drive Molly home. I walked over and stood by them.

"Joe asked me to tell you he would meet you at home later."

She nodded and stepped away from Molly, guiding me by the arm.

"I figured as much," she confided. "This is not something he can walk away from. He hasn't been sleeping much since all the murders started. He's got a whiteboard with names and theories, but it makes no sense to me. He doesn't have a clue what's going on or who might be behind all this, and he's afraid that he doesn't have the resources he had in the past. The Sheriff is totally in over his head. The only murders the Sheriff has had to deal with in the past are drug related gang stuff or domestic violence. Always open and shut cases."

This did not give me a sense of comfort. If the investigators had no clue who was behind the killing, what chance did we have? I wasn't exactly panicking, but I was close. Were we supposed to wait while the killer struck again and again, until he finally made a mistake? So far, whoever was behind this was careful, if not downright clever. What if he never slipped up? Some murders do go unsolved for years. Then you see the case on *Unsolved Mysteries* and some new leads come in that help catch the killer. Unfortunately, that seems to happen years later. Who knows how many more bodies there can be in that time?

I wasn't keen to wait around and find out.

I picked up my gear and left. I wanted to be alone with Butch.

Pickleball Tip # 20 – Too Much Force On Attack Shots

A common error of players at almost all levels is to try to crush put-aways. It's satisfying and exciting to hit a clean winner, but a high percentage of those easy put-aways go into the net or travel far or wide. A better strategy, although less satisfying, is to hit at only 75-80% of your capability, rather than 100%. The ball will stay in play, and you might even still win the point outright. Chances are, even if the point gets extended, you've put your opponent on the defensive and will likely get another chance to put it away, rather than bailing them out with an unforced error.

Chapter 21

I got back home and immediately started telling Butch what happened. He yawned. He clearly wasn't getting the severity of what had just taken place, but then I didn't think he understood what had happened up until that point either. He groaned, got off the couch, and stood by the back sliding door. When I didn't immediately jump up and let him out, he groaned again and sat down. I may be slow, but I'm not dumb. I let him out and watched him do his business. When he was done, he came back in, expecting a reward. I complied.

In every scary movie, there is always that moment where the audience screams at the main character to pack her bags and move out of that haunted house, or to get the heck out of that creepy town. I could almost hear the audience screaming at me, telling me to move out. Move out now! If I did listen to the audience, there would be no way I could become the next victim. But if it was too late? What if the director was just letting the audience think there was a way out, only to have the killer suddenly appear behind the hero as he heads out the door?

I futzed around the house with no real purpose in mind, as Butch followed me, probably wondering what was going on. Were we going on a walk or what? He finally tired of the game and settled back onto the couch for a well-earned nap. When I finally tired of pacing, I sat down at my computer and started doing searches on the internet. The first thing I looked up was other places with pickleball that had good weather year-round. I started out with *Places to Play*. If a town had a decent number of courts, I pulled up Wikipedia to see what they had to say about the area. I followed that up with Weather.com. I was done with snow, no matter how many courts they had. If a town had good weather and good pickleball accommodations I wrote it down on a piece of paper. California was getting the most hits, after Arizona.

Then it dawned on me. Why limit myself to one location? Butch and I could become pickleball nomads. I remembered meeting someone in Denver who lived full-time in an RV and traveled to different places to play pickleball. He followed the good weather and never stayed anywhere more than three months. He claimed he was having the time of his life, and he was actually a pretty good pickleball player.

The next search on the internet was for sites specializing in RV living.

"Butch," I called, waking him from his slumber. "How would you like to live in an RV and see the country?"

He lifted his head and stared at me briefly. He didn't say a word, but he turned his head sideways as if trying to understand what I was telling him. Then he raised his eyebrows and sighed. I took that to mean, *Whatever you want, dude. Count me in*. He had always been very supportive that way.

After an hour of going down the rabbit hole reading articles about RV's and living on the road, I was sold. I surfed over to sites that offered RVs for sale and lease and got familiar with a dozen different ones that I thought would meet our needs. I was amazed at how elaborate or basic they could be. I was going to shoot for something in between. I wanted all the comforts of home in an easy to drive rig that was still big enough not to feel too cramped.

"Butch," I woke him again. "We're going RV shopping next week."

One thing I was sure of was that we were getting out of Rio Viejo. I'd had enough of the drama there. It didn't matter where we went really. Not if we were in an RV. We could go somewhere, check it out, and as long as no one was dying, we'd stay for a while. That was the plan. I looked over my shoulder. No one was standing there ready to bludgeon me with a pickleball paddle.

Joe and the Sheriff had told me to stay put, but the hell with them. In my mind, I wasn't a suspect and unless they locked me up, they couldn't stop me from leaving. With any luck we would be somewhere new before the next body dropped.

I always felt better after I'd made a tough decision, and I felt great then. I got up from the computer and stretched. It wasn't too hot, so I woke Butch up a third time and told him to get ready for a walk. I don't think he believed me or maybe he didn't hear the word walk, because he just sat there staring at me. I said it again and emphasized that word. Worked every time. He jumped off the couch and stood by the door waiting. I leashed him up and we were out the door, with no direction in mind. We ended up at the market. Tom and Martin were sitting on the patio outside drinking beer when they spotted us and waved us over.

"Al, how you doing?" asked Tom, pulling another chair over to the table for me.

"OK I guess, considering." I didn't need to finish the thought.

"Yeah, pretty wild around here these days," agreed Martin. "We are thinking of taking a little trip to get out of town until this all blows over."

"I was thinking the same thing," I answered. "In fact, I'm thinking of getting an RV and just hitting the road permanently. You people are too damn crazy here."

Martin laughed. "You people?"

I couldn't resist. "Yeah, damn old white people killing each other."

That got them both laughing. It was good to see you could still draw a laugh, considering people were dropping like flies.

287

"It would be a shame to see you go, but I can't say I wouldn't do the same if we could afford it. We would need to sell our house though. Leslie and I lived for a year in an RV before we bought a place here and we had a great time."

"I didn't know that," I said. There was a lot I didn't know about these people. I supposed I could ask Joe for a dossier on everyone. "I might come to you for advice on RV's if Butch and I decide to do it."

"Sure, happy to help, Al."

"So, Martin and I have been sitting here trying to play amateur detective, since Joe and the police don't seem to be making any progress."

"And?" I asked hopefully.

"We are thinking Brian looks awful suspicious," said Tom. "He had a beef with Ethelwolf and gets hit in the head, so he goes back for a little revenge, but hits him too hard and kills him."

"I considered that too," I agreed. "And then he goes off the deep end when we get back and tell everyone what happened to Little E. But what I'm having trouble with is why would he kill the others?"

"Maybe he didn't," said Martin. "What if the murders are unrelated?"

I nodded. "Joe was thinking that might be the case too." That kind of thing happens in murder mysteries all the time. Could real life be imitating fiction? "OK, if we assume Brian knocked off Little E, then who did the other murders?"

"Joe said there was some suspicion it might be the Mexicans," said Martin. "He said he had done some background checks on them. From what he could find, since they aren't actually US citizens, Julio and Jesus both have ties to cartels, but nothing that the law could prosecute them for. This could be drug related."

"Why would they want to kill Nathan, Anna, and Nancy?" I asked.

"According to Joe, Nathan had financial problems ever since he got out of jail for the DUI in Canada. He's been wondering how Nathan could afford to live here without a job," answered Tom. "I told Joe that Nancy had been helping Nathan for years, but he still thinks that there might be some drug trafficking going on."

"When did Joe say that?" I asked.

"A couple days ago. Before Little E was murdered."

"I don't think he still thinks this is drug related," I said, but started to wonder if maybe Joe was giving us different theories.

It was possible Nathan was dealing drugs on the side, but it didn't meet the smell test to me. Nathan didn't fit the profile of the stereotypical drug dealer, but these days I guess that doesn't mean much. If Nathan was suspected of drug dealing, would Joe's background checks discover that? I remembered Colin, a friend from my brokerage days in Denver that was a computer genius. He had boasted to me once that there was nothing he couldn't find out about someone if he really wanted to. That gave me an idea.

"Guys, I need to know everyone's full names. Do you have them?"

"Sure. But why do you need that?" asked Tom.

"I've got a friend in Denver that is an internet wizard. The guy can find out anything about anyone. I just need a little information about them to give to him."

"That's creepy," said Martin.

"Hey, nothing is safe on the internet and these days everything is out there. The guy can hack into databases that you wouldn't believe existed."

"What do you need to know?" asked Tom.

"Well, for sure first and last name. I doubt you have social security numbers, but age, addresses, last place of residence. I suppose if you know their last profession and phone numbers that wouldn't hurt."

"I think we can give you most of that. Certainly, phone numbers, names, where they told us they last lived," offered Martin, pulling out his phone. "Who do you want to check on?"

I thought about it for a moment. "Let's start with Jack, Rory, Brian, Nathan, Jane, Nancy, Ethelwolf, and Anna," I answered slowly. Then I added Joe as an afterthought. It made sense to check on the deceased, to look for any past connections they had with each other. I wanted to know if Nathan, Nancy, and Anna had any past drug convictions, or if they were ever investigated for that. I wanted information on Brian and Ethelwolf because they were rumored to be in some business dealings together, and of course because of their feud. I didn't think Jane was much of a suspect, but why not check anyway? She was definitely a Royal. I wanted to know about Rory because he seemed to have anger issues, and about Jack because he didn't. Jack seemed a little too nice. I wasn't sure how much Colin could learn about Mexican nationals, but thought I'd give them a try as well. "Do you have names and phone numbers for Eddie, Julio, and Jesus too?"

"What about Tom and me?" joked Martin, as he scrolled through his phone contacts.

"I'm making a guess you aren't part of this. Please tell me I'm not wrong," I laughed.

"Of course not," replied Tom. "What about some of the others, like William?"

"Can you really see William pulling something like this off?" After I said it, I had second thoughts. Wouldn't it be just like a mystery novel if the least likely person was actually the killer? They say truth is stranger than fiction and William as the killer would be strange indeed.

"No, not really," replied Martin. "But I can't imagine who would. And Joe? He's a homicide detective. You can't think he's behind all this."

"I see your point, and I know this sounds crazy and maybe even a bit paranoid, but I've read so many detective novels that I feel like you can't leave anyone out. I mean, think about it, Joe hates pickleball, his wife hates the Royals, and do we know that he really was a homicide detective? Even if he was, you can't tell me all cops are clean."

"Shit, Al," exclaimed Tom. "You are fucking creeping me out. There is something off about Joe. I've never really warmed up to him, but I never thought he could be a murderer. What do you think, Martin? You play golf with him."

"He's OK when you get to know him. He can be intense, and when he's been drinking, he does get a little loose-lipped. I know there is more to the story about when he got shot and left the force, but he clams up when I bring it up. But you never know about people. Could you have ever imagined Little E hitting Brian on the head with his paddle?"

We let that sit for a minute. While Tom and Martin compared notes on everyone, I went inside the market and asked to borrow a pen and paper to write with. When I returned to the table, Martin and Tom rattled off full names, phone numbers, and even a few birth dates for the group we were targeting. Evidently people shared birthdays there, and the group would have community cakes. At least until the Royals took the joy out of the group. Because of sketchy memories, they weren't as helpful coming up with things like place of birth or previous places lived, and there was some disagreement as to careers, but I still had quite a bit to go on. I took it all down and then said I was going to call Colin.

Colin answered on the second ring and sounded genuinely glad to hear from me. He had a slew of questions about what I had been up to and how I was doing. He was getting tired of the snow in Denver and asked what I thought about Rio Viejo. When I informed him about the rash of murders, he quickly decided he was no longer interested in leaving Denver. In fact, he offered to put me up, to get me the hell out before something happened to me. I assured him I was safe, although I wasn't quite convinced of that myself.

"How are your hacking skills these days?"

"Why?" he asked.

I told him what was going on and what I needed.

He laughed, "Well, funny you should ask. I've been writing some new programs that let me into a ton of servers and block any trace it was me. I've been playing around with it, and I think I can generate more information on a person than those sites that charge for background checks. I might even start a side business offering the service."

"Awesome. I think I can be your first client. How long does it take?"

"It's mind-blowingly fast. I can get the basic results in minutes, depending on how much information I have on someone. Some information takes a little longer, and depending on what you're looking for, it may take some cross-referencing if there are people out there with similar names and locations. So, the more information you can give me about each person, the easier it will be. Oh, and no charge, my friend."

I told him what I had gathered.

"That will work. If you can add stuff about appearances, like hair color, height, etc., that will help if we get multiple hits."

I told him to give me a few minutes to type it all up and I would email it over.

292

"Perfect. I should have some results for you by this afternoon."

Pickleball Tip # 21 – Have A Plan And Hit With Purpose

Most players just react to the ball, rather than hitting a shot that will produce the desired result, i.e., a ball you can easily put away.

If your opponent has a weak backhand from the baseline, target that with your service return.

If your opponent can't handle low shots, aim for their feet with drives or dinks.

If your opponents have trouble deciding who takes the middle, aim for the middle.

Etc., etc. It may seem obvious, but players rarely discuss strengths and weaknesses, either their own or their opponent's. Discuss with your partner who takes what shot in each situation before the game starts. Keep communicating strategy as the game progresses. If a weakness in one of your opponents presents itself, make sure to talk about it with your partner so you have the same game plan.

You'll have more fun, and your opponents will fear you.

Chapter 22

"Wow," exclaimed Martin, as I finished up the email to Colin. "You know someone that can get that kind of information?"

"The guy is a genius. He's written programs for all sorts of companies. He did a lot of work for my brokerage firm back in the day and we became good friends. I bet he sends me back a report in a couple of hours."

"Amazing," said Tom, shaking his head. "All that information is that easy to get?"

"Most of it is easy. People volunteer information on social media all the time. Nothing is really secure. But Colin can also get into a lot of corporate and government web sites that have little or no security. It's really funny when you think about all the people accusing Bill Gates or Mark Zuckerberg of planting chips and all that nonsense, when in fact they don't need to. We've already given the information willingly. Like phones. They track you all the time and we tell the phone it's OK." I went on to explain more of what I had learned from Colin over the years and from running a brokerage firm that relied heavily on technology.

We hung out, drinking beers, trading pickleball stories and golf achievements (or lack thereof), and talking about our previous careers. We were all transplants from other areas of the country, even Martin, who at one time or another had lived in five or six different states after emigrating from Spain when he was still in his teens. He spent a career in education teaching history at the high school and then junior college levels. Tom was a Vietnam vet who was wounded trying to help a buddy get in a rescue helicopter. The wound got him back home without too many lasting side effects. He considered himself one of the lucky ones. He came back to the states and landed a management job in the trucking industry that allowed him to travel extensively before retiring with a healthy pension. The two of them had met at the golf resort putting green and driving range, and soon became good friends. From what they told me about scores and handicaps, I learned they were both better than average golfers. Tom discovered pickleball by accident one day, when Nathan and Nancy were playing in the parking lot in front of his condo with chalked lines and a temporary net. Martin tried it, but never warmed up to the game, although his wife, Celeste, became quite addicted. Tom's wife, Leslie, never fell in love with the game either.

Tom talked about the birth of pickleball in Rio Viejo. How they graduated from the parking lot to painting lines on a county tennis court that was rarely used. For a while that worked out well, until the pickleball group grew. Soon they had painted lines on both the tennis courts and had convinced the county to build four more. Now the little town had developed a reputation in Southern Arizona for nice courts, friendly people, and decent competition. The local tennis players, like Roger and Richard, tried to mount a fight against this encroachment, but their efforts with the county fell on deaf ears. The problem was there were too few tennis players amidst a growing revolution. Pickleball attracted all types of people with or without racket skills, and many with no previous athletic endeavors. Some players, if you watched them closely, could barely walk without a limp. Older people, looking for something athletic and social, took to pickleball with incredible speed and passion. For them, tennis required too much skill and physical exertion to play and enjoy. Rio Viejo had plenty of older people for the game to appeal to.

That was all very well and good for a few months, as the group grew from a small core of eight to ten players into a group of eighty to a hundred people who played at least once a week. It was that kind of growth that

296

convinced the council that pickleball was here to stay, and they would get more bang for their buck by supporting it with city funds. It also didn't hurt that one of the players was the mayor of Nogales, who frequently made the trek to Rio Viejo to play with the group. He was still trying to arrange some land in Nogales for a ten-court complex.

Then things in paradise started to go sour.

Nathan and Nancy decided there needed to be more structure to the group. They formed an official club with them as president and vice president. Then they handpicked the rest of the board (their loyal friends Brian, Little E, and Jane), who supported anything they wanted done. With that came rules and dues, and anyone that didn't cough up their share was shunned. They couldn't legally keep people off the courts, but they could make it unpleasant for you if you didn't pay. Other players started to gripe about the rules: how the courts were designated by skill, playing times, amount, and use of dues and equipment. As the grumbling and in fighting increased, the board and their sycophants got dubbed The Royals. It was never meant as a compliment.

This was not uncommon at pickleball courts across the country, but I was fascinated by the dynamics. It explained a lot. Nathan and his court ruled without much input from the rank and file but acted like it was such a great sacrifice on their part. Even if they didn't know they had been dubbed Royalty by their membership, they acted the part. They thought they were better players than everyone and, subconsciously or not, they flaunted it. If they had an idea to improve the club, they weren't really interested in anyone else's opinion, unless it agreed with theirs. When they started to play in tournaments and bring back medals, they expected the other players to shower them with compliments and appreciation. I could see how their actions and attitude would turn everyone away, but did that animosity rise to the level of murder? Hard to imagine. But then people are strange, and pickleball players are no exception.

We were well into our third beer when my phone dinged, alerting me that I had an email. I took another draw off my beer and opened the email. Colin had been thorough, and the information was illuminating. Before I could read much and share the information it contained with Tom and Martin, my phone rang. It was Colin.

"Hello, Colin," I answered. "That was way quicker than I would have thought possible. Thank you."

"You're welcome, Al. I'm waiting on some more spiders I wrote that are still combing the web."

"Spiders?" I asked, thinking about tarantulas.

"A spider is a web crawler. Essentially, a program that searches the web for a phrase or term. Just like a search you might do on a retail site like Amazon, but instead of just looking at that store or website, this looks through the entire web. They can be slow, but my program will return the results as they come in. I don't need to wait for it to search everywhere or finish before I can start using the info. I called because I wanted to alert you that information is coming in on everyone you gave me, except that fellow Jack. Are you sure you got his name right? And you did say he was from Ohio, right?"

"That's what he has told people. Why?"

"Well, there are some Jack Swensons from Loveland, Ohio, but none come even close to your description of him or his age. Could it be spelled wrong?"

I checked with Tom and Martin, and they confirmed that Jack had talked about some small town in Ohio called Loveland. They checked their phones to make sure it was Swenson and not Swensen. I conveyed that back to Colin.

"Well, my friend, your boy Jack doesn't exist then. At least not in Loveland, Ohio. I'll keep checking, but it's a common name. Without a birth date, it could be that he was born somewhere else and moved there. The other thing I can do is rerun the search and not be so specific. Let me try all of Ohio. And I'll increase the birth-date range to include anyone between the ages of sixty-eight and eighty."

"That's great, Colin. How long will that take?"

"I already started the spider. It shouldn't take too long since those parameters are relatively narrow."

"Awesome. We'll look over the information on the others while we wait on Jack."

I told Tom and Martin about the revised search and about spiders. Not surprisingly, neither of them had ever heard of spiders or web crawlers. I don't know if it was the beer and the slight buzz we were getting, but they seemed fascinated. We also had a little debate about how old we all thought Jack really was. Maybe he was older than he claimed? Do guys lie about their age?

The information we were getting was confirming most of what we knew about our group. Nathan had in fact been in a nasty car accident while driving drunk and had hit a car with three teenagers; two of them died at the scene and a third one survived but lost a leg. Nathan served only one year in prison due to some clever legal defense. Later, he declared bankruptcy and moved to Rio Viejo, where he had lived until his recent demise.

Turned out Rory also lived in the same town in Canada and was, in fact, Nathan's attorney. There was an article about Rory that said he was disbarred for ethical violations stemming from that case, as well as others. He left Canada a few months after Nathan and also settled in Rio Viejo.

"Well, isn't that interesting. Rory was Nathan's attorney. Gets him off with only a year in jail for a double manslaughter DUI and ends up losing his license over some malfeasance associated with the case," exclaimed Tom, followed by a long draw on his beer. "I knew he was shady."

"You think Rory is our guy?" asked Martin. "It would seem he had a beef against Nathan."

"True," I replied, not fully convinced. "I suppose he would have hard feelings about losing his license by helping Nathan." Then I recalled the conversation Rory had with someone where he accused Nathan of not paying his legal bills. "And on top of that, it sounds like Rory still has anger issues over not getting paid."

"Yes," agreed Tom, "Rory has often intimated that Nathan was a deadbeat who didn't pay his bills. Nathan has been accused by a few people here of being a leach."

"So, you think maybe Rory moved down here to follow Nathan and kill him? If so, why wait almost two years to do it?" It did have a ring of plausibility to it. "Joe's been doing his own background checks and I would assume he knows this too. But he didn't mention that to any of us."

"It's possible," agreed Martin, "but Joe and the Sheriff probably aren't sharing everything they know with us. And even if it's true, it only points to motive. The Sheriff will still need some evidence tying Rory to these crimes."

Another swig of beer went down, and I was starting to feel a buzz.

"OK. What else is in that report from Colin?" asked Tom.

I looked at the screen on my phone. "Brian and E," I started, deciding to call him E rather than Little E, out of deference to the newly departed, "appear to be who they said they were. There are some articles about them concerning some questionable land dealings they were involved in together in Florida. Turns out Brian did do some time and had to pay some big fines for embezzling."

"Isn't he the pickleball club treasurer?" asked Martin.

"He is," answered Tom.

"Perfect," I said. I still hadn't paid my dues, but in my defense, no one had asked me again since Nancy told me about them. Now I was glad I hadn't.

"OK, so the two of them have had a nasty history, which would explain the fight and the antagonism between them, but how does killing Nathan, Anna, and Nancy fit in?" asked Martin.

I had to ponder that a minute. All I could come up with was the plot of some murder mystery where the killer murdered a bunch of random people to obfuscate his motive for killing his main target. He was one of those killers who thought he was so clever that no one could ever catch him. They are always proven wrong in the end.

"OK, I get that," I said, nodding my head. "Here's a theory. Let's say the killer is actually Brian. He wants E dead but doesn't want any of the suspicion directed at him, so he kills Nathan, Anna, and Nancy to throw off the authorities. He's obviously planned this for a while, which would explain obtaining the poison from Mexico."

"If that's the case," said Tom, swirling his beer bottle, "then the killing should be over. His intended victim is dead, and the police are baffled. He's made them suspect the Mexicans and drug dealing as the motive."

"Hmm," said Martin. "I don't know. They may have suspected the drug cartels at first, but where's the proof? None of us have ever seen any of the four of them do drugs. You would think if they were involved in drug trafficking there would be some evidence, even circumstantial. I can't believe Joe and the Sheriff are going to hold onto that theory."

"Why else would Eddie, Julio, and Jesus be missing now? It definitely looks suspicious," Tom pointed out. "But Brian couldn't have known they would disappear."

301

"Well, given the quick to judge society we are living in these days, I'm not surprised that Julio, Eddie, and Jesus haven't been around. They probably figured they would be the first suspects, given all the rumors about them and their ties to drug cartels, even if the rumors are false. I have some intimate knowledge of being prejudged," I said.

My phone rang, it was Colin.

"Dude, I'm still not getting any hits on your boy Jack. I'll expand to the surrounding states if you want."

"No, thanks anyway. Hold off and let me see if I can find out more about his background. Maybe we have his name wrong. I don't want to waste your time."

"As for your Mexican friends, I did get some more hits. Eddie is a legit produce importer. Doesn't mean he isn't involved in the drug trade, but I couldn't find any ties to cartels. If he was shady, I think there would probably be some articles about investigations, and I don't see any. Jesus is, in fact, an attorney and he has defended some cartel figures in the past. It looks like he is involved with a case now in Sinaloa. I didn't see anything about charges against him anywhere, so he may just be a clean attorney for a bunch of shady people."

"Thanks. What about Julio?"

"Julio is a trip. He is in the US or maybe back in Mexico, who knows? He's on an expired visa. Other than that, he doesn't have any charges filed against him."

"So, he could just be paranoid anytime police are around," I surmised.

"That would be a good assumption. Anything else I can do for you, my friend?"

"Oh. Did anything else come in on Anna or Jane?"

"Clean as a whistle. If anyone has any beefs with Anna, they aren't official. She moved there with her parents when she was a toddler, legally. Her parents were teachers at the university in Tucson and she applied and was granted citizenship while she was in high school. Not so much as a parking ticket on record. Jane is clean too. She had a messy divorce about five years ago and then nothing. I'll let you know if the spiders come up with anything later, but I don't expect it to change much. Oh, and I almost forgot. Your homicide detective is a piece of work. He had a clean record until a few years ago. Then he got caught up in an internal affairs issue. They redacted most of the information from the official report, so I can't tell what scandal he was involved in. But whatever it was, it forced him to resign or retire early. He does have a full pension, so I can't imagine it was too egregious, but who knows? Up until then, he had a great reputation for getting results and closing cases, although I saw a couple things that suggest he was known to use excessive force."

"Anything about him getting shot on the job?"

"Didn't see anything."

"Wow. OK. Anything else?"

"Give that dude a wide berth, if you can."

"Colin, you have been great, as usual. I'll get back to you soon. And if you need to get out of Denver for a vacation, you are always welcome here. Butch would love to see you." After I said it, I wanted to kick myself. Butch and I had already decided to leave the first chance we got.

"Thanks, but not right now. Call me when the killer has been apprehended. In the meantime, I'm going to stay safe in Denver." He let out a hearty laugh, but I knew he was serious.

I shared what Colin had told me with Tom and Martin.

"How does this help us?" asked Tom.

"That's a good question," I answered. I'm not a detective and I'm not sure what I thought I was doing. I didn't exactly know when I asked Colin to get all this information what I would do with it once I had it. Did I think doing a background check on everyone would reveal that someone had a history of murder? Nathan's conviction for manslaughter didn't qualify, and besides, he was the first to get killed. "Well, we know that Brian and E have bad history together. None of the Mexicans really look guilty to me and I don't see this as the work of Jane. Guys, I'm baffled."

"All the victims are Royals," said Martin. "We've noticed that before and I don't think you can ignore that fact. Someone is killing the Royals and it could be that that someone isn't one of the people you have done background checks on."

"Do we just assume it could be anyone?" asked Tom.

"Someone who has been wronged by the Royals and takes pickleball too seriously," replied Martin.

"From what I've seen and heard, everyone that plays here is on that list. At least the part about being wronged by the Royals. Maybe it's someone who hates pickleball and blames the Royals for its growing popularity here."

"I know what you are thinking," said Tom.

"Richard and Roger," I said.

"Bingo."

"You think?" asked Martin.

"I don't know for sure, but I think they slashed Brian's tires and they have made it known how much they hate pickleball."

"Geez. That would explain a lot," said Martin. "But you know who else really hates pickleball?"

"Who?" Tom and I asked in unison.

"Joe," said Martin, looking quite proud of himself.

"The detective?" asked Tom.

"He's the only Joe here, isn't he? Think about it. Joe has complained about pickleball and what he calls the "fanatics" since you all got this thing going. He's made it clear he hates that his wife is so enthusiastic about playing. Every time they go out together, they run into other players and all they discuss is pickleball, and I can tell he's bored and fed up with it. I know he made it clear when you all passed the hat asking for donations to buy paint and nets for the courts. He balked, and Samantha had to kick in over his objections. If you ask me, he's a very intense dude and definitely physically capable of inflicting harm. He knows police procedures and knows how to cover up a crime of this nature. His wife hates the Royals and is always criticizing them."

Tom and I remained silent.

Martin continued, "And who better to do the investigation than the killer himself? He could hide critical evidence if it implicated him. Who would actually suspect him?"

"You," I said.

"But not until now, and if that report from your friend hadn't mentioned how unstable Joe was and how he lost his career under suspicious conditions, I wouldn't have thought it was him either. But after hearing about his past, I'm convinced it's him."

"Is that the beer talking?" I asked, looking at the all the empty bottles we had on the table. Martin laughed, but I don't think he actually thought it was funny. "What do you propose we do with your theory?" I asked.

"Fuck if I know. I'm sure going to the Sheriff with my suspicions would not go well. He would confront Joe, and I would be outed as his accuser. I don't want that shit coming down on me or Celeste." He shook his head violently. "Nope. This has to stay between us. We share this with anyone, and I guarantee we become targets."

Everything that Martin said made sense. I had had my suspicions about Joe before, but then I'd suspected just about everyone at some point. But I had to agree with Martin. This new information about Joe's past, both known and unknown, did cast some suspicion his way. If this was about killing Royals and not some other motive, than it should be about over. There weren't too many Royals left to kill. Of course that begged the question, who decided who was a Royal? If it really was about the Royals, then Brian and Jane were certainly at risk.

But I still wasn't convinced. Of course, Stephanie would be telling me right about now that I was hardheaded and couldn't see what was right in front of my face. She wouldn't be wrong.

"What about Jack?" I asked. "Isn't it odd that Colin couldn't track down anything about him?"

"You didn't ask your friend to do background checks on William or Molly, or a couple dozen others. No, Jack's not the killer," said Tom, laughing, "any more than William is. I mean can you imagine William pulling something like this off? No, Jack is about as mild-mannered a player as we have out there. I would suspect Rory or Brian before Jack. Jack never gets mad at anyone, about anything. It's probably just that we got his name wrong or where he's from."

"I say it's Joe," reiterated Martin.

"So, what do we do?" asked Tom, looking nervous.

"Nothing. I say nothing," Martin advised. "We go quiet, and we stay away from the courts. I'm going to insist that Celeste refrain from playing until the killer is found and I suggest you two do the same."

"Nancy and E weren't killed at the courts," I pointed out.

"Leslie and I have guns," said Tom. He didn't need to say more.

"You have Butch," said Martin. "I'm sure he would protect you."

"As long as the killer didn't bring him a meaty bone."

It was starting to get dark, and I realized I hadn't fed Butch. He wasn't going to be happy eating dinner late, and if I wanted him to protect me, it was probably best to keep him happy. Besides that, the conversation was giving me a headache. Or maybe it was the beer? In any event, I felt like we were just going around circles, throwing off names and working ourselves into a tizzy, but getting nowhere. We weren't detectives and we had no clue what we were doing.

"Guys, I'm not sure we are getting anywhere. If it is Joe, we need to keep an eye on him for now and keep quiet about our suspicions. I'm not sure staying away from the courts helps. We should play." Was that me being fanatical and not wanting to stop playing, or was it a good idea? "But we should keep our eyes and ears open and watch each other's backs." Then I remembered the water bottles. "And keep an eye on your water bottle. Don't let anyone touch it. Keep it close to you. But for now, I gotta go. Butch needs his dinner." Butch looked up eagerly. He obviously agreed with me.

They both nodded and we all agreed to meet again to share any suspicious behavior we witnessed, and of course, to update everyone if Colin called with more information. We paid our bills and departed. It was already dark, and I mean dark. The minimal outdoor lighting in Rio Viejo made a walk home at night quite an adventure. I hadn't brought a flashlight, so I was going to have to depend on what little light came off the moon. Butch and I rushed home, but carefully, for fear of stepping on a snake or tarantula. It did occur to me that I could be ambushed by the killer in this darkness, and I would never see it coming.

But, Butch had great hearing and I was sure he would alert me to any two legged dangers. Whether or not he would jump in front of a speeding bullet or knife to save me was another question.

Pickleball Tip # 22 – Charging The Net After The Return Of Serve

All of us were told when we first learned the game to rush to the NVZ. We were instructed to hit the ball and charge the net without a thought to where we had just hit the ball or the position of our opponents on the other side. Even now, many teachers still preach to get to the net at all costs. It was never the best advice, and it still isn't. The top pros and instructors now give the following tips, although they may use different terminology:

1. Look at your partner

2. Watch or assess what kind of shot they are attempting

3. Ascertain if they succeeded in either hitting a drive deep or an effective drop shot

4. Decide to either advance to the net, advance a few steps, or wait at the baseline with your partner.

It does no good to rush the net and be caught moving if your partner has set up your opponents for a slam or a shot at your feet. It is difficult to hit a ball on the move, and invariably, if you do return a shot aimed at your feet, you will likely pop it up for an even better offensive shot by your opponent. It is also not advisable to create a large gap between you and your partner. If your partner is stuck back at the baseline because of a great service return, you need to be back there to help defend until you or your partner can hit a reset shot that will allow you to advance to the net together.

If your partner tries to hit a drive from behind the baseline while backpedaling, the likelihood is that he or she will hit a weak shot that has no chance of intimidating your opponents, who can then attack you either while you are moving to the NVZ or after you have reached there and are now a sitting duck.

Want proof? Watch any pro match and you will see them watch and assess before charging to the net.

Chapter 23

We made it home in record time, and fortunately did not encounter any snakes, tarantulas, javelinas, or a killer ambush. I vowed that next time I left the house in the afternoon, I would bring a flashlight. I was winded when we walked in but went directly to the treat closet. Butch chomped down on the Milk Bone while I prepared his dinner – dry kibble topped with a can of beef stew.

While he scarfed down his treat, I summarized the call with Colin, who he had met before and enjoyed playing with, and the details of my talk with Tom and Martin. I was pretty sure he had slept through the entire discussion at the market, and I wanted to bring him up to speed. I assured him we had decided not to do anything rash at this point, but we would be on the lookout for anyone who looked suspicious or dangerous. He grumbled when I told him his job was to keep me safe. I took that to mean that he was up to the job and how dare I even question it.

He gobbled down his dinner while I gave him the lowdown on who we might have to worry about. He didn't seem worried or daunted at all. That gave me more confidence. He finished his meal and sat by the treat cupboard to tell me he needed a Dentabone to clean his teeth. He had always been very concerned about his dental hygiene, as he hated to visit the vet. He finished cleaning his teeth and then marched over to the front door to tell me it was time for his after-dinner walk. I didn't want to go back out in the dark, but I had trouble saying no, so I grabbed a flashlight and leashed him up. I may have a fear of night-time critters, but Butch didn't.

311

Butch led the way. I tried to direct him to go where I wanted, but when you have a dog of Butch's weight and strength you go where he wants to go. I could tell by his determination that it was not going to be a short walk. The trip to the market had ended up more talk than walk, so I owed him. If it hadn't been so dark, I wouldn't have minded. Fortunately, the flashlight was big and had a bright, wide beam that helped me conquer my fear of unseen wildlife, though there didn't seem to be any out that night.

I noticed my flashlight was starting to dim, and I had no intention of walking down pitch-black streets without a functioning flashlight. I stopped Butch with a sharp tug on the leash and was about to explain to him why we needed to head straight home, when I noticed a car pull up in front of a mobile home across the street. A woman exited the car, marched purposefully up to the door, and knocked. There was only a dim front porch light, but I could still see enough to tell that it was Jane, one of the pickleball Royals. I felt like a Peeping Tom, so I turned off my flashlight so I wouldn't be noticed. Jane knocked a second time before the door opened. Jack appeared at the door and started talking to her. We were too far to hear the conversation, and I longed for one of those hearing aids that let you hear things going on thirty feet away.

Even without hearing the words, I could tell they were having a heated discussion. Jane was waving a piece of paper in Jack's face and raising her voice, but all we could hear was gibberish. Jack was waving his arms back at her. This went on for a couple of minutes until Jack opened the door completely and she barged in, or possibly was pulled. It was hard to tell from where we stood. Jack looked around quickly but didn't spot us, then slammed the door shut.

I was torn. I wanted to get home and out of the dark, but the encounter we had witnessed had me intrigued. At the courts, the two of them always looked like friends, but this exchange was anything but friendly. I'm not normally a nosy person, but with all that was going on in Rio Viejo, I couldn't help myself. Was there an affair going on between Jack and Jane?

As far as I knew, these were two single, consenting adults. They could do whatever they wanted. Jack was clearly a flirt, always wanting to play with the ladies and bringing them treats and water bottles, and Jane, well I didn't know. Seemed to me she was a flirt too, and if I wasn't mistaken, she had directed some attention my way. Other than her obsession with pickleball, I had no idea about her life. She wasn't a bombshell to look at, but she wasn't hard on the eyes either. She was very fit, constantly on the move. I could see Jack making a move on her, even if he was twenty years her senior. But what were they arguing about? Was it a lovers spat?

I should have accepted that it was none of my business and moved on. But I didn't.

Butch and I remained across the street, watching the house after they both went in. We scooted a little closer to get a better view. One of the windows in the front had flimsy drapes, allowing us to see silhouettes of the two of them. They were still very animated and clearly still arguing. They seemed to be yelling at each other, but nothing was discernible from where we stood.

Suddenly, the voices stopped. They had moved away from the window, so there was no action that we could see. Whatever they were arguing about was apparently finished, and I decided Butch and I should get on home. I certainly didn't want to peek in the window and see the two of them kissing, or more.

Then the front door opened and Jack stepped out onto the porch. Not wanting Jack to know we had been spying on him and Jane, I signaled Butch to be quiet. It was one of the many hand signals I had taught Butch while Stephanie was ill and trying to sleep. She needed all the rest she could get and having Butch remain quiet during those times was really useful. It certainly came in handy that night. We stood across the street, frozen and silent, and watched as Jack came down the steps with something in his hands. He looked around furtively but didn't see us. Satisfied no one was watching him, he walked briskly to his car and kneeled down. He removed the front license plate and replaced it with the one he was carrying. He repeated this on the rear plate. I resisted the urge to call out to him and ask what he was doing; instead, I just stood there, fascinated and curious about what I was seeing. Why would he be changing license plates at this late hour, and in the dark no less? Even if it was time to put on new plates, it certainly wasn't something that needed to be done at night, and especially when he had a guest over. I wondered where Jane was. At least they weren't arguing anymore.

Butch and I stayed quietly in our position as Jack finished the job and hurried back into the house. Again, I considered leaving. Spying felt creepy and I certainly didn't want to be discovered there. Then Jack reappeared on the front porch, this time carrying two large suitcases. He paused and looked around briefly, then carried the bags to his car. I repeated my quiet command to Butch. He had previously been able to keep quiet on command for up to two hours. I was grateful for that training, as I wasn't interested in talking to Jack at that point. Jack appeared to be satisfied that he was alone. The bags must have been heavy, as he struggled to get them to the car and into the trunk. He partially closed the trunk enough for the light to go out and then ran back to the house. A couple minutes later, he re-emerged from the house carrying two more suitcases. He maneuvered them into the trunk with the other bags and closed the door. Once again, he ran back to the house and repeated the process, this time putting the bags in the backseat.

Not sure if I was more confused or concerned. Was Jack leaving town in the middle of the night? Even under normal circumstances that would seem odd but given the recent murder spree it was very suspicious. And still no sign of Jane. Something was definitely going on and I had to find out what it was.

Jack finished loading up the backseat, shut the door quietly, and hurried back to the house. I told Butch to sit and stay, another command he had learned perfectly, while I went to confront Jack. I knew it wasn't the smartest thing I could do in that situation, but my curiosity and concern for Jane got the better of me. In my defense, I had imbibed four or five beers earlier and wasn't quite as sharp as I might have been.

With Butch sitting quietly at attention across the street, I walked up to Jack's house and was about to knock, when he opened the door. I don't know which of us was more startled by the timing.

"Al," he stammered. "What are you doing here?" He looked surprised and afraid at the same time.

I wasn't expecting the door to open before I knocked, so I was tongue-tied at first.

"Uh, I was just taking a walk and saw you packing your car. Are you heading out on a trip?" I finally managed to say.

"Uh, yes. I was thinking of taking a little road trip." He stood by the door and kept it mostly closed, so I couldn't see in. I was wondering where Jane was and why she was being so quiet.

"Looks like you don't travel light."

"Why do you say that?"

"Looked like you put everything you own in the car," I said, pointing at it.

"I was thinking of a long trip. You never know what you will need. Look Al, I'm kind of in a hurry to pack up and hit the road. Is there anything else you need?"

"Late start for a road trip," I commented, ignoring his question. "Personally, I hate driving at night."

"Hmm. Well, I like it. Roads are empty. No traffic and you can make good time," he said, as he started to close the door.

"I'd be happy to help you pack up," I persisted.

"No. Al, I really can handle it. But thanks anyway."

I wasn't about to give up yet. I probably should have taken the hint at this point and walked off, but my curiosity was nagging me. Where was Jane and why was he changing license plates? And the big question that I probably shouldn't have asked was about the argument with Jane. Maybe they were having a lovers spat about him leaving town so quickly and it was none of my business. But I couldn't let it go.

"Jack, I thought I saw Jane go in earlier and I heard you guys arguing about something. Is everything OK?"

"Are you spying on me, Al?"

"No, I uh..."

"Al," he interrupted before I could finish, "it's none of your damn business. Jane's not here." He paused. "She already left."

"But that's her car, isn't it?" I turned and pointed at a car parked by the curb. Another bad move on my part. I turned back to Jack just as he swung a pickleball paddle at my head. Where did it even come from? He hit me with so much force my legs buckled, and I went down to my knees. I wasn't knocked out, but I was out of commission. Out of the corner of my eye, I could see Butch come flying across the street barking and growling. If I hadn't been half passed out, I would have really appreciated how graceful and ferocious he could be at the same time. Jack must have spotted Butch, too. He grabbed me by the shirt collar and tried to drag me into the house. Butch leapt from five feet away, jaws wide open, with a look that could kill. He landed on Jack and knocked him back into the door jam. His teeth were locked onto Jack's leg, and he quickly drew blood. Jack screamed but was able to retrieve the paddle and started whacking Butch on the head. Butch howled in pain and released his grip on Jack's leg long enough for Jack to drag me the rest of the way into the house and slam the door shut. Butch remained outside barking angrily. I was conscious enough to be relieved that he was okay.

Dazed and groggy from the wallop I took to the head, I struggled to stand up, but my legs said no, and I fell back to the floor. Jack was cussing and screaming in pain, but he noticed my attempt to stand and whacked me again with the paddle. Everything went dark.

Pickleball Tip # 23 – Contact Point When Hitting Drives

Too many people hit shots while backpedaling or off balance, causing the ball to float too high or go too long, or giving the opponent an easy put-away. Part of the problem is waiting until the ball has bounced before preparing to hit it back. Taking your paddle back late causes balls to go wide, or forces you to swing too fast, losing control of the direction of your shot.

Rather than waiting till the ball has bounced, try getting your paddle in a ready position sooner. Once you know if it's going to be to your backhand or forehand, bring your paddle back and prepare to hit the ball slightly in front and to your side, with a smooth stroke and follow through.

Chapter 24

I woke up and my head was pounding. I was lying on a couch with my hands zip-tied together. I struggled to sit up and could hear Butch outside barking like I'd never heard him before. He was running from the front door to the side of the house and back again; snarls and barks alternated with loud thuds that I could only imagine were caused by him ramming the front door in an attempt to knock it down. Part of me wanted him to succeed in breaking down the door and part of me was worried what Jack might do to him if he did.

My eyes cleared and I could see Jane on the love seat across from me. She, too, had her hands zip-tied together, but she also had a gag in her mouth. She had a look of terror in her eyes, which were full of tears.

"Are you OK?" I asked her in a shaky voice. She nodded but wasn't very convincing. "Where is Jack?" She nodded toward the kitchen. I looked over to see Jack returning with a large kitchen knife in his hand and what I assumed was going to be a gag for me in the other. There was blood all over his leg and it looked like he had duct-taped a kitchen towel over the wound that Butch had inflicted on him.

"Al, why couldn't you have just left when I told you to?" he asked in a whiny voice. "I always liked you and I didn't want to harm you. You forced me to do this!"

"I forced you?" I asked, incredulous. "I didn't tell you to hit me over the head."

"You persisted in asking questions. If you had just left, you wouldn't be caught up in this."

"What is this that I'm caught up in, Jack?

I could easily guess what it was, but he didn't know that. I needed to buy time. All my hopes rested on Butch alerting the neighbors, but I didn't remember seeing any lights on in any of the other houses.

"Jack, I don't understand, what's going on? Why is Jane tied up and gagged? I thought we were friends. I thought she was your friend."

"Al, you're an OK dude, but I can't let you live knowing what you know."

"Knowing what?" *Keep him talking*, I said to myself. Bad guys always make a mistake when they talk too much.

"That I killed Nathan. Are you that dumb?"

"Why would you kill Nathan?"

"Oh Al, it's a long story."

"I've got time and I'd really like to understand. You know Jack, I like you, you're a good guy, you must have had a reason to do these things."

Jack paused and let out a deep sigh. "Well, I guess it would be nice for someone to hear my side of the story. You're right Al, I am a nice guy. I'm not really Jack from Ohio, my name is actually Leroy Martin and I'm from Toronto. Same as Nathan. Nathan is the bad guy in this story, not me. Remember when I told you Nathan was a heavy drinker?"

"Yes, but what does that have to do with anything?"

"I'm getting to that. Patience, my friend. Nathan got in a wreck when he was drunk. Killed two kids and seriously wounded a third. They were just teenagers on their way home after a high school football game. Two of those girls were my nieces."

320

"I'm really sorry, Jack, I mean Leroy, but didn't he go to jail for that?"

"A year is all he did! He needed to pay a bigger price. If the law wouldn't punish him, then I had to."

"But why kill Nancy, and Anna, and Little E?"

"Well don't feel sorry for Nancy. She was an enabler. She coddled Nathan when he should have been tossed out on his ass. You know he beat her a few times when he was drunk? She kept talking about throwing him out but kept forgiving him. It was just disgusting. Not to mention her being one of the Royals. They all disgust me. But her real crime was that she wouldn't accept that Nathan died of a heart attack. She kept asking questions. I was afraid she wouldn't give up until she proved that Nathan was murdered."

Jane made a noise, it sounded like she was trying to say something through her gag. "Shut up, bitch!" Jack screamed, "And then this bitch had to interfere as well."

"I don't understand, what did Jane do?"

"For one thing, she is a Royal and deserves to be punished. These people and their holier-than-thou attitudes and rude behavior need to go."

"Geez, Jack."

"You can call me Leroy with the time you have left."

"OK, Leroy. I still don't understand why Jane is here?"

"She," he pointed at Jane, "was really good friends with Nancy. So, she was over at Nancy's, cleaning up the place, and found a letter from someone in Canada that knew me," he took a piece of paper from his pocket and held it up for me to see. "I guess the shithead was here for Nathan's funeral and spotted me. He didn't recognize me at first, but then he did some digging and found an article with my picture in it. He wrote to Nancy but fortunately she didn't open the letter before she died. I dodged a bullet on that one, until this Royal bitch decides to clean house and finds the letter. She made the fatal mistake of confronting me with it."

"You were in the newspaper?" I asked, trying to keep him talking but also curious as to how all this came together.

"I had some legal issues in Canada."

"What kind?"

"You sure are curious, aren't you? Why do you care? You're going to be dead shortly and it doesn't matter anyway."

"Please indulge me, Leroy. At least let me die knowing why."

"Fine. I was implicated in a murder up there along with some drug dealing. I skipped town before my trial and decided to track down Nathan. So here I am, and he's finally paid the ultimate price for killing those kids."

"But Leroy, why Anna? Why did you kill her? She seemed like such a nice person."

"Another sad circumstance. She was the one who introduced me to the poison I used to kill Nathan. She had a big mouth, though, and kept telling that story to everyone, making the police suspicious. I stole the poison from her."

"Why would she have poison?"

Leroy shook his head. "This is getting tedious, Al. OK. She had the poison from her Mexican friend Jesus. She was pissed off at Nathan and was going to drug him to punish him for going back to Nancy. Anna wanted him for herself. She knew a small dose of the poison would incapacitate the victim and she could inflict a little pain, but she had no intention of killing him. I guess in Mexico some ladies use it that way on cheating husbands. She even told Nancy about the poison, probably hoping Nancy would do the deed for her. Anna was going to figure out that I had stolen it from her. I knew they both had to go but I didn't have enough of the concoction to kill them both. So, I spiked the water bottle I gave to Anna at the court that day. That left me just enough to drug Nancy and make it easy to strangle her."

"Why Ethelwolf?"

"Ethelwolf was a little piss-ant. He thought he was so great at pickleball and had this disgusting attitude, along with being a Royal. You can't tell me you liked him?"

"I hardly knew him. I'm new here."

"Too bad you came here, Al. Well, if you knew him much longer you would have hated him too. When he had that fight with Brian, I thought it was the perfect time to kill him. There was a rumor going around that the killer was targeting Royals, so taking out Little E would encourage that theory. Of course some might suspect Brian did it, but I can't stand that guy either. If I had had more time, I would have killed all the Royals. It made a perfect cover. No one would suspect me. I was the nice guy on the pickleball court. I was really starting to enjoy being here and playing pickleball with everyone, but the Royals kept spoiling it for me. And for everyone else too. You know that's true. Nobody's going to miss them."

"What happens now, Leroy? Jane and I won't do you any harm. We won't say anything. You could just leave town, you don't need to kill us."

"Sorry, Al, but I do. No one knows who I really am. I can disappear and restart my life in another town, but not if I think you will talk, and the police will start tracking me down."

"Leroy, you know they will find out you aren't who you say you are. They're not dumb."

"What? You mean that hick Sheriff? They don't have a clue."

"If I figured it out, they could too."

"What do you mean you figured it out?" said Leroy, with a confused look. He came over and stood right in front of me and pulled out a revolver.

"I had a friend do some checking. We knew that there was no one named Jack Swenson from Ohio. Joe was checking his sources, too, and would have discovered you soon enough. And you know, he's very suspicious and protective of Samantha. He's been doing background checks on all of us. I'm sure he knows who you really are by now."

Leroy grimaced. "Shit. Really?"

"Yes. I think if you run now, by the time we get out of these binds and are found you could be halfway across the country."

"No. I don't think so. You're lying. Joe doesn't know shit." He left the room, and I looked over at Jane. She was sobbing quietly through her gag and looked petrified and exhausted.

Leroy returned a few minutes later with some bottles of alcohol and lighter fluid and it became apparent to me what his plan was. All this time, Butch was still going crazy outside trying to get in. As hard as he was trying, I didn't think he could ever break down a door, but I still had hopes that someone would wander by and see him, or at least hear the ruckus he was making.

Leroy set down the bottles near us. He was acting more and more agitated.

"Al, you need to shut that damn dog down."

"Let me go and he will calm down."

"Nice try. Stop him making all that noise or I'm going to go out there and shoot him."

"Leroy, he's just a dog. Please don't hurt him," I begged.

324

"Then do something."

I had to think fast. We were running out of time. I had no doubt if Butch kept up barking and ramming the doors Leroy would shoot him. Butch knew the command to sit and wait and be quiet, but did I really want him sitting by the door waiting for Leroy to murder him? I wish I had a better idea, but I was running out of time and I knew it.

"Leroy, I can tell him to go home," I lied. Butch had never learned to go home on command. If I told him that he would just be confused. "I need to go over to the door so he can hear me."

"Fine. Get up and tell him to go home or he's dead."

I struggled to get off the couch with my head aching and my hands zip-tied in front of me. I pretended to be in even worse shape than I was, hoping to lull Leroy into a false sense of security, like trying to get your opponent to go for a low percentage shot in pickleball. I made it off the couch and limped over to the front door, where it sounded like Butch was banging his head against the door and growling.

"Butch," I yelled. He stopped barking when he heard my voice. "Sit." Then I quickly said in a loud voice that I knew Leroy would hear, "Be quiet and go home."

In my mind I could see Butch sitting quietly on the porch, staring at the door and waiting for the next command. Although he knew sit and quiet very well, I had never taught him to go home. He wasn't going to leave without me, but Leroy didn't know that. My hope was that when Leroy went outside to finish packing his car, Butch would attack. Once Butch pounced, I would break my binds, giving me a chance to take out the older, weaker man. The possible flaw was the zip tie on my wrist. The plan was dependent on the validity of a YouTube video that I had seen which showed a teenage girl break free from zip ties all on her own. If she could do it, why couldn't I? I had never tested the technique and if it didn't work, we were all going to die. But it was a plan, and I was going to go out fighting. Besides, other than hoping the cavalry would arrive, I had no other ideas.

Phase one of the plan was working. Butch was quiet and Leroy had calmed down.

"Now what?" I asked.

"Get back on the couch and stay there. I'm going to finish packing and if you two are really good, maybe I won't kill you before I leave."

I heard a sigh of relief from Jane, but I knew Leroy was lying. He had no intention of letting us live. I had noticed that among the items he had laid out with the alcohol was a candle. I figured that his plan was to light the candle so that when it burned down it would ignite the alcohol. This would give him enough time to escape before the resulting fire would alert the police.

I tried to reason with him again. "Leroy, you don't have to kill us. You can be miles away before we are found. They'll know it was you anyway. Killing us doesn't help."

That seemed to make him pause, like he was considering it.

"Maybe you're right. Behave, and I might just do that."

I wished I could believe him. I wanted to, but I didn't. We knew he was Leroy Martin from Canada, and we could give the police enough information to be able to find him. If we died in the fire, they would suspect Jack Swenson did it, but Jack Swenson didn't exist. The car had new plates, probably stolen. I'm sure he thought it was a perfect plan. But I had a plan too.

Butch was still being quiet, but I had no doubt he was there, waiting and angry. He had taken a chunk out of Leroy's leg, and if he had another chance, he'd bite the man's nose off. I watched Leroy gathering more things to take out front. I reviewed in my head the YouTube video. The girl, smaller and weaker than me, was sitting in a chair with her hands tied in front of her with a zip tie. She raised her hands above her head and quickly dropped down her arms, causing a chicken wing effect. The zip tie snapped at its weakest point, the locking mechanism, freeing her. She no doubt practiced before making the video, but I had only one shot to get it right. Now I just needed Butch to create the diversion.

Leroy looked over at me and I almost panicked. Did he know I was up to something? He went into the kitchen and came back out carrying a dish rag and duct tape. He was limping and it was clear he was in pain. I shook my head. "You don't need to gag me," I pleaded. "I'll be quiet."

"Not taking any chances with you, Al. Sorry."

He shoved the rag in my mouth and ran duct tape around my head to keep it in place.

"Now I know you'll be quiet," he said, with an air of satisfaction.

Pickleball Tip # 24 – Shift To Cut Off The Court

Often times in doubles, one team will identify and target the weaker player, essentially freezing the stronger player out of the game. If you are the player being shut out of the play, you need to squeeze the court smaller. Move closer to your teammate, giving your opponents a smaller target to aim for and a smaller margin for error. It will give you an easier opportunity to poach. Your partner should also slide a little, giving you more room to operate. With this formation, your opponents will have a harder time keying in on the weaker player. They might try a difficult passing shot that also has a low margin for error. Good strategy and court position will tempt your opponents into difficult, low percentage shots.

Chapter 25

I was getting incredibly nervous. Would my plan work? All our lives depended on it. After gagging me, Leroy finished staging the rest of his belongings by the front door, while I waited anxiously to make my move. I pictured what would happen when Leroy opened the door and found a vicious beast waiting to attack and save his companion.

I held my breath in anticipation as I watched Leroy put the gun in his pocket. He opened the door a crack to peak out but evidently didn't see or hear anything. I prayed that Butch hadn't gotten distracted by a squirrel or something and wandered off. If he did, we were all doomed. Leroy left the door ajar and turned around to pick up his stuff. He stepped outside, and not a moment later, he let out a blood-curdling scream. If I hadn't hated Leroy and wanted him dead, I would have felt sorry for him.

Leroy wasn't expecting Butch's attack and fell back into the house, sending the bags he was carrying flying everywhere. Butch's jaw stayed clamped onto Leroy's arm as he hit the ground. Growls and snarls and a tearing sound told me that Butch was trying to rip the man's arm off. This was my cue. I raised my arms and dropped them quickly to my lap, swinging my elbows out. Nothing happened, other than a rush of severe pain. The zip tie didn't snap open, but the motion tore some skin from my wrists. Blood followed. My heart sank and I began to panic. I needed to get free and help Butch before Leroy could extricate himself and pull the gun from his pocket. I tried again, this time with more force and more determination. It had to work, dammit.

Snap. The zip tie broke and I was free. I ripped the duct tape off and pulled the gag from my mouth. Jumping up from the couch, I scanned the room for a weapon I could use. A table lamp. I ripped the cord from the wall and called out to Butch to back off so I could have a clear line at Leroy. He obeyed the command, but first gave a little extra tug on Leroy's arm. I thought I heard a bone crack. Leroy, now free from the monster's jaws, was reaching in his pocket for the revolver with his other hand. It was awkward, as the gun was in his right pants pocket, but because of the damage Butch had done to his right arm he had to reach across with his left.

Just as he started to pull the gun free, I reached him and swung the lamp like a forehand overhead slam. I was aiming for his head, but in the excitement of the moment I missed and hit him on the shoulder. I wasn't sure if it was the lamp breaking or the man's clavicle, but the sound was deafening. But it wasn't over yet. Somehow Leroy was able to pull the gun from his pocket and he started shooting wildly. Luckily he missed me and Butch, giving me time to swing what was left of the lamp and this time I landed a clean blow to his head. Leroy looked at me with a confused expression that was almost sad. I don't think he believed he could lose. Then his eyes shut, and he toppled over.

I followed him down. Leroy hadn't missed me completely; I just hadn't felt it with all the excitement and adrenaline flowing. My shoulder suddenly hurt like hell. I looked carefully at Leroy to make sure he wasn't getting up, fully prepared to crack him in the head again regardless of the pain I was now in. Butch came over and licked my face while also keeping a wary eye on Leroy, who still wasn't moving. There was a growing puddle of blood around his head. I was going to call 911, but Leroy must have taken the phone out of my pocket when he knocked me out.

I heard a noise and glanced at the front door. To my surprise, Joe was standing there. He was holding a gun and pointed it from side to side as he entered the room. When he realized that Leroy was down, and I was sitting next to him holding a broken lamp, he slipped his gun in his pocket, kicked Leroy's gun to the side, and bent down to check him for a pulse. He shook his head.

"Dead?" I asked.

"He's dead."

I sighed and hugged Butch. "I was just about to call 911, but I can't find my phone."

Joe grabbed a towel from the bathroom and applied it to my shoulder, instructing me to stay still and hold it there. I complied while he called 911. Then he called the Sheriff.

Joe had me wait on the floor for the paramedics while he went to check on Jane. She was slumped over on the love seat, and I was afraid she had taken one of the wild bullets from Leroy's gun. He removed her gag and cut the zip tie with his pocketknife. She woke up and hugged him.

Joe came back to check on me.

"Is Jane OK?" I asked.

He nodded. "She passed out, but I didn't see any wounds and she's breathing fine. I think she just fainted. There was a bullet hole in the couch right next to her. Missed her by six inches."

"Wow," I sighed. So Leroy hadn't succeeded in killing another Royal.

"How did you get here?" Joe asked.

I told him about my friend doing background checks for me and how he couldn't track down Jack Swenson. Why Butch and I ended up in front of Jack/Leroy's house that night, I was not really sure. Was it chance or my suspicions that drove me there? I'll never know. I told Joe how Butch and I spotted the fight between Leroy and Jane and went to investigate. I admitted it wasn't the smartest thing I had ever done, that my curiosity and concern for Jane had got the better of me. I explained how Leroy panicked and attacked me when I asked too many questions. Then I went into great detail about how Butch saved the day with his heroics. If it wasn't for Butch, Jane and I would likely have been burning to death by then.

"What brought you here?" I asked Joe. Before he could answer, Samantha entered the house. She looked around in disbelief.

"What happened?" she asked.

"I'll explain later," Joe answered. "We're waiting for the ambulance now." As he turned back to me, we heard the siren in the distance. "I had done my own background checks on everyone, but nothing ever came up on Jack. So, my suspicions aroused, I got a sample of his fingerprints. Samantha and I were out to dinner tonight when I got the call from a friend in Phoenix telling me there was a match. Jack, or rather Leroy Martin, was a criminal from Canada. He was wanted for murder and a number of racketeering and drug charges. He's been on the run for over a year."

"How did you get his fingerprints?" I asked.

"Jack was always handing out bottled water to people, so I took one and had it analyzed. He acted like he was the nicest guy. Totally above suspicion. The guy no one would ever suspect, but I didn't like the fact that I couldn't confirm his story. Why would he lie about where he was from? So, when I got the call at dinner about his history, I immediately called the Sheriff and told him to meet me here. I was waiting outside in the car for just a minute or two, when I heard the gun shots and came in the house to find," he paused, nodding his head toward Leroy's body, "this."

The paramedics arrived just before the Sheriff, and they started to give me medical attention to stop the bleeding. I was losing a decent amount of blood at this point, but I was surprisingly pumped up. Butch was sitting next to me, keeping an eye on the paramedics to make sure they weren't hurting me. Jane was in shock and getting some attention from the paramedics too, but she was okay and would live to play another day.

I was still a little leery of the villain coming back to life to attack again when everyone's guard is down, just like they always do in the movies. I kept asking the paramedics to check once again and confirm Leroy was dead. They assured me that he wasn't going anywhere, at least not on his own. I was still trying to process the fact that I had taken another person's life. On the one hand, I was appalled that I had just killed someone, but on the other I was glad he was no longer a threat to anyone. It was still hard to believe that the mild-mannered court custodian we had all come to like was really a monster. He had a legitimate gripe against Nathan, and all the Royals were certainly annoying, but none of that justified murder. But then what does?

Almost as if he was reading my mind, Joe said. "Al, you did good. Leroy was going to kill you and Jane if you hadn't acted when you did."

I nodded. I could rationalize my action by saying it was self-defense and with him gone everyone else was now safe, but I had still taken someone's life.

"Thanks. I appreciate that," I answered gratefully.

He must have understood I still was having doubts.

"Look Al, I won't bother telling you about the first time I killed someone in the line of duty, but just believe me when I say, I know what you are going through. It's tough under any circumstances but give it time and you'll come to peace with it."

I smiled and then groaned as the paramedics strapped me to a gurney.

A paramedic motioned to Joe, saying, "We need to get him to the hospital now."

Joe stepped back to give them room to wheel me out. Butch got up and followed us out to the ambulance, with Joe and Samantha right behind.

"He can't come in the ambulance," said one of the paramedics.

"I can't leave Butch alone," I pleaded.

"He can't come in here with you. Regulations," the paramedic reiterated.

"You don't understand. Butch and I live alone and besides, Butch is the real hero today. If not for him," I started to cry, "we'd be dead."

"I'll take him home and take care of him till you are released," said Samantha. I could see Joe wasn't that thrilled to have a house guest, but he didn't complain. Then I passed out.

Pickleball Tip # 25– Communication Is Critical For Success

Communicate before and during a match. Talk with your partner before the match begins and discuss strengths and weaknesses and who will take what shot in each situation.

Being in sync with your partner is key if you are going to win points and games. Calling "mine" or "yours" during the point eliminates any confusion as to who is going to take the shot. Sometimes it is based on positioning and sometimes it's based on who has the better shot. Proper communication should help avoid those shots down the middle where both players assume the other is going to take it and instead it splits the middle, with both players saying "yours" after it has gone for a winner.

A key part of communication is talking to your partner about strategy – who is going to take shots in certain situations and why. It might be that someone has a weak backhand and needs their partner to cover more of the court to prevent them from hitting weak shots. Another area that needs to be discussed ahead of time is who is going to return deep lobs, so that their partner doesn't run into them or cut them off from a full swing.

Lastly, it is important to discuss what happens when one player poaches. If a player poaches, they should continue to that side of the court and call switch, telling their partner to cover the vacated area.

Chapter 26

Jane was sleeping in a chair next to my bed when I opened my eyes. The sun was peeking through the blinds in the window behind her. I had the headache to beat all headaches and my shoulder was throbbing. It took me a moment to realize where I was and remember what had happened. I was thirsty and pushed the little red button by my bedside. The beep woke Jane up.

"Hey there," she said, as she wiped the sleep from her eyes.

"Hi," I managed to croak, my throat dry and rough.

"How do you feel?" she asked, as a nurse came in to check on me.

"Head, throat, and shoulder all hurt like hell," I managed to say.

"We had to put a tube down your throat during surgery, but that pain should go away soon," the nurse informed me. "The shoulder might hurt for a few days, but we'll give you something for that and the headache."

"Surgery?" I was still a little hazy.

"Yep. They took the bullet out and the doctor said it didn't do any permanent damage."

"Okay." I remembered Leroy shooting me, but everything after that was a blur.

The nurse gave me some water and a cup with some pills that I assumed were pain killers, then she left.

"Have you been here all night?" I asked Jane.

She nodded. "After what you did to save me, I couldn't bear to leave you alone."

"Thanks. Is Butch okay?"

"He is doing fine. He's with Samantha and Joe and they are taking good care of him 'til you come home."

"When is that?

"The doctor said he wanted you to stay here a couple more nights. Even though the bullet missed any critical areas, he wants to make sure you don't develop an infection or something."

I wanted to tell her that I was ready to go home now, but I didn't really believe it, and arguing with Jane wasn't going to get me anywhere anyway. We chatted about what happened the night before and she filled in the details that weren't quite coming back to me yet.

"Even after Jack shot you, somehow you were still able to hit him over the head with a big lamp."

"You mean Leroy?"

"Yes. I still think of him as Jack. I can't believe that nice old man was really a killer. Anyway, you cracked his skull wide open. He died pretty quickly."

"OK. I remember that." Or thought I did.

"Joe came in right after that happened. He's the one that released me and called 911."

There was a light tap on the door and Tom, Leslie, Martin, and Celeste shuffled in, carrying flowers and what looked like a box of chocolates.

"Hey there, hero," said Leslie.

"Hi." I waved with my good arm. Lucky for me, Leroy shot me in my left shoulder and not my right. Pickleball came to mind.

"Tell us what happened," asked Martin. "Inquiring minds want to know."

I told them as much as I could remember or knew, and Jane filled in the blanks where I was sketchy. The nurses wanted to keep the visitors to a minimum, but stretched the rules to allow more of the pickleball community in. With each new visitor, Jane had to retell the story, and by the time everyone was brought up to date I had a clear vision of how it all went down. Like Jane, everyone was shocked that the killer was Jack, except William. He tried to claim he was suspicious of Jack from the start.

"I suggest we pass the hat and erect a monument at the courts commemorating the bravery of Butch and Al."

I hoped he was joking. "Please don't."

By the time they all left, I had a room full of candy, cookies, and flowers, which ended up making me quite popular with the nurses. The outpouring of concern and love I was getting almost made me reconsider leaving Rio Viejo. Almost.

Jane stayed a little longer than the others. She had a lot to get off her chest that she didn't want the others to hear.

"I had no idea that everyone hated us so much," she said, sounding like she might cry. "Just before you came in, Jack was telling me how much we were hated. He said he wanted to kill all the Royals before he left. He kept calling us Royals. I feel so bad that we were so rotten to everyone that he wanted to kill us. I feel partially responsible for all their deaths."

Whoa. I didn't see that coming.

"You can't blame yourself. His real vendetta was against Nathan, and he was obviously a sociopath."

"But he said everyone hated us."

"That's a stretch Jane."

"I don't think so, but thanks for saying that. I'm going to be a better person from now on. I don't want to feel this way again."

I believed her. She was ditsy and probably driven by Nathan and Nancy to be a pickleball queen, but I didn't think she was a bad person. The Royals as a collective unit were jerks, but they didn't deserve the fate that Leroy had planned for them.

"Jane, thanks for hanging out here all night, but you look beat. Go home and get some rest. I'll be okay." The truth was I wanted some rest myself. It had been a steady stream of visitors and I needed a break. She left, vowing to return in a few hours. I wanted to tell her not to bother, but as usual, I held my tongue.

With the room cleared out, I had time to think. I was grateful that I had made some good friends in Rio Viejo, but I was also soured on the place. When Stephanie died, I had felt the same way about Denver. I was ready to move on. As bad as Leroy was, I still was shaken by the fact that I had killed a man. I wasn't sure if that was something I could easily get past. Everyone assured me he deserved it, and the world would be a better place without him. Who knows how many more people would have died at his hands? All true enough.

As promised, Jane returned a few hours later, carrying an afternoon edition of the Nogales newspaper.

"You're a celebrity," she said, handing me the paper.

It was the cover story and bled into two more pages. It talked about the pickleball murders in Rio Viejo and how this newcomer, me, and his dog Butch, arrived about the time the murders started. According to the article, had it not been for our brave actions, The Pickleball Killer, as they dubbed him, would have gone on killing.

"How did they get all this?" I asked. "No one talked to me."

"Oh, they tried to get in, but the nurses and doctors wouldn't let them near you."

"I'll have to thank them for that."

I read the rest of the article. "Looks like they did their homework."

"Oh yeah. They talked to everyone they could find that knew anything, but I think most of the details came from Joe and the Sheriff."

Almost everyone interviewed for the article, except William, was shocked to learn that Leroy had a serious criminal past in Canada. He was described as the nicest guy on the courts; the thought of him as a murderer was inconceivable. The lone dissenter was William, who claimed that he had never trusted him. He also described himself as my best friend.

The parade of visitors was repeated that afternoon, and by the time the room cleared, I was seriously ready for some peace and quiet. The hero thing was exhausting, and as nice as it was to be appreciated, I had made up my mind to leave town. Using my phone, I revisited the RV websites and found a number of suitable choices with all the right amenities. None of which would break the bank and threaten the financial security that Stephanie and I had built over the years. My savings, along with the day trading I had become adept at, would keep Butch and I from starving. A quick search on the web about San Carlos, Mexico, and I had a destination all picked out. I planned to mull it over a few more days before making my move. I couldn't really do anything from a hospital bed anyway.

The next day I awoke with almost no pain. Thanks to a sleeping pill administered by my nurse, I had slept like a baby. With the doctor's blessing, I dressed and waited for Tom and Martin to come by and shuttle me home. When we arrived, Joe and Samantha were there with Butch. Somehow Butch knew I was wounded, and although he was excited to see me, he approached cautiously and refrained from jumping on me. We kissed and I gave him a one-armed hug.

"How was he as a house guest?" I asked Joe and Samantha.

"He was a perfect angel," she replied. "If it weren't for the fact that Joe doesn't want another dog, I would have tried to steal him. He can stay with us anytime."

I was beaming with pride. "He's a great buddy, but he's mine and you can't have him," I joked, and hugged him again.

"Everyone at the pickleball court thinks he's a hero," said Samantha. "They think he should be our official mascot. They want him to come to the courts."

"Maybe a parade in his honor," joked Martin.

"I'll bring him by," I assured them.

As I healed over the next few days, I took short walks close to home. I had been told not to overdo, and for the most part I heeded the doctor's advice. Once they removed the stitches, I walked Butch all the way to the pickleball courts to see the action and receive his much-deserved admiration from everyone.

The courts were packed, and the laughter was infectious. Play was interrupted when everyone spotted us, and we were swamped. We were even given a cheer of some sort. Jane came running up and hugged me.

"So good to see you out and about," she said, smiling from ear to ear. "And you, my little hero." She gave Butch a huge bear hug.

I was a little uncomfortable with all the attention, but Butch was enjoying it. Everyone was giving him treats and hugs, shaking his paw and getting him to do tricks. As I watched, I wondered if taking him away from his adoring fans was fair.

Rory came off a court, triumphant and bragging about his victory. "Good to see you, Al. All healed?"

"Almost," I replied.

"Are you ready to play?"

"I wasn't going to yet. I didn't bring a paddle."

"No problem. I have a spare." He didn't even wait for an answer. He turned and rooted through his bag and pulled out an old paddle. "Come on. You can be my partner against William and Peggy. She's new and can use some of your expert advice."

I wasn't entirely sure this was a good idea, but the allure of playing again was more than I could resist. The stitches were out. What damage could I do?

"I'll keep an eye on Butch for you," offered Jane.

I followed the group onto the court and was a little embarrassed that everyone was watching me. Peggy was definitely new to the game but was enthusiastic and determined to learn.

They allowed me a few minutes to warm up and when I felt comfortable, we played. It was meant to be a slow, friendly game, no pressure on me. And for the most part it was. I offered Peggy a little advice but tried to keep it simple. I also let Rory hit most of the balls on our side of the court which he seemed to appreciate. We finished the game with a win, and I decided to quit while I was ahead.

Tom was standing there watching when we came off the court.

"How did that feel?" he asked.

"Like it was probably a mistake, but I don't think I did any damage."

"When will you be up to full speed and back to beating us all again?"

"I think I need a few more days to rest up. But I've been meaning to talk to you. I think I remember you saying that you spent a year traveling in a motor home."

"Yep. Before we moved here."

"Well, I was wondering if I could pick your brain about that?"

"Sure." He looked at me with a little sadness showing on his face. "Are you thinking of doing a road trip?"

"More than a road trip. I was thinking that Butch and I should get a motor home and do some traveling."

"For how long?"

"'Til we don't like it anymore."

"You just got here. And besides, it's safe now, thanks to you."

"Not sure about that, but with all that we went through, I think getting away will be a good idea. I was waiting 'til my arm healed to hit the road. I've been doing some research online and would just like some expert advice before I pull the trigger. so to speak. Will you help me with that?"

He took a big breath and let it out slowly. "With regret, I will. We will hate to see you leave. We were just getting to know you and becoming friends. But I understand. After my stint in Vietnam, I did the same thing. Traveled that is. When do you plan on doing this?"

"I'd like to buy something next week and be on the road soon."

I could see that he was sad, and so was I, on a certain level. I liked Tom and enjoyed playing with him. There were some others, like Leslie, Celeste, and Martin that I would miss as well, but my mind was made up.

The following week came, and my shoulder felt almost as good as new. I arranged a time for Tom and Martin to join me and Butch on a trip up to Tucson to find our new home. Butch looked as excited and anxious as I

343

did. He marched up the steps of each model we looked at and even jumped onto the captain's chair and the bed to test for comfort. With each model we looked at, the sales rep tried to close the deal, while Tom shared his thoughts with me. When my decision was made, he helped me negotiate a good deal. I ended up with a thirty foot, used Sunstar with low miles, for well under my budgeted $100k. I bought a tow bar for my car and drove it back to Rio Viejo, with Tom giving me advice the entire way and Butch sprawled out on the bed. By the time we got home, I was ready to pack up and go.

A week after the RV purchase, the pickleball group threw Butch and me a going away party. Most everyone was there, and surprisingly to me, a few tears were shed.

"When you come back, you are welcome to park that big rig in front of our house for as long as you want," offered Joe. "You are always welcome here."

"I'll extend the same invitation to all of you to come down to San Carlos and visit us while we are there."

"Well as it turns out Al," said Joe, "Samantha and I have a place in San Carlos. I keep my fishing boat there. I'll take you out next time we are down."

"That sounds great Joe. I have always wanted to learn to fish."

"And there is a great pickleball community down there," added Samantha with a huge smile.

"Awesome," I replied. Of course I already knew about pickleball in San Carlos. That was one of my reasons for choosing it.

Two days later, we were on the road. I had rented a space at an RV Park in San Carlos, right across the road from the beach and a short walk into town. The border crossing was simple. The guards looked at Butch and waved us through, not wanting to find out if the big dog was friendly or not. We made the trip to San Carlos in an easy six-hour drive. The toll road was well maintained, and we had no problems. As soon as we arrived, I took Butch for a walk and found a taco stand that served burgers for Butch and tacos and a beer for me. We sat by the edge of the Sea of Cortez, eating our meal and enjoying a spectacular sunset, while Zac Brown Band's *Toes* played on my phone.

Pickleball Tip # 26 – Making Good Pickleball Decisions.

Everybody wants to hit the big put-away to win the point. It's oh so satisfying, but so often we over-hit the ball, sending it out or into the net. The smarter move would be to hit the ball with some angle to move the opponent out of position. That way you can either hit the next ball where no one can touch it, or place a dink that forces them to hit another shot. But just as getting over exuberant and trying to smash the ball for a clear winner, only to hit it into the net can be demoralizing, so can letting a smash opportunity go to waste. When you are at the NVZ and your opponent hits you a weak volley, don't waste the opportunity by letting the ball come too far or too low before punching it back. Take the ball out in front of you while it is still high, and hit down at your opponent's feet. Don't hesitate and allow your opponent to get back in the point. You have earned the advantage, so jump on it.

The End

Pickleball resource list

This list is by no means complete and in no particular order. New sites are popping up every day and you may have a local club with a site of their own. These sites have not been vetted. Please let us know about other sites that should be added to the lists below.

Facebook Groups

Pickleball Forum
- https://www.facebook.com/groups/1340630926008388
Pickleball Clinic
- https://www.facebook.com/groups/thepickleballclinic
Pickleball Underground
- https://www.facebook.com/groups/1375588089184813
The Kitchen
- https://www.facebook.com/groups/thekitchenPB
US Senior Pickleball
- https://www.facebook.com/groups/usseniorpickleball
Pickleball Rules -
 https://www.facebook.com/groups/pickleballrules
Pickleball Forever
- https://www.facebook.com/groups/478524982758048
Pickleball Classifieds
- https://www.facebook.com/groups/1098117483721911
Bite Size Pickleball
- https://www.facebook.com/groups/bitesizepickleball
Pickleball Humor
- https://www.facebook.com/groups/1249960438692539
World Pickleball Tour Players
- https://www.facebook.com/groups/worldpickleballers
Third Shot Sports
- https://www.facebook.com/thirdshotsports

Pickle Madness -

https://www.facebook.com/profile.php?id=100090851865060

Pickleball Buddies

- https://www.facebook.com/groups/1068716196571785

Pickleball Memes

- https://www.facebook.com/groups/8121839367857504

OnCourt Off Court

- https://www.facebook.com/oncourtoffcourt

Pickleball Librarian

- https://www.facebook.com/PickleballLibrarian

Web Sites

Pickleball Central

- https://pickleballcentral.com/

Total Pickleball

- https://www.totalpickleball.com/

Pickleball Portal

- https://www.pickleballportal.com/

USA Pickleball

- https://usapickleball.org/

Pickleball Galaxy

- https://www.pickleballgalaxy.com/

Pickleball University

- https://www.pickleballuniversity.com

Pickleball Tournaments

- https://www.ckleballtournaments.com/

Pickleball Exchange

- https://www.thepickleballexchange.com/

Pickleball Global

- https://pickleball.global/

The Dink - https://www.thedinkpickleball.com/

The Pickler

- https://thepickler.com/blogs/pickleball-blog

Better Pickleball

- https://betterpickleball.com/blog/

Pickleball Max

- https://www.pickleballmax.com/2020/01/top-10-pickleball-blog-posts-of-2019

Pickleball Pirates

- https://www.youtube.com/@ThePickleballPirates

Pickleball Cafe

- https://www.pickleball.cafe/

Third Shot Sports

- https://www.thirdshotsports.com/

Pickle Madness

- https://picklemadness.com/

Pickleball Buy Sell Trade

- https://www.facebook.com/groups/picklebst

OnCourt OffCourt

- https://oncourtoffcourt.com/

Pickleball United – Tournaments

- https://www.facebook.com/pickleballunited/

YouTube Channels

Pickleball Channel -

- https://www.youtube.com/@PickleballChannel

House of Pickle -

- https://www.youtube.com/watch?v=JD7afQs7JbA

Briones Pickleball -

- https://www.youtube.com/@BrionesPickleball

That Pickleball Guy -

- https://www.youtube.com/watch?v=JGMLn68RZS8

PrimeTime Pickleball

- https://www.youtube.com/@primetimepickleball

Cliff Pickleball

- https://www.youtube.com/@CliffPickleball

Pro Pickleball Media

- https://www.youtube.com/@pickleballmedia

Enhance Pickleball

- https://www.youtube.com/@EnhancePickleball

The Kitchen

- https://www.youtube.com/@TheKitchenPickleball

Pickleball Librarian

https://www.youtube.com/c/PickleballLibrarian

If you enjoyed this book please be so kind as to leave a review on Amazon or Barnes and Noble. You can find Gary's other book, *All In A Day's Work*, at Amazon or Barnes and Noble. You can keep abreast of future work by Gary at

https://www.facebook.com/GResnikoff/

If you find yourself in Port Hueneme please stop by Moranda Park and say hi.